SHE COULD NOT RESIST . . .

"Come here," he said in a voice almost soft enough to turn the phrase into a request rather than a demand. She looked around wildly, seeking an avenue of escape, then he closed the trap with a single word. "Please."

Like a sleepwalker in a trance, she obeyed him, approaching his outstretched arm, letting his embrace enfold her until she sat stiffly on his lap. His thighs were firm and hard beneath her legs, though she sat as primly as a schoolgirl with her back straight and her shoulders squared, her hands knotted tightly in her lap.

He tugged her closer to his chest until she could feel his heart pounding as furiously as her own. She looked away from him, unable to handle the myriad sensations flooding her body and mind—his scent and feel, his closeness; her excitement and the heated swirl of emotions rocketing through her—sudden desire and enervating fear.

"What do you want?" she whispered. . . .

Diamond Books by Anne Harmon

DESERT FLAME
WYOMING WILDFIRE

WYOMING WILDFIRE

ANNE HARMON

DIAMOND BOOKS, NEW YORK

This book is a Diamond original edition,
and has never been previously published.

WYOMING WILDFIRE

A Diamond Book / published by arrangement with
the author

PRINTING HISTORY
Diamond edition / April 1993

ISBN: 1–55773–883–1

Diamond Books are published by The Berkley Publishing Group,
200 Madison Avenue, New York, NY 10016.
The name "DIAMOND" and its logo
are trademarks belonging to Charter Communications, Inc.

PRINTED IN THE UNITED STATES OF AMERICA

10 9 8 7 6 5 4 3 2 1

In memory of my parents,
Anne and Milton Shinn,
for teaching me that reading is the
door to the world

To my sisters,
Leora
Daphne
Danielle
Judy
for their enthusiasm and support

WYOMING WILDFIRE

ONE

GRAYSON BENEDICT RAN a hand through his thick, dark hair and sighed. God, he was tired. He really should have headed back to his ranch, but Sam had asked him to join the boys for a drink, and he hadn't had it in him to refuse.

"Here's your beer, boss," Sam said as he plonked the glass onto the table. "The boys will be right over, once they've gotten an eyeful of Ruby in her new dress. May take a while, though. Seems like she's barely got the good parts covered."

"I guess that's why this crowd's larger than usual," Gray said as he leaned back in his chair. Business was always good at the Golden Plumb, but today the place was packed even though it was still daylight.

Sam grinned. "Reckon so, though it's a mite early in the day for this many rowdies." Even as he spoke, a squabble broke out between some of the men across the room.

Gray shook his head as the fight subsided almost as quickly as it had begun. "You'd think there'd be enough excitement out here without their having to start more."

"That's the Rolling R's crew. Just got in last night from Texas with a bunch of cattle for old man Rafferty. Guess they got full pockets and an itch to spend. Ruby knows her business. She'll have every last cent out of 'em before dark."

"I just hope Rafferty knows his. I wouldn't leave any

1

new cattle alone on the range, not with the problems we've been having of late." Gray scowled as he thought of the recent losses. That was one of the reasons he was so tired. Riding the range all night and doing his business all day left precious few hours for sleep.

"Won't be long now 'fore the vigilantes get involved," Sam opined.

Gray merely grunted as he sipped his beer.

Sam gave him a look. "Don't you want them rustlers stopped?"

"Of course I want them stopped. I just don't always like the way those vigilantes do it. Seems to me they're little better than the men they hang."

Sam looked even more puzzled. "But they're on the side of the law," he protested.

"Are they?" Gray replied. "I always thought the law required a judge and a jury before a man was declared guilty. Once a lynching's over, there isn't much room for an appeal."

"Well, that's true, I reckon." The younger man frowned as he mulled over this new perspective. "I just figured they only went after the guilty ones."

"I hope you're right, son," Gray replied, feeling every one of the fourteen years between him and his newly hired, twenty-two-year-old ranch foreman. Had he ever been that idealistic or naïve? Probably. But not anymore. Felicia had taken care of every bit of innocent naïveté he'd ever had. Now he prided himself on his realistic view of the world. He didn't expect too much from life, and so far, he'd seen nothing to change his mind.

"I'll be heading out to the Whispering Winds tonight," he told Sam. "I don't want to leave Amelia alone at the ranch too long, especially with those rustlers hanging around God knows where."

"Maybe you should bring her into town until those men are caught," Sam suggested. "It might be safer."

"If the repairs on my house were further along, I'd have brought her on this trip. She certainly wanted to come."

"It's too bad about your roof blowing off like that in the last wind. How much longer before it's fixed?"

"Not too much, but until the workmen are done, I'd just as soon have Amelia at the ranch."

Now it was Gray's turn to frown. At sixteen, Amelia was becoming a young lady. Soon she would be of marriageable age. Already she was attracting the attentions of young men, both here in Cheyenne and out on the ranch. Gray wasn't sure where she would be safer—at least out on the ranch she was near him. Soon enough she'd be married and in a home of her own.

Gray didn't like to ponder that thought. For so many years it'd been just him and his daughter. She'd been his reason for carrying on, for coming out West to make a new life for himself—and for her. She'd blossomed under his care, and over time he'd taken new interest in the world around him, letting go of the bitterness and looking forward to the next day. Now he faced loneliness again. It was just a matter of time.

"I'd better be going," he said, coming to the decision even as he spoke. There was no point in getting maudlin over a glass of beer. He raised his glass to swallow the last drop, but before his hand was halfway to his face, another ruckus broke out.

"Damn," Sam swore softly as the men of the Whispering Winds ranch squared off against Rafferty's bunch, fists flying. "We'd better go break them up before Ruby has a fit."

He waded into the brawling crowd, separating the men with a shove or a shout, and Gray followed suit. Ruby's bouncers helped keep the two groups of men apart while the lady herself screamed at the men that they would pay for any damage so they better stop.

By the time the melee was over, glassware lay shattered on the floor and the smell of raw whiskey filled the air.

"They started it!" Roy Wilson shouted, and Sam had to physically hold the ranch hand back as he lunged at one of Rafferty's men.

"That's enough!" Ruby cried. "I want you boys to leave. And tell Rafferty I'm putting the bill for this mess on his tab," she added as the drunken group of Rafferty's men jostled across the floor, glass crunching underfoot.

Gray and Sam lingered for another minute to make sure none of their men went after Rafferty's, then went back to the table to get their hats.

"Maybe we'd all better head back," Sam said. "We can't afford to have any of the men busted up right now, not with the extra watches we need at night."

"Let's just give them another minute or two to settle down. I don't want another brawl in the street," Gray answered as Ruby sauntered across the room to their table.

Sam was right about that dress, Gray thought. It left nothing to his imagination.

Ruby sure was a looker, and she knew it. She leaned against the back of Sam's chair, flaunting her endowments barely two inches from his face. Her eyes, though, locked onto Gray's, passing explicit messages of invitation, an invitation he'd taken up a time or two in the past. But not today.

"Thanks for breaking it up, you two," she drawled and ruffled a hand through Sam's hair. His face turned red, and he stared into his empty glass.

Gray would have grinned at his foreman's plight, but a sudden scream from outside made him look the other way instead. Cries and shouts were not uncommon in this part of town. Sixteenth Street boasted more than its share of saloons and varieties, but this was different. This was a woman's cry, and filled with terror.

Through the swinging door, Gray caught a glimpse of a couple of Rafferty's men and a flash of red hair.

"Come on, Sam! Looks like real trouble this time!" he shouted over his shoulder as he sprang from his chair and headed for the door.

Lily Avenel walked down the plank sidewalk with some trepidation. Cheyenne was every bit as wild as she'd feared, at least in this part of town. She looked down at her companion. Though Dun Edwards was as gallant and honorable as any man of full height, she feared the dwarf would be scant protection in this town.

"I hope we find the city fire marshal soon," she said, pretending not to hear the ribald catcall shouted at her from across the street.

Dun looked no more comfortable than she felt about their predicament.

"If not, we'd better head back for the town hall and wait there," he said. "We don't need the permit for several days yet. After all that rain, the others won't get here for at least a week."

Lily and the small Englishman had been sent ahead of the circus caravan to make final arrangements for the troupe's stay in Cheyenne. The caravan of wagons, performers, and roustabouts was making its slow way west from the center of Nebraska where they'd last performed.

The rain had been only the latest catastrophe to hit their circus troupe. The first had been Hilda Bruner's death nearly a year and a half ago. Her husband, Otto, had yet to recover from the blow, and the fortunes of Bruner's Munificent Menagerie and Family Circus had declined with his spirits.

Lily and Dun turned onto Eddy Street and headed for Sixteenth.

"There's McDaniel's place, just like the man promised," Dun pointed out as they passed the landmark.

Like so many of the establishments in Cheyenne, the one-story building had a false front, but McDaniel made good use of it to advertise his wares. The entire wall was filled with signs and pictures, inviting all and sundry to come for entertainment, everything from singers to lecturers to drinks and cigars.

"No wonder he calls himself 'The Barnum of the West,' " Lily commented as they made their way past the crowd of miners and cowboys, cattlemen and down-and-outers. "He seems to put on quite a show."

Dun must have picked up the worry in her voice. "Don't fret. We'll do fine. A circus from out of town can always compete with the local entertainment. All we have to do is advertise Old Bess, and we'll have all the customers you please. It's not every day that an elephant comes to town, you know. How can McDaniel possibly compete with that?"

"You're right," she conceded. "But I've heard he has all sorts of . . ." She let her voice trail off.

"Curiosities?" Dun supplied in a wry tone.

Lily nodded unhappily. The dwarf by her side served that same function in their circus. He was a good and honest man, well-read and educated, with a formal British accent, but that was not why the crowds came to see him. All they cared about was that he was a man full grown, yet stood barely three feet tall in his stocking feet.

"Don't feel bad," he said reassuringly. "I make a good living this way. It's better than some of the other things I could be doing."

Lily knew he was right. People reacted in strange ways to those who were too different, and often those ways

6

were cruel and hurtful, denying the humanity of those who were "freaks." Dun rarely left the confines of the circus, preferring to be with people who knew him to braving the outside world.

"I appreciate your coming with me today," she said as they neared the next corner. "I never realized what Otto went through to get these bookings."

She grimaced as they stepped around a supine cowboy sleeping off his drunkenness on the sidewalk.

"I'm glad to do it. Besides, no one else could be spared, not with the mess the roads are in. It'll take long enough to get all the wagons into Cheyenne as it is."

The sun was shining today for the first time in over a week, but the damage had already been done to the back country roads the circus caravan used to transport everything they owned, from the canvas for the tops to the animal acts to their own personal belongings. Thirty-seven wagons in all, and each had to be brought over sloppy roads from one town to the next.

"I hope nothing else goes wrong," Lily said with a sigh. "This has been a hard year."

Dun shot her a sharp look. "How's Otto been doing lately?"

"I don't know. Most of the time he stays holed up in his wagon." She didn't add "with a bottle," but she didn't have to. The circus was a tight-knit group, of necessity, and there were few secrets that stayed outside of common knowledge. "He leaves all the decisions to Bryce, but I'm not sure Bryce understands the complexities of running a show this size." Bryce Mason was the new circus manager, a position Otto had created after his wife's death. Until then Otto had done all the managing himself. "I wish I'd realized sooner how things were going. I might have been able to do something."

"Like what?"

7

"I don't know. Maybe checked on our regular bookings back East. I never thought Otto would forget to make them. By the time I realized what happened, our competition was booked instead." She shook her head sadly. "If we hadn't lost those bookings, we wouldn't have had to come out to these uncivilized parts. . . . Everything's so muddy and unkempt out here, and the people are different. I liked it better when we had families coming. Out here, you hardly see any women compared to the men."

As if to confirm her words, a crowd of men came pouring out of a saloon door.

"Listen, Lily, maybe we should turn around and wait for the fire marshal at his office," Dun said just as she noticed the name of the place: the Golden Plumb.

"No, wait. We're here."

In her eagerness to find the fire marshal and get her business over with, she pushed her way through the crowd of men, hoping Dun was behind her. Suddenly her path was blocked, and in front of her loomed a huge man. His breath smelled of whiskey, and she didn't even want to think about what his body smelled like.

"Hey, little lady. What's your hurry?" he asked. "Why don'tcha come along with us? We'll show you a right nice time." He leered at her, showing stained, crooked teeth.

"No, thank you," she said quickly and tried to slip around him.

He grabbed her roughly by the arm, tearing her sleeve at the seam near her shoulder.

"Not so fast. All I want is a few minutes of your time, ain't that right, boys?"

"You tell 'er, Blackie," another voice rang out, and a chorus of bawdy shouts joined in as the men pressed in on them.

"Please, let me go," Lily pleaded, truly frightened now. "I'm meeting someone in there."

The men were all drunk, their words slurring as they spoke. But it was the sporting look in their eyes that made her heart climb to her throat. They had the look of starving predators who had just caught sight of their prey.

"Don't worry. I'm sure he won't mind waiting for ya," the big man said and grabbed her other arm as well, turning her to face him, his fetid breath blowing in her face.

Lily turned her face to the side. She was strong—she had to be for her bareback riding act—but her strength was no competition for the man they called Blackie. Every time she tried to pull away, he merely tightened his grip. She was afraid to struggle too openly, knowing instinctively that it would only incite the men even more.

"Hey, Blackie, you losing your touch? The lady don't seem to like you none. Why don't you give someone else a chance?" a new voice called out from nearby.

The new man latched onto one of her shoulders and tugged, but Blackie refused to let go. Instead, he jerked her closer, anchoring her to his side with one arm while he shoved the newcomer away with the other.

"Get lost, Travis. I saw her first. You want a piece, go ask Ruby to fix you up with one of her girls."

"How about we ask the lady?" Travis countered, shoving back.

At that moment Dun finally managed to work his way through the throng.

"Let her go," he demanded. In his hand he held a small, custom-made pistol pointed at Blackie's chest.

Blackie looked down on him and laughed. "Who's gonna make me? You?" He laughed again, squeezing Lily tightly, his hand massaging her breast. "Hey, boys, take a gander at this runt. What happened, Shorty, your mama step on your head when you was a baby?"

"I said, let her go. Now."

Dun cocked the gun and aimed right for Blackie's heart. But the big man was unfazed.

"Here, Travis, now we got one apiece. I'll keep the lady and you can have him."

With those words he lashed out with one foot and kicked Dun into the man called Travis, catching him off guard. As Travis went down under the unexpected weight, Blackie turned his back on the pair and started dragging Lily down the sidewalk.

"Stop!" she shrieked as she heard the sound of fists landing on flesh behind her. "Stop, they're hurting him."

But Blackie didn't pause. "Don't worry about ol' Travis. He can take care of himself. You just worry about takin' care of me, and we'll get along fine."

Lily struggled against him and managed to look back only to see Dun being tossed from one man to another, as if he were a large ball. Some of the men pretended to miss catching him and just let him drop to the ground; others took a moment to punch or kick him before throwing him to the next man.

Lily screamed again, and Blackie put his hand over her mouth to silence her. In all her twenty-seven years, she'd never been so frightened or so angry. Fueled by her fear and fury, she bit the large man's palm and kicked out at his shins, heedless of his greater strength and size.

Cursing fluently, he yelled out his pain, then grabbed her by the back of the neck with one meaty hand while he drew the other back to strike her. She closed her eyes, bracing herself for the shock of pain, but it never came. Instead, she was suddenly set free. Disoriented, she staggered a few steps until she reached the outside wall of the saloon. She leaned against it, her breathing ragged and her throat aching from all the screaming. She was vaguely aware that the drunken group of men was dispersing, but everything seemed to come from a distance, muffled by the roaring in her ears and the clammy feeling settling over her.

"Put your head down," a male voice ordered as large hands eased her into a sitting position with her head between her knees. These hands were different from the ones that had grabbed her before. Their touch was gentle, even if impersonal. "Now, take a deep breath."

She did as she was told, and the roaring in her ears diminished.

"Again," he ordered quietly. She didn't think of disobeying. The voice was mesmerizing, deep and rich, the hand tangled in her hair warm and reassuring. The spots before her eyes faded and the world came back into focus.

All the men were gone, except the two who had saved her life. A dark-haired man with slate blue eyes sat next to her, coolly assessing her condition, his expression closed and a little forbidding. A younger man with blond hair stood looking down at her from a little farther away.

"You all right?" the older one asked. He looked to be in his thirties, judging from the mere handful of gray hairs she spotted and the radiating lines etched near the outer corners of his eyes. He wasn't exactly what she would call handsome, but there was a rugged self-sufficiency to him that more than compensated for any lack of looks.

She nodded and struggled to her feet. The man looked like he was about to protest, but he said nothing as he helped her to her feet.

She looked around, searching for Dun. At first she didn't see him, then the fluttering of a torn piece of blue material by the edge of the sidewalk caught her eye.

"Oh, my God," she said in a whisper.

Gray didn't know what to make of the woman. What was a lady like her doing in this part of town? Didn't she know any better than to go wandering unescorted on these

11

streets? Hell, these blocks of Sixteenth and Seventeenth were known for every type of saloon, bawdy house, and variety hall known to man. She'd been asking for trouble, and it had found her.

Well, it was none of his concern. He'd had more than enough trouble from women in his life, and he knew better than to let a pretty face turn his head. And, he had to admit, she had a very pretty face—small and heart-shaped with large brown eyes framed by a riot of flaming red hair that blazed like a prairie fire.

He suppressed a sudden urge to run his fingers through it, to savor its silky texture. She'd just been through a terrible experience, one that would have shattered most women. For a moment she'd looked as if she was about to faint, but now she seemed recovered.

When she made a move to stand, he automatically reached for her upper arm to help steady her, as though she were fragile and a bit helpless. His experience with women was that their helplessness and fragility were often a ploy to get men to do their bidding. He waited to see what she would do, fully expecting her to take advantage of him for whatever she could get.

But to his surprise, once she was standing, she ignored him, looking around instead with a worried expression on her face. Perhaps she had lost some valuable ornament in the struggle with Blackie. He was about to ask what she was looking for, when, with an indistinct whisper, she suddenly headed for the edge of the road.

"Where are you going?" he demanded. Didn't she understand her vulnerability? Where did she think she was going?

He'd barely taken two steps toward her when she flung herself down on the road next to what looked like a bundle of old clothes.

Gray caught Sam's questioning look and shrugged. As

far as he could tell, the fiery-haired lady had taken leave of her senses.

And then the bundle of rags gave a very human groan.

"What the hell! What is it?" he demanded as Sam knelt in the street next to the moaning bundle.

"It's a . . . a man. Injured bad, from what I can tell."

"No, oh, no," the lady cried, and for the first time, tears appeared in her eyes and spilled down over her cheeks. "Dun, speak to me, please," she implored.

"Shh, he'll be fine," Sam said as he stood and pulled her awkwardly away from the small man. Looking up at Gray, he added, "You'd better take a look. He's pretty beat up."

Sam tried to keep the lady away from the dwarf. When Gray knelt to get a better look, he could see why. The man had been beaten to a bloody pulp.

"Please, let me help him," she was saying to Sam. "He's hurt. He needs me. Please."

"We're trying to help him, ma'am," Sam replied. "Just give us a minute here to figure out exactly how bad he's hurt."

"I don't think anything's broken," Gray said, after checking the injured man out as best he could. "But he may be bleeding inside. We need to get him off the street. Where're you staying, ma'am?"

She looked anxiously from Gray to Sam and back. The tears had left a dusty track on her cheek, but instead of making her look unattractive, it added to her vulnerability. Gray didn't want to respond but couldn't help himself. The need to protect surged through him. He clenched his jaw; he'd been down this road before and knew where it led: to pain and sorrow.

"I don't mean no disrespect," Gray added when she stayed silent, "but the sooner your friend is in his bed, the better off he'll be. If you tell me where you're staying, I'll arrange for him to be taken there."

"I-I'm sorry, but . . . we didn't have a chance to find a place yet." She chewed on the inside of her lip, looking nervous and a bit lost, and Gray knew he had no choice. Like it or not, by default he'd been selected to care for this woman and her friend.

He sighed. "I see. In that case, Sam, you'd best bring the buckboard around. See if you can't find a couple of blankets to pad the back. It's going to be a mighty uncomfortable ride out to the ranch for him as it is."

"You want to take them back with us?" The younger man couldn't quite keep his surprise out of his voice.

Gray glanced at the lady, but she was more concerned with the little man than with anything the two of them were saying.

"Uh, ma'am," he said. She looked at him with her fathomless brown eyes, her worry and concern evident. "Under the, uh, circumstances, I think you and your friend had best come with us. The men that attacked you have had a mite too much to drink today. You don't want to stay here too long in case they come back."

She looked around anxiously. "You think they might?"

"I don't rightly know. Ruby's place is kind of popular right now so . . ." He shrugged to let her know anything was possible. "I'm sending Sam, here, to get the buckboard and then we can go. All right?"

"Go? Where?"

"To my ranch. Whispering Winds."

She shook her head, then jumped to her feet. "Mr. . . ."

"Benedict," he supplied. "Grayson Benedict." He tipped his hat.

"I want to thank you for all you've done. I mean, I don't know what would have happened if you and—" She looked over in Sam's direction.

"Sam Carter," Sam said. "I'm his foreman."

She gave him a quick smile. "You and Mr. Carter saved our lives today, I know that," she said, a shudder shaking her body. "And I thank you both—but you shouldn't feel obligated. We'll manage just fine."

She gave a quick glance in the direction of her companion, as if he could bolster her claim, but the small man was still unconscious.

"Where will you go?" Gray asked. For some reason, he felt he couldn't abandon her, no matter what she said. "Where did you come from?"

"We'll go back to our friends. Please, it's what Dun would want. He doesn't like to be with strangers. Don't you see? He needs to be with his own people. The outside world doesn't always accept him."

"What people? Where are they?" he asked. She was too evasive. If he had any sense, he'd leave her to her own devices, as she seemed to want. Unfortunately he was discovering he didn't have half the sense he ought to. "This man can't travel any distance to speak of. And if you stay in town, I guarantee Blackie and his friends will find you. They won't take lightly to having been bested by us, and out here a woman, especially one who looks like you, doesn't exactly fade into the woodwork, if you get my meaning."

Lily got his meaning, all right. From the moment she had appeared on the streets of Cheyenne, she had been the object of more male attention than she'd realized existed, on either side of the Mississippi. Like it or not, there were at least ten men for every woman in this godforsaken place. It didn't even matter if a woman was pretty or plain, despite what Mr. Benedict implied. All the men cared about was that she was female.

"I suppose you're right. We really don't have a choice." He scowled at her. Belatedly she realized how rude her words had sounded, but before she could apologize for seeming ungrateful, he was barking out orders.

"Get going, Sam. Bring the buckboard over here, then round up the boys. I'd just as soon have a bit of protection on the way out."

Sam nodded, then turned to her. "Do you have anything you want to bring out to the ranch with you?"

"I'm not sure—"

"Do you have luggage or a wagon?" Grayson Benedict said, cutting her off. "Just tell Sam and he'll arrange transport to the ranch. We don't have time to waste." He looked meaningfully at Dun.

For a moment Lily wished she were back in her own tidy wagon, among her friends, where her responsibilities were clear. Then she shrugged off the helpless feeling. She was a woman grown, capable and independent, or so she liked to think. If life had taught her nothing else, it had taught her to stand on her own two feet. And now she had to care for Dun as well, to figure out what was best for him, whether he would like it or not.

"We have a couple of trunks at the train station," she said. "The stationmaster said he'd keep an eye on them for us."

And just like that, it was decided. She was going to a ranch in the middle of nowhere with two strange men. She had no idea why she should trust them, but somehow she did. Maybe it was the obvious reluctance of Grayson Benedict to invite her to his home, or the calm, respectful way he treated her. Or maybe it was the admiring way his foreman looked to him, seeking his approval as though Mr. Benedict were a force to be reckoned with, a man of consequence. Regardless, the decision had been made, and now she would have to make the best of it.

"I'll have Roy fetch the trunks out to the ranch in the

freight wagon," the foreman said before he took off down the street, leaving her alone by the side of the road with his boss and Dun.

Dun moaned again. Lily knelt beside him and stroked the hair off his forehead as he struggled for consciousness. He tried to open his eyes, but because of the swelling he couldn't manage more than narrow slits.

"What happened?" he croaked. "Where are we?"

"We're still in Cheyenne," she told him in a calm voice. The last thing she wanted was for Dun to be worried about her. "You've been hurt, but you're going to be all right. We're going to a ranch in a little while, and then everything will be just fine."

"You're . . . okay?" He spoke haltingly, as if in great pain.

"I'm fine," she reassured him. For the first time since the attack she became aware of her appearance and self-consciously pulled together the front of her traveling suit. Not only had the sleeve been ripped in her struggles, but several buttons had popped off the jacket as well, leaving the front gaping open more than was proper.

Sam came barreling down the street in the buckboard and pulled the horse up sharply, the wagon's brakes making a screeching sound.

"Roy's getting the last of the supplies loaded, then he'll get the trunks and join us up on the trail. The rest of the men will be here in a minute," Sam announced as he jumped down from the seat. "I got a couple of blankets spread out in the back, and I put some hay under 'em."

"Good job," Gray said, and the younger man beamed. "Now, if you could check with Ruby and see if she has any ice to spare, maybe we can do something about the swelling. I didn't want to leave them while you were gone."

"Oh, you should have told me," Lily said, feeling badly. "I could have gotten it."

Gray gave her a narrow-eyed look. "We've had enough trouble here today. You'd best let Sam handle this. Haven't you realized yet that this part of town is no place for a lady?"

Lily had no answer to that. She looked away from the man's sharp scrutiny. She knew he was judging her and finding fault, but she honestly had thought she and Dun could handle traveling into Cheyenne alone. This was the first time she had taken responsibility for handling the details of the circus's stay in such a large town. And though she'd done her best, circumstances had conspired against her, but she was determined to work things out before the circus arrived next week.

"Is there some way I can help?" she asked.

Gray came to her side and once again looked Dun over. "Why don't you check on the wagon," he told her. "Make sure Sam laid everything out all right." As she stood to do his bidding, he added, "Maybe bring one of the blankets here. We can use it as a sling to lift your friend into the wagon bed."

She walked to the buckboard where Sam had fixed up a place for Dun. Grabbing the nearest blanket, she brought it back.

"Here's the blanket, Mr. Benedict," she said, handing it to him.

"Just call me Gray," he said and reached for the blanket without looking up. "We don't stand much on formality out here."

"All right. And I'm Lily Avenel," she replied, remembering belatedly that, with all the excitement, she had never introduced herself by name. Just then Sam came out of the saloon carrying some ice wrapped in a tattered piece of material.

"It's a pleasure to meet you, Miss Lily," Sam said with a smile. "Here's some ice, Gray. Ruby said to let her know if you need more."

Gray looked up at his foreman. "Looks fine to me. If you'll take care of him, I'll help Miss Lily into the wagon. Then we can sort things out here."

He gave Sam a man-to-man look, and Sam nodded as he moved to Dun's side. Gray rose to his feet and turned to Lily. "This way," he said. "Now, watch your step."

Lily understood that they were trying to protect her sensibilities. Little did they know that she had seen and cared for all sorts of injuries during her years with the circus.

Still, she had to admit that her knees were shakier than usual, and her hands trembled when she didn't clench them into tight fists. The combination of Blackie's attack and Dun's injuries had undoubtedly taken its toll, and since the men seemed to have everything under control, there was no reason for her to fight them.

Gray's hand felt strong and reassuring when he took her arm. From this close, she could see the fine lines etched by the sun near his eyes and smell his clean, masculine scent. She shivered, unsure of the cause, whether it was his touch or the excitement of the day.

He handed her up onto the wagon's hard seat and, after she thanked him, joined Sam by Dun's side. The two men spread the blanket out on the ground and rolled up the two long edges until only a center section the width of a man was left smooth.

Lily watched the men as they worked. Sam was dressed in his range clothes: jeans, scuffed boots, a flannel shirt, and a heavier vest. Gray Benedict, in contrast, was dressed for the city in dark wool slacks, a pristine white shirt, and a tie. He'd removed his topcoat a while ago, and now Lily could see the play of his muscles beneath the light fabric of the shirt. His shoulders were broad, broader than those of the lanky younger man, and they tapered to slim hips.

Lily was used to seeing muscled me. She worked with animal trainers, acrobats, and tumblers every day. But she'd never been aware of them the way she was of the man kneeling before her. His dark sable hair caught the sunlight and reflected it boldly in shiny highlights. She wondered how it would feel to the touch—if it would be thick and plush like her own or sleek and smooth like that of the circus's black panther.

Probably the latter, she decided. He even moved like the panther, all strength and masculine grace with no wasted motion. As she watched, the two men arranged themselves on either side of the blanket, one at Dun's head, the other at his feet. At Gray's nod they gently lifted him a couple of inches and hoisted him onto the blanket. Dun moaned and Lily's stomach clenched.

Gray looked up at her, as if sensing her worry. His eyes were a darker shade of blue than before. "He'll be all right in a minute," he tried to reassure her. "Then we'll put him in back and be ready to go. You okay?"

She nodded, puzzling over the mystery of this man who was helping them. Not many men would go out of their way to befriend two strangers as he was, especially not for someone like Dun. Yet she was aware of some reluctance, as if he were willing to help them, but only from a distance. She couldn't blame him. She would be wary, too, about taking strangers to her home. She was grateful, but she was curious, too, curious to know more about this man, to learn what forces had shaped him, to discover why he made her so aware of herself—and of him.

Now, like it or not, it looked as if she was going to get an opportunity to do just that. Something inside of her quaked at the thought, worried by barely remembered nightmares from her childhood, but another part tingled with excitement, eager for the adventure. She felt poised on the brink of something wonderful yet frightening, the same feeling she had in the instant before she did a flying leap from Lancelot's back as the steady-gaited horse ran round the ring to catch her again before she fell to the ground.

The two men bent, then hoisted Dun and the makeshift stretcher onto the wagon. Once Dun was settled onto the blankets, he lay very still. Lily clambered over the seat to his side.

"He's unconscious again," she said and felt for his pulse.

"Better that way," Gray said. "The road out to the ranch ain't half bad, but in his condition, even the tiniest bump will be painful."

"Yes, but what if—"

"Take my advice, ma'am, don't borrow trouble. Let's get him into a real bed, and then we'll be better able to tell how he's doing."

Lily knew he was right, but Dun was like family, and he'd been hurt trying to help her. She felt responsible for what had happened to him.

"Here's the ice, ma'am," Sam said as he came around to the side of the buckboard. He handed her the dripping bundle. "Think that'll be enough?"

"I don't know. How long will the trip be?"

"Oh, 'bout half hour to an hour, I'd guess. Maybe a bit longer. We'll have to go kinda slow on account of we don't want to jostle your friend too much."

"I think this will be plenty, then."

Sam nodded and saluted her from the brim of his hat. "You just give a holler if you want us to stop or anything, you hear?"

"We'll be fine," she said, though in her heart of hearts she wasn't at all as confident as she tried to sound.

Sam climbed onto the wagon seat, and once Gray retrieved his topcoat, so did he. The wagon took off slowly and headed west out of town.

Lily spent most of the ride holding the lump of ice against Dun's swelling face, moving it from one place to another when his skin felt too cold to her touch. Dun groaned on occasion but, for the most part, lay quietly, lost to the world. She worried about that most of all. She knew the dangers of head injuries—she'd heard circus stories all her life. The sooner Dun was awake, the better she would feel.

Within the hour they had reached the ranch, and Lily took in the sight of a large two-story house of alternating dark and light stripes. The dark stripes were the weathered logs used to build the house, while the light were from the plaster used to seal the chinks between them. The house was larger than she'd expected and built in a sprawling style. Around the back she could see a series of large corrals and various outbuildings.

Sam pulled up in front of the house, near a covered porch leading to the front door. Gray jumped down.

"Wait here a second. I'll make sure a room is ready for Dun. We don't want to move him any more than necessary."

Gray went to the house, Sam following in his wake. As they approached the door, it flew open. In the dim light of the porch Lily could just make out the silhouette of a woman. As Gray drew near, she flung herself into his arms, and he caught her to him.

The sudden hollow sensation in her stomach caught Lily by surprise. She had no claim on Gray Benedict, so why did she feel this disappointment, as if something special was lost to her? She shook her head to free herself of these unwanted thoughts and turned her attention to Dun. He seemed to be regaining consciousness and was struggling to open his eyes and sit up.

"Lie still," she murmured. "Don't try to move yet. We're here now."

"Here where?" Dun croaked through cracked, swollen lips. "What happened?"

"Do you remember anything at all?"

Dun started to shake his head, then stopped with a grimace of pain.

"Never mind. Just lie still and let me do the talking." She placed the ice over his left eye, and Dun slowly reached up a hand to push it away. "Don't, Dun. You were beaten pretty badly this afternoon. The ice will help."

He stopped fighting her. When she was satisfied that the melting ice wasn't dripping down his neck, she gave him a brief account of the day's events. Just as she finished, Gray returned with Sam.

"Everything's all set," he said. "Amelia is turning down the sheets on the bed in the west bedroom. We'll take Dun up there. If you like, you can stay in the bedroom across the hall from him."

"You're most generous. Thank you," she replied.

She sidled toward the back of the buckboard, intending to jump down that way. Suddenly strong hands held her by the waist and gracefully lifted her in an arc, setting her down on the ground. Her breath hung suspended inside her as Gray's hands lingered a moment longer than absolutely necessary. She could feel his breath on her cheek and smell his enticing masculine scent. She looked up into eyes bluer than the sky and felt herself begin to sway toward him.

"What's keeping everyone?" she heard a feminine voice

call from inside the house, and she jerked guiltily out of Gray's hold.

The voice brought Lily back to her senses. She quickly pulled the remnants of her suit jacket together and hoped she was ready for whatever lay ahead.

TWO

LILY LOOKED ABOUT Dun's new room, impressed but a little intimidated by all she saw. The furniture had elegant lines and intricately tooled brass handles. In the corner hung a cabinet with a mirror mounted on its door, its backboard carved in the pattern of interwoven vines that extended nearly a foot above the cabinet itself.

Looking at her face in the mirror, Lily was taken aback by the frazzled young woman she saw, her red hair disheveled, her cheeks pale. Behind her the reflection showed the canopy of the high-post bed. Standing on tiptoe, Lily could barely make out the diminutive figure of Dun, his bruised face centered on the pillow, his body covered by a beautifully embroidered quilt.

This house was a surprise—its size, its presence, the feeling of permanence it exuded. It was a house built to last, to be passed on from one generation to the next. There was nothing makeshift here; Grayson Benedict had put roots deep in the Wyoming soil.

She knew now that the young woman at the door earlier was his daughter. Amelia, he'd called her, but they'd had no chance to meet. Dun had to be settled in his bed, and she'd wanted to wash off his wounds, especially where the skin was broken.

Now she was exhausted. So much depended on her: Dun's health, the circus's permit, the livelihoods of so

25

many people. She prayed she could handle all this responsibility and keep the circus together.

Lily could barely remember her life before the circus. She'd come there as a young child, running away from home with her older sister, Rosemary, and she'd never looked back. The circus folk had taken them in; Otto and his wife, Hilda, treated the two girls like their own children. They'd taught Lily everything there was to know about circus life and kept her safe. And though sometimes a nameless yearning caught up with her, she thought of the circus as home. She couldn't envision any other life for herself or her friends.

After tidying up her hair as best she could, Lily turned away from the mirror to look again at the room. She wondered what it would be like to live in a place like this—to wake every morning and know that the view outside the window would not change, that the beautiful tree you'd found a quarter mile away would still be there, waiting for you, that you'd be around to see the flowers you planted sprout and then bloom.

Permanence and stability. The concepts were so foreign to her, she almost couldn't imagine them. And then she thought of all she'd have to give up to get them: her friends, the sense of family that extended over all the members of the troupe whether they were along for only one season or had been with Otto for many years, the adventure of seeing new places, of making new discoveries, of exerting herself to her physical limits developing some new trick, one never done before from the back of a horse.

She squared her shoulders. She would have faith in herself. After all, she'd taught her horse to jump through a ring of fire, taught him to bravely continue in the face of his worst fears; surely she could expect no less of herself.

A knock sounded at the door, bringing Lily out of her

thoughts, and she went to answer the door. Gray stood awkwardly in the hall holding a covered tray.

"How are things up here?" Gray asked as he stepped in. "Do you have everything you need?"

"Yes, thank you. The room is lovely. I can't tell you how much I appreciate all you've done."

"How is Dun?"

"He's resting quietly. He doesn't remember all that much about what happened."

"That's probably for the best. You look tired yourself. I thought you might prefer dining here rather than coming downstairs. That way you can rest and keep an eye on your friend. I'll show you to your room later. If you want, I can ask my housekeeper to spell you so you can get some sleep."

"Oh, no. I couldn't possibly leave Dun. He's already so confused about everything. He wouldn't know what was happening if he woke to find a stranger."

Gray frowned and his gaze swept around the bedroom. "Well, if you're planning to spend the night here, I'll have a day bed brought in."

"That's really not necessary. I don't want to be a bother, and your wife might not like having the furniture moved."

"That's not a problem. My wife's been dead for some time."

Just when Lily was about to say how sorry she was for his loss, he quickly continued, as if he didn't want to discuss that subject. "Here, sit and eat and I'll make the arrangements." He lowered the lid of the slant-front desk and put the tray down on it. "I'll be back in a few minutes. Don't let the food get any colder."

With those words he left, and Lily found herself no closer to understanding him than she'd been before. Though he took every pain to ensure their comfort, he hadn't once met her eyes the entire time he was in the room.

Was her appearance so distasteful that he couldn't bear to look at her? She remembered the sight in the mirror just a few minutes ago and sighed. All right, maybe she did look pretty awful, but it was probably all for the best. Too much curiosity about someone outside the circus could only lead to trouble—she'd seen the dire results of that too often. Still, there was something about the tall rancher that made her want to ignore the warnings in her head and listen to the longings of her heart.

Not knowing what else to do, for either Dun or herself, she decided to obey Gray's orders and eat. Things would look better on a full stomach and a night's sleep. In the morning she'd figure out her next step. For the moment Gray seemed to have everything well in hand, so she'd let him make the decisions.

Gray watched as Lily quietly took her seat at the breakfast table the next morning. She looked even more beautiful than she had the night before. He still marveled over his reaction to this spirited, mysterious woman. He'd never met anyone like her, nor had he ever felt such an immediate physical and emotional response. Truth to tell, he'd thought Felicia had killed that part of him, their marriage having been such a disaster. It was reassuring to realize she hadn't.

He'd gone to bed last night but found he couldn't sleep. Lily was all he could think about—her red hair in wild disarray, her dark brown eyes like fathomless pools beckoning him, her trim, firm figure calling for his touch. Her skin was milky white with a freckle or two where he'd caught a glimpse through the tear in her jacket. It looked so soft, so feminine, not hard and tanned like his own.

Gray had tossed and turned for an hour, haunted by visions of Lily, and then, giving up on sleep, he'd saddled his horse and ridden out to the range, knowing Sam could use some company as he guarded the cattle against another round of rustling. This time of year was one of the worst, before the last season's calves were branded at the spring roundup. It was all too easy for someone to ride through his herds culling unbranded calves. Orphans were the most susceptible since without the mother's brand, it was impossible for an owner to claim the calf. And the unscrupulous had no qualms about creating new orphans by the use of a bullet.

But even away from the ranch house, images of Lily wouldn't disappear. He saw her as he had that first moment in town, knowing she was trouble but unable to stop himself from helping her. And now she was seated across the table from him, so close he could smell the delicate feminine scent that clung to her hair and skin.

She wore a pale yellow dress dotted with small green flowers. The material hugged her form from shoulders to waist, outlining the perfection of her figure in precise detail. Her hair shimmered in the early morning sunlight, its fiery redness mesmerizing him. He'd never seen anyone with quite that color and was unable to look away. It wasn't until Mrs. Bellows entered the room that he realized how long he'd been staring.

"Now, miss, is there anything else I can get you?" Mrs. Bellows asked as she bustled about the dining room.

Lily, who'd been staring at her plate as if aware of his scrutiny but unsure how to react, looked up at the housekeeper and smiled. "No, thank you. Everything is lovely. I appreciate all you've done. You've been very kind."

"Weren't no trouble, but *someone* should have called me last night when you arrived," Mrs. Bellows said gently, then turned to Gray and added in a sharper tone, "I can't imagine what that *someone* was thinking of, having a

29

guest make up her own bed. Some folks just don't know the proper way to behave."

Gray was about to protest, then thought better of it. He couldn't very well say he'd wanted time alone with this beautiful stranger and that's why he hadn't called Mrs. Bellows. Instead, he lifted the platter of eggs and passed them to Lily.

"Care for some eggs, Miss Avenel? And maybe a biscuit?" Gray asked, looking pointedly in the housekeeper's direction even though his words were directed at his guest.

"I think your gesture is a matter of too little, too late, young man," Mrs. Bellows said in a huff before turning on her heel and heading back to the kitchen.

Gray looked at Lily and caught the hint of laughter in her eye. He smiled, sharing the moment, and she smiled back.

"You'll have to excuse Mrs. Bellows," he said. "She likes things done a certain way."

"Yes, she made that quite clear." Lily smiled again, and Gray sensed her approval over Mrs. Bellows and her place in his household—more as a gruff mother than a servant.

A warm sense of comfort settled over him, dissipating the tension that had pervaded the room earlier. For the first time since meeting Lily, Gray forgot about watching his every move and keeping his distance. Somehow, in the light of day, he couldn't remember why he'd thought this lady was a threat. Instead, he savored the chance for conversation with someone who would be less taciturn than his closed-mouth cowboys and less interested in gowns and parties than his active daughter.

The pocket door on the hall side of the room slid open just then, and his daughter peeked in.

"Good morning, Papa," Amelia said hesitantly as she slowly walked into the room. Her eyes darted to Lily and then back to him.

Gray sighed and rose from the table. Amelia's interruption was probably for the best. He didn't know what was getting into him, but he certainly wasn't acting like himself. While women were always an interesting distraction, he'd never found any other to have this spellbinding effect on him.

"Amelia, I want to introduce you to Miss Avenel. She and her friend Mr. Edwards will be staying with us for a few days."

His daughter shyly smiled her welcome and sat down in the chair he held out for her.

"Thank you for having us," Lily said.

"Oh, you're very welcome," Amelia answered, filling her plate with eggs and biscuits. "We don't often get visitors. This is a special treat. Will your friend be coming down to breakfast soon?"

"I'm afraid not. He was involved in an unfortunate accident in town. Your father was kind enough to offer him a bed until he is up and about."

"How badly is he hurt?"

"Not as badly as we'd first feared, I'm happy to say."

"I might be able to help," Amelia offered. "I've had some experience with the Ladies Aid Society. They teach us how to tend the sick, you know."

"You're kind to offer, but Dun is a very private person. I think he would prefer someone he knows, but if I have any problems, I'll be sure to ask for your help."

Gray appreciated Lily's tact with Amelia. Though Lily could handle Dun's needs alone, she was kind enough not to hurt his daughter's feelings by completely turning down her offer. Watching Amelia converse with Lily made him realize that his daughter was almost fully grown. Soon her girlish infatuations would turn to real love and she would want a home of her own. He'd be alone again. Was this all there was to life?

He'd thought so once. Now, though his cattle outfit was prosperous and he'd found a niche in society, he still felt something was missing, something even Amelia didn't satisfy. Wondering what else he could possibly want, he lost track of the conversation around him until he heard Amelia ask Lily, "Do you live near Cheyenne?"

"No," Lily replied with just the slightest hesitation.

"Did you come to Cheyenne on business?"

"You'd better stop talking and start eating if you want to get to school on time this morning," Gray admonished his daughter gently. He knew she could talk the hind leg off a mule, given half a chance, and having visitors at the ranch was the only excuse she needed.

"I was just making polite conversation, Papa," Amelia said, then turned to Lily. "Isn't that right, Miss Avenel?"

"Please, call me Lily, and I'm sure your etiquette teacher would be most pleased with you. I've been quite comfortable, really," she added to Gray.

Amelia flashed him a triumphant look, and he settled back in his seat, resigned. If his guest didn't want to be saved, he'd leave her to her fate. Next time she'd know better, especially if she wanted to get a bite of her meal before everything got cold.

"Did you come here on business?" Amelia resumed, as if their conversation had not been stopped. "My father often goes to town on business."

"As a matter of fact, I have."

"What kind of . . ." Amelia started to ask and then stopped. "Is it impolite to ask what kind of business?"

"In most circumstances it is, but with practice you'll learn how to use just the right phrase to get the answer you want."

"So that's how you ladies find out all you need to know, is it? By using a secret questioning code?" Gray asked just to tease.

"We'll never tell, will we, Amelia?" Lily responded, sending the younger girl a conspiratorial wink, before glancing at him from beneath lowered lashes.

"That's right, Papa. This is a lady's secret," Amelia corroborated, smiling at Lily, clearly reveling in the company of another female, especially one so attentive to her.

The eager look on Amelia's face made him realize how much his daughter was missing by having only a father. She needed a woman's influence, a woman's hand to guide her. Why had it taken him so long to see it? Had he blinded himself to his daughter's needs because of Felicia? His wife had died years ago. Maybe it was time to put her truly in his past. Maybe the yearnings he'd felt of late meant he was ready to trust a woman again. Looking across the table at Lily, he was almost ready to believe that was true.

"Why are you in Cheyenne, Lily?" Amelia said, looking expectantly at the woman across the table.

"My friend Otto Bruner is ill, and I'm making some arrangements for him," Lily told her.

Amelia thought for a moment before responding. "It's so nice having you here. I hope the arrangements will take some time?"

Lily laughed. "I see you learn quickly. The way you phrased that question, Amelia, it would make me seem rude and unmannerly if I didn't respond. And, yes, I will be in town for a while. I'm arranging location permits in Cheyenne for our circus."

"The circus!" Amelia exclaimed, her eyes widening at the prospect. "How wonderful! How long will it be in town? Can we go and see it, Papa? Of course, we will, how silly of me. You must tell us all about it. Do you perform? Have you traveled all across the country? It must be so exciting, traveling with the circus. Why, I can't think of anything that would be half as much fun."

Lily bit back a smile as Amelia chattered on. "Fun" was what you were supposed to think when you saw the circus. The reality was far different—the circus required stamina and hard work, but it did have its rewards. How could she tell the girl that without destroying her illusions?

Before Lily could figure out what to say, Gray snapped open his watch case and said, "It's half past seven. When do you need to be at school, Amelia?"

Lily looked up at his words, then glanced at Amelia. The girl seemed unaware of the sharp undertone Lily was sure she'd heard. Lily decided she must have been mistaken; the events of the past couple of days had just left her overly sensitive.

"Eight-fifteen. I have to be at school early today," Amelia explained, turning back to Lily. "Miss McCann wants me to do some special work on my Latin—I've got the highest grades in class—but I wish I could stay here and talk to you instead."

"I've always admired people who have a grounding in the classics," Lily said. "You should be glad you have the opportunity to excel in your schoolwork. We can talk some other time."

"Are you sure? I really don't want to miss hearing all about your life. It must be so exciting, much more so than living on a ranch all the time."

Lily wasn't so sure about that last sentiment. With a man like Gray Benedict around, life on a ranch must be quite exciting. She glanced at him from the corner of her eye and was surprised to see him glaring at his empty plate. What had happened to his easygoing mood of a few minutes ago? Maybe she had heard something in his tone, after all.

Just then Sam walked into the room.

"My, those biscuits sure smell good," he said, moving toward the empty chair beside Amelia. "Mornin', everyone," he said, gazing shyly at the girl, and then added, "Ma'am" in Lily's direction.

"Amelia needs to get to school early today, Sam," Gray said. "You'd best go hitch up the buggy. Mrs. Bellows will keep your breakfast warm."

"Uh, sure, boss," Sam replied, but Lily could tell he was surprised at the order by the look he shot Gray before he left the room.

"Oh, Papa . . ." Amelia started to complain with a pout.

"That's enough, Amelia," Gray said in a tone that brooked no argument. "You don't want to keep Miss McCann waiting."

Amelia got the message. "Yes, Papa." She stood and brushed the crumbs off her skirt. "I'll see you when I get home from school," she said to Lily. "Then you can tell me everything about the circus."

"I'm looking forward to it." She smiled at Amelia, and the girl smiled back, her expression eager, her cheeks lightly flushed. She looked a lot like her father, with the same blue eyes and intent way of looking at people, but her hair was several shades lighter. Lily wondered what her mother had been like, but since Gray's curt reply to her comment about his wife, she didn't feel she could ask.

Amelia smiled back. "I'll see you later."

She followed Sam out the door, and Lily turned to Gray, the smile still on her face. Whatever she had expected from him at that moment, it was not the look of sheer fury she found on his face. He threw his napkin on the table and stood up, leaning over the table so he towered over her.

"Just what do you think you're doing?" he asked, separating each word so it hung menacingly between them.

Lily stared incredulously at Gray and couldn't think of anything to say. What had come over him?

"Well, are you just going to sit there?" he demanded, taking a step in her direction.

"No, I'm not," she returned in much the same tone of voice, and in a flash was standing beside her chair, though she had no idea what they were battling over. All she really wanted was to go back to those few minutes before Amelia had come into the room, when there had been such a . . . rightness between them. She couldn't explain it any other way, though at this moment, she wasn't sure her memory hadn't been playing tricks on her. "Why don't you tell me what you think I've done?"

"Don't play dumb with me. You know you're trying to entice Amelia with all your tales of the circus."

"I—"

"I won't have my daughter's mind corrupted with stories of your life with some disreputable traveling carnival of grafters and other petty criminals, Miss Avenel."

Lily drew herself up to her full height, incensed by his slurs.

"I was merely being polite and answering her questions, Mr. Benedict. And I'll have you know Bruner's Munificent Menagerie and Family Circus is not a disreputable operation. We've toured some of the finest countries in the world and played before kings and queens."

"I don't care if you've played before the Queen of England. I don't want my daughter's head filled with such nonsense."

"That's Her Royal Highness to those of us who've met her, and she thought we were wonderful," Lily retorted, unable to resist the jab, but he either didn't notice or chose to ignore her quip.

"It's still nonsense and I won't have it. I don't want Amelia corrupted." Gray's voice rose in volume with each word.

"I have no intention of corrupting your daughter or anyone else," Lily said in a gentler tone, all the fight leaving her. "I think it would be best if Dun and I leave for town immediately. We have no wish to cause you or your family pain."

Her words stopped Gray in his tracks. What was he doing? When he'd seen his daughter question Lily so ardently, a primitive protective instinct had suddenly come to life warning him of a dangerous threat. For the first time he'd seen a resemblance to Felicia in Amelia's eagerness—something he had never seen before. His daughter was very much like him, both in looks and temperament, so he had thought he was safe, that his daughter was nothing like her mother, that she would never have the urge to exhibit herself shamelessly, to forsake everything she held dear for a fleeting chance at glory.

Then Lily Avenel had come into his life, and suddenly nothing was quite the same. She brought out longings he never thought to have again, yearnings for a different life, a fuller one. And he was not the only one affected. Amelia was showing the same eager attentiveness Felicia had shown when she had talked about the theatrical world. But Felicia's fascination with the theater had had dire consequences, taking her away from her family and friends, and ultimately leading to her death. He'd be damned if he'd let the same thing happen to his daughter.

When he'd seen Lily and Amelia smile at each other as if they had a private understanding, he'd lost all control. This upstart from nowhere wasn't going to put any funny ideas in his daughter's head. He'd see her in hell first. Whatever attraction he'd felt for her was buried under his fear for Amelia.

But her quiet tone of voice and subdued manner reached through his anger and brought him up sharply. In fairness, Lily had not gone behind his back to lure his daughter away. She'd merely answered Amelia's questions politely, just as she'd said.

"I'm sorry," Gray said stiffly, taking a step away from her. "My outburst was uncalled for."

"It's all right. We've imposed on your hospitality long enough. If you could arrange for a wagon, Dun and I will be ready to leave within the hour."

For a second Gray didn't speak; he just stared at her, sure he'd misunderstood. But her determined expression left no doubt in his mind. "Are you out of your mind, woman?" he said, making no attempt to hide his surprise. "Your friend is in no shape to be taken from his bed."

"I'm sure Dun would want us to leave immediately if he knew the circumstances."

"What circumstances?"

"Why, that we're imposing on you and your daughter."

"You're overreacting, and I absolutely refuse to let you move your friend."

"Please," she said, her tone beseeching. "We really—"

"Didn't you say you had to get permits of some sort?"

"Well, yes, but—"

"Then we'd better make plans for going into town. To-morrow will be soon enough. By then your friend should be well on the mend, and you'll be able to leave him for a longer time."

Lily didn't know quite what to say. His complete about-face on the subject of the circus was unnerving, and while she appreciated the use of his home, she didn't want to subject herself or Dun to any more unpleasantries.

"Besides, even after he's feeling better, Dun won't be able to help you complete your business, will he?" Gray added with a superior look, knowing he had clinched the argument.

And he had. Dun would find it very difficult to return to Cheyenne and once again try to track down the recalcitrant fire marshal. For the time being, she'd best leave things the way they were and wait and see what happened. In the meantime, Dun needed her full attention. With a terse nod Lily swung around and walked upstairs to attend to Dun.

Lily sat by Dun's bed and helped him eat his breakfast, though he seemed more interested in talking than eating. He seemed smaller than usual, the outline of his body under the coverlet barely reaching halfway down the bed and his battered face looking even worse against the stark background of the white pillow.

"You shouldn't make such a fuss, Lily. I'm feeling much better," he told her after taking a sip of his coffee.

"And you look wonderful, too, what with those two black eyes and your face swollen to almost twice its size."

"I didn't say I looked ready to stand in the ring, only that I was feeling a bit better," Dun said, easing himself up against the pillows. Even that slight movement caused him to groan.

"And I think you've probably done something to your ribs as well."

"A few wraps of cotton and those will be good as new. This isn't the first time I've cracked a couple of bones."

"Be that as it may, I want you staying put for a few days."

"What about getting those permits?"

"Mr. Benedict has offered to help us get them. I think he's planning on going into town tomorrow."

"Seems like a nice chap, that Mr. Benedict. Came around to look in on me this morning, right before you came with my breakfast. Said if I needed anything, I had only to ask. He wanted the doctor to come out and make sure I was all right, but I told him it wasn't necessary. He insisted, though, and wouldn't take no for an answer."

"Oh?" The man was a complete enigma. Just when she

39

thought she had him figured out, Gray did something to change her mind. She could have sworn he wanted nothing more than to see the back of them, and then he goes and tells Dun to stay as long as he needs to.

"Yes, a right nice chap," Dun continued. "As a matter of fact, everyone's been extremely welcoming."

Certainly Sam, Amelia, and Mrs. Bellows had been, but Lily was reserving judgment on Mr. Grayson Benedict.

"How's the patient this morning?" Mrs. Bellows asked as she walked into the room with a fresh towel and linens.

"Quite well," Dun answered.

"Better," Lily said at the same time.

"Now, isn't that just like a man," Mrs. Bellows said in a confiding whisper to Lily. "Why is it they can never admit to feeling poorly?"

"Must have something to do with never admitting they do *anything* wrong," Lily teased, knowing Dun was hearing every word.

"Give a gentleman some leeway, ladies. Here I am, on my deathbed—"

"Not ten minutes ago you were telling me you were fine," Lily interrupted.

"—on my deathbed and all I get is bedeviled."

Both women merely shook their heads, not listening to a word he said.

"Men," Mrs. Bellows said and rolled her eyes, then she turned back to Lily. "Why don't you take a turn about the house, Miss Lily? You haven't been away from this room for more than a half hour since you arrived. It'll do you good to get some fresh air."

"Do go, Lily. I'll be fine."

"I'll keep an eye on him," Mrs. Bellows offered. "As a matter of fact, I was hoping he'd tell me what it's like in his homeland. We have a number of ladies and gentlemen from London right here in Cheyenne, and I wouldn't mind hearing more about England."

"If you're sure?" Lily asked.

"Go on with you," the older woman said, shooing her out of the room.

Lily reluctantly agreed. She didn't want more time to think about Gray Benedict, and when she had Dun to fuss over, she was able to keep thoughts of him out of her mind. On her own, it would be more of a challenge.

The warm spring air felt good against her face. After a week of clouds and rain, it was nice to look up and see a blue sky dotted with white, fluffy clouds. She hoped the weather would hold for the circus's week of performances. They always pulled in larger crowds when the weather stayed nice. After the way things had been going, they needed every dollar they could make. It seemed as if nothing had gone well since they left St. Louis, just one catastrophe after another.

She needed to see about getting the location permits so the canvas could go up as soon as the troupe hit town. They couldn't afford to waste a day. And then she'd have to make sure the long rest between shows hadn't hindered her horses' performance. She hoped Elena and her husband weren't having any trouble taking care of her mounts. Leaving them in someone else's care had been Lily's one concern when she'd volunteered to go to Cheyenne, but someone responsible had had to go, and she'd been the most likely choice.

While she trusted Elena and Roberto Santelli, and knew they were one of the best acrobatic acts on the road today, she couldn't expect anyone else to give her horses the special treatment she always did. Besides, she was worried about Lancelot; he'd been showing signs of coming down with something, but she hadn't been able to put her finger on his problem. She'd asked Gustav, Old Bess's trainer, to keep an eye on him, too. You could never be too careful with your stock. They were your livelihood as well as your constant companions. On occasion artists jumped from one circus to another, looking for better pay or a better billing, but your animals stayed with you always.

Lily rounded the corner of the house and strolled toward the barn and corral that stood about one hundred feet away. She caught sight of a young filly racing along an inner fence and walked over to get a better look.

Resting her hands on the top rail of the fence, Lily leaned her chin on her hands and examined the young horse. She was a lovely chestnut color with long sleek lines. She moved with a grace and effortless beauty that drew the eye. Lily recognized the horse's potential immediately.

"She sure is fine looking, isn't she?"

Lily turned at the sound of Sam's voice and smiled. She'd liked the younger man the moment she'd met him. His straightforward manner and quiet confidence had endeared him to her immediately in a brotherly sort of way.

"She is that," she agreed. "What plans do you have for her?"

"The boss has a soft spot for her. He hasn't said anything yet, but my bet is he'll give her to Miss Amelia. She's already given her a name. Cleopatra, after some queen or something. Says it's because the mare looks so beautiful."

Lily laughed. "I can see why. Cleopatra was reputed to be the most beautiful woman of her time, and this mare certainly qualifies, doesn't she? I bet she'll make a good riding horse." And also a great horse for the ring, Lily added silently. If the opportunity presented itself, she'd ask Gray about the mare. If he did intend to give her to Amelia, she'd say nothing, but if he didn't ... it would never hurt to feel him out.

"Do you like horses?"

Lily almost laughed at the question. "You might say that. I handle the equestrian act with the circus."

"The circus! I've never met anyone from a real circus before. What does an equestrian"—he stumbled over the word—"do?"

"I work with the horses—training them and riding them in the show."

"You do?" Sam's voice held a touch of wonder and skepticism. "Then maybe . . ."

"What?" Lily prompted when Sam stopped speaking.

"I just thought if you knew about horses . . ."

Lily looked at Sam. It was almost as if he were afraid to ask, but then, some men had fixed ideas about women. Having been brought up in the circus, she sometimes forgot that in the outside world, men didn't always think ladies were capable of doing the same things as men.

"Is there something I can help you with?" she asked.

"Well, you see, one of the horses is sick, and if it wouldn't be too much trouble, would you mind looking at her?"

"I'd be glad to, Sam. After all you and Mr. Benedict have done for Dun and me, it's the least I can do," Lily assured him, though she did have her doubts. She wasn't sure Gray would feel the same way about her involvement. He'd been pretty protective of his daughter. Would he feel the same about his animals and think she was interfering?

It didn't really matter what he would think, she decided, since for her it was a form of repayment for all that had been done for them. "Where is the horse?"

Gray slowed his horse to a walk as he neared the ranch. He'd sent the men back a good hour before, but claimed a limping steer needed his attention and delayed his return for as long as he could.

With this as an excuse, he had managed to stay away from the ranch house and Lily Avenel. She was a threat to his peace of mind, and he wasn't too proud of the way he'd acted this morning, either. He knew that the way he'd behaved was uncalled for, but in his heart he was afraid— afraid for his daughter and where Lily's fanciful stories might lead her. But he was also afraid for his own sake, that history would repeat itself and he'd be left with nothing.

When he'd married Felicia, he'd thought they'd been idyllically happy. They'd had a modest but pleasant home in New York, and he was willing to work hard to improve their standing. Though Felicia had married beneath her station, at least as far as her parents were concerned, she seemed satisfied with their life together. When Amelia was born, Gray's happiness knew no bounds.

At first, Felicia seemed to share his joy. He was doing well at work, had even been promoted. Felicia spent her days seeing to the baby's every need. But as time passed, she became less enchanted with the notion of being a mother and started looking for more exciting adventures.

Before long she'd taken up with a troupe of traveling actors, marveling over their wonderful and exciting lives. One man, in particular, captured her fancy, and before Gray realized what was happening, she was gone.

She'd left Amelia with a neighbor and written him a short note. Six months later she'd returned home, critically ill and wasted. Her lover had tossed her aside for another, and she had nowhere else to go. Gray had taken her in and nursed her, but before the month was out, she was dead.

He'd never forget the horror of that time, of seeing his dreams crumble before his eyes, of having his illusions torn from his heart. Now Lily Avenel represented everything he feared. Until this morning he'd never thought that Amelia might follow in her mother's footsteps. In fact, he'd never even told Amelia what had happened to her mother, only that she had died from a respiratory problem when Amelia was two years old. Having Lily at the ranch reminded him of all he wanted to forget. Worse, she reminded him that he was a man, a man with wants and needs.

Gray couldn't put off going back to the ranch forever, and as he rode toward the barn, Gray remembered he'd promised Sam he'd look in on a mare who hadn't been well for a couple of days. His confrontation with Lily had completely driven Sam's request from his mind.

Gray dismounted and directed his horse into the barn, deciding to check on the mare before facing the household over lunch. When he got halfway to the back of the barn, he heard the voice of the one person he was hoping to avoid.

"You're right, Sam. There's definitely a problem," Lily was saying as Gray drew closer. "Let me take a look; I just want to check something."

He stood by the side of the stall, unobserved, and watched as Lily walked over to the back wall and scrutinized a pile of dung lying on the straw-strewn dirt floor. Then she moved back to the horse and gently tipped up its head, murmuring nonsense words in a hushed tone. Slowly she opened the animal's mouth and peered inside.

"Do you see anything?" Sam asked.

"It's kind of dark in here, but I think it's much what I expected. The inside of her cheeks are a bit torn up. The thing to do now is check her back molars. Can you hold her head?"

Gray decided he'd better intervene. Though it hadn't taken him long to realize she knew her way around horses, she was now risking too much. This mare had been exceptionally nasty the last couple of days, and if Lily thought she could stick her hand into its mouth just like that, she was crazy. He had no intention of standing idly by and letting her do it.

"I'll take care of this, Sam," he said and stepped into the stall. "Why don't you go get your meal? The rest of the boys are already inside."

Sam shot him a speculative look but made no objection. "Sure, boss," he said and headed for the door of the barn.

Lily had jumped at the sound of his voice, but made no comment about his arrival. Gray was acutely aware of the tension that sparked between them, and he, too, remained silent. She stood by the horse, watching him as he approached. Her red hair was more tamed than he'd ever seen it, in an intricate topknot of cleverly spun braids, but a few rebellious tendrils had already made their escape.

In the dim light of the barn her eyes looked almost black and her skin had a translucent glow. He took a step closer.

"What do you want me to do?" he asked, looking down into her wide, dark eyes.

"I just want to check her teeth."

"Step aside and I'll do it," he said, moving in even closer. Her feminine scent reached his nostrils, obliterating the earthier smells of barn and horse.

"I can handle this, you know," she said. "I do it all the time."

Her tone was defensive, but at the same time she stepped back, giving him room to approach the mare and allowing some space to separate them.

He closed that space, moving toward her rather than the horse. "But you don't do it to this horse. She's been particularly bad-tempered lately."

At that moment the horse gave a nervous shudder and stepped forward, forcing Gray to turn his attention from her.

"Steady there, girl," he said to the beast. "Don't be afraid."

As Lily had before him, he crooned soothingly to the mare and patted her side.

"She's in a good deal of pain," Lily commented.

"So Sam said."

"I think it might be sharp tooth."

"Hmmm?"

"She has cuts on her cheeks and tongue."

Gray opened the mare's mouth as she spoke and examined the inside. "Yep."

"And she's not digesting her oats."

She looked so earnest as she listed each of the horse's symptoms. Gray knew he should have gotten out here as soon as Sam had mentioned the problem, but with the rustling trouble, his mind had been elsewhere.

"And your recommendation?"

"Well, file down the teeth, of—" Lily suddenly stopped speaking and looked up at him.

"Sounds right," he agreed, not looking at her.

"Of course, it's right, but you knew that all along," Lily said in an indignant voice.

"I suspected as much," he replied in a lazy tone. He was enjoying baiting her, seeing her spirited response. Suddenly he didn't want to leave the warm intimacy of the barn; he was too enthralled by this woman who looked as if she'd stepped out of a bandbox, but didn't mind sticking her hand into the mouth of a horse.

"Why did you let me go on and on like some kind of show-off?" she demanded.

Gray didn't answer. He couldn't very well tell her he was enjoying listening to her talk. He didn't even want to admit it to himself.

"I think I'll wait until I can get one of the boys to help before filing down her teeth," Gray commented, easing the horse back to the center of the stall. He motioned for Lily to step outside and then closed the stall door behind them.

Before she could move away, he reached for her hand, then splayed her fingers over his palm. Though he felt their tensile strength, they looked exceedingly fine-boned and feminine against his larger hand.

He no longer understood himself. Hadn't he decided just this morning not to let her get too close? He was afraid of the impact Lily, and her career, would have on his life, but the physical attraction was overwhelming.

"I wouldn't want you to lose any of these pretty fingers." His voice sounded husky.

He brought her hand up to his shoulder, then reached around her waist and turned her to face him. She looked up through half-closed lids, her expression a blend of confusion and curiosity. Her lips parted as she took a sudden breath, and then he saw no more. Everything became feeling as his mouth closed on hers. For the briefest moment she stiffened, then as his lips gently nibbled and his tongue subtly probed, she parted her lips and sank against him with a sigh.

She tasted sweet and fiery all at once. She lit a fire inside of him and the heat of her mouth burned him, making him ache for more. The more he kissed her, the hotter the blaze grew, consuming him with no sign of abating. He stroked her back with one hand and dimly registered the firmness of her muscles, the suppleness of her flesh, for he had a softer goal. His hand swept down her side and around her waist before starting to climb again.

Mere inches from the fullness of her breast he stopped, distracted by the pounding noise from inside the stall.

Slowly he withdrew from the kiss, raising his head and leaning back so he could look over the stall rail. The mare was kicking up a storm, sending dust motes and bits of hay flying through the air.

"Damn!" he muttered.

He gazed back at Lily. She appeared slightly dazed, her eyes not quite focused, her lips swollen and moist from his kiss. He wanted nothing more than to continue where they'd left off but knew he couldn't. The mare would injure herself if she wasn't stopped, and there was no one else around.

As he stood silently cursing his fate, Lily suddenly came to life and pulled out of his embrace. She looked mystified and unsure. She put her hand to her mouth, and her eyes grew round. Giving him a disbelieving look, she turned on her heel and darted down the center aisle of the barn toward the front door.

Before Gray could say a word, she was gone.

THREE

AFTER THEIR KISS in the barn, Lily and Gray barely spoke more than two words to each other. For her part Lily wasn't quite sure what to say. Never had a man's touch affected her the way his had, making her lose all sense of time and place, all knowledge of right and wrong. Never had she fallen so prey to her emotions, to desires and passions she'd only read about.

Gray seemed to be avoiding her, too. On the few occasions they were together over the next two days, he made no mention of going into town to get the circus's permit. Since Lily was no more eager to spend time alone with him, she didn't bring it up either.

But as the days passed, a restless energy filled her. She was used to a lot more physical activity, and her muscles were begging to be stretched and worked until they were pleasantly sore. Unfortunately, without her horses around, practicing her act was out of the question. But that didn't mean she had to spend the day doing nothing.

Determined to do some stretching and balancing exercises, Lily waited until everyone was busy at their appointed tasks and Dun was taking an afternoon nap. She felt strange sneaking out the back door, but she didn't want anyone to see her—especially Gray.

In all her dreams, when she'd thought of meeting a man she could love, she'd always envisioned finding someone who shared her love of performing, of traveling from place to place, of following the circus from season to season. Though Gray hadn't said anything more, she knew he was still uncomfortable about her circus connections—just as she was unused to staying in one place all the time, no matter how she had longed for it.

How confused everything had become. What she needed was a good practice session to take her mind off Gray's body and focus it again on her own, on the skills she needed to stay on the back of a galloping horse. Behind the barn she found the perfect place. A runoff from a small creek watered a patch of grass that the horses kept clipped short. Today all of the horses were out, leaving the small corral clear. Taking off her regular shoes, she slipped on a pair of soft leather slippers that molded to her feet without restricting their motion. She'd dressed lightly today, too, leaving off her corset and layers of petticoats in favor of a free swinging skirt that gave her more freedom to move.

Ordinarily she would practice in a short performance costume that barely cleared her knees, but here on the ranch she was too self-conscious to attempt wearing such skimpy attire. She spent the next half hour loosening her muscles with a series of stretching exercises and calisthenics. A light sweat soon covered her skin, and her body felt pleasantly warm and invigorated.

Unable to resist she tried a couple of tumbling runs but was not pleased with her performance. Though light, the skirt still got in her way, twisting round her ankles and tripping her up. Reaching down between her legs, she brought the back hem through and up, over the front of the skirt, then tucked it into her waistband. The skirt pulled snugly against her legs, like a pair of full-cut trousers. She looked around to make sure no one could see her. Satisfied that she was alone, she launched into one of the routines she and Elena had worked out when they wanted to practice together. Though their acts were different, both relied on a combination of balance, flexibility, and various acrobatic tricks. They had found that the same exercises were useful to each of them, and working together eased the tedium of the endless practicing.

As she finished the routine, sliding to the grass with one leg stretched in front of her and the other straight behind, she heard clapping. Scrambling to her feet, she quickly looked around to find Amelia leaning against the corral fence, her expression rapt.

"That was wonderful, Lily," she crowed. "I've never known anyone who could do things like that!"

"When did you get home?" Lily asked, not sure how to handle the situation. Amelia's face was flushed with excitement and her blue eyes glowed.

"Just a few minutes ago. I came out to see Cleopatra and caught sight of you doing your tricks. Do you think you could teach me a few?"

Lily couldn't think of anything to say. The last thing in the world she wanted was to disappoint this eager young woman. On the other hand, incurring Gray's displeasure was something she wanted to avoid.

"I don't think that's such a good idea," she said to Amelia. "To learn tricks properly you have to practice a lot, and that takes time. You have so much to do between your schoolwork and social responsibilities."

"No, I don't, not really. I mean, I have to go to school, but I don't have very many other responsibilities."

Lily had to bite her lip not to smile. Just yesterday Amelia was happily complaining about her enormous responsibilities and the various social gatherings that demanded her attention.

"I thought you were planning for a big party in just a few weeks," Lily said, remembering the details of the conversation.

Amelia's eyes widened, as if she had forgotten what she'd described as the party of the year. "Well, that won't take up *all* of my time."

"What about your ranch chores?" Lily asked.

"You've been listening to Papa," Amelia accused, but the smile on her face let Lily know the point had struck home without angering the girl.

"And so should you," she said, returning the smile. "Come on, let's go back inside and see if Mrs. Bellows needs any help getting dinner ready."

"Oh, you're not stopping, are you? I hoped you would at least show me something from your act."

"I'm afraid I can't do that. I do an equestrian act, so I need Lancelot to perform."

"Who's Lancelot?"

"My horse."

"Is he anything like Cleo?"

Lily laughed. "Not one bit, I'm afraid. Lancelot is a temperamental old thing except when he's in the ring. Then I trust him with my life. The rest of the time I stay away from him as much as possible, and so does everyone else. Especially if Merlin is not around."

"Is Merlin another horse?"

"I wish he were. No, Merlin is a small, very smelly goat, but Lancelot can't live without him."

"Does Merlin also do tricks?"

"Not the way you mean. Merlin doesn't perform, but you can't turn your back on him either. That little goat is so full of vinegar and spite . . ." She let her voice trail off as she realized she was doing exactly what Gray had asked her not to—telling Amelia about her life with the circus. From the expression on the girl's face, she could tell that her stories were only increasing the girl's interest.

"I can't wait until your circus comes to town," Amelia said, confirming Lily's thoughts. "I'll have Papa take me right away. Can we visit you and meet Lancelot and Merlin, and all your other friends?"

Lily decided her only recourse was to be diplomatic. "If you come, I'll be glad to introduce you to everyone." She'd been honest without pointing out to Amelia how unlikely it was that her father would bring her anywhere near Bruner's Munificent Menagerie and Family Circus.

At that moment they heard the sound of approaching hoofbeats. Lily's first reaction was one of relief, thinking the new arrival would be a distraction from their conversation. Her second reaction, however, was not as sanguine as she recalled how she was dressed and what a mess her hair must be in.

"Oh, no! I'd better get to the house before someone sees me like this!" Lily exclaimed and hastily undid the hem of her skirt from her waist. She shook down the skirt, then headed for the house at a run. "You coming?" she called back to Amelia.

Amelia nodded and raced ahead of Lily to the back door, all decorum forgotten.

At dinner that night Lily discovered her restless energy had not abated in the least despite her physical exertions earlier in the day. As soon as Gray walked into the room, that same sense of anticipation filled her, as if something mysterious and exciting lay just beyond the horizon, waiting for her. When she looked at him, her pulse beat more quickly, colors seemed brighter and more vivid, and life seemed to move at a quicker pace. In the hours he was gone, time slowed down, even dragged a little as she worried about Otto and the circus or cared for Dun.

"How's Dun today?" Gray asked. Without looking directly at her, he passed her the bowl of potatoes.

"He's doing much better. We should be able to resume our work in a day or two."

Deep inside, where even she was afraid to look for fear of the secret yearnings she might find, a small part of her hoped he would suggest they stay on anyway.

"We still haven't been to town to get your permit," he said instead. "Let's plan on going tomorrow. Sam can handle things here, and I know you want to get things settled. Is that all right with you?"

Lily swallowed her disappointment, knowing she had no right to the feeling. After all, just this morning she'd been worrying about how to broach the issue of the permit with Gray. He had made no mention of the trip since their kiss, and she wasn't sure he was still interested in helping her.

"That would be fine, if it isn't too much trouble for you."

"No trouble at all. Be ready around eight."

When she nodded, Gray breathed a sigh of relief. Now all he had to do was control his baser urges for another day or so, and then he could send Lily and her friend on their way, knowing he'd done all he could for them.

He'd spent the last couple of days in turmoil. If he'd thought he had trouble keeping Lily out of his mind before their kiss, he found it impossible afterward. All he had to do was catch sight of her, and his whole body would shake with the memory of having her in his arms. He'd feel again the silkiness of her hair and remember her taste, sweet and feminine and enticing, and his loins would tighten.

Worst of all he knew she was wrong for him. Oh, she knew about horses, all right, and got along well with his crew and his daughter, but that meant nothing. It was the novelty of the situation. Soon enough, just like Felicia, she'd get bored and look for more excitement. A steady, hardworking man, no matter how much of a success he might be, would never satisfy them. And he wanted more.

He wanted permanence, a deep commitment to a life together.

So he had no choice. The best thing he could do for all concerned was to hasten her departure—before Amelia grew too fond of her, before he gave his own heart to a lost cause, before the circus came to town and brought along its dangerous magic.

He managed to keep his eyes averted from Lily for the rest of the meal. As soon as he finished eating, he found an excuse to leave the house.

Sam found him a while later in the barn, checking up on the mare whose teeth had been filed.

"Everything all right, boss?" Sam asked from outside the stall.

"Everything's fine. I just wanted to see how this mare was doing."

"She looked okay this afternoon. Mouth's healing up nicely and she's chewing her food again."

"Let's give her another day, and then she can be put back to work."

"Okay."

Gray rubbed the mare's nose and let her nuzzle his palm as she searched for another treat. With her pain a distant memory she had reverted back to her usual disposition, and Gray knew she was well on her way to a complete recovery.

"I'm taking Miss Lily to Cheyenne tomorrow," he told Sam. "She wants to work out the details of the circus's stay, and I might as well drop in on the Cattlemen's Club and catch up on the latest news."

"You fixin' to stay the night?"

Gray looked up sharply at that but saw nothing insinuating in his foreman's expression. Apparently Sam had asked the question innocently enough, not to confirm any ideas he had about Gray and Lily.

"No, I think we can make it back before supper without any problem. I don't want to be out on the roads after dark, not with those rustlers hanging around and an eastern tenderfoot on my hands."

"Miss Lily ain't hardly no tenderfoot, boss. You saw how she handled that horse. Just walked right up to it like she knew her business."

Sam's voice was full of admiration and respect. For some reason that rankled Gray. "Taking care of a horse doesn't mean much. This is her first trip west of the Mississippi, and as far as I'm concerned, that makes her a tenderfoot whether she can ride or not."

"Well, if what she says is true, she sure as hell can ride, I'll say that for her."

Gray knew he shouldn't ask but couldn't stop himself no matter what ideas he might be giving Sam.

"Oh? She been talking much about that circus of hers?"

"Not so's you'd notice. Getting her to talk about it is like pulling teeth, though I don't know why. Sounds like her life is exciting enough, and she sure has some danged funny stories."

Sam chuckled as if he were remembering one of those stories right that minute. Gray didn't like it one bit. Not only was his daughter under threat from the circus, now Sam was just as enthralled.

"Well, funny or not, this is hardly the right time to be lollygagging around doing nothing and listening to wild yarns. Those rustlers could be out there picking off the best of our herds even now."

Sam drew himself to his full height at Gray's words and narrowed his eyes. "You not happy with my work, boss?" he bit out.

Gray sighed and ran his fingers through his hair. Now he'd done it! Insulted Sam without meaning to, and all because of that redheaded siren.

"Now, Sam. I didn't mean that, not at all. I guess I'm just worried about all that's going on, what with planning for the roundup, watching out for rustlers, and handling things around here. There's a lot to do this time of year. That's why I hired you in the first place, and I haven't changed my mind."

In fact he'd taken a chance, hiring such a young and relatively inexperienced man to be his second-in-command. But there had been something steady and mature about Sam, a sense of strong values and faith in himself that appealed to Gray. Experience was something you could learn, character was something you had to be born with, and as far as Gray could tell, Sam had been born with more than his share.

"Them rustlers are bound to be caught soon. They're getting too bold," Sam said, relaxing his stance at Gray's explanation. "Besides, once the roundup is over, they won't be able to steal so easily."

"I don't know about that. Some of them are damned good with a running iron. I've heard they can work over a brand so's you'd never know it'd been doctored. And make the new mark look as old as you please just by putting a piece of wet blanket on the animal first."

Sam scratched his head. "So what're you going to do?"

"The only thing I can do. Keep up the patrols on the range and see what I can find out from some of the other cattlemen. That's why we formed the Cattlemen's Association, after all."

"You want me and the boys to do anything special?"

"Just what you've been doing. Keep a watch on the place and look out for signs of unusual activity, especially the remains of fires that burned hot and long. Whatever else he can do, even a brand blotcher can't do his work without a fire."

Sam nodded and took his leave while Gray busied himself in the barn until he saw the lights go out in the main house. Then he went inside and prepared himself for another fitful night of wild dreams that left him hot and bothered and more tired in the morning than he'd been the night before.

Shortly before eight o'clock in the morning Lily came downstairs dressed in a warm traveling suit. The dark brown wool coat was trimmed with fur, and she carried a matching muff to keep her hands warm. Beneath the coat she wore a short-trained walking dress with a snugly fitted basque top in shades of russet and brown. A small hat sat on her neatly coiffed curls. She'd spent the past hour taming her hair, curling her bangs neatly in the current fashion and weaving her long tresses into several braids which she then wrapped round her head like a bandeau, tucking the ends of each braid beneath another.

She wanted to look her best today—for the city fire marshal, of course. She wanted him to take her seriously, to give her the permit without taking advantage of her, without adding fees no one else had ever heard of, or setting conditions the circus could never meet. The fact that Gray was coming with her had nothing to do with it. She'd decided the night before that she and Gray lived in fundamentally different worlds and that their differences could never be bridged. There was no point in tempting fate by thinking otherwise.

In her handbag she had copies of the letters exchanged between the Cheyenne officials and Otto authorizing their visit, subject to their paying the various use fees required by the city. She also carried some money, in case she needed ready cash, and a letter of credit from Otto's bank.

"Here, now, Miss Lily, you ain't going to town without eating breakfast, are you?" Mrs. Bellows demanded as Lily reached the bottom step.

"I'm afraid I'm not very hungry today." She smiled at the large woman.

Mrs. Bellows frowned back. "Then come have some hot coffee. A body needs warming before venturing out in our cold weather. The sun may be out today, but the wind's right wicked. Listen, you can hear it blowing something fierce."

Lily cocked her head and listened as the housekeeper requested. Sure enough, she could hear the wind as it gusted around the outbuildings and raced past the open area between them to hit the main house full force.

"No wonder this place is called the Whispering Winds," she said.

"Shoulda been 'Roaring Winds,' if you ask my opinion. But of course, no one does," the housekeeper responded with a snort of derision. "Come and get that coffee," she added as she went down the hall to the kitchen.

Lily followed, not so much because she wanted the hot drink as that she appreciated the interest and attention of the older woman. Today more than before, she felt lonely and homesick for her friends and her home, even if it was only a small wagon that moved from place to place. At least it was hers and she felt she belonged.

"Have a seat," Mrs. Bellows said and placed a cup of coffee and a plate with buttered toast in front of her. "Hang on a minute and I'll get some of my strawberry preserves."

"Oh, that's really not necessary. . . ." Lily let her voice trail off since Mrs. Bellows wasn't listening anyway.

Once the preserves were laid out in front of her, she really couldn't resist. The sweet, fragrant smell and bright red color were too enticing.

"This is really wonderful," she said after taking a generous bite.

60

Mrs. Bellows smiled her pleasure and gave her a rather smug look.

The outside door opened, letting in a gust of frigid air, and Gray stuck his head in. "Oh, good. You're ready."

Mrs. Bellows looked up. "And here's another one," she said, "that doesn't want no breakfast. What's folks gonna think? I have a reputation to uphold, you know."

"I'll just have a cup of coffee," Gray replied and stepped into the kitchen, shutting the door behind him.

"And where have I heard that before?" Mrs. Bellows said with a sniff. "Sit and I'll pour you a cup. Then I'm going where my efforts are appreciated. You don't find that fine Mr. Dun refusing my good food. Small as he is, he eats better than the lot of you."

She set a cup of coffee near Gray and pushed the plate with the toast closer to the middle of the table. Then she picked up a tray with a teapot and two covered dishes on it and headed for the back stairs.

"Have a safe trip," she said over her shoulder. "I'll keep dinner warm. Hopefully by then you'll have found your appetites again."

The words carried a hint of warning in them. Mrs. Bellows was not about to be insulted by having her culinary skills ignored a second time.

Now that they were alone, Lily had no excuse to avoid looking in Gray's direction. She meant to just sneak a quick glance at him, just long enough to notice how well he looked in his city clothes. But she hadn't seen him in a suit since the day he brought her and Dun back to the ranch, and she couldn't keep herself from staring. His dark coat had the newly fashionable wider lapels, and he wore a matching wool vest beneath it. She could see a gold watch chain crossing his chest where the coat hung open. His trousers were lightly checked and were obviously hand-tailored.

Lily's gaze wandered to Gray's face, and she caught him·looking at her. She quickly turned her head, but not before noticing that he did the same.

"I'm ready to leave any time you want," she said.

He took a last swallow from his cup. "Right now is fine. You have everything you need?"

"Yes."

They both stood up at the same time.

"I'll get the carriage," Gray said. "Sam's hooked up the team for us. I'll drive around to the front to get you."

"All right." She went toward the front of the house, and Gray slipped out the back.

The drive to Cheyenne passed with the same still formality between them. Lily should have been happy with this turn of events. After all, it made it that much easier for her to keep her distance. She kept reminding herself of that fact as the ranch land gave way to the open range and then to the outskirts of the burgeoning city.

When they drove into the central part of town, Gray said, "I have some business at the Cattlemen's Club. If it's all right with you, I suggest we find the fire marshal so you can make your arrangements. Then we'll lunch at the club."

"That would be fine," she replied, secretly relieved that he would be coming with her. After her last attempt to find the marshal, she had no eagerness to be on her own in this wild place.

As luck would have it, the fire marshal was in his office. After he and Gray exchanged pleasantries, she got down to her business. In a short while everything was arranged. All that remained was for the troupe to reach Cheyenne, and they could set up in one of the large parks near the edge of town.

"Will you be round to the club?" Gray asked the marshal.

"I reckon I might."

"We'll see you there, then."

The fire marshal nodded, and Gray waved good-bye. Placing his hand on her elbow, he escorted Lily out the door and down the few blocks to the building the Cattlemen's Association was using as a regular meeting place.

As he walked in, several people greeted him. One of them, a man a bit taller than Gray but every bit as impeccably dressed, came over.

"Gray, it's good to see you. I can see why you've been scarce these past few days."

He gave Lily a look of respectful admiration and smiled. She couldn't help but smile back. He had the kind of handsome looks that made women respond without their even knowing it.

"Hello, Hank. This is Miss Lily Avenel. Lily, this is my friend Henry Farrell. He's also a rancher. Owns a spread a few miles north of mine."

"I'm pleased to meet you, Mr. Farrell," Lily said.

"No more pleased than I, Miss Avenel. And please, call me Hank."

He took her hand in his and raised it to his lips in the European fashion. His mustache tickled the top of her hand, making her smile.

"Then you must call me Lily."

"I would be most charmed. You are as beautiful as the flower for which you are named. Won't you join me and a few friends for lunch?"

Lily looked up at Gray for a sign as to what he preferred, but he was glaring at her hand still nestled in Hank's. She felt herself blush as she withdrew her hand from the other man's. "I'm afraid I don't know what Gray's plans are. You'll have to ask him."

"Well, Gray, what do you say? Surely you'll join us. Prescott will be there and Franklin Pollock and Zeke Martin. We're hopin' John Dixon will also stop by with his wife."

Gray faced a dilemma. Those were the very men he'd come to town to see. Though the thought of watching Hank shamelessly flirt with Lily over the entire meal was almost more than he could bear, responsibility won out over his emotions.

"We'd be glad to join you. That is, if you have no objections, Lily."

Gray saw her look from him to Hank. Hank gave her his most winsome smile. Gray clenched his jaw.

"I would be delighted to meet your friends," Lily said.

"Good," Hank responded and held out his arm. "Allow me to show you the way. I've already reserved a table."

Gray gritted his teeth as Lily placed her hand on Hank's arm and sent a questioning look his way. He merely shrugged in response and followed the pair into the dining room, then greeted the other men and women.

Prescott Warford-Smythe's reaction was every bit as fawning as Hank's had been, and he had the advantage of nobility on his side, as he was British and a relative, however distant, of the reigning queen. The other two men, Franklin and Zeke, were married and less inclined to flirt, but Gray could tell Lily was charming them all.

"Will you be stayin' in our fair city long?" Hank asked her during a lull in the conversation.

"No more than a couple of weeks, I'm afraid," she said.

"That is a pity," Prescott put in. "But at least you will be here for my sister's party on Thursday. Do say you'll come. Cybil's so anxious for it to be a success. This will be a party to celebrate her return from the East."

"It's kind of you to invite me, but are you certain that your sister won't mind my coming?"

"Oh, no. Cybil loves a social occasion. The more

guests, the better. If I know Cybil, she took this last trip just to have an excuse for another party."

"Thank you and I am delighted by your invitation."

"Where are you staying? I'll arrange to have you escorted."

Prescott smiled at Lily, and Gray found himself resenting the lascivious gleam in the man's eyes. Before Lily could speak, Gray intervened. "Lily is staying with Amelia and me. She won't need an escort. We'll be happy to bring her."

"But—"

Lily looked as if she was about to protest, and he understood her surprise. He'd spent the day making her feel as much of an outsider as he could. He certainly hadn't extended an invitation to her to stay, nor had he planned to. If he'd been smart, he'd have let Prescott or Hank escort Lily to the party from some hotel in town. Either would have been thrilled to do so. Only Lily seemed naïvely unaware of the undercurrents flowing round the table, but based on his experience, it all could be an act. Felicia had been a master at that, why should Lily be different?

Still, he felt impelled to step in, an unanticipated sense of possessiveness or some primitive male instinct driving him. "Since you have no plans until your friends arrive in town, you might as well stay at the ranch and go with Amelia and me."

Lily gave him a puzzled look. Granted, it wasn't the most polished invitation, but he wasn't feeling very polished right at this moment, not with his closest friends panting over the lady *he'd* brought.

Lily smiled apologetically at the other two men. "I fear Gray is right. My friend Dun and I did not plan our trip well enough. Gray's been most gracious to put up with us for so long, and if he's willing to have us stay on, how can I refuse? But I thank you both for your hospitality."

She smiled again and both men grinned back. Gray scowled.

"Where's that waiter?" he demanded of Hank. What was wrong with Hank today? He knew they had important business to discuss. All Gray wanted was to get this meal behind them and go to the club room where they could have some privacy to really talk.

Hank looked back, unperturbed. "Here he comes. May I take the liberty of orderin' for you?" he asked Lily. "The chef has some exquisite specialties I'm sure you'll enjoy. Better than anythin' you might have had, even back East."

Lily nodded and murmured her thanks, then spent the next few minutes reminiscing about England with Prescott. It seemed she really had visited there with the circus as she'd once mentioned to Gray. The only satisfaction Gray got from the whole episode was seeing Hank as irritated as he was that the British nobleman had entranced their new guest.

The meal seemed interminable to Gray, but obviously not to Lily. She basked in the attention of the others. Even the wives seemed taken by her. Only Gray seemed outside the circle of her warmth, though she kept sending him questioning glances. But he had no answers either for her or for himself. All he knew was that his heart was at war with his head, and he had no idea which would be the victor.

After lunch the men and women separated, the men going into a special room to smoke and converse while the women disappeared to another part of the building.

"Well," Prescott said between puffs on an extremely pungent cigar he was trying to light, "have you heard any more about those rustlers?"

"I heard John Dixon lost a couple of young bulls he'd been keeping an eye on," Franklin said. "Found one cow dead and the other seriously injured. Had to put it down himself."

"Seems like just last week Dixon was bragging on them bulls," Prescott observed, his cigar finally drawing to his satisfaction. "Damned shame to have lost them so quick."

"Did he talk about them here?" Gray asked.

"Why, I don't recall precisely," Prescott replied. "I remember we were having lunch. Hank, old chap, you were there, were you not?"

"Where, Prescott?" Hank called out from across the room, where he was deep in conversation with another cattleman.

"Why, at lunch the day Dixon told us of his bull calves."

"Can't say," Hank called back. "Are you sure it was me?"

"No, no. Must have been someone else. Sorry to bother you." Prescott shook his head. "Bloody hell. Now, who could have been with us? I was so sure it was Hank."

"Well, it makes no difference now, does it?" asked Franklin. "The animals are long gone and the rustlers with them, I would guess."

"It makes a difference if Dixon mentioned it here," Gray put in, deciding to feel out his colleagues and see what they thought of his suspicions.

"Why?" Prescott asked, looking puzzled.

"Because all of the rustling has happened to members who—"

"But, old chap, nearly everyone who has cattle is a member here," Prescott interrupted.

"Yes, but the ones who've been selected by the rustlers all had something different or special going on at their ranches."

Hank walked up at that moment. "Well, men, what are

you so serious about? Don't you think it's time we rounded up the ladies and made plans for the evenin'?"

Though Hank was one of his oldest and dearest friends, Gray was ready to strangle him. Whether it was because he'd ended the conversation about the rustlers before Gray got the information he wanted or because he clearly wanted to spend time with Lily, Gray didn't venture to guess.

Prescott, however, had no such reservations about their discussion. His face lit up as he said, "Ah, yes. The ladies. Mustn't keep them waiting, must we? Listen, Gray, this rustling thing will work itself out one way or the other. I wouldn't worry about it if I were you."

No, *you* wouldn't, Gray thought uncharitably. No wonder the local ranchers felt a certain resentment toward the foreigners who invested in beeves but ran their businesses from afar. Prescott was not a totally absentee owner in that he did come to Cheyenne for a good portion of the year. He rarely ventured out to his ranch, though, preferring to spend his days here at the Cattlemen's Club or similar venues. Moreover, Prescott seemingly did not care about or did not understand the ranching business. Perhaps he had enough other sources of income that a loss now and then made no difference to him. But for most of the ranchers, too much thieving and a bad winter or two could bankrupt them.

"You havin' problems with rustlin'?" Hank asked him.

"No, but we're keeping an eye out, just to be safe."

"Have you seen any signs of anythin'?"

"No, I'm happy to say."

"Good, I'm glad to hear that."

"How about you?" Gray asked. "Any problems?"

"None but the usual. I only wish I had enough cattle to interest a rustler," Hank said with a strained laugh.

Gray clapped him on the shoulder. "Don't worry, friend.

You've got the makings of a fine outfit. Just give yourself a bit of time. If my new breeding program works out, I'll sell you a few of my cows at a good price."

"Have those new cattle arrived yet?"

"Yes, just last week." The day he'd met Lily, Gray thought to himself.

The conversation ended as they met up with the ladies in the common room.

Lily looked up as the men walked in. She picked out Hank and Prescott right away, Hank because he was so tall and Prescott because of his very British looks, but when Gray entered, Lily saw no one else. He was neither as tall nor as handsome as Hank nor did he carry himself with the natural arrogance of the British peer. But there was a compelling attraction about him that went beyond mere looks or social standing. Even the other ladies in the room turned their gazes to Gray, Lily noticed when she was finally able to draw hers away.

She hoped he would come sit by her side since there was an empty chair right next to her. Until the men entered, the conversation had been interesting with the women discussing ranch business. The men would probably have been surprised at how much these women knew, for as soon as the first male had entered this chamber, all talk of rustling and beef prices had ceased. Now the sounds of flirtatious laughter and teasing were all that could be heard.

Gray did walk over, but instead of sitting down, he leaned over and murmured, "We should probably be heading back to the ranch soon. It still gets dark early this time of year, and I don't want to be out after sundown if at all possible. How soon can you be ready?"

"I'm ready now," Lily said, feeling flushed from Gray's closeness. "Do you want to leave?"

Gray nodded and Lily stood up. In an instant Prescott

and Hank were by her side, entreating her not to go so soon. The attention embarrassed her. She was not used to such blatant flirting, nor to being the center of attention when she was not on the back of her horse. She was more comfortable dealing with people one to one.

"Ah, look, she's blushing!" Prescott exclaimed a little too loudly for Lily's taste. "You are really the most charming young miss. Now, you won't forget to come to Cybil's party, will you? I shall be counting the minutes."

He kissed her hand as Hank had when she'd first arrived, and Lily snatched it back as soon as she could, aware of Gray's icy stare. Surely he didn't think she encouraged this man's interest? One look at Gray's face told her that he did and was none too pleased about it.

"I'm afraid we have to hurry on. Amelia is expecting us," Lily put in as she edged her way out of the room. "It was a pleasure meeting all of you."

Once they were in the buggy and on their way back to the ranch, Lily couldn't resist asking Gray about the rustling.

"Where'd you hear about that?" he demanded.

"Why, from the ladies, of course. Did you think they didn't know about it?"

"I wasn't sure. The men are pretty protective of their womenfolk around here."

"And how is it protective not to let them know what's going on?"

He looked at her as if she was daft. "What point is there in having them worry unnecessarily?"

"Unnecessarily! How can you think that? Their livelihoods depend on the fortunes of the ranches as much as their husbands' do. Besides, if there's danger on the range, shouldn't they be told so they can protect themselves?"

"That's what they have menfolk for."

"Well, I never heard of anything so . . ." She stopped in

midsentence, aware that she was about to call her host some unflattering names.

"You were saying?" Gray prompted.

From the way his lip twisted on one side, she knew he was trying hard not to smile because he knew exactly what she was going to say. "You know very well what I mean. *I* would certainly want to be told if there were problems with my ranch."

"Didn't know you had a ranch."

"That's not what I meant and you know it."

"I guess I did at that," he admitted and smiled.

It was the first smile she'd seen since their kiss. Her stomach fluttered, and she laced her fingers together to keep both hands where they belonged—on her lap rather than reaching out to brush back the errant lock of dark hair that fell over his forehead.

"So, what do you think of my ranch?" he asked, and she began to hope he was no longer seeing her as a threat to his daughter or himself.

"It's very impressive. The house is so solid. Built to last forever. And your men pull together and work hard. They seem extremely loyal to you, especially Sam."

In some ways the place reminded her of the circus: everyone working toward a common goal with a spirit of camaraderie that extended beyond the workday. Just like the circus, the men bunked together and ate together as well as worked together, day in and day out. She wished she could tell Gray how similar their lives were, but she sensed he wasn't ready to hear that, so she merely told him her impressions of his ranch and his daughter and the horse Cleo. In turn he told her how he ran the ranch, how they worked the cattle and trained the horses, surviving summer's grueling heat and winter's bitter cold. And then, all too soon they were home.

He helped her down from the carriage, and for a second

71

she was afraid that he would revert to his distant self
again. Instead, he said, "Go on in and let them know we're
back. I'll unhook the horses and come join you."

She smiled and watched as he drove off to the barn.
Only then did she realize she'd thought of their arrival as
coming home.

FOUR

"So how was your day in Cheyenne?" Dun asked when she dropped in to see him after dinner.

"Everything went well. I paid the fees, and the fire marshal is allowing us to set up in a park." The fire marshal was the designated official for giving the circus a permit in most towns. He would collect their fees and tell them where to set up. The fees covered any costs the city anticipated might result from the circus's stay.

"Any trouble finding him?"

"No, he was in his office this time. I must confess I didn't even see a saloon today. Cheyenne is certainly a city of contrasts. You wouldn't believe how cosmopolitan the Cattlemen's Club is. Everyone wears the latest fashions—even the men—and the women looked straight out of *Harper's* magazine!"

"Sounds very posh, indeed. How was the food, or shouldn't I ask?"

Lily laughed. "You would have felt right at home. Half the people there seemed to be English, and they all want a touch of home in their menu."

"Ah, now you have me envious."

"Just don't let Mrs. Bellows hear you say that. Why, just this morning she was singing your praises. Seems you eat better than all of us downstairs."

Poor Dun turned bright red at her words. "Mrs. Bellows

is a fine cook," he said. "Besides, there hasn't been much else I could do these past few days other than eat."

Lily frowned. "I'm sorry, I should have asked immediately. How are you feeling?"

"Now, Lily, I didn't say that to make you feel bad. I'm doing just fine. My shoulder hardly aches anymore, and I'm more than ready to get out of this bed. If we don't get back into town, how will Otto find us?"

"I left word for him with the fire marshal. Besides, Gray has invited us to stay on a bit longer. There's a party in Cheyenne later this week. An Englishman is holding it for his sister. Seems they're out here building the family fortune. . . ." She didn't know how to proceed. After all, she'd been invited to the party, but the invitation had not been extended to Dun. She was sure an invitation would be tendered if requested, but she didn't know what Dun would want.

Ever sensitive, Dun came to her rescue. "Sounds like a dreadfully boring affair, especially if everyone has to dress to the nines. I'm looking forward to a relaxing evening myself. Miss Amelia has offered me the use of her library now that I can see again."

"Are you sure you wouldn't like to accompany us?"

"Now, Lily, you know better than that. I don't know what's worse, being beaten by a group of cretinous louts or being stared at, poked, and prodded by the so-called upper classes. Neither of them care one whit for me. One way or the other I'd just end up being pitied or derided. I'd much rather stay here unless you object."

"No, that's fine. It's just that I hate to see you miss out on things. There's more to life than just the circus."

"That's not what you used to say." He studied her through narrowed eyes.

She caught his look and understood it. She'd spent most of her years with the circus, coming there when she was a child. She'd never openly questioned whether her life with the troupe was complete—maybe because she'd never realized there was so much more.

For his own reasons, Dun, too, had chosen to confine his life to the circus tent, rarely venturing outside unless forced to by circumstance, as in this case.

"Don't worry," she reassured him. "It's not what you think. It's just that this is an opportunity to see something of the world outside, and I just wanted a glimpse. No one knows better than I the perils of that world. After all, I lived there once."

Dun did not look reassured, but had the grace not to pursue the subject, to Lily's relief. She wasn't ready to explore the feelings coming to life inside her. First she had to sort them out in her own mind, then she would know what to do.

Gray awoke to the sound of birds singing and lay in his bed without moving. Thoughts of Lily filled his mind—the sound of her laugh when she was amused, the fire in her hair when the sun shone through it, the light in her eyes when she looked at him. The trip home from Cheyenne had been different from the trip out. Instead of silence and strain, there had been conversation and laughter. She'd answered his questions honestly, and he'd enjoyed hearing her voice, its cadences so different from his. What she'd said had intrigued him as well, and he was glad the Whispering Winds had impressed her. More remarkably, she'd noticed what made it home to him—he'd tried to set down roots, to create a place of permanence, and she'd seen that first thing. She liked his cowboys, too, had noticed their loyalty and pride. He'd worked to create that, too, to make his hands know that they were an important part of the ranch.

While he dressed, his thoughts turned to the new cattle

he'd just shipped in. They were part of his plans for the future, a way to build up his herd to get the best characteristics of two breeds: the hardiness and ability to forage of the range cattle and the more muscular, meatier build of the imports. Today his imported *cows*—for that's what the cattlemen called them, regardless of gender—would be taken out on the range for the first time.

"You ridin' with us today, boss?" Sam asked when he entered the kitchen a short while later. It was still dark outside, but the eastern sky was beginning to lighten.

"Yeah, I want to get a good look at the new cows and check out Glader Canyon." The canyon was a secluded valley with high cliffs surrounding three sides so that entry to it was controlled.

"Roy was out there yesterday with a couple of the boys. Said it looked fine. Plenty of grass and the stream's full to overflowing up by the north corner." Sam was seated at the table, tackling a stack of pancakes.

"We should leave a couple of the men out there with them until we get the branding done, don't you think?" Gray suggested as he sat across from Sam.

"I told Roy and Jud to take their bedrolls along and plan to stay the night. I figure two men ought to be enough since the herd is so small."

"Sounds like you have everything well in hand."

Sam grinned, obviously pleased to have gained Gray's approval.

"You eatin' today or just having more of that coffee you're so fond of?" Mrs. Bellows asked Gray as she came in from the pantry.

"A few of those pancakes would be mighty welcome. I'm riding out with the boys and don't expect to be home before supper."

Mrs. Bellows turned to her stove. Her frown disappeared and she started to hum as she poured out the batter.

Amelia came in wearing a cashmere wrapper against the morning chill. She yawned, noticed Sam at the table, and blushed.

"Pardon me," she said, putting her hand over her mouth. "I didn't realize anyone was here."

"Please don't leave on my account," Sam said as she started to back out of the room. "I can go now."

"But you haven't finished your breakfast," she protested.

"I don't see the problem," Gray said. "Amelia, come in and sit down. You, too, Sam. Finish your breakfast so we can leave on time."

Sam flushed but did as he was told, as did Amelia, but Gray sensed a lingering tension in the air. He looked at his daughter, who sat staring at the tablecloth in front of her, her cheeks a bright pink. Her face had slimmed over the last year or so, gaining maturity. The blue wrapper she wore set off the color of her eyes and brightened her hair, bringing out its blond highlights.

The wrapper was a gift from Prescott's sister Cybil. She'd brought it with her on a previous trip home to England and assured Amelia it was in the latest fashion. The robe had a high neck and buttons all the way down the front. The hem was scalloped and ended a foot above the floor, revealing a box-plaited underskirt of a lighter blue. But it was the snug-fitting bodice that caught Gray's eye. Even with the matching fichu crisscrossing over the front, there was no mistaking his daughter's shape.

No wonder Sam's face was red—and Amelia's, too. He gave his foreman a second look but found nothing to increase his worries there. Sam might be aware of Amelia as a young woman, but he was taking pains to keep that awareness from her. Although Gray had thought that his daughter might be ready to leave home soon, he hadn't realized just how right he was.

"Have you seen Lily yet this morning?" he asked Amelia.

"No. Would you like me to check on her?"

Amelia looked as if she would welcome the excuse to leave, so Gray nodded and said, "If you like."

"Please excuse me," she said to Sam, then hurried out of the room and up the stairs.

"She's growing so fast, I can hardly believe it," Gray said.

"She's still pretty young," Sam replied without looking up. He finished his last pancake. "I'd best go see how the boys are doing."

He left just as Mrs. Bellows put a heaping plate in front of Gray. "Thank you," he said absently.

"That Sam is a good man," Mrs. Bellows observed.

He looked up at her. "I know that."

"Well, sometimes it's hard for a father to keep track of what's important in these situations. Sam wouldn't do or say anything he shouldn't."

So, she had also noticed it. He didn't know whether to feel reassured or even more uneasy at her words. "I know that, too."

"Good. Then you can relax and enjoy your meal. I didn't wake up extra early this morning to cook over a hot stove just so's you can let my good food get cold. I take my responsibilities around here seriously."

"Yes, ma'am," he said and started to eat, knowing he had an ally who was as concerned about the two young people as he was.

Having made her point, Mrs. Bellows gave him an approving look and went back to her hot stove.

Lily didn't wake until Amelia knocked on her door, much to her chagrin. She'd especially wanted to see Gray this morning, to see if the tentative friendship that had sprung between them the day before had survived the night. But by the time she reached the kitchen, having washed and dressed, Mrs. Bellows informed her that Gray and Sam had already left with the other men to move the new cattle out to the range. A few minutes later Amelia appeared at the table, also dressed, but she couldn't stay long since she had school.

Lily felt at loose ends and spent the rest of the morning helping Mrs. Bellows around the house and talking to Dun, who ventured from his bedroom for the first time. In the afternoon, feeling the need for some fresh air, she headed for the barn. The mare she'd helped treat was gone, undoubtedly put back to work now that she was better.

Not ready to return to the house, Lily wandered out the back of the barn toward the horse corrals. There she got the shock of her life.

Amelia was sitting atop Cleo and trying to get her feet under her so she could stand. Afraid to shout at the girl for fear she would startle the horse into a sudden movement, Lily could only hold her breath as Amelia squirmed around on the mare's back, trying to gain her balance. She managed to get up into a squat, but then Cleo took a tentative step forward and Amelia teetered.

Lily gasped but muffled the sound with her hand. One foot slipped out from under Amelia, and she fell down onto her bottom, her legs splaying on either side of the horse. The mare tried to escape the unfamiliar burden on her back by trotting a few steps, and Amelia slowly bounced off, sliding down the animal's rump to land on the ground behind her. Cleo stopped with one rear hoof cocked as though she was ready to kick out.

"Oh, Cleo, you silly horse," Amelia sputtered as she picked herself off the ground. "I told you not to move. Can't you understand anything?"

The girl rubbed her tail bone as she walked over to the mare, and Lily noticed she had imitated her practice dress from the day before with her skirt hem pulled up from the back and tucked into the front waistband. Grabbing the horse's head, Amelia shook it gently back and forth.

"What am I going to do with you?" she asked, her tone filled with affection.

"What am I going to do with *you*?" Lily said, walking up to the pair.

Amelia looked up, her eyes wide with surprise. "I thought you were inside."

"I was. Then I came out. And I couldn't believe what I just saw. What did you think you were doing?"

"Nothing much," Amelia answered, her expression both guilty and defiant.

"Well, that particular 'nothing much' could get you seriously hurt."

"I'm not afraid of a little pain."

"And how about your horse? She could be injured, as well. Surely you care about her?"

Some of the defiance left Amelia's face. "How could she get hurt?"

"Any number of ways. She may be trained to the saddle, but she isn't used to having someone stand on her back. If you make her skittish enough, there's no telling how she might react. And if she ends up hurting you, what's your father going to do?"

"He'll probably get rid of her right away," she said quietly, looking down.

"That, or worse." Lily paused to let her words sink in. She knew just how protective Gray was of his daughter—and so did Amelia.

"I guess you're right," the girl admitted reluctantly. Then she looked up at Lily with a sly gleam in her eye.

"Of course, if you taught me how to do it right, none of that would have to happen, would it?"

"Now, Amelia, we've been through that—"

"But, Lily, don't you see? This is something I really *want* to do. Please?"

Lily felt torn. She knew Gray would be furious if he learned she'd gone behind his back to teach Amelia circus tricks, but if she didn't, Amelia could be gravely hurt trying to learn them on her own. And the girl was just stubborn enough to do that.

"All right. But—"

"Oh, thank you, thank you." Amelia flung her arms around Lily and danced her in a circle.

Lily laughed at Amelia's exuberance. The mare cocked her ears forward and stared at the two humans.

When they finally collapsed onto the grass, Cleo ambled over to nuzzle at Amelia's hair.

"We're going to teach you some new things, Cleo old girl. What do you think of that?" Amelia asked and rubbed her palm along the mare's forehead.

"Not so fast," Lily warned. "You never let me finish my sentence. I'll teach you some tricks, but you have to promise me two things."

"Anything you want," Amelia said earnestly.

"First, you have to do exactly what I say."

Amelia nodded her agreement.

"And second, you won't try anything when I'm not here to watch you—and especially not anything with the horse. It's just too dangerous. Do I have your word?"

Amelia frowned. "But how will I practice?"

"You'll practice when I'm here spotting you. Even in the circus no one works alone. We can't afford injuries, and neither can you, so either give me your promise or I won't be able to teach you."

"All right. I promise." The words were reluctant but

seemed sincere. Then Amelia clambered to her knees and said, "Can we start now?"

Lily laughed and tousled the girl's hair. "Yes, I suppose so."

They spent the rest of the afternoon together, working on Amelia's balance—but not on the horse—and on teaching Cleo the short-strided canter essential to a good ring horse.

"Now, the most important thing is to have her run in a circle," Lily explained as she attached a line to the mare's bridle. "First we'll teach her to canter at the end of this line. Once she's used to it, you can ride her while she runs."

"Why is the circle so important?"

"Running in a circle tilts her just the right amount and pushes the rider out. It makes it easier to stay on her back than when she's running in a straight line. In fact, if you look at the size of the ring when you come to the circus, you'll see it's purposely laid out in the perfect size for riding bareback."

"Do you do this with your horses?"

"Yes. Not only in the beginning when I was training them, but even now. You want to get rid of bad traits before they become habits. I also have to make sure nothing scares the horses in the ring. You can never trust the audience or, for that matter, some of the other animals. If something unexpected happens, I need my horses to ignore it and keep on going exactly the way they've been taught."

Lily started the horse trotting in a large circle at the end of the line while she stayed in the center, turning slowly so she always faced the horse. Amelia sat on the rail fence and watched.

"How can you teach a horse about unexpected things?" she asked after a while.

"I can't, but I can make sure the horse has learned to ignore distractions. Sometimes I get the clowns and children to help by making noise and running around near the ring. But nothing is perfect. There's always a risk. That's why I want you to be so careful."

"Should I make some noise now so Cleo learns to ignore distractions?"

Lily chuckled. "Why don't we let her learn the basic steps first?"

"I guess so. It just seems as if it will take forever before the two of us get to do any real tricks."

Lily remembered having the same feeling of impatience when she was first learning to ride. "I know it's hard having to wait, but it's important. Discipline is the key to any trick, not just to riding; you need discipline and patience, and before you get on the horse, you need the balance skills we worked on earlier. You can work on most of those any time you want."

Amelia perked up. "I can, can't I? Would you mind if I went and practiced now?"

Lily smiled. "No, go ahead."

As Amelia went off to do her practicing, Lily couldn't help but feel flattered at the young woman's interest. She only wished Gray could accept that interest without feeling threatened. Amelia was headstrong and spirited and needed a way to release some of her energy. Riding could be that outlet.

She sighed. Her wish was not very realistic. She turned her attention back to the horse.

By the time she had finished the mare's first lesson, Amelia was back. Together they walked the horse until she cooled down, then turned her into her stall.

"You know, I've been thinking," Amelia said as they headed back to the house before supper.

"About what?"

"About Cleo and getting her trained. I'm sure she'd

83

learn things much faster if you rode her. What do you think?"

"Well, she might, but I thought you wanted her for yourself."

"I do. I just thought we could share her while you're here. Besides, I'm not even around most of the day. If you rode her and taught her some tricks while I was at school, I'd still have plenty of time to work with her once I got home."

Lily couldn't resist the chance to work with the well-formed mare. "If you're sure you don't mind, I'd love to work with her. She's really a beautiful animal—she'd make a perfect rosinback."

"What's a rosinback?"

"That's what circus people call the ring horses used in equestrian acts because sometimes we use rosin on our shoes to keep from slipping around when we land."

"Oh! Could you get me some rosin, too?"

"All in good time. As soon as you're ready, I'll make sure you have everything you need. Just remember your promise, okay?"

"Don't worry, Lily. I'll do everything exactly like you tell me."

Sincerity showed in Amelia's eyes, and Lily felt tremendous relief. She'd been so scared when she'd come upon Amelia this afternoon. If nothing else, she'd impressed on the girl the importance of being careful, and that was the most important lesson of all.

"Good," Lily said as they climbed the two steps to the back porch. "Let's go in and get some supper."

Though they'd never discussed what to do, neither mentioned a word about their afternoon activities at the evening meal. Afterward, lying in her bed, Lily wasn't sure how good an idea that was. She felt as if she was betraying a trust in going against Gray's wishes, but she felt she had no choice. Telling Amelia not to try a trick or two clearly wasn't going to stop her, and if Gray learned what they were doing, he would certainly put a stop to it. But what would happen then?

For the first time Lily realized the awesome responsibilities faced by parents. Gray was so different from her own father. Gray instilled pride and a natural confidence in his daughter; she believed in herself and in her judgment. That was a precious gift, and Gray had given it to his daughter all on his own. Now that same spirited independence was going to cause problems between parent and child—and Lily was caught right in the middle of it. She only hoped she was doing the right thing.

The next morning the sun was still in the east as Gray left the ranch house and rode toward the hilly section of his land in the north. He'd come home to check on his guests only to find that Lily had left on Cleo for a ride on the range. How could she be so foolish? She'd heard about the rustlers from the women at the Cattlemen's Club. What made her think she'd be safe on her own?

In all honesty, he felt partly to blame himself, especially after their conversation on the way home from Cheyenne. His comment that women did not need to be told about dangers on the range because their menfolk could protect them was now coming back to haunt him. He'd never laid down the rules to Lily, never thought it necessary.

Since Amelia had shown little interest in going off on her own, he'd assumed the range held little interest to women. Certainly none of the women he knew had ever expressed any desire to see the wilder parts of his ranch. Of course, he usually spent time with ladies like Cybil Heath, Prescott's sister, and she didn't even venture outside of Cheyenne if she could help it.

Where would Lily go? he wondered. His only clue was

that Mrs. Bellows had seen her ride toward the hills. He wished now that he'd impressed on Mrs. Bellows the folly of anyone riding the range alone with the rustlers about, but he'd never seen the need, and he hadn't wanted to frighten the older woman. Now he was paying the price.

Fortunately the usually arid ground was softer than usual because of the rains a week earlier, and as Gray crossed a washed-out gully, he caught sight of fresh hoof marks and followed them to the edge of a tiny stream that led into the low hills on this side of his property. Here the hoof marks ran parallel to the stream and into the hills.

As Gray rounded a bend in the stream awhile later, he glimpsed a flash of red, and there she was, lying on a large, flat boulder sunning herself, her glorious hair spread out on the rock like an angel's halo. Cleo grazed calmly a few feet away, her reins tied to a nearby willow. Gray's mount whickered softly, and the mare raised her head, suddenly alert to the intruders.

Lily also sat up, her hair falling to her waist like a red curtain. He knew the instant she recognized him from the nervous smile on her face. He nudged his horse's ribs with his heels, and the animal ambled forward.

"Gray, what are you doing out here?" she called and scrambled to her feet on the rock.

He squinted up at her as she stood silhouetted against the sun. The light outlined her figure, setting off each feminine curve. Gray felt a tightening in his loins and shifted slightly in the saddle.

"I planned to ask you the same question. You're pretty far from the ranch."

"I guess I needed some time on my own and didn't notice how far I'd come. Cleo's a wonderful horse."

"You should have left word where you were going. The weather out here is pretty unpredictable this time of year.

It's not unheard of to have blizzards in April and May, you know."

As if to confirm his words, a cloud chose that moment to hide the sun. They both looked up.

"I'm sorry," Lily said. "I didn't expect to be out here that long. I guess we'd better get back That cloud looks kind of dark."

A chill wind picked up, lifting her hair and blowing it wildly around her face.

"Do you have a jacket of some sort?" Gray asked.

She looked down at her blouse, and her face flushed. "Why, yes. I just took it off. The sun was so hot just a minute ago, especially on this rock." Her cheeks turned a darker red. "Let me get it," she added and scooted out of his sight to the opposite edge of the boulder.

Gray dismounted and put his horse next to Cleo, then returned to the boulder. Lily was sitting on the edge of the flat area, preparing to jump down. She was wearing her jacket now but had only fastened the bottom few buttons.

"Here, let me help you," Gray said and reached up to grab her by the waist.

The first thing he noticed was that she wasn't wearing a corset beneath her flannel riding habit. She didn't need to. Her body was firm and sleekly muscled, and her full breasts were high. As he lifted her down from her perch, his hand slipped under her basque jacket to the cotton shirtwaist below. Only a thin layer of fabric kept him from touching her skin.

Her warm, feminine scent surrounded him. She smelled of the sun and the earth, vital and alive. His pulse quickened as he lowered her, and when she was standing on her feet, he couldn't bring himself to let her go. Her eyes grew round as she watched him, and her tongue darted out to trail a swift path across her lower lip. He felt a bolt of desire surge through him.

Lily looked up at Gray and almost didn't recognize him. Gone was the cool, controlled man she was used to. In his place was a man with flushed cheeks and burning eyes and a gaze that bore into hers, sending messages of passion and desire she could not ignore. A gust of wind swept up a lock of her hair and whipped it across his face. She lifted a hand to brush it away, but he caught her hand with his and pressed her palm to his lips.

His mouth felt warm; his breath hot. When his tongue reached out to taste her skin, she thought her knees would buckle. The sensation was unlike anything she'd ever known. Her palm tingled and she felt more alive than ever before in her life. Her heart was pounding and her breath fluttered in her chest. And all the time his blue eyes seared her, heating her everywhere his gaze lingered—on her face, on her lips, on the top of her chest and lower. She felt her breasts swell in response and tried to pull her hand back, embarrassed by her body's reactions.

"Don't," he whispered, his voice sounding raw and male. He let go of her hand, and for a moment she thought he was setting her free, but instead he reached for her waist and brought her against him. Her hands went to his shoulders, though whether it was for support or to push him away, she didn't know. She knew what she should be doing, but her body refused to obey her. It listened to its own needs and desires, and she knew in her heart they were what she wanted, too.

Ever since their first kiss in the barn, she'd yearned to be back in Gray's arms, to feel his hard-muscled frame shelter hers, to once again taste him, dark and enigmatic and undeniably male. At the same time she feared this moment, knowing its consequences. Would he withdraw from her as he had before? Would their fragile friendship wither and die beneath the weight of passion and desire?

She had no time to consider the questions, for no sooner

had they formed than he was lowering his head, and in the next instant his mouth was on hers, gently insistent as his lips parted and his tongue darted out to caress her. Her lips opened in response, and he took full advantage, deepening the kiss as he pulled her more tightly to his frame until her pliant body was fitted to his.

He was everything she'd remembered and more. Her hands slid up past his shoulders to his neck, then farther until her fingers tangled in his hair. It was as thick and plush as it looked, and smoothly silky as it slid between her fingertips. His tongue felt like rough velvet as it caressed hers, then withdrew, only to return and tease again until she breached his mouth with her tongue. His taste filled her, as dark and mysterious as before, urging her to discover his every secret, to unravel the mystery of him.

She strained on her tiptoes, needing to be closer. Because she'd planned to ride, she'd dispensed with the usual layers of petticoats fashion decreed, and now she felt almost naked as the ridge of his arousal pressed against her. A liquid warmth pooled low in her abdomen.

The world around her disappeared and a kaleidoscope of colors danced behind her closed eyelids. Gray's hands stroked her back, and every muscle flexed beneath his touch. She wanted so much more. She wanted him to touch her in places that were aching for contact. She wanted to arch into him, but he held her too close for her to move. Then his hand glided past the opening of her jacket to the front of her shirtwaist and up to cup her breast, and she knew her wish had been granted. She moaned his name as sensation raced through her.

Gray thought he would explode when he heard his name on her lips. She was all fire and passion in his arms, and he wanted nothing more than to lay her on the ground and make love to her. Even through the cotton fabric of her shirtwaist, he could feel her nipple pucker and harden in response to his touch. He trailed a line of kisses across her eyelids and over her cheeks, past her jawline until he reached the pulse point on her neck. She arched back and he lingered there, savoring her unique taste, slightly salty and definitely sweet.

Her unbound hair, buffeted by the wind, swirled around them with a wildness that matched the feelings surging inside him. He raised his head to look into her face. Her eyes were closed and her expression rapt. Her lips were bright and slightly parted. Her breath came as rapidly as his own, and he could feel her heart beat against his chest—or at least that was what he thought it was until the familiar rhythm registered in his mind. A horse was galloping along the streambed south of them.

"Someone's coming," he said, straightening reluctantly. He put her behind him, against the boulder where she wouldn't be seen. "Stay here," he commanded and headed for his horse and rifle.

He looked in the direction of the hoofbeats just as Sam rounded the bend.

"Gray, I'm glad I found you," the young man called out between labored breaths. "Mrs. Bellows wasn't sure where you'd gone."

"What happened?" he asked as the younger man rode up beside him.

"We found signs of the rustlers up near Glader Canyon. We thought you'd want to know right away."

As Sam spoke, another horseman rounded the bend. "Over here, Jud," Sam called out and waved his arm at the ranch hand.

Jud came up and nodded to Gray, then took off his Stetson as he noticed Lily. "Miss Avenel," he said in greeting.

Gray looked over his shoulder and noticed she'd done up her jacket and her hair. Looking at her, no one would ever guess what they'd been doing scant minutes ago, not unless they knew what to look for. He tried not to think about that but to concentrate on what Sam was saying.

The rustlers were near his new cattle. That meant they had found out where he'd moved them almost right away. Gray didn't like to think what that might mean since he'd told very few people where he was taking his new herd— only the men on his ranch and the few at the Cattlemen's Club knew the particulars.

"Who's out there now?" Gray asked.

"We left Roy keeping an eye on things. They snuck up on Jud here last night and conked him out good. I thought he'd be better off back at the ranch, but when we couldn't find you, he decided to come along."

"Sorry 'bout that, boss. I shoulda kept a better lookout."

"I'm just glad you weren't hurt worse," Gray replied. "I'd better get up there right away and see what's going on. Jud, if you wouldn't mind escorting Miss Lily back to the ranch, I'd be mighty appreciative."

"Sure thing, boss."

"Sam, just give me a minute and we can go." Gray turned and walked back to Lily. "You heard?"

She nodded.

"That's why I was worried about you. This is exactly the kind of thing I've been afraid would happen. These rustlers have gotten too brazen, and someone was bound to get hurt. I'm just glad it wasn't you. Promise me you won't ride out here alone again."

"I promise. You be careful yourself."

The worried look on her face warmed him. It had been a long time since anyone had cared about him in that way. Most of the people on the ranch looked to him for leadership and strength. They expected him to find the answers and take care of problems. And to the best of his ability, he did. Even Amelia assumed he knew what was best and did it. This was the first time in a long time that someone showed concern for him.

"I'll be careful," he promised. He walked her back to her horse, and slipped behind it with her, where the two men couldn't see. He pulled her into his embrace and gave her one last sweet kiss. "You be careful, too, okay?"

She nodded and he helped her onto her horse.

"I'll try and get back this evening," he said.

"I'll look for you," she replied, and desire sprang to life in him again.

"You do that," he said, making it into a promise. Then he rode out to Sam, and the two of them cantered off toward Glader Canyon and whatever trouble waited there.

FIVE

GRAY'S SPURS BIT into the sides of his horse as he urged the animal forward. He raced across the flat stretch of land but knew he wouldn't be able to outrun his thoughts no matter how far or how fast he rode. The thoughts that plagued him had nothing to do with this latest rustling attempt. While he should have been thinking about how best to capture the thieves that were robbing him and the other ranchers blind, all he could picture was Lily as she'd been only minutes before.

He could still feel the heat of her body next to his and taste her sweetness as he'd deepened their kiss to the most intimate. He hadn't expected the swirling excitement, the mad rush that filled his body with a hunger he hadn't felt in a long, long time.

What amazed him most was that Lily had seemed as caught up as he in the sensations that were exploding between them. He would never forget the sound she made the first time their lips touched. He'd been aware of her every movement, her every breath, and that awareness had surprised and intrigued him, making him want more— much more.

If Sam hadn't arrived when he did, who knows what might have happened. And if he'd arrived a few moments later . . . That thought didn't bear thinking about, at least not now when there were other things that should be occupying his mind.

Gray looked to his right. Sam rode hunched over his saddle, his attention on the path ahead. Though they were racing as fast as their mounts could go on this terrain, Gray knew they would be too late to apprehend the rustlers. His main hope was that they'd left some clues behind this time. He'd lost more cattle than he liked to think about to those wily bastards.

When they reached the secluded valley where Gray had pastured the new animals, they found Roy had gathered the small herd together near the entrance to the canyon.

"Glad Sam found you, boss," Roy called out when they rode up to him.

"Did you see anything or recognize anyone?" Gray asked as he pulled up alongside Roy.

"Nope. They clipped Jud from behind when he stumbled onto their camp, and then they hightailed it out of there. By the time I found him, they were long gone. How'd you figure they'd be coming after this lot?" Roy asked, nodding to the cattle.

"Good guess, I suppose," Gray replied, but it had been nothing of the sort. He'd noticed a pattern some time ago and had decided it was better to be prepared than to suffer another loss. "Let's spread out and see if we can find anything. Roy, you stay here by the cattle, and Sam can show me where the rustlers camped."

"Sure, boss," Roy replied.

"Do you think we'll find anything?" Sam asked as they rode toward the rustlers' camp.

"I doubt it, but it doesn't hurt to look," Gray said.

"They certainly are a lucky bunch," Sam commented as they neared the high ridge marking the side of the canyon.

"I'm not sure luck has anything to do with it."

"What do you mean?" Sam stopped his horse and turned in the saddle to look at Gray.

"I mean no one could have guessed these cows were pastured here, and they haven't been here long enough for someone to have stumbled across them. We only brought them up yesterday," Gray said, looking back over his shoulder toward the herd.

"What are you saying?"

"I think their 'luck,' as you put it, might be based on someone's loose tongue."

Sam frowned when he realized where Gray was headed with his comments. "But who could it be? Not someone you know?"

"Maybe, maybe not. The way I figure it, it has to be someone who knew my plans. I intentionally didn't tell the hands in case they'd mention it when they were in town. I'm afraid the only people who heard about this new shipment were a few other members of the Cattlemen's Club."

"You think it might be someone at the club?" Sam asked with astonishment. "But they're your friends."

"Yeah, but that doesn't mean they didn't talk where they could be overheard." Or used the information themselves, Gray added to himself, though he didn't like to think anyone at the club would do such a thing. He'd hoped nothing would happen to his cattle because the only people who had known about this shipment had been men he knew and respected, and most of them were the cream of Cheyenne's social register. Still, you never could tell. He certainly had his work cut out for him now.

"What are you going to do?" Sam asked.

"First, let's see if we can find anything at the camp. Then I'll make a visit to the club. We'd best keep this between us for now, though."

Sam nodded his understanding, and they set the horses in motion again.

More than ever, Gray was afraid that the club was where the information had gotten out. He tried to imagine who might want to take advantage of fellow ranchers this way, who would be desperate enough or immoral enough to have no compunctions about harming his friends. No face came to mind, but then he didn't know the members as well as he might. He preferred to spend most of his time at his ranch rather than in town.

He'd have to get Hank Farrell to help out. Hank spent a lot of time at the club and might be able to come up with some useful information. The whole point of the Cattlemen's Association was to fight this sort of intrusion. What an irony it would be if their club was being used for nefarious purposes, if someone was taking advantage of the unsuspecting nature of the cattlemen toward one another.

When he and Sam reached the rustlers' camp, everything was just as he'd expected. No clues had been left behind to help them trace the thieves. These men were good at their jobs—too good. It would take cleverness and possibly even trickery to trap them, but Gray swore right then that they'd met their match if he had anything to say about it.

"What should we do now?" Sam asked him as they rode back to rendezvous with Roy.

"We'd better post more guards around this canyon. Why don't you stay up here with Roy, and I'll send a couple of the hands up to relieve you. That okay?"

"Sounds good to me. While you're gone, Roy and I will move the cattle deeper into the canyon so they won't be as easy to pick off."

Gray nodded his approval. "Let's ask Roy if any cattle are missing, and then I'll head back to the ranch." *And Lily.* He'd managed to keep his mind on his business while they were searching the rustlers' camp, but now that his thoughts turned back to the ranch, he just naturally pictured her there, waiting for him.

Without conscious thought, he dug his heels into his horse's side and hurried him along. The sooner he finished checking with Roy, the sooner he'd be back at the ranch.

Lily rode back to the ranch in silence. She still wasn't sure what had happened. One minute she and Gray had been talking about the perils of going away from the ranch alone, and the next she was in his arms with her mouth pressed to his. From that point on, she'd done little thinking. All she'd known or cared about were the myriad sensations coursing through her, the feel of Gray's hard body pressed to hers, the heat of his mouth, the taste and scent of him.

She felt her face turn pink at the memories and looked over at Jud, hoping he hadn't noticed. He was looking straight ahead. Like many of the cowboys she'd met, he was a man of few words—and fewer still when a lady was near. He seemed just as happy not to be forced into a conversation.

Still, Lily felt self-conscious about her thoughts and wished she could put them aside until she was alone. But every time she tried, Gray's image would fill her mind, and she'd relive the episode all over again. She'd never felt such pleasure before, such a sense of rightness, as if she'd finally found her place in life. The knowledge left her feeling both embarrassed and guilty.

It wasn't as if this were her first kiss. There'd been a young aerialist who'd joined Otto's show when she was twenty-one, some six years ago. She'd thought she was in love with him. They'd kissed, too, but looking back, Lily realized that what she'd felt with Jacques Frénier had been but a pale shadow of the emotions she'd experienced today. And then Jacques had died, killed by the very ambition the young Lily had found so exciting. Jacques had aspired to do the triple somersault and had accomplished two and a half turns successfully. But the last half turn eluded him, with fatal results.

Her memories of him were bittersweet. He'd been so young and dashing, so full of enthusiasm and daring. How could any young woman resist him? Would she have fallen in love with him—so deeply in love that no one and nothing would have come between them—if they'd had more time together? She'd certainly thought so in the first months of grief following his death. Now, with painful clarity, she had to wonder.

Unwilling to pursue this train of thought until she was in the privacy of her room, Lily turned to her riding companion. "It's awfully pretty out here, isn't it?"

Jud turned his head and squinted at her from beneath the brim of his hat. "I reckon," he said.

"I never realized how beautiful the colors could be," she continued, undaunted by his terse response.

He looked around the area where they were riding, which was fairly drab now that they'd left the region watered by the stream. "If'n you say so, ma'am."

"I didn't mean right here," she said, holding on to her laughter. "I meant all around on the plain."

"Yes, ma'am, on the *plain*," Jud said in a strangled tone as they pulled up to the front of the ranch house.

Lily was trying to figure out what Jud meant when Amelia came running out of the house, her light brown hair flying as she raced down the steps.

"Oh, Lily, I'm so glad you're back," Amelia said, out of breath in her rush from the house.

"And I'm glad to be back, too," Lily replied, dismounting from Cleo. "Though I did have a wonderful time out on the plain."

Amelia put her hand over her mouth and looked at Jud.

The older man merely shook his head and took Cleo's reins from her hand.

"I reckon I'll take these here animals to the barn," he said and ambled off in that direction.

Before the horses had moved more than a few steps, the laugh Amelia was trying to hold back escaped.

"What is it?" Lily asked, putting her hand to her hair, thinking something was out of place.

The sound of Amelia's laughter filled the air, and still Lily could find nothing out of place on her person, much to her relief. She wasn't ready to provide explanations of what had happened this morning to Amelia.

"I'm sorry, I shouldn't have laughed, but we must work on your vocabulary if you want to be a true westerner. The phrase is 'out on the *range*,' not *plain*."

"No wonder Jud gave me such a strange look," Lily said with a chuckle. "Well, whatever it is, I really enjoyed my time there, but I do want a quick wash. The *range* is mighty dusty."

"When you're done, will you have a few minutes to talk?" Amelia asked as she put her arm around Lily's waist for the walk into the house. "I've just heard the most marvelous news."

"I can't wait," she replied, giving the girl a hug. "Let me just freshen up and drop in on Dun, and then I'll have as much time as you want. Will that be all right?"

Amelia nodded her head. "I'll meet you in the front parlor. I'll fix us a special tea, and we can have our chat."

Lily smiled as the girl turned and raced up the steps into the house. Had she ever felt that young and excited? Maybe not that young, but that same kind of excitement was not reserved just for the very young; it coursed through her veins even now. She felt like running and laughing with happiness and joy.

Suddenly she was seeing all kinds of new possibilities;

things she never before dared to dream now danced enticingly before her. For the first time, those elusive dreams—dreams of home and love, of building something lasting and sharing it with another—seemed so close, almost as if she could reach out and touch them.

She skipped up the stairs to her room and quickly washed off the light covering of dust that clung to her face and hands, then changed into a pale blue house dress. The calico dress was trimmed with lace at both neck and cuffs, and though it wasn't particularly fancy, she felt feminine and attractive in it. She fastened her hair into a neat topknot, then impulsively loosened a few strands to trail down her back.

The face looking back at her from the cheval mirror was decidedly different from the face she'd seen just a week ago in Dun's room. This face was vital and alive, with snapping eyes and rosy cheeks. This face carried a sparkling grin. Anyone looking at her now would guess immediately what had happened to her today.

She forced herself to assume a more serious expression. There, that was better. Now she looked just like herself, her usual self, that is, not this new person whose insides bubbled like the best champagne and whose heartbeat raced at the mere mention of Gray's name.

Satisfied that she looked appropriately sedate, she left her room and crossed the hall to Dun's. She'd spend a few minutes with him, then find Amelia and hear her "marvelous" news. And then ... why, by then Gray should be back home!

She knocked on Dun's door and entered the room at his bidding to find him sitting in a chair by the window fully dressed, including a vest and tie.

"So, I heard you'd effected a miracle cure for one of Benedict's horses," he teased her. "Has he hired you on as his new hand yet?"

Lily smiled as she walked in and sat down on the rocking chair near his bed. He was obviously feeling much better, though he still bore the marks of his beating. The swelling on his face had almost completely disappeared, but both his eyes looked like the hues of the rainbow. Though he'd never admit it, Lily knew his ribs must hurt considerably, too.

"Since I did nothing more than look on, he hasn't discovered my hidden talents, and therefore, no offers of employment have been tendered. But once I show my worth as a ranch hand, I'm sure he'll offer me more money than any of us has ever seen," Lily teased back.

"More money than Dan Rice?"

"No one makes more money than Dan Rice," Lily said in a suitably awed tone. Dan Rice, the well-known American clown, was rumored to have a weekly salary higher than that of the President of the United States. "Besides," Lily continued, "Gray wasn't exactly happy when he found me treating his mare. I'm not sure whether it's me or my connection to the circus. Though I must admit, lately he hasn't made an issue of it. Maybe he doesn't think women should have anything to do with the rougher side of handling animals."

"Not everyone has the same ideas, that's for certain. Look at circus people—I've always considered them to be among the most open-minded, but there are always some who have prejudices. That doesn't make them bad, just opinionated."

"Well, all I know is that countries have gone to war over differences of opinion, but I hope it doesn't come down to that."

Dun laughed, as she'd intended him to, and the remark served to ease them off the subject of Gray. Her feelings were too new, too precious for her to share, even with someone she'd known as long as Dun.

"Now I want you to tell me about everything you've seen out here," Dun insisted. "While this room is quite nice, I've had more than enough time to memorize every square inch of it. Since I'm chained to the house, tell me what it's like beyond these four walls."

Lily could imagine how hard it was for Dun to be confined. He was used to a different life, as was she, with a lot of travel and activity and rarely a moment to oneself. While she found this interlude a delightful change, she knew what a hard time she'd have if she'd been stuck inside the house for days on end.

"Well, I know you'll find this hard to believe, but in many ways it reminds me of our life on the road. For one thing, everyone pitches in and works together. And Gray told me about this thing they call a chuck wagon. It carries all the food the hands will need when they're out on the range for any length of time. When it's time for a meal, the men all gather around this wagon in much the same way as we do at the food tent."

"How often do they do this traveling?"

"Not too often. Gray says they have a series of roundups a couple of times a year. They work one section of the range at a time, gathering up all the cattle. In spring they brand the new calves and do the tally so they know how many survived the winter, and in the fall they choose the animals to send to market. Gray says the longer drives require twenty-odd men all working together. It sort of reminded me of when we put the canvas up, how we all have to work as one unit.

"And the horses. You wouldn't believe some of the fine livestock they have here. Those animals can turn so sharply and stop so quickly you'd fall off if you weren't paying attention. In their way those horses know as many tricks as ours, except they use theirs for a different purpose. And Gray takes such good care of them. Seeing him with them reminds me of Gus with his bears."

"Lily, don't make the mistake of thinking that ranch life is like our life with the circus. There are far more differences than similarities."

"I realize that. I was just surprised at how well everyone seems to work together. This ranch is really a great responsibility."

"Yes, and as far as I can see, Mr. Benedict takes his responsibilities very seriously."

"What does that mean?" Lily asked, not sure she wanted to hear his answer. For the first time in her life, she was daring to look outside the narrow confines of her daily routine, to wish for something she'd long thought was out of her reach. She didn't want anything to change those dreams.

Dun sighed. "Don't get me wrong," he said. "Benedict did take me in, and I certainly appreciate it, but to be completely honest, I think you were the reason for his generosity. He took one look at you and that was it. And I think you took one look back and felt the same."

She wanted to protest but knew she couldn't, not with Dun looking at her in that funny way of his that never allowed her to get away with anything. She'd tried to put things over on Dun before and never succeeded. She wasn't surprised he saw through her now, especially when she'd practically mentioned Gray's name every other sentence. In a way, it was a relief that Dun suspected something.

"I'm glad you know," she said to him, "though I didn't think I was being so obvious. I wasn't sure I'd be able to keep it to myself much longer anyway."

"You weren't all that obvious, except maybe to someone who knows you . . . and cares. I don't want to see you hurt." Dun leaned forward in his chair and winced from

103

the pain. Lily watched him take a long breath and lean back again. He might put up a brave front, but it would be some time before he could get back into his regular routine. "The point I'm trying to make is that Gray is tied to this place," he went on after a couple of breaths. "Just listen to yourself—you know it, too."

"I understand what you're saying, but this isn't something I've done on purpose. It's just that . . . well, Gray is different. He's a good man, don't you agree?"

Lily gave the small man a hopeful look. She respected his judgment. He could spot a grafter a mile away, and Otto often asked him to keep an eye out to make sure the paying public was not shilled by a faker toting a game of three-card monte at their circus. Now she wanted to know that he concurred with her assessment of Gray.

"Yes. I think Benedict's a good fellow," he admitted.

"Because of what he did for *both* of us in Cheyenne?"

Dun nodded in agreement. "And he's also treated me as a regular person. As you know, that doesn't happen too often outside the circus."

"Surely that says something about him. You've said yourself that people outside the circus are less tolerant of differences like yours. And you're mostly right. No one can deny that after what happened in Cheyenne. But it hasn't happened here, and Gray's the reason why."

"Don't misunderstand me, Lily. I'm not criticizing Benedict or you. I just want to make sure you're aware of what you're getting into."

The concern in his eyes touched her deeply, and she struggled to explain to him everything she was feeling. "So much has happened since we've arrived, I don't quite know how to describe it." She looked toward the ceiling, as if she could find the words she was looking for written there. Dun sat quietly, waiting for her to gather her thoughts.

"Everything's so different out here. Do you know what I mean?" she finally said and looked at him.

He shook his head and looked more worried than before.

"It's so vast out here—I've never seen anything quite like it. Even I seem different. It's like I'm playing a part in a play—it's new and exciting, but I don't always know all the lines or the exits and entrances. I have all the butterflies of a first-night performance, and they never seem to stop." Lily hesitated for a moment, unsure what else to say. "But, Dun, sometimes I feel this is the role of a lifetime, my lifetime, if I could only learn the part."

"And I take it Gray Benedict is the source of all this?" Dun asked when she didn't continue.

"There's no denying that, but there's more to it. Ever since Rosemary brought me to the circus, I've always thought it was the life for me. I never dreamed there could be anything else. The circus was our salvation when we were children, but now Rosemary is gone, and sometimes I wonder if there isn't something more to life. Do you think I'm being disloyal?"

"Your sister would have wanted you to be happy. That was more important to her than anything else. It's why she brought you with her when she ran away from home. She never intended the circus to be a prison—and neither do I, but I want you to remember something I've always lived by: Circus people stick to their own. We take care of each other when no one else will. It's easy to put your trust into another's hands, but it's just as easy to have that trust betrayed. Just be careful."

Lily considered his words, turning them over in her heart. He was right on one score: The circus did take care of its own. But that didn't mean there was no one else you could trust. She thought back to the way Gray had intervened on their behalf outside the saloon. He could have walked away, as had so many others, dismissing the events as just one more brawl on the city's crowded streets. But he hadn't. He'd taken the time and trouble to ascertain what was happening, then he'd waded into the fight with no thought for his own safety. Everything she'd seen and experienced told her Gray was an honorable man.

"I'm flattered, Dun, that you worry about me. You're a true friend. But this time I think I'm in safe hands."

"You could be right. I hope you are. Just remember, if you ever need me, I'll be there for you."

Her eyes filled at this avowal of friendship from one who'd seen so much trouble in his life. "Thank you," she said, her heart lightening. This was as close as Dun would get to giving his approval, and she knew it was a mark of his esteem for Gray that he didn't push the issue further.

They spent a while longer talking about the ranch and speculating on the arrival of the circus, which should be pulling into town any day. Then Lily caught Dun trying to suppress a yawn and decided to end their visit so he could rest.

"I'd better go now. Amelia is waiting for me. She has some exciting news, or so she said when I first came home."

"In that case, I'm afraid I've kept you overlong. Please extend my apologies to the young miss."

"Can I get you anything before I go?"

"No, I'll be fine. Don't keep your friend waiting any longer."

Lily left his room and hurried downstairs to find Amelia. The girl was pacing impatiently in the front parlor when Lily came in.

"I thought you'd never get here!" Amelia exclaimed when she saw Lily enter the room.

"I'm sorry. It took longer with Dun than I expected, but he's feeling much better."

"Oh, I'm glad. I would have asked myself, but I'm so excited, I've almost forgotten my name. Please excuse my bad manners. Have a seat while I pour the tea."

Lily sat down on the velvet emerald-green sofa and waited while Amelia sat and drew the tea tray in front of herself. She watched the poised young girl prepare each cup as if she did it every day of her life. Lily envied her. Never had she been given the opportunity to have friends over and serve them tea with this kind of formality. At the circus they would grab a bite to eat or something to drink as they worked, as often as not using a banged-up metal cup or chipped dish. Each day she stayed here, she realized how much she had missed.

"Sugar?" Amelia asked as she looked up.

"Yes, please. Two."

After handing Lily her cup, Amelia could no longer contain herself. "I've just heard the most wonderful news," she said breathlessly.

"Well, don't keep me in suspense," Lily prompted, catching the younger girl's excitement.

"We've been invited to Prescott's party."

"Oh?" Lily wasn't sure how she was to respond to that. A party shouldn't be such a great event to someone with Amelia's social calendar.

"Yes, and it's to be at Prescott's house in town tomorrow evening."

"Oh, yes, the arrangements were made when we were in town the other day," Lily said, suddenly remembering the plans that had been agreed to at the Cattlemen's Club. So much had happened since then that it had slipped her mind, but obviously not Amelia's, and she was beginning to understand why from the emphasis the girl placed on Prescott's name each time she mentioned him.

"You must help me pick out my dress," Amelia said. "It has to be perfect." She stopped speaking and looked

107

around as if she wanted to make sure no one else could overhear them. "Can I tell you a secret?" she whispered when she was satisfied they were alone.

Lily smiled and nodded, enjoying the younger woman's fervency. "Secrets seem to be our specialty," she said, remembering their afternoon of circus tricks.

"They do, don't they?" Amelia grinned mischievously, then leaned over and took hold of Lily's hand. "But this one is very special. I haven't told *anyone* else."

Lily squeezed Amelia's fingers to let her know she would keep whatever she was told in confidence. "In that case, I'm especially honored that you want to tell me."

Amelia looked around once more, then said in a low voice, "I think Prescott is the most wonderful man I've ever met."

Lily bit down a smile and said, "He seemed very nice when I met him."

"Oh, he's more than nice. He's so suave and cosmopolitan. Every time I see him my heart does this strange little flip. Do you know what I mean? I believe I'm finally in love. What do you think?" She sighed and looked expectantly at Lily.

Lily didn't know what to say. She wanted to give Amelia the best help she could, but advising people on their love lives could be potentially dangerous if the advice wasn't what the person wanted to hear. Worse, she knew Gray still thought of Amelia as his little girl, and Lily could only imagine what he would think if he overheard this conversation.

"I think it's different for each person," she began tactfully. "The important thing is to take things slowly. You have a lot of time to make such an important decision."

Amelia stood up and twirled away. "But I don't want to wait. I want to know now. Surely some things must be the same for everyone, don't you agree? Have you ever been in love, Lily?"

That was the question Lily had been dancing around all day herself but hadn't dared ask outright.

"I've certainly thought myself in love," she equivocated.

"Did you feel your heart doing flip-flops? Did you want to dance and sing?" She twirled again into the middle of the room, then turned to face Lily. "When I think of Prescott, I could almost swoon."

"I think love is different at various ages," Lily replied carefully. "Sometimes people are more in love with love than with the person, if you know what I mean."

Amelia drew herself up stiffly. "You mean because I'm only sixteen I don't know what true love is," she said in a small, hurt voice.

"I don't feel that way at all, Amelia. Love is a wonderful thing no matter when you experience it."

"Then you think I might be in love?"

"I can't tell you that. You have to listen to your heart. It's not something you decide one day; it's something you just know. When it happens, you don't have to question it. It's just there." Lily held out her hand to the girl. "Now come sit next to me and tell me all about your Prescott."

Amelia must have liked her answer, for she sat back down beside Lily and launched into a long and dreamy description of Prescott and his life in Cheyenne.

"And he has a sister, too. Her name is Cybil," Amelia said when she ran out of things to say about Prescott himself. "She's been back East for the last two months visiting friends. That's the reason for Prescott's party, to welcome her back. It's been really dreary without her around. She's *so* interesting."

"In what way?" Lily asked, knowing Amelia expected her to show an interest.

109

"She's the most cultured lady I've ever met," Amelia answered. "And you'll just love her accent. Of course, you must be used to it, what with Dun being English and all, but I'll never forget the first time I heard her speak. Both Father and I were completely enthralled."

Lily's brow furrowed. From all she had gathered, Gray had had no permanent ties since the death of his wife, but she could be mistaken, especially since Prescott's sister had been out of town.

"Of course, her children are absolute angels, too," Amelia continued, unaware of Lily's distress.

"Oh, she's married, then?"

"Widowed. That's the reason she came to America and then out West with Prescott. She couldn't bear to stay on in England with all the memories. And she wanted Peter and Lorna to experience more breadth in their lives than could be found in a small English hamlet."

Lily could almost hear an English accent tinging those words. It was apparent Amelia idolized this woman and took all her comments to heart. Lily couldn't help but wonder how well Gray knew her. "I understand there are quite a few transplants from England living in Cheyenne. That must make her feel at home."

"Oh, yes. I think she likes the Wyoming Territory and may want to live here permanently. At least, she's hinted as much to me."

"Has she?"

"Mmmm," Amelia said and took a last sip of her tea. "But I don't know for sure. She never goes out to their ranch. Isn't that strange? You'd think she'd want to see it now and then. Father says he would wither and die if he was stuck in town all the time. In a way I know what he means, except *I* would wither and die if I could never go to town!" She laughed and Lily joined her, glad the wonderful Cybil had a fault or two, at least from Gray's perspective.

"Well, I can certainly understand your father's feelings. If I owned a beautiful place like this, I wouldn't want to spend all my time elsewhere, either."

Amelia thought about that for a second. "I guess you're right. I mean, I wouldn't want to *never* come here. I guess I have it best of all since we have our house in town as well as the ranch out here. In winter Papa often lets me stay in Cheyenne with Mrs. Bellows so I won't get stuck out here in the snow. That's how I got to know Cybil so well."

Amelia looked ready to launch into another set of stories about the wonderful Cybil when her words were interrupted by the ringing of a bell.

"What in the world—?" Lily started to say as Amelia jumped to her feet.

"That's Dun. My teacher was kind enough to lend me a bell today when I told her about Dun's incapacitation. When he needs something, he only needs to ring the bell, and one of us will come running."

"In that case . . ." Lily said, also rising.

"No, you stay. You're probably tired from your outing. Besides, he probably wants me. I promised I'd play a game of checkers with him before dinner and completely forgot about it when I got the news about Prescott's party."

The girl hurried toward the stairs with the same enthusiasm she'd shown earlier. Lily had to smile. One minute Amelia wanted to be all grown up, in love with a handsome young man and ready to start a life of her own; the next minute she was a young girl again, running up the stairs for a game of checkers. She was a jumble of confused feelings, still half child but with a growing sense of herself and her desires. A volatile combination, indeed. No wonder Gray was so protective of her.

No sooner did Gray's name pop into her mind than all her thoughts turned to him. Was he safe? She wondered if he had found the rustlers he was after. She almost hoped not. She'd heard the penalties for rustling were most severe, so only a desperate man would willingly take the risk. And desperate men became dangerous men when they were cornered.

She walked to the window and looked out. It made her feel closer to Gray, though she had no idea where Glader Canyon lay in relation to the ranch. For all she knew, Gray might ride up on the other side of the house and she would never even know it, but that didn't matter. The fact was, she felt closer to him here, as if her thoughts could protect him from harm, so she kept her vigil.

And then at last she saw something—a small cloud of dust in the distance growing larger as it came closer. Soon she could make out more detail, a man and a horse galloping toward the house. It was Gray, alive and well and clearly in a hurry. Her heart raced in cadence with his approach. Soon he would be here. Soon she would be in his arms again.

She ran upstairs to her room, determined to look her best now that she knew he was safe. Hurriedly she changed her dress and combed her hair. Then, taking a deep breath, she went back downstairs.

SIX

WHEN GRAY GOT back to the ranch, it was late in the day. He felt tired and as grimy as a bear after a winter's hibernation. The thought of a hot bath was immensely appealing, and he didn't stop to wonder why he should feel the need to be so clean all of a sudden. Usually ranch work was fulfilling and gave him a sense of accomplishment, the dust and dirt that went with a day on the range never bothering him. Not so today.

Since there was no time for the luxury of a bath before the evening meal, he did the next best thing. He took some hot water from the reservoir at the back of the stove when Mrs. Bellows was out setting the dining room table, then skedaddled to his room for a quick wash. He didn't need anyone to see him and ask unwanted questions.

The loss of some of his cattle to the rustlers continued to plague him, but there was nothing he could do about it tonight. He focused his attentions on preparing for the evening ahead. A short while later, wearing clean clothes and a hint of bay rum, he headed down to the front parlor.

When he entered the room, he caught sight of Dun. "Why, this is a pleasant surprise," he said, shaking the smaller man's hand. "I take it you're feeling better."

Dun grinned. "I decided I'd lose my chance with these lovely ladies if I allowed you to monopolize them much longer."

Gray looked over at Amelia and Lily. They were indeed lovely ladies. His daughter looked so grown up, sitting there in one of her best dresses. Gray guessed she wanted something from him to have gone to all this trouble.

Lily, too, looked beautiful. But then, he was finding that she looked beautiful to him no matter what she wore. In fact, his mind couldn't help conjuring up her image at her most beautiful—wearing nothing at all. He could feel a flush steal over his cheeks to match the one he saw on hers and wondered if she was remembering their kiss of this morning, too.

"Good evening, ladies," he said before his thoughts got him into trouble. "Dun is certainly right about how lovely you both look."

"Oh, Papa, you always say that," Amelia said with a teasing pout. "I could be wearing a sack on my head, and my father would tell me how nice I looked. Fathers are like that. Don't you agree?" she asked Lily.

Gray thought he saw a flash of pain cross Lily's face, but it was gone so quickly he was sure he must be mistaken.

"Most fathers, I'm sure," Lily replied, but her smile did not reach her eyes, and Gray wondered what was bothering her. Before he could pursue the issue, she changed the subject. "Did you find anything up at the canyon?"

"The canyon? What canyon?" Amelia demanded, and looked suspiciously from Gray to Lily.

"There was a small problem out by Glader Canyon, that's all. Nothing for you to worry about," he said soothingly.

"That's where you put the new cattle, isn't it?" Amelia persisted.

Gray sighed. He thought they'd kept it all a secret, but if Amelia knew, then there was no telling how far word had gotten round. "Yes, but how did you know?"

"I'm not a child, Papa, no matter how much you may like to think so," she said in her most adult voice. "This ranch is my home and I've always been interested in what's going on here."

"Of course it's your home," Gray said, relieved to find she felt that way. Sometimes lately he'd worried that she was falling under the influence of the Cheyenne social set and would soon refuse to stay at the ranch.

"Then why shouldn't I know what's going on here?"

The simplicity of her question caught him off guard. She sounded suspiciously like Lily had the other day, as if being a female didn't mean she needed protection from the harsher realities of life. He glanced at Lily, but she was carefully keeping her face bland. Only someone who knew they'd discussed the need for women to know as much as their men would detect the gleam of amusement in her eyes.

"I just didn't want you to worry unnecessarily," he said, sounding defensive even to his own ears.

"Does that mean there's nothing to worry about or that you don't want to tell me what it is?"

When had his daughter become so astute? She was turning into a woman before his eyes, with all of a woman's obstinancy and perspicacity, especially when they sensed they had a man pinned.

"At the moment there's nothing to worry about. We spotted the remains of a campfire up near the canyon, and one of the young cows is missing. That's all. I've doubled the guard up there, and I'm not expecting any more trouble. Satisfied?"

"I've heard about the rustling," she said, nodding her head. "Prescott says it's nothing to worry about, too."

Prescott's a damn fool, he almost said aloud, but bit back the comment, knowing his daughter's fondness for Prescott's family.

115

"He does, does he?" he said instead, annoyed that his daughter would take the Englishman's assurances over his own.

"Speaking of Prescott," Lily broke in, "Amelia reminded me about his party tomorrow. Will you still want to go?"

"Of course he wants to go!" Amelia cried out, jumping to her feet. "You're not changing your mind about that, are you, Papa?" Her blue eyes opened wide with dismay, and Gray thought he could see tears glistening in their depths.

"Don't worry, we'll go."

"And will you take us to town early so we can stop at the dress shop? Mrs. Parsons has been working on a new dress for me. It should be all but ready by tomorrow. I couldn't possibly go in any of my old things, not to Cybil's house."

"No, I don't imagine you could," he admitted wryly. "All right, then, we'll make a day of it."

"Oh, thank you, Papa, thank you," Amelia said and threw herself into his arms.

Lily smiled at him over the younger girl's head, and he knew he'd been neatly had. What could he do? She was his only daughter, after all. At least he now knew why she'd dressed so carefully this evening.

"We'll plan on spending the night in town as well," he added, then inquired of Dun, "Would you like to come along?"

"Not to the party, if it's all the same to you, but it might be a good idea to stay in town. The troupe should arrive any day now, and I'd just as soon be on hand in case they need my help."

"In that case, let's plan on staying a few days. I can make arrangements with Sam to keep me posted on any goings-on here at the ranch. It'll give me a chance to see how the other ranchers are faring, as well."

"Oh, Papa, that's a wonderful idea! Don't you agree, Lily?"

Gray looked over at Lily. "Do you agree?"

He hoped she would. In the city they would have more time together, private time. He knew his daughter would be making the most of the social opportunities available in town, especially with Cybil there.

"I wouldn't want to impose. If you're going into town, perhaps Dun and I should consider moving to a hotel."

"You won't be imposing, not in the least. Will she, Amelia?" Gray asked, shamelessly using his one ally.

"Of course not, Lily. Don't you want to stay with us?" Amelia turned her pleading gaze in Lily's direction, and Gray could see her objections melt away.

He smiled in satisfaction. "It's settled, then. After dinner we'll all pack for tomorrow, and then we'll leave right after breakfast. How does that sound?"

"Sounds fine," Dun put in. "We'll be ready."

Dinner was a boisterous affair, what with Dun joining the usual crew and Amelia full of excitement about the upcoming party. Though Gray wanted nothing more than to spend a couple of moments alone with Lily, he had no opportunity until the meal was over and everyone went their separate ways.

He noticed her slipping out the back door after helping Mrs. Bellows with the dishes. Amelia was up in her room deciding what she absolutely could not do without in Cheyenne over the next few days, and Sam had gone off with some of the other men to set up guard duty for the night.

Gray followed Lily out, waiting only long enough to arouse no suspicions. He found her down by the barn scratching Cleo's head.

"You seem to have grown fond of that mare," he said softly, not wanting to startle her.

117

She looked up at him. "She's a wonderful animal. Amelia dotes on her."

"So she tells me." He took a couple of steps closer and reached out to stroke the horse's neck.

"Are you going to let her keep Cleo?"

"I don't see that I have much choice, not if I want to live in the same house with her."

"She's a wonderful girl. You're very lucky; the two of you have a very special relationship."

Gray remembered the bleak look in her eyes when Amelia had mentioned fathers earlier that evening. "How about your own family? Are they with the circus, too?"

The silvery light from the full moon illuminated the barn so that he could see the expressions crossing her face in quick succession—first fear, then wariness, then sadness covered by a neutral expression designed to hide her innermost thoughts.

"My sister Rosemary was with the circus until she died some years ago," she said in a flat voice.

"That must have been a painful loss," he said, but knew there was more to the story. "You must have been fairly young. Who took care of you?"

He could see the relief on her features. This, then, was a safe direction, but what was she so eager to hide? He put his curiosity aside for another time and gave her his full attention.

"Hilda and Otto Bruner took care of us from the very beginning. I think I mentioned that Otto owns the circus?"

He nodded but didn't speak, afraid she would use that as an excuse to stop talking.

"Well, Hilda was his wife. She had the equestrian act in those days, and she was the star of the show. You wouldn't believe some of the things she did from the back of a horse. The first time I saw her, I thought she was a fairy the way she stood on the back of this tall white steed,

118

dressed in a pink, gauzy skirt that floated in the breeze. She was wearing a silver crown pinned to her hair so it wouldn't fall off when she jumped and somersaulted over these four-foot-wide banners. She seemed to float in the air as if she had wings, and then she landed on her tiny feet right on the back of that galloping horse. It was a sight to see."

Gray could almost imagine it just from Lily's rapt expression—the mystery and magic were painfully exposed. "Is that why you started to work with the horses yourself?" he asked, keeping his voice soft, so he wouldn't break the spell. He wanted to know everything about her, if it meant hearing—even about the circus.

Lily laughed. "That's when I started to *dream* about working with the horses. Hilda wouldn't let me near her pampered pets until I'd learned to muck out their stalls. Then I graduated to cleaning out their hooves and brushing their coats. Finally she taught me how to braid their manes and tails and dress them for the ring. I had begun to lose hope that I'd ever get to ride one, then one day she walked in with that imperious air of hers and demanded to know why I'd put off learning to ride for so long."

"She sounds like a fascinating lady."

Though she couldn't make out Gray's face, Lily could hear the interest in his voice. The only light came through the open door behind him. She'd thought about lighting a lantern when she'd first come in the barn, but now that he'd joined her, she welcomed the sheltering darkness, especially with the direction their conversation was taking.

"Oh, she was fascinating, no question about it. And generous, too. She took in both Rosemary and me and treated us as if we were her own children—circus children, to be sure, but hers nonetheless."

"And what makes circus children so different from others?"

119

"Well, they move around all the time, and they learn how to perform almost from the day they're born. Most families expect to pass their act on to the next generation. The children also have to help out during the performances and on the road. There's not a lot of time to do nothing."

"It's not that different out here," Gray said reflectively. "Most ranchers expect to pass their ranches on to their children, and the children help out, especially in the smaller outfits." He paused for a moment as if absorbing his own words, then asked, going back to the original subject, "And where is Hilda now? Is she coming with the rest of the troupe? I'd love to meet her. She did so much for you."

"And I'd love for you to meet her," Lily answered, sorrow heavy in her heart. "But I'm afraid that won't be possible. You see, she died more than a year ago. That's why Dun and I have been making the arrangements for the circus. In the old days Otto took care of everything, but since Hilda's death . . ." Her voice trailed off, then from deep in her heart came the words, "I miss her still."

Gray's arm slipped around her, and she felt the heat of his body as he moved closer. Gently he pulled her into his embrace, his arms around her waist, her head tucked into the hollow of his shoulder.

"It's hard to lose someone you love," he murmured, and she wondered whom he meant for she knew he wasn't referring only to her loss. Could it have been his wife? She wanted to ask, but as they stood in the silvery darkness, just outside the reach of the iridescent moonlight, she kept her silence. More than knowledge of each other, they needed peace together, the peace of this moment.

As they stood gently swaying, she became more and more aware of him, of the steady beat of his heart beneath her cheek, of his masculine scent with the subtle overlay of bay rum, of the sound of his breathing in the quiet barn with its background of shuffling hooves and snuffling horses. Most of all, she became aware of the heat emanating from him everywhere he touched her, along her front where her breasts pressed against his chest, across her hips cradled by his, and around her back where his arms crisscrossed to her waist.

She raised her head to look up at his face and met the greatest heat of all as his burning mouth came down on her lips. She parted them in welcome, and he stoked the embers of her passion, thrusting his tongue past her teeth to tangle hotly with hers. The kiss was alternately dark as the night and silver as the moon, with all the mysterious beauty of both. This time she knew his taste, knew the velvet textures of his touch, recognized his need as a reflection of her own wild desires. This time she knew when to follow and when to lead, when to give and when to take all he offered and ask for more.

Just when the kiss would have become too much, would have lasted too long and led to something neither was ready for, Gray eased back until only their lips touched, until the passion of the previous minutes burned low, until their breathing slowed down and their heartbeats matched. Slowly he lifted his head and with one hand eased her head back to his shoulder where it had lain before. He rested his cheek against her hair and wrapped his arms around her. Once again they stood silently together.

Minutes passed, but Lily lost all sense of time. The complications and worries that had plagued her fell away. All she knew was the utter sense of completion she felt standing here in the dark with Gray, of belonging as she never had before, of having found her place and never wanting to leave it. But all too soon reality began to intrude. The night chill entered the barn on a burst of wind, a horse nickered close by and another answered, a shout of laughter from the bunkhouse echoed in the air.

"We'd best head inside," Gray whispered.

She nodded, knowing he could feel the motion against his chest even if he couldn't make it out in the dark, but she made no other move. Neither did he as they stood, treasuring this moment out of time. Then, as if by mutual consent, they turned and left the barn arm in arm, stopping only to close the huge doors before making the short walk to the house.

The next day passed quickly, more quickly than Lily would have liked. The thought of making her debut in Cheyenne society on Gray's arm was a bit daunting. She hoped her dress was adequate, especially after seeing the clothes at the seamstress's shop. The styles were straight out of the latest issues of *Harper's Bazaar*. If she hadn't known she was out West, she never would have believed it. The transcontinental railroad had only been completed a few years ago, yet Cheyenne had grown from a small, wild shantytown at the end of the railroad track to this large cosmopolitan city almost overnight.

Gray's house in the city was no less imposing than the one on his ranch. It was in the eastern part of town on Seventeenth Street, where several other stock growers had already built their mansions and others were planning to. This part of town bore no resemblance to the area where Dun and Lily had been accosted. The few houses rising from the treeless prairie looked out of place against the barren landscape, as if they'd been transplanted from another place. Most had barns behind them, and Lily noticed that several owners had planted their front yards with grass and set out quick-growing trees and shrubs.

There were houses of brick and stone as well as of wood. Some had been enlarged from smaller cabins built when Cheyenne was first settled; others were simply built on a grander scale by cattle owners who were already coming to wealth on the rich Wyoming grasslands. They rose to heights of two or three stories and were as different from one another as their owners. But none was as grand or ostentatious as the one occupied by Prescott Warford-Smythe and his sister, Cybil.

"Wait until you see the inside," Amelia whispered to Lily as their carriage drew up in front of the ornate iron fence and joined the line of vehicles waiting to discharge their passengers. "I just hope Cybil likes my new dress."

"Why shouldn't she?" Lily asked, frankly surprised. The dress was in the latest fashion, with a snug-fitting, low-cut bodice that accentuated Amelia's feminine curves and set off the alabaster skin of her neck and shoulders. The short sleeves were shirred and hugged her bare upper arms. The green poult-de-soie overskirt fell in flounces over a modest bustle and was edged with pleated ribbons of a slightly darker green. Silk flowers delicately trimmed the edge of the bodice and the side of the overskirt, trailing down onto the underskirt of gathered tulle that fell to the floor.

Already Lily could see the promise of great beauty in her face and in the way she held herself. Who could object to such youthful grace?

"Oh, Cybil won't say anything. It's just . . . she has this way of looking at you so you know something's not quite right. And she's such a wonderful dresser herself. She always knows the latest styles. I'd just hate for her to be disappointed."

"Well, I may not know as much about the latest styles, but what's more important is that you look simply enchanting. Isn't that what really counts?"

Amelia gave her a doubting look. "I suppose." Then she brightened. "Do you really think I look enchanting?"

Lily laughed. "You know you do. After all, Mrs. Parsons spent the better part of the day ensuring that you would. Surely you have faith in her judgment, don't you?"

"Oh, yes. That's why I go to her. Cybil says she's the only dressmaker in this whole town who really has an eye for style."

Though Lily had yet to meet Cybil Heath, she was rapidly forming an impression of her that was less than flattering. Had the woman nothing more to worry about than dressing in the latest fashion?

"I hope I won't be an embarrassment," Lily commented, looking down at her own dress. Compared to the fussiness of Amelia's, hers was austere, the cream lace and brown silk a more subtle combination that fit with her hair, taming its fiery color. Though equally snug as Amelia's, the bodice of her dress revealed far less skin with its lacy edgings and long, narrow sleeves. Velvet trim decorated both bodice and overskirt and the cream-colored underskirt had three flounces of knife pleats.

"Your dress is lovely," Amelia immediately replied. "It makes your eyes look so dark. I wish I had your figure, then I wouldn't need all of these"—her hand fluttered above the silk flowers and lace that enhanced the top edge of her bodice—"to make it look as if I did."

"You're too hard on yourself. You just wait and see if the men don't all flock to your side tonight."

"I don't really care about all the men, but do you think Prescott will notice me?"

"He'd have to be blind not to," Lily replied, though she secretly felt the Englishman was a bit jaded for this fresh young girl.

At that moment the carriage pulled to a stop, and Gray knocked on the door.

"Ready for your big entrance, ladies?" he asked as he opened the door and helped Amelia down.

"Oh, yes, Papa. I can hardly wait! Hurry, Lily, I can hear the music already playing inside."

Gray reached up to help Lily alight from the carriage. He'd bought the rig for Amelia's sake. She'd claimed to need a fancy covered carriage to travel in to the endless parties she seemed to love so much. Usually he avoided such scenes, preferring to let Cybil or some other responsible female acquaintance chaperone his daughter. But tonight he was glad he had come, not so much because he wanted to discuss the latest rustling attempt with the other stockmen, but because of Lily.

When his hand touched hers, a jolt ran up his arm and sent tremors coursing over his skin. In the light from the ornamental torches lit by the gate, he saw her eyes widen, the dark irises turning even darker. He grasped her hand to help her down, then nestled it in the crook of his elbow and held out his other arm to his daughter.

"Okay, Amelia. We're all set. I'm going to be the envy of every man there, coming in with the two loveliest ladies."

"Oh, Papa. Don't start that again," Amelia said with a blush that told him she really appreciated his words.

Gray thought his daughter looked especially radiant and mature tonight, and he felt something of a loss.

"I'll introduce Lily to everyone if you want to talk to Cybil," Gray offered, knowing his daughter would be eager to share all the latest gossip and fashion news with their hostess.

"Oh, but I want Lily to meet Cybil, too. And I know Cybil will want to see you. After all, she's been gone for so long."

Gray chuckled. "Two months is hardly a long time, at least not for someone my age."

"You're not that old, Papa. Why, you're barely thirty-six. Besides, you haven't seen Cybil in even longer than that. I'm so glad you've come to her party."

She squeezed his arm, and Gray smiled down at her, then looked over at Lily and winked. He could see the corners of Lily's mouth curve with affectionate amusement. He thought he just might enjoy this evening, with Lily by his side. For a change he was actually looking forward to the dancing, to the chance to hold Lily in his arms. He liked it that she didn't take this frenetic social scene too seriously, yet honored his daughter's feelings.

He looked over at Amelia and saw her face shine with anticipation, eager for the adventure that awaited her beyond the high stone walls of the house they were about to enter. In truth, he shared that anticipation, that hunger for life and all it had to offer, that impatience to get on to the next step and savor its fullness. These were not feelings he'd had for a very long time, and he had only to glance to the side to know in his heart where they came from. Every time his lips touched Lily's, he hungered for more. Every time he held her in his arms, his dreams increased until they encompassed his every thought.

There was something magical in the air tonight, something more than just the fantasy of going to the ball with the lady of your dreams. Tonight, the line between reality and fantasy was gone; the two seemed to merge, and life was full of possibilities.

"Come on, you two, we don't want to be late," he said, quickening his pace.

They walked up the outside stairs to the large double doors that stood open ready to admit the guests. The foyer soared two stories and was lit by a beautiful cut-glass chandelier that glittered like a million stars above their heads. Lily couldn't help but be impressed. A manservant waited on either side of the entrance to take their wraps, and then they were directed up the stairs to the large ball-room.

The winding staircase was of walnut with bronze medal-lions that sparkled in the light from the chandelier. Above the walnut wainscoting that ran along the stairway hung pictures of Prescott's ancestors, each bearing a remarkable resemblance to the current heir. At the top of the stairs the landing opened onto the ballroom. Here, more chandeliers glittered, and the music, only dimly heard from outside, became clear.

"Cybil must be trying for a more cultured effect," Gray murmured under his breath. "A string quartet, no less."

Amelia darted him a look. "Don't you like the music?" she asked, a frown furrowing her brow. She looked unsure about how to interpret his remark.

"It's lovely," Lily said before he could reply. "The play-ers sound extremely accomplished."

"Of course they are," a woman's voice wafted out from just inside the room. "I wouldn't settle for anything less." Then the woman herself came out of the ballroom, a tall, willowy blonde with a classical peaches-and-cream com-plexion. "Why, Gray, it's so good to see you again," she continued and lifted her cheek for a kiss. "And, Amelia, you look lovely, as well." She took the girl's hands in hers and held them out to the side as she spoke.

Amelia seemed to bloom under the praise, and Lily re-vised her opinion of Cybil. Apparently the lady was not without feeling after all.

"And, of course, you must be Miss Avenel. I've heard so much about you. Do introduce us, Gray."

She smiled prettily at Gray, and Lily felt the sting of jealousy pierce her heart. Then she turned her gaze to meet Gray's, and all her worries fell away. The blaze in his eyes when he looked at her told her she had nothing to fear, at least not from Cybil Heath.

Gray made the formal introductions, and then Prescott came up. "Good evening, all. I'm so glad you were able to attend, Miss Avenel. Didn't I tell you it would be a delightful romp? Have you met everyone?"

"Don't be ridiculous, Prescott. Why, she's only just arrived," Cybil said.

"In that case, why don't I do the honors?" He bowed slightly at the waist and held out his arm.

Lily looked to Gray, uncertain what she should do. She really didn't want to go with Prescott, nor did she want to be openly rude.

Gray raised one eyebrow almost imperceptibly in question, and she shook her head just as subtly.

"If you don't mind, Prescott, I'd just as soon show Miss Avenel around myself. After all, she's been a guest in my house for a week now, and I feel responsible for her. I hope you don't mind."

Lily had the distinct impression that Cybil did not approve of Gray's interference, though she didn't say a word. For his part, Prescott looked a bit flustered, as if he couldn't quite believe any woman would possibly turn him down, but to Lily's relief, he nodded once and said, "Certainly, old chap. Why don't I take you around, Miss Amelia? The Martin girls were just asking after you when I came through from the garden."

Amelia's eyes glowed and her cheeks flushed. "I'll see you all later," she said as she placed her hand on Prescott's arm.

"She's such a dear, Gray," Cybil said in a fond voice as the pair walked off, whatever displeasure she felt at Lily's continued presence put aside. "I really marvel at how well you've done with her. I wish I could say the same of Peter and Lorna. They do so feel the lack of a father."

"It's good that they have Prescott in their lives," he said.

"Oh, yes," she replied, moving closer to Gray. "But it's

not quite the same, is it? I mean, it's not as if they have someone there every day to give them a sense of security and discipline. You know how children can be, especially boys." She sighed and her white breasts rose and swelled above the very low-cut bodice of her modish dress. As Amelia had promised, Cybil had donned a spectacular dress fresh from Paris, its cut just this side of scandalous. The top edge of the bodice dipped dangerously low, so low that when she breathed in too deeply, one could not help but wonder if the top would stay in place.

"Has something happened with Peter lately?" Gray asked.

"You won't believe this. He tied some cans around a dog's tail, then chased it into Converse and Warren's. You couldn't conceive of the commotion!"

Gray started to laugh, then explained to Lily that Converse & Warren's was the furniture and dry goods store. "That's just a normal, little boy thing to do," he added.

"Perhaps out here, but it's hardly proper, especially when the dog in question belongs to Mrs. Dixon. Why, she came down in a faint when she heard of it."

"How'd her dog get away? I'd heard she keeps that runt on a little satin pillow by her side."

"Oh, Gray, you know it's not a runt. It's a highly bred Dutch pug. And she dotes on it, you know. But that's not all. You must come over here where we can sit. I have so much to tell you," she said, indicating a little alcove with her hand.

She led them to a small niche fitted out with two silk damask-covered chairs on either side of a small matching settee. Cybil arranged herself on one of the chairs, carefully draping her voluminous skirts and long train so they wouldn't get wrinkled. She gestured to the other chair and said, "Do have a seat, Miss Avenel."

"Please, call me Lily," Lily replied.

"Oh, you Americans," Cybil said with a little chuckle. "You're so informal. In England we place much more importance on titles and such. It shows our appreciation of better breeding, don't you think so? But I suppose that since I'm now living here, I really should try to adapt to the local customs. So, Lily it is.

"Now, Gray, do sit down or I'll get a crick in my neck from having to look up at you, and there's so much I want to tell you. We haven't seen each other in ages," she explained to Lily, "so I hope you don't mind indulging us for a few minutes."

Cybil didn't wait for Lily to agree or disagree. She simply assumed everyone would fall in with her plans and immediately launched into a series of stories and reminiscences about all the times Gray had helped out with Lorna or Peter, the times they had gone on outings together or stayed in the house engrossed in some activity. Lily was effectively excluded from the conversation and suspected Cybil had done it on purpose. With Gray on the settee, he could only look at one of them at a time, and with Cybil doing all the talking, his attention stayed in her direction. Beyond that, Cybil seemed to be using the conversation more to make sure Lily knew how involved Gray was with their lives than to inform Gray about all the goings-on since they last met.

After a few minutes of indulging his hostess, Gray said, "I'll have to make sure to drop in on the children now that you're back. Maybe I'll take them to the circus. It should be arriving any day now."

"The circus?" Cybil said. "Why, yes, I did see some notices tacked up around town. But are you sure it's a proper place for children? I've heard the most terrible things go on there—charlatans and pickpockets abound."

"That's not true." The heated words burst out of Lily.

"The circus is a fine place for families—at least Bruner's Munificent Menagerie and Family Circus is."

"Well, I'm sure I don't know the specifics of any particular circus, but you can't deny what I say is true. Everybody knows it."

Lily had always known that the outside world was often suspicious of circus folk, but she'd never before run into those suspicions head-on when it mattered so much. She sent an anxious glance in Gray's direction. Only a few days ago he'd expressed similar opinions of the circus. Did he hold to them still?

"Now, Cybil, I have it on the best authority that Bruner's circus is safe, whatever else may be true," he was saying. "I shared your opinion not long ago but knowing Lily has shown me I was wrong, at least in this case." His gaze was open and friendly as he turned to look at Lily. "I'm sure the children will be just fine and will enjoy themselves enormously. Don't you agree?"

Lily basked in the warmth coming from him. "Oh, yes," she concurred and breathed a silent sigh of relief. "Children seem to enjoy the circus most of all. They see the magic with such fresh eyes."

"Magic?" Cybil asked, stiffening her back.

"I don't mean there's real magic. I mean that they latch on to the fantasy, to the magical wonder of it all. That's the whole point of a circus, after all, to make you believe the most wonderful, spectacular things can come true."

"And how do you know so much about it?"

"Lily is part of the circus troupe, Cybil. I thought Prescott must have told you."

He reached across the settee and took Lily's hand in his. His hand felt strong and manly, and definitely reassuring in the face of Cybil's reactions.

"Of course. Now that you mention it, I do believe he said something of the kind," Cybil said with a smile, but the smile did not reach her eyes, and Lily realized Cybil had known all along about her circus connections. "And what do you do with the circus, if I may ask?"

Her tone carried an edge to it, though Lily wasn't sure which emotion had produced it—wariness, distaste, or anticipation that whatever Lily answered would only serve Cybil's purposes.

"I do all sorts of things, including the equestrian act."

"Oh, so you ride, then?"

"She rides very well," Gray said. He squeezed Lily's hand and sent her a veiled, heated look.

Lily could feel a blush rise to her cheeks as she remembered what had happened the last time she had ridden on Gray's ranch—that day on the "plain" when he'd found her sprawled luxuriously on a rock, dreaming of him.

"Don't tell me you use one of those awful Western saddles!" Cybil exclaimed with a shudder.

Gray laughed. "Now, Cybil, you know our saddles serve a very important purpose. We use them for work, not chasing after a poor, outnumbered fox for sport."

"Really, Gray, you know as well as I do that foxes can be most destructive. It's not as if the hunt doesn't serve a useful purpose."

"Well, this is an old argument that I'm sure we won't solve here. Besides, I doubt very much that Lily uses a Western saddle in her work, do you?" he asked, neatly turning the conversation to include her once again. The heat in his gaze more than made up for Cybil's coldness.

"I'm afraid I don't use any saddle at all, most of the time."

"No saddle? Doesn't that bother the horses?" Cybil asked.

"No, they're trained to it. I work with them almost every day."

"Every day? That doesn't leave much time for anything

else, does it? I would never want to be so preoccupied that I didn't have time for my family or children. Don't you agree, Gray?" Cybil seemed bent on ignoring the fact that Gray was holding Lily's hand as she made another bid for his attention. "I mean, it's all well and good to be busy, especially for a man, but women are needed for other things. We must frame a welcome home for our family and make sure the household is run properly. Surely you must find that hard to do in addition to your other duties, Lily."

"I don't actually have a household as such. We travel from town to town, so there isn't all that much to take care of, at least not inside the wagons."

"It's a very vagabond sort of life, isn't it?"

"We do a lot of traveling, if that's what you mean."

"Well, yes," Cybil said. "That's what I meant. Here today, gone tomorrow, that sort of thing. No?"

Lily didn't answer. Cybil was using the conversation to make sure Gray realized she was not a permanent member of their tight social circle, not because she was interested in Lily's life or opinions. Fortunately, Hank Farrell picked that moment to join them.

"Good evening, ladies, Gray," he said with a courtly bow. "I wasn't sure if you had made it, Miss Lily, what with Gray hidin' you here in this corner. And you, too, Miss Cybil. You have been sorely missed these past few months—you certainly breathe life into this town, if I dare say so. It's good to have you back, and if I may, you look more beautiful than ever, doesn't she, Gray?"

Gray nodded as he rose to his feet, drawing Lily up beside him. Cybil smiled up at Hank. "You are most gracious, Hank, if one can believe even half of what you say. This man is the very devil with words," she added archly.

"Ah, it's merely part of my charm." He grinned and his teeth gleamed white beneath his dark mustache, giving

133

him a piratical air. "It's even good to see you, Gray. How are things at your ranch?"

Gray let go of Lily so they could shake hands, then said, "I'm glad you asked, I wanted to talk to you about—"

"Now, now, boys. This is a party. I will not have you talking of cows and such tonight," Cybil said, rising to stand between the two men. She took advantage of Gray's preoccupation to link her arm through his, shutting Lily out. "Your business can wait for another day. Right now, the music is playing and the food is laid out. You have better things to do with your time."

Hank laughed. "Like dance with the ladies?"

"Certainly. Why else do you think I invited you if not to please the ladies?"

"In that case, I will do my humble best." He stepped over to Lily's side and added, "If you would do me the honor of havin' the next dance, I would be most pleased."

Lily had no choice. Social etiquette dictated that she couldn't refuse, even if she would rather dance with Gray. So she did the only thing she could: She smiled and accepted Hank's invitation.

As she left the alcove on Hank's arm, she saw that Cybil was leading Gray in the opposite direction, toward the doors that led to a secluded balcony. Lily chanced one glance over her shoulder to catch Gray's eye, but he never looked back, and then Hank was taking her out onto the dance floor, and she could look no more.

The rest of the evening became a blur. She was caught in a social whirl, every man present wanting a dance with the star attraction of the upcoming circus. Gray managed to sneak in two dances, but it seemed every time he was about to ask Lily to dance, Cybil admonished him for monopolizing their guest and not allowing anyone else a share of her time.

By the time the evening came to an end, Lily felt as if

she'd seen Gray for all of ten minutes. It appeared Cybil had done her best to keep him to herself. If it hadn't been for the telling glances he'd sent her way, Lily would have thought Cybil's innuendos might be based on fact. Tomorrow she would talk with Gray and sort out all she was feeling.

SEVEN

LILY CAME DOWN to breakfast in the morning to find Gray dressed and ready to go out.

"I've been called to an important meeting," he said apologetically. He placed his hands on her waist and drew her into his embrace. "I had hoped we could spend the day together."

"I'd hoped so, too," she confessed shyly as she straightened his collar and smoothed his jacket over his shoulders.

"Maybe later, then," he said, his blue eyes dark with promise. "I'll try to hurry things along." He bent his head as if to kiss her, but before their lips could touch the sound of Amelia's approaching footsteps reached their ears. "I guess we'd better wait," Gray said ruefully as he stepped back. He touched her cheek with one fingertip. "Think of me?"

She flushed and nodded. "I'll see you later," she said, and her voice sounded huskier than usual.

"That's a promise," he replied as he went out the door.

But events worked against them for, halfway through the morning, one of the older boys from the circus came to Gray's house to let her know the troupe had arrived in Cheyenne and were setting up. She and Dun hurried right over to the park grounds. She'd been on the move since then, checking on her horses and making sure her equipment had survived the trip intact.

Her week with Gray seemed like a dream now that she was back. Everywhere she looked she saw well-loved faces and familiar scenes, but the sense of coming home, of fitting in perfectly, was no longer with her. She knew the circus hadn't changed, not in the short time she'd been gone. The changes had occurred inside her, changes she both welcomed and feared.

She walked around the "backyard" of the circus, taking in the bustle and familiar noises of the troupe setting up for their stay in Cheyenne. Groups of roustabouts were hard at work, one raising the canvas for the top where the performances would take place while others worked on the other two major display tents that housed the museum and menagerie. Smaller tents would be set up on the periphery for the use of the circus troupe as well as the public.

"Elena," she called out as a diminutive, dark-haired woman hurried past. Elena Santelli was her closest friend at the circus, and she was glad to see her at this moment. The Frenchwoman had married an Italian acrobat, and they had combined their talents into one of the most exciting acts in the circus.

"Oh, Lily, zere you are! I 'ave look all over for you. 'Ave you seen your 'orses? Are zey all right?"

"Yes, they're fine, except for Lancelot. He's in an even worse mood than usual. I hope he didn't give you any trouble."

"No. We leave 'im with Merlin just like you say. Something is wrong wiz him?" She gave Lily a worried glance.

"Whatever it is, it's not because of anything you did or didn't do," she reassured her friend. "I think he may be coming down with something, but I hope I'm wrong. I haven't had a chance to speak to Gustav yet."

"Gustav, 'e check on your 'orses every day, but 'e never say anything about Lancelot." She looked over her shoulder, then stepped in closer to Lily and continued in a lower voice, "But I tell you, zis trip was *très difficile*. Bryce push and push and everything go wrong."

"What happened?" she asked.

"No one told you?" Elena looked surprised. "Zat Bryce!" She shook her head in disgust. "Come with me, we go somewhere more private. I tell you about it."

They found a secluded nook out beyond the food tent and grabbed a couple of stools to sit on.

Elena dropped onto hers with a sigh of relief. "I tell you, lately I am so tired I fall asleep anywhere. Is good to just sit and rest." She leaned back against a length of board propped behind her stool and lifted her face to the sun. "Mmmm, nice. I could sit 'ere all day."

Lily worried about her friend's uncharacteristic lethargy. Was there something Elena wasn't telling her? She and her husband, Roberto, had toured with Otto for several years as one of the star acrobatic attractions, refusing other offers as their fame spread. Lily and Elena had become close friends over that time and often confided in each other.

"How is everything with you and Roberto?" Lily now asked.

Elena opened one eye and looked at her friend. "So far, we are managing, but like your Lancelot, I 'aven't been feeling well lately."

"Should you be in bed? Is there anything I can do?"

"Zere is nothing. Just time, I think." She smiled reassuringly at Lily.

"You mentioned that this was a hard trip. What happened?"

"Nothing you can point a finger at and say, 'Zis is it.' Just many little things." Elena sat up and looked at Lily. "I 'ate to be ze one to tell you, but your costumes, zey are ruined."

"Ruined? But how? I packed them all neatly away."

"Yes, and where you put zem?"

"In the wardrobe wagon with everyone else's."

"*Alors.* We were crossing the river, and the water she was deep, even at . . . what do you say, where the water is short?"

"Ford?" Lily answered hopefully.

"*Oui*, ford. But you know Bryce. Zat man, 'e did not stop, not even for a small time. All 'e did was yell and push at everyone. And when zat was still too slow for 'im, 'e wanted a new way so more wagons could go together."

"What happened?"

"Well, no one wanted to do it. It was too 'ard to do even one wagon. We needed all ze men and even Old Bess to push ze 'eavy ones through. So Bryce, 'e took ze wardrobe wagon, and 'e drive it across 'imself. Next thing, ze wagon is falling into ze river. Everything is wet."

"Including mine."

"Especially yours. Your trunk was not tight. One clasp she was open, and ze mud and water just poured in. I tried cleaning, but ze mud was really bad. I am so sorry."

Lily couldn't believe it. She'd worked so hard on her costumes, saving her money to buy just the right materials, fabrics that would flow as she moved yet not get in her way. Worse yet was the loss of the costumes Hilda had given her. They were the truly irreplaceable ones, for they had been made by Hilda's own hand. She clearly remembered closing both clasps of her trunk. What twist of fate had resulted in one of them opening?

"Where are the costumes now?" Lily asked, blinking back her tears.

"Come and I show you. I wouldn't let Bryce throw anything out. I knew you want to see yourself."

The two women stood up and threaded their way past the groups of men and animals hoisting the top. As they went by Otto's wagon, they caught sight of Bryce Mason. He scowled when he saw them approach.

"Bryce, can we have a moment of your time?" Lily called out.

"What do you want?" he demanded. "Can't you see I'm busy?"

In fact, he looked anything but. Unlike the other men on the grounds whose clothes and brows were sweat-streaked, Bryce was immaculate. Even his hands were unsullied by the slightest stain.

"I just wanted to check how the trip went and to give Otto the various receipts we got from the fire marshal."

"The trip went fine and Otto's resting. Why don't you just give me the papers? That's what Otto'll do, anyway."

Even though Lily knew he was right, she couldn't bring herself to circumvent Otto. This was still his circus, and she harbored the hope that one day he would shake off his sorrow and take charge again.

"Thank you, but I'd rather wait until Otto is available. If he chooses to give you the papers, that's his decision."

"Suit yourself." He turned as if to go.

"Wait a minute," Lily said, forestalling him.

"What now?" He took a watch out of his pocket and snapped open the cover to check the time. Lily noticed the mellow color and realized it was a real gold watch, not one of the imitations.

"I just heard about the costumes. How did it happen?"

"It was an accident, that's all. I was doing my best to get here as quickly as possible, but we ran into some trouble. It's to be expected when you're working with a caravan of this size."

"It's never happened before."

His eyes snapped angrily. "Maybe not, but you've never been out West before, either. Now, if that's all—"

"It's not. What did Otto say?"

"Otto's a man. He understands what it's like out on the road. He was there, don't forget." Lily had to back down at that. Besides, this argument was getting them nowhere. It was more important to get the costumes replaced than to fight about whether they could have been better protected to start out with. "You women would do better to stick to what you know and stay out of my end of the business," Bryce added for good measure.

"All right, then tell me, what's being done to replace the costumes?"

"Look, we've barely pulled into town, it's already Friday, and I have to have the parade ready to go by tomorrow. I've enough problems to handle right now."

"Without the costumes, there won't be a parade, at least not one that will attract the crowds we need. Are any of the costumes usable?"

"How the hell should I know? I can't take care of everything."

Lily bit back her sharp retort. In fact, his job *was* to take care of everything, but what good would it do to antagonize him even more? "All I want is to find out if I can be of some help. I haven't had a chance to assess the damage yet myself, but Elena tells me only about half the clothes can be salvaged. That means we need to replace the rest. There's an excellent seamstress in town, and I'm sure she could work with us if we ask."

"Well, I can hardly believe this—Lily willing to spend some of Otto's precious money. You sure about this, girlie?" Bryce's voice was full of venom.

Elena stepped between them. "We need ze costumes, Mr. Mason. You know zat as well as we do. And we need zem soon."

"All right, all right. Hire your seamstress and get her down here as soon as possible. Now can I get on with my work?"

"Merci." Elena stepped back out of his way, and he took off without a backward glance.

141

"You see?" Elena said to his back. "It would appear 'e is trying, but nothing works out right."

"I know what you mean, but Otto won't listen to anything against him. I've tried talking to him before. I guess Hilda's death hit him much harder than anyone imagined." Lily sighed. "Let's go look at those costumes, and then I'll contact Mrs. Parsons."

The costumes were laid out on ropes strung between posts set in the ground, since there were few trees in the area. Lily could see at a glance that many were ruined, especially the fancier ones. The mud had stained the delicate fabrics beyond repair.

"I think I'd better get Mrs. Parsons down to look for herself."

" 'Ow you meet zis Madame Parsons?" Elena asked as they walked past the rows of costumes. "You 'ave not spoken of your stay in Cheyenne. Was it all right? Dun, 'e looked not so good."

"You'll never believe what happened," Lily said to her friend, and then told her about the fight outside of the Golden Plumb and how Gray and Sam Carter had come to their aid. By the time she finished telling of her stay at the Whispering Winds, Elena was looking as worried as Dun.

"You seem quite *enchanté* by zis Monsieur Benedict," she said.

"I guess I am," Lily admitted. In fact, she was more than fond of Gray. With very little effort on her part, she could easily fall in love with the man.

"And 'ow does 'e feel?" Elena asked, her expression softening.

Lily looked away. "I don't know, exactly. He leads a very different life from us. On the ranch I didn't notice it as much, but in the city everything changed. You should have seen the party last night, the way the people dressed,

142

the food, the conversation ... It wasn't like the circus at all."

All Lily could think of was the way Gray had looked next to Cybil, as if he belonged, as if they were part of the same world, refined and sophisticated in ways that she wasn't. Faced with Cybil's cool beauty, Lily had felt out of place, her hair too flamboyantly red, her dress too far from the current faddish style, her manner too straightforward. She'd never learned the coy flirtatiousness that seemed to come so naturally to Cybil's social set.

When she'd danced in Gray's arms, none of these worries had plagued her, but away from him, the doubts returned.

"Is not my place to say," Elena said, "and I don't know zis man, but ..." She took a deep breath before plunging on. "Don't be 'urt. Put 'im out of your mind while you still can. Is 'ard enough to make a life with a circus person, but what will you do when you 'ave to leave? 'Ave you thought about zis?"

"You're right, I know. I think of little else."

Elena must have heard the desperation in her voice for she walked up to Lily and put her arm around her shoulders. "Oh, *ma petite*, what 'ave you done?" she whispered as she hugged Lily close.

Lily had no answer, at least none that she was willing to acknowledge, but she knew one thing for certain: It was already too late to put Gray out of her mind now that he'd found a home in her heart.

"Do you think I could walk uptown and see if anything's happening?" Amelia asked Gray on Saturday morning, two days after Cybil's party, and two days since he'd last seen Lily.

His daughter hadn't stopped talking about the circus and

Lily since she'd gotten home from school the day before. Nor had Mrs. Bellows. Neither wanted to miss seeing anything they'd heard Lily and Dun describe.

Despite their chatter, Gray had never been lonelier. Last night they'd gathered together for dinner and then spent a quiet evening at home—too quiet, Gray thought. He missed Lily's presence more than he'd imagined he would. She'd been at his ranch for only a week, yet he was already used to having her nearby. He missed talking with her in the early evening, hearing her laughter at the dinner table, and just watching her.

He missed holding her, feeling her softness, having her sweet feminine scent waft by on a breeze, hearing her voice in laughter and delight . . . and passion. Now, for the first time in a week, she was no longer in the next room, no longer within reach whenever he needed to see her. Instead, she was a city's length away, and he found he didn't like it.

"Papa? Are you listening?"

"I certainly am," he said, not wanting to admit to his daughter that his mind had been on Lily. "And I don't think going by yourself is a very good idea. If you'll wait about an hour, until my meeting's over, we can go up together."

"Oh, Papa. You weren't listening. Mrs. Rossiter and Elizabeth have asked me to go shopping with them until the parade starts."

"Shopping?"

"I thought I might stop at Mrs. Parsons's Dress Shop and see if she has anything new."

"You were already there this week. Surely you don't need another new dress so soon?" Gray queried, knowing the answer he would receive. He enjoyed seeing Amelia's delight in her purchases and admitted to himself that he sometimes spoiled her. As long as the spoiling was having a positive effect, he'd continue.

"Well, I need a new dress, what with my party coming up soon, but to be honest, Elizabeth said she'd heard something scandalous had arrived at the shop, and all the ladies are aghast. Mrs. Rossiter said it was probably nothing, since it didn't take much to scandalize a group of old bid—" She bit her lip and looked up at him sheepishly.

Gray tried to hide his amusement behind a stern warning. "Mrs. Rossiter is a fine woman, but I don't think it would be wise to quote her quite so freely."

"Yes, Papa," Amelia replied, her blue eyes sparkling. She did not look the least bit repentant, but Gray knew she was usually more tactful.

"Well, since Elizabeth and her mother will be with you, I'll meet you in front of Mrs. Parsons's at twelve-thirty."

Though Gray's worries about the circus had eased as his relationship with Lily deepened, he was still wary of having Amelia attend the parade alone. If she met him at twelve-thirty, though, they would have plenty of time before the parade began.

He watched Amelia hurry off to her room to ready herself for her excursion. He was glad to see she was keeping up her usual pursuits. It was a sign that her life was going on in its usual patterns, free of outside influences of the wrong sort. He was also happy that she would be outside of the house when Hank and the others came over. He wanted her as far away as possible from anything that had to do with the rustling. He wanted her aware of the danger, but he didn't want her to know more than was necessary despite her protestations. Her safety was his paramount concern.

The thefts had been happening with more regularity in

the past few weeks. Since Cybil had banned all talk of the cattle business and anything related to it from her party, he decided to have some of the more prominent members of the Cattlemen's Club to his house, where they could talk freely. Hank had come up with the idea of using his ranch and some new cattle as bait. Gray had reluctantly agreed, realizing that no one could find out about it except a few select members of the club. That way, if someone made an attempt on Hank's cattle, the club's staff could be eliminated from suspicion. That would narrow the field down to members of the club or someone they might have talked with.

Within fifteen minutes of Amelia's departure, the first of the men arrived, and soon the front parlor was filled with smoke from their cigars. Mrs. Bellows had quietly filled their coffee cups and retreated to the kitchen.

"Well, Gray, old man, what is it you think we'll accomplish here?" Prescott asked as he sipped his coffee.

"Maybe nothing, but it never hurts to share what information we have."

"Gray's right," Hank put in. "I've got two mighty fine bulls that I hope will be the start of something big on my ranch, and I don't want them wanderin' off in the night."

"I say, that's great news, old chap. When did you come by them?" Prescott asked.

"They're comin' in on Monday, and I don't want some no-good runnin' off with my future."

Gray nodded. "As most of you know, the rustlers staged a raid on my place early this week. We were lucky. They only got one cow, but one of my men was pretty shook up."

"You have any ideas who's behind this?" Franklin Pollock asked from his position on the sofa.

"Not many. I just thought if we all got together and

146

shared what we'd heard, we might come up with something."

"All I know is I lost some of the best damn bulls I've ever laid my eyes on to those bastards, and I want them caught," John Dixon complained, then turned to the sheriff and added, "Have you come up with anything?"

"I've followed up on each theft, but they don't leave a whole lot to go on," Sheriff Tyler replied. "They know what they're doing and exactly when to move in."

"Doesn't that strike you as peculiar?" Gray asked.

"I say, Grayson, what are you getting at?" Prescott put in.

Gray turned to face Prescott. "That they always seem to know when there's new cattle in the area."

"And?" Prescott asked, not understanding where Gray was leading.

"I think they may be getting some of that information through the club."

"Through the club?" Prescott sputtered. "You're not bringing that up again. Shouldn't we be—"

"Yeah, Gray's right," Dixon broke in, looking pointedly at the sheriff, as if he should have come up with the idea. "My bulls were gone almost before I knew I had 'em, and I did a lot of talking at the club."

"Dixon, I want these fellows caught as much as you," the sheriff said, defending himself. "It don't look too good for me with all these cows disappearing right under my nose."

"We all want these men caught. We just need to keep our ears and eyes open," Franklin added.

"Franklin's right. Let's meet again Monday night at the club and see what we come up with," Dixon suggested.

"Just remember I don't want any of them vigilante shenanigans from this group," the sheriff put in.

All the men agreed, but Gray suspected some of them were more partial to the vigilantes than they'd ever admit. Their whole future depended on the size and quality of their herds. And some of them were willing to do anything to make sure they kept what they had.

"You're taking a chance, you know, allowing the bulls on your spread," Gray said to Hank after the rest of the men had left for their afternoon appointments.

"Hey, I'm willin' to do anything to stop this thievin'. These incidents are makin' everyone itchy."

"I hope this works. Your scheme might very well narrow down who's letting the information out, but I'm still not sure it's a good idea." Gray had had his doubts about this plan when Hank first suggested it, but since he couldn't come up with anything better, he'd gone along with it. "I'll send the bulls over Monday, but I want you to be careful. Don't go and take any foolish chances."

Hank smiled. "Don't worry, I won't."

Gray didn't like the looks of that smile. He just hoped Hank didn't do anything harebrained.

An hour later Amelia was standing in front of Mrs. Parsons's just as Gray had requested, waiting for him. He hurried along the main street to her side, anxious that he might have missed seeing Lily in the parade, since he'd heard the band playing for the last few blocks. He hurried his steps as his urgency increased.

"Papa, you're late," Amelia complained when Gray reached her side.

"I'm sorry, sweetheart. The meeting lasted longer than I thought it would." The parade was just beginning, to Gray's relief. He watched the clowns as they passed by, running, jumping, and doing somersaults for the approving crowd. He leaned forward craning his neck, trying to see what was coming next but could see no further than a coach being pulled by two pure-white horses directly behind the clowns.

He felt increasing impatience with the slow-moving column. He craved the sight of Lily. Even with his concern over the rustling and this morning's meeting still fresh in his mind, his thoughts strayed to her. When he should have been listening to what the sheriff was saying, he'd found himself wondering what Lily might be doing at that exact moment. He realized he didn't know much about her everyday life, and suddenly what she ate for lunch and when she practiced her routines became very important. If he'd missed seeing her in the parade—

"Papa? Are you listening?" Amelia's voice brought him back to the present.

"Of course, dear."

"Is everything all right?" she asked in a worried voice. "Lately, you seem so preoccupied. Are you worried about all the rustling that's been going on?"

"Yes, a little, but it's nothing you need to be concerned about right now," Gray said, patting the hand she'd slipped into the crook of his arm. "You just enjoy the parade."

Gray found it amusing that he was more intrigued by the parade than his daughter was, particularly in view of his earlier fears of the circus's allure for her. It seemed now that the circus held him in much deeper thrall than it did Amelia, and all because of Lily.

While Amelia chattered on about her shopping and socializing, Gray searched the faces of the passing performers looking for the only one that truly mattered to him.

"Have you seen Dun yet?" he asked his daughter.

"He was one of the first clowns to come by. They were pulling him in a small wagon. I'm sure he was riding because of his injuries. I hope he isn't doing more than he should."

"I'm sure Lily is looking after him. By the way, has she gone by?" Gray said in a casual tone, hoping his interest wasn't too obvious.

"Not yet. Oh, here comes the band," Amelia said, almost jumping up and down in her excitement. "Can we go to the band concert? Mrs. Rossiter says the band will play in the ring right before the circus starts."

"We'll see," Gray answered distractedly while the brightly painted bandwagon passed. He was more interested in what was to come. As time passed, his pulse quickened and his muscles grew taut. He wasn't sure what he was going to say or do when Lily finally came by. All he knew was that he had to see her again, to hold her in his arms, to kiss her.

If he closed his eyes, he could see her again in a swirl of different images—at his ranch and in the city, with her hair in a neat knot and flying wildly in the breeze like a bright red flame, laughing and serious, in passion and in anger. She had so many faces, so many moods, and he knew he could spend a lifetime and never tire of them all.

"Oh, look! There's Lily."

As Amelia's words registered, Gray blinked his eyes open and looked up, searching for her. And suddenly there she was, not ten feet from him as he stood on the muddy side of the road. He wasn't prepared for the vision she made atop the jet-black horse. His heart jerked to a stop at the very sight of her, and he willed her to look in his direction.

His gaze never left her as her horse started forward toward the next intersection. He couldn't believe she was moving away with no sign, no contact between them. He almost called out to her to get her attention. Then the bandwagon preceding her came to a halt, and her horse stopped directly in front of him—him and fifty other people. He watched as she smiled and waved at the crowds. Her horse stood perfectly still as if he was enjoying the appreciation of the crowd as much as the human performers.

Lily was sitting sideways on the back of the horse as if she were riding sidesaddle, only she was perched on the animal's bare back. Her pale blue dress reached to the middle of her calf, revealing legs covered by blue stockings and feet encased in soft white leather slipper shoes. As his gaze traveled back up to her face, he realized she had finally seen him. She had stopped waving and was looking directly into his eyes.

Then the smile that had been only on her lips reached her eyes, and he knew her smile was especially for him. He wouldn't have believed it if he hadn't seen it himself, but this smile was so much more radiant than the one she'd sent to the rest of the crowd. And at that moment he knew he didn't want to live without her.

"Oh! Doesn't she look stupendous? And look at her costume! Have you ever seen anything more beautiful?" Amelia interrupted his thoughts, exclaiming loudly enough to be heard over the band, which had just started a new number.

"No. Never." And he hadn't. Never in his life had he seen anyone more beautiful nor felt what he was feeling at this exact moment. He knew in that instant that he wanted to share his life with her. There had to be some way they could be together.

"I see your friend is certainly getting her fair share of the crowd's attention." Cybil's mocking tone drew his attention away from Lily as she placed her hand in the crook of his free arm.

He looked down at the woman beside him ready to make a suitable retort when he noticed the two children clinging to her skirts. He wanted to defend Lily and let

Cybil know he felt her acid comments were not welcome, but he refrained. Neither four-year-old Peter nor eight-year-old Lorna deserved to witness his disdain for their mother's attitude. He had known Cybil for well over a year and never noticed this particular trait before. Had his better judgment been taken in by her cool beauty? Or hadn't he cared enough about her to notice?

When Gray didn't reply, Cybil continued, "I don't think I could ever put myself on such display."

"Oh, I think she looks wonderful," Amelia said, not recognizing Cybil's less than sincere tone and taking her comment as a compliment.

"And not all of us have the talent that affords us the opportunity to entertain others," Gray returned, allowing Cybil's hand to drop from his arm. He had had enough of Cybil's caustic remarks at the party and had told her so at the time, but apparently she chose not to heed him. He moved to Amelia's right, putting his daughter between them to close off further conversation.

Suddenly the parade started moving again, and Lily was giving all her attention to her mount. With the merest flick of her wrist she sent the animal into a smart prance and began edging forward. Before she was completely out of eye range, she turned and her gaze met Gray's again. The smile in her eyes was dimmed, her expression filled with confusion. He knew he'd have to see her again soon to make sure she didn't misinterpret what she had just seen with Cybil.

"Are you going to the band concert?" Amelia asked Cybil as they watched the rest of the parade.

"The children would like to attend, but I find them so hard to control all by myself," Cybil said, looking over at Gray.

"Yes, I can see where that could be a problem," Gray said, taking Cybil's lead. "But I know just the thing.

Amelia can go with you and help with the children. Is that all right?"

"But, Gray—" Cybil started to say.

"I'd love to," Amelia said at the same time, stopping Cybil from finishing her protest about the arrangements. "But aren't you coming, too, Papa?"

"I have some business to take care of. Why don't I meet you when the circus starts its performance?"

Gray gave Amelia some money to purchase treats for the children, then walked them to Cybil's carriage, which was parked on a side street. He didn't start for the park until he'd seen them safely off. Then he walked as quickly as he could in the direction of the circus tent whose colorful banners were just visible over the tops of the nearby buildings.

Lily left her horses and Merlin with one of the roustabouts and headed for her wagon to change into her show costume. She and Elena had managed to salvage one or two costumes, piecing them together from the cleanest remnants of her collection. Her footsteps were slow as she wended her way to her wagon, which had been placed on the outermost corner of the lot since she hadn't been there to object. Lily didn't mind the location; in fact, right now she was glad to be so far away from everyone else. She needed time to think. Burned into her mind was the image of Gray and Cybil as she'd last seen them, her arm entwined with his. Standing with her two children and Amelia, they'd looked very much like a family.

When Lily had first seen Gray standing on the side of the street, he'd appeared happy to see her. She could have sworn the look he'd given her held a promise, a pledge of what they would share together. And then she'd noticed Cybil. Had she been there all along? Lily wasn't sure.

When she'd first seen Gray, she'd been so mesmerized by the look he'd given her, she'd seen nothing but him.

Everything between them was so up in the air. She wished they'd had more time to talk, but between his meetings and her duties at the circus, they hadn't been free to meet for even a moment. When she'd seen him at the parade, her heart had soared. He hadn't forgotten her, not if the messages she'd read in his eyes were real. And then she'd seen Cybil, and her fledgling hopes had wavered.

Lily wasn't so naïve that she didn't realize Cybil had plans for Gray. It had been obvious to Lily from their first meeting. If anything, Lily had felt sorry for the woman because she'd seemed so taken aback when Lily had arrived with Gray. Now she had to wonder if she was the one who had been assuming too much. Was it a mistake to have concluded that Gray and Cybil were only friends? Had it been only her wishful thinking that made her think Gray could be hers, that he was a free man?

Though she and Gray had talked of many things, of the past and of the present, they had never spoken of the future. Lily hadn't noticed the lack until she returned to the circus. There was so much she wanted, so many dreams she'd never dared entertain, and now that those dreams had been given life, she had no idea if they were only her own or if he shared them. She felt cut off from him and unsure.

She was just about to step on the wooden box that served as the step-up to her wagon when she heard her name called in Dun's familiar voice. "You've got company!" he shouted as she was opening her door. Her heart leapt, but she tamped down her excitement. Had Gray come?

She turned to see who it was, but all she saw was Dun. Her heart dropped, then Gray rounded the corner of the large red wagon sitting directly ahead of hers, and her excitement rekindled.

"I told you she'd sneak back here for a rest before the show started," Dun said in a confidential whisper more than loud enough for Lily to hear.

"What have I told you about spreading my secrets to all and sundry?" Lily said to Dun in the same teasing tone, her heart suddenly light. Dun merely shook his head and laughed. She felt giddy inside and filled with excitement.

Gray clapped Dun on the shoulder. "Thanks for helping me find her. I'll see you after the show?"

"My pleasure," he said, nodding to Gray, then turned to Lily. "I'll see you at the main tent before the performance?" Dun asked before he turned to head back to the public promenade area.

"Of course," she called to him. She had the idea he was asking more than where she would be an hour from now, but she wouldn't let Dun's oblique reminder dim her joy at seeing Gray.

"I didn't expect you," she said as soon as Dun was out of sight. She had so much she wanted to tell him but was afraid. She hoped his being there was a good sign.

"After I saw you in the parade, I knew I had to come see you."

"Did you?" she prompted.

Gray nodded as he stepped up beside her.

"Why?" she asked when he didn't speak. His nearness was having a decided effect upon her. Her pulse had picked up its rhythm, and her cheeks felt warm. Warmer still was the ache deep inside her. It burned her very center and spread in ripples of want through her entire body. It wasn't fair that just the presence of this man produced such immediate reactions within her, not when she was still unsure of Cybil's place in Gray's life.

For a moment Gray just looked at her. Then he looked

around and noticed they were attracting attention. He tipped his head toward the wagon and asked, "Do you think we might go inside?"

"Oh, of course," Lily replied, all flustered. She should have invited him in immediately, but she'd been so shaken by his nearness she'd completely forgotten her manners. As she stepped up into the wagon, she realized that once they were inside, they'd be alone, truly alone, with no fear of interruptions or prying eyes. Her heart skipped a beat at the thought.

Lily could feel Gray directly behind her as she moved into her small home. She wondered what he would think of it. This had been the only home she'd known for the greater part of her life, and she'd never looked at it from an outsider's point of view. Suddenly it became very important for him to approve, though looking around her now, she realized how tiny and cramped everything was.

She had tried to make the cabin into two rooms by hanging a curtain across the middle of the wagon, only this morning she had forgotten to close it. As a result, the area she used as a bedroom was visible. There was a small bunk-style bed attached to the wall and a low chest that stored some of her clothes and doubled as a couch when she covered it with cushions and an afghan.

On the other end were two chairs, quite comfortable and upholstered in a cheery pattern, as well as a table which held an oil lamp and a picture of herself and her sister both in costume, taken just before her sister's death.

She motioned for Gray to take a seat and hastily pulled the curtain, blocking his view of her bedroom. He didn't immediately sit down, but turned and looked around her home.

Lily had always known her wagon was small, but until the breadth of Gray's shoulders filled the room, she'd never realized how tiny it really was. With his arms stretched out, Gray could practically touch the walls on either side, and his head just missed hitting the ceiling.

"The wagon's small. If you'd rather, we could go over to the food tent," Lily offered, thinking he might be uncomfortable in such a cramped space.

"This is really amazing," he said. "Everything's so compact."

"If it wasn't, there'd be no room to walk."

"I never thought about what it would be like living and traveling at the same time."

"I'm sure most people don't think about what the performers do after the show's over. They probably don't realize we live in all the wagons they see as they pass by on their way home."

Lily looked around the room and then peeked at Gray. She wasn't sure what she should do or say next, what he expected of her. Her home was so different from his; nothing could have set out their differences more pointedly. She wondered if her tiny home had reminded him of all the reasons why they shouldn't be together. Was that why he was silent?

And then he turned to face her and ran a hand through his hair, leaving it boyishly tousled. "Dammit, Lily. I didn't come here to talk about your wagon, as nice as I think it is. Or the circus. Or the weather."

"Then why did you come?" she asked, almost afraid of his answer. If he'd come because of Cybil . . .

"I suppose I came for this," he said as he wrapped one arm around her waist and pulled her close to his body. His other hand came up to circle her jaw, lifting her chin so her eyes looked directly into his. Then, without further warning, his mouth covered hers.

For an instant his sheer masculine power overwhelmed her, and she could do nothing but stand in the circle of his arms and savor his nearness. This is what she had wanted since the first moment she'd seen him watching her at the parade. It was what she had secretly longed for, every moment since leaving his house, what she needed to make her life complete. All thoughts of Cybil were pushed to the farthest reaches of her mind.

His mouth moved over her lips as if the taste of her would never satisfy him. His tongue dipped and traced, never stopping long enough to satisfy, only making her want more.

She closed her arms around him, and the entire length of their bodies touched. Every line, every muscle melded. The burning urgency of his kiss left an ache in her center, melting away all thoughts of resistance. His fingers slowly trailed down the side of her neck, hovering over her pulse point, then moving on relentlessly, until his hand came to rest on the curve of her breast.

She heard the raggedness of his breathing and knew it matched her own. She felt his heat, but it wasn't enough. As if he sensed her innermost desires, his hand moved to her back, and he began unfastening the long row of buttons that ran along her spine. One by one she could feel each button give way and the cool air touch her skin. Then his fingers stopped moving.

"Lily?"

She knew what he was asking and knew what her answer would be. She loved this man, and she was willing to take what he offered, even if they only had this small amount of time together. If memories were all she could have, then she wanted her memories to be so full of Gray, they could fill her dreams for years to come.

"Yes," she whispered. The last button opened, and Gray's hand slid inside. She felt his skin against her, warm where she was cool, slightly rough and calloused where she was smooth and soft. His closeness heightened her awareness of their differences, of his hard masculinity and her softer femininity, of his angles and her curves. Then his hands moved up and pushed the dress from her shoulders, allowing it to drop to her waist.

Gray looked down, and she knew he could see her breasts through the nearly transparent cotton of her chemise. She watched his face as his gaze moved from her shoulders to her puckered nipples pressing against the thin fabric. His eyes were a smoky blue, his cheeks flushed with desire.

His earlier urgency was gone as he slowly reached out and gently touched the rigid point of one nipple, tracing its contour with just the barest touch. She thought she might faint from the excruciating sensations radiating throughout her body, a pleasure so keen it bordered on pain.

He kissed her mouth again and fondled her breast until she felt as if molten lava flowed from her very core to heat her blood and tighten her nerve endings. And in her very center there was an aching emptiness crying to be filled, an emptiness only Gray could fill. She pressed her hips against him and felt the ridge of his arousal as he pressed back.

Her hands moved inside his suit jacket and over his shoulders. She could feel his muscles through the fabric of his shirt, but it wasn't enough. She wanted to touch his skin as he was touching hers, to learn the different textures of his body and know he was hers. She was reaching for the buttons of his shirt when the sounds of raucous voices directly outside of the wagon reached their ears, bringing them both back to reality. Gray's lips slowly lifted from hers, and she opened her eyes. She was tempted to pull him back, but knew the spell had been broken. There was also her performance to consider. The first act would be starting soon, and she had so many things to do.

"I-I . . ." Lily stammered, feeling awkward and unsure as Gray pulled her dress up over her shoulders.

He gently placed his finger over her lips, silencing her. Slowly he ran his fingers over her swollen mouth, mesmerizing her with his movements. The look in his eyes eased whatever embarrassment she might have felt. "We picked the wrong time," he said in a soft, soothing voice. "Next time—*and there will be a next time*—we'll choose better."

With unsteady fingers he raised her chin and touched his lips to hers. Then, slowly turning her around, he began fastening the long row of buttons down her back.

Lily stood completely still, not saying a word while he finished his task. When she felt the last of the buttons close, she moved away from him, coming to stand by one of the chairs. She needed to put some distance between them if she was to compose herself enough to face the world outside. Checking the clock that stood on the table between the chairs, she realized she didn't have much time. "I have to get back to the main tent. There are things I need to do before the performance starts."

Gray nodded silently. When he didn't speak, Lily felt her nervousness return. When she was in his arms, anything seemed possible, but when she looked reality in the eye, the problems seemed insurmountable. How did he see their future?

"I have to go," she said and started for the door. As she neared him, Gray reached out and pulled her into his arms.

"I'll see you soon?" he asked with a hint of uncertainty in his voice, and her breath caught. Maybe he was as uncertain as she. Maybe he wanted the same things she did, but like her, he didn't know quite how to get them.

Leaning back in his arms, she looked up into his eyes and smiled. "I'd like that," she said.

"Me, too," he replied, then set her free and opened the door for them both.

They hadn't set a place or a time, but both of them knew their next meeting wouldn't be very far into the future. With a brilliant smile on her face, Lily led the way outside.

EIGHT

LILY'S SMILE WAS short-lived. As she and Gray headed for the main tent, they heard loud voices again from over by the ticket wagon.

"I'm telling you I bought a ticket," a gray-headed man was saying to anyone who would listen. His arms flayed about as he spoke, attracting a large crowd of onlookers who had come to see the next performance.

"And I'm telling you, you have to hand a ticket in at the door, and you didn't!" Bryce Mason was shouting back.

Lily hurried her steps. She knew a scene like this wasn't good for the circus's reputation. They didn't need any more problems, and creating ill will within the community would only hurt them in the long run.

"Bryce! What's going on?" she called out as she came around one of the animal wagons with Gray by her side.

At the sound of Lily's voice the two men turned. The gray-haired man was obviously ready to place his argument before a new pair of ears.

"Nothing you need to concern yourself about, Lily," Bryce said. "I can handle this."

"It certainly doesn't sound like it to me."

Just as Bryce seemed about to throw out some nasty comment, Gray spoke up, forestalling him. "What seems to be the problem, Ned?"

"This here fellow says I didn't pay my entrance fee."

"He tried to get into the main tent without a ticket," Bryce stated, a stubborn look on his face.

"I'm sure there's just a small misunderstanding here," Gray said. "Ned Bates is as honest as the day is long."

"Dang right, I am. Paid that fella for my ticket and was about to go into the tent when I remembered I'd left my lunch in my wagon. I went back for it, and when I tried to go into the tent, this here man stopped me," Ned said, jerking his finger in Bryce's direction.

"He didn't have a ticket. This is not a free show," Bryce said through clenched teeth. His gaze moved from Gray to Lily, his hostility plain to see.

"I did so. I handed it to a young fella and then told him I'd be back after I got my boxed lunch."

"Which young fellow, Ned?" Gray asked.

"Why, a little yellow-haired fellow, about so high." Ned raised his hand to waist level.

Gray looked to Lily. "Sound familiar?" he asked.

She nodded. "It could be Bobby Elston, Claudette's son. Claudette's our low-wire act," Lily clarified when she realized Gray didn't recognize the name. "He usually collects the tickets at this side. Let me see if I can find him."

Lily looked over to the tent entrance and saw that Polly Anders was now taking tickets. Her gaze moved around the immediate area, checking to see if Bobby was anywhere in sight. She wanted to solve this problem as quickly as possible. If it had been up to her, she would have let the man go in without question, but Bryce could be very inflexible, and she didn't want to start another argument.

While Lily was looking for Bobby, Gray walked over to the ticket wagon and bought another ticket. "Here, take this," he said, handing it to Ned.

"But I paid for my ticket."

"I know you did. This lady," Gray said, pointing to Lily,

"is a friend of mine. When the lad returns, he'll set everything straight, and I'll get my money back. Is that all right with you?"

"I guess," Ned said, not really happy with the arrangement.

"But—" Bryce started to say.

"Not now, Bryce," Lily murmured just loud enough for him to hear, not wanting him to start the brouhaha all over again.

Bryce looked from Lily to Gray and Ned, then back. His face was flushed an ugly red, but he held his tongue. The crowd was looking on with avid curiosity at this free show, so Lily was relieved when Bryce turned on his heel and stomped off.

"I'm really sorry about this," she said to the man. "I'll find Bobby and get everything straightened out. Please try to forget about this and enjoy the show."

"She's right, Ned. Why don't we go in together? I wouldn't mind some company. Lily, I'll see you later?"

Lily nodded and watched as Gray guided the other man toward the tent entrance. The milling crowd of onlookers followed them. Just before he went inside, Gray looked back and sent Lily one of his rare smiles.

She smiled back but couldn't let go of her worries. This story would be all around town by evening, magnified out of all proportion. From Cybil's disparaging comments, Lily knew the circus had to fight to maintain its good reputation even without any problems, and incidents like this had to be avoided at all costs.

Bryce should know that. Otto certainly did. In the past he would have fired anybody who treated an obviously well-to-do patron so shabbily. But Otto was nowhere in sight, so Bryce was free to do as he wished.

This was not the first time Bryce had been at the center of some conflict with the townspeople. The last couple of days had been filled with such minor incidents, small when viewed by themselves, but taking their toll nonetheless. When people started talking about their experiences here, Lily was afraid that too many would have a negative story to tell, and the circus would be the one to suffer.

Lily didn't know what to do. At the moment, though, she had no choice. She could already hear the band striking up the introductory music and knew she was late for the opening procession. Promising herself that she would tackle Otto once again about resuming his rightful place in running things, she hurried off to make sure her horses were ready to go.

Nothing was going her way, nor had it for the past two days, not since Gray had held her in his arms in her wagon, Lily thought as she dragged her feet toward the food tent. She'd tried talking to Otto, but to no avail. All she'd accomplished was to increase Bryce's animosity toward her and her "interfering ways."

She hadn't seen Gray since that afternoon performance when she'd spotted him with Amelia and Ned sitting halfway up the tier of benches. She'd waited for him expectantly after the performance, but he hadn't come. Although he'd never said exactly when he would be back, she'd assumed it would be soon. Now, not having seen him for two days, she wondered if she'd misunderstood him. Or perhaps he had decided the barriers between them were too high to even try to knock down.

She wished she'd never gone to Cybil's party. Maybe then she wouldn't have these high and low moods, feeling everything was within her reach one minute, knowing that nothing was the next. Her stomach made a growling sound, and she decided she'd feel better after eating, then noticed the flag was down. She sighed. She'd be lucky if she got a cold biscuit now. The rule was: You came when the flag was up. If the flag was down, you didn't eat. At least the cook had a soft spot in his heart for her and often put something aside when she didn't make it for a meal. She hoped he remembered her today.

She hadn't missed breakfast by choice. She'd spent the early morning with Lancelot, putting up with the horse's bad humor in the hopes of discovering what was wrong with him. She'd been using Galahad whenever she could to spell Lancelot, but the big horse wasn't improving and she could find no cause for his discomfort. She needed someone else's opinion and had planned to ask Gray, but since he hadn't shown up, she'd have to find someone else.

Gray again. He was never far from her thoughts, whether she was performing, or grooming her animals, or helping Elena and Mrs. Parsons work on the new costumes. She wanted to see him again, needed to. If only she could see his face, look into those clear blue eyes of his, then she would know where she stood. If only . . .

Lily stepped inside the tent and stopped in her tracks. Her heart started its familiar cadence in anticipation of being with Gray, for there, much to her surprise, sat Amelia eating a plateful of food, Elena by her side. And if Amelia was here, Gray must be, too.

"Ah, 'ere she is now," Elena was saying as she stood up from her seat and motioned Lily over. "Amelia 'as been looking for you," she said as Lily drew near.

Lily raised her eyebrows in silent inquiry, but Elena merely shrugged, indicating she had no idea why the younger woman was there.

Amelia looked up at that moment. "Oh, Lily, I'm so glad I found you," she said in a rush. "I never realized how big a circus was. And how many people it took to run one."

"And she 'as seen every one of zose people," Elena

added with a laugh. "I found 'er with Gustav and 'is animals, asking more questions than even Gustav could answer."

Lily laughed. Both Elena and Lily knew that Gustav liked nothing better than talking about his animals. To make him run out of words was a true feat.

"It's truly amazing what he does, isn't it?" Amelia said, looking up at Lily.

"It certainly is. I'm glad you had a chance to meet him." She gave the girl an affectionate smile.

"Me, too," Amelia said with an impish grin. "After we talked, I asked about you, and he brought me here. Then Mrs. Santelli said I could have some breakfast. This is just so wonderful. I can't believe I'm really here, getting to see a real circus."

"Did you come with your father?" Lily asked.

"No, I came on my own. Mrs. Bellows went to have lunch with a friend, and I was bored. Besides, I wanted to see you."

Though she was disappointed that Gray wasn't here, Lily couldn't help but be gratified by Amelia's words. "I'm glad you came," she said and gave the girl a hug. "Is your father coming to take you home?"

"I was hoping you could. He's been so busy lately, what with all this rustling, he doesn't have time for *anything*. He spent all day yesterday out at the ranch and even missed Sunday services!" The girl pouted, but Lily detected real loneliness beneath the complaints. "He did say he would be back in town later today, though," Amelia added in a more hopeful tone.

Lily caught her breath. If she took Amelia home, maybe she would see him. It would give her the perfect excuse to go to his house without feeling she was pushing her presence on him. Knowing he'd been out at the ranch on business reassured her. He hadn't been avoiding her after all.

"I'll be glad to take you home, but I have to be back here in time for the afternoon performance," Lily warned the girl.

"I should probably be back by then anyway. Cybil said she might drop by for a visit if the children aren't too cranky. I wouldn't want to miss her."

Lily hoped Cybil wouldn't be there when they arrived. She didn't relish another round of verbal sparring with the woman; it only left her tense and unsure of herself. The Englishwoman would be no happier to see her, Lily knew without being told. Cybil didn't appear to be the type who gave up on something she wanted, and she had given all the signs of wanting Gray.

"Since you're here now, would you like the grand tour?" Lily asked when Amelia pushed her empty plate aside.

"I'd love it." Amelia quickly stood up and deposited her dirty plate and silverware in a pan sitting on a side table. "Where shall we start?"

"I thought you might like to see my horses."

"And Merlin, too?" Amelia gave her a look of eager anticipation.

"Merlin, too," Lily confirmed.

Amelia smiled happily, reminding Lily so much of Gray that her heart turned over. She'd become very fond of Amelia in the short time they'd spent together. That she was Gray's daughter only made her more special.

"I go now," Elena said. "I promised Roberto I would practice ze new tumbling routine again. 'E wants it all perfect." Elena grimaced, then laughed.

"Thank you, Mrs. Santelli, for finding Lily for me. And for getting me breakfast."

"It was my pleasure."

As Elena walked away, Lily thought longingly of the

breakfast she was now going to forfeit in favor of Amelia's tour.

"Shall we go see my horses?"

Before Amelia could answer, Lily heard her name called.

"Miss Lily? Don't think you can leave here without a bite of something to eat," the cook said as he approached them from the back of the tent. "I don't appreciate you ignoring my food."

He held out a small bundle wrapped in a white cloth napkin. Lily could tell from its size that it contained a biscuit and, if she was lucky, maybe some honey. "Oh, thank you," she said as she accepted the cook's offering.

"Next time don't you miss breakfast, you hear?"

"No, I won't."

The cook went back to the kitchen, and Lily and Amelia walked to the exit.

"He treats you just like Mrs. Bellows treats me," Amelia commented. "I'll probably get the same lecture about not eating my breakfast this morning when I get home tonight."

"But don't you feel lucky that we have people who care about us like this? If we didn't, we'd both go hungry."

"I know." She looked away, then added more softly, "I just wish sometimes that the someone who cared was my mother."

"Your father loves and cares for you."

"Oh, I know he does. I just wish I had my mother, too," Amelia said in a wistful tone.

Lily and Amelia threaded their way between the wagons and animals crowding the lot on which the circus was camped. All the performers were out preparing for the afternoon performance. Some were limbering up, while others were practicing their craft.

"I sometimes think we're never happy with what we

have," Lily commented as they made a wide circle around the dog act. "We assume everything would be better if this or that had happened. Most of the time that isn't true."

"I know that, and I wouldn't trade my father for anything. He is wonderful, isn't he?"

Lily definitely agreed, though she and Amelia were looking at him in two completely different lights. "I think your father would do anything for you. And that shows how much he cares."

"He came out to Wyoming just for me."

"He did?"

"He said after my mother died, he wanted me to have the best of everything, and when he heard about Wyoming, he knew that was where we should settle. I don't really recall the move. I was very small when my mother died and don't remember very much about her."

There was a sadness in the younger woman's voice with which Lily could identify. It was obvious Amelia wanted just a tiny bit of her mother to hang on to. Lily had felt the same about her own mother—the same sense of loss, the same need to know and understand who and what her mother had been.

"I don't remember my mother, either," she confided with some hesitancy. Talking about her mother always brought with it the pain of remembering her other life, the one before she and Rosemary joined the circus.

"You don't?" Amelia asked, clearly wanting to know more.

Lily shook her head. "She died when I was very young."

"So you don't even remember what she looked like?"

Again Lily shook her head.

"I'm lucky, then, aren't I? I can remember my mother smelled so wonderful, like roses. And I can see her face if I think very hard. I know she had blond hair, and she wore it swept up on the top of her head. Papa never talks about her, but I suppose it hurts too much. They were very much in love." Amelia had a dreamy look in her eyes as she spoke, as if she were reciting a fairy story she'd heard many times before. She looked over at Lily. "Do you know what your mother looked like?"

For a moment Lily didn't answer, her mind still holding the picture of Gray and his wife together, and then she shook the image from her head. "I know what my sister told me. In fact, my sister said I look almost exactly like my mother."

"Oh, I wish I did," Amelia said. "I've always wanted to look like my mother. Papa says I should be happy with the way I look because I'm beautiful in my own way. But I think all fathers say that."

Lily knew better, but she wasn't ready to divulge all her secrets, nor was Amelia mature enough to know them. Lily's father had been nothing like Amelia's. He'd wanted sons and never forgave his daughters for being girls. Lily remembered him as a distant and forbidding figure, but she hadn't stayed with him long, for as soon as he'd shown an interest in her, Rosemary had run away to the circus, taking her along.

"I'm sure most fathers say that about their daughters," Lily agreed, having observed numerous families in her years with the circus. "But in your case I think it's perfectly true."

Amelia blushed at the compliment. "Do you think Prescott thinks so, too?"

From what Lily had seen of Prescott Warford-Smythe, she was sure he thought only about himself. She'd never met a man more concerned about how he looked and the impression he made than this very stuffy Englishman, though she couldn't very well tell Amelia without offending her.

"I barely know Prescott, but anyone looking at you could hardly fail to notice."

"You're so nice, Lily. I'm really glad you came to Wyoming."

"I'm glad, too. And speaking of beautiful things," she said, intent on changing the subject, "this region is one of the most beautiful I've ever seen."

"You only say that because you haven't been here in the winter."

"Why? Are the winters really that bad, or is that just another of your tall tales for fooling Easterners?" Lily asked, glad Amelia was diverted from continuing on about Prescott.

"Some winters are terrible here in the Territory. It can snow so hard we get stuck out at the ranch for weeks on end. I miss a lot of school when that happens, so we try to spend most of the winter in town. But if we do get caught out at the ranch, Papa handles my lessons. Can I tell you a secret about Papa?"

Lily looked over at the young woman and saw a hint of mischief on her face. She wasn't sure she should hear what Amelia was about to say, but nodded her head anyway, unable to deny herself even the smallest tidbit of information about Gray.

"I think he really likes doing my lessons with me. He says he learns something new every time," Amelia confided.

They stopped to watch a family of tumblers build a human pyramid.

"Look at that! I'd be afraid to be the one at the top," Amelia said.

"I'd be afraid to be the one at the bottom," Lily countered in a wry tone.

Amelia examined the pyramid more closely. "You do

ave a point. I guess the men must be very strong to hold everyone up like that."

"It takes strength and timing, as well as balance, especially for the ones on top."

They walked on as the pyramid came apart and the men set up their equipment for the next part of their act.

"What's that I smell?" Amelia asked as they rounded a corner.

The scent of freshly popped popcorn wafted through the air around them, luring the hungry and curious toward its source. "Mmmm, smells like popcorn to me," Lily said. "Would you like some?"

"What is it?"

"You've never had popcorn? You're in for a treat. I still remember the first time I tasted it," Lily said and grabbed Amelia's hand. "Follow me." She pulled the girl toward the public promenade.

Just as she had thought, Ed Senak had the popcorn stand open and was getting ready for the crowds that would soon pour through the main gate demanding more popcorn than he could quickly provide.

Lily grabbed a handful of popped kernels and gave them to Amelia. She put a couple in her mouth rather warily, and Lily watched her face for a reaction. After two bites Amelia smiled.

"This tastes wonderful. I'll have to have Father save some corn from the kitchen garden. Do you think you could teach me how to pop it, Mr. Senak?"

"I don't think you'll get much from your garden corn," Ed told her. "You need a special kind of corn. See this?" He held up a small ear of corn with tiny kernels. It measured no more than four inches long.

Amelia ran her finger over the kernels. "They're hard," she said in surprise.

"And they're just like that when you pick them off the

173

stalk," Lily said. "I'll see if I can't get you some seeds.
Then your father can plant them and you'll have it to eat
anytime you feel like it."

Amelia smiled her thanks through another mouthful of
popcorn.

"Speaking of your father, when does he expect you
home?" Lily asked.

"He didn't say, and I'm not ready to go home yet. Besides, he's probably not back yet himself, and I really want
to see Merlin. You promised me I could."

"If you're sure no one will be upset, we'll go see Merlin
and the horses, then we'll worry about getting you home."

"And Dun, too."

"And Dun, too," Lily conceded. Was there anything she
wouldn't do for this young woman?

Obviously not. For the next hour they walked around
visiting Lily's friends and looking at all the animals.
Gustav even put Amelia up on Old Bess's back and had
the elephant take her for a short ride. Amelia talked of
nothing else for the rest of her visit. By the time Amelia
had seen all the "behind the scenes" sights "up close," as
she put it, Lily found she had barely enough time to get
ready for her performance.

She dragged Amelia away from one of the clowns who
was trying to teach her how to juggle three balls, and hus-
tled the girl off toward her wagon. She'd have to see that
Amelia got home, but she couldn't take her now; it was
too close to showtime. Amelia helped her get dressed and
was enthralled with her small home. She talked endlessly
about how lucky Lily was to have such a wonderful life,
and wasn't it exciting to move from place to place, seeing
new things and meeting new people.

Her enthusiasm and excitement reminded Lily of her
first day at the ranch, when Gray had been so angry about
Amelia's interest in the circus. She remembered promising

him that she would not encourage the girl with tales of circus life, and suddenly Lily felt a shiver run down her
spine. What would Gray think about the morning they had
just spent? How would he react to Amelia's shining eyes
and sparkling smile? What would he say if he knew about
the tricks she had taught Amelia?

In fairness, Lily had tried to tell her about the less pleasant aspects of being on the road, moving from town to
town, never knowing what you were getting into, never
having friends outside the members of the troupe or a
place you could really call home. But Amelia did not want
to hear that, and Lily was unsure what to do next.

Gray walked to his front door, unsure what to do next
but knowing he had to do something. Amelia was gone
and he had no idea where. He'd been so sure she was with
Mrs. Bellows, he hadn't even thought of looking for her
earlier. Then his housekeeper had come home from a visit
with her friend, and Amelia wasn't with her.

At first he'd assumed she was somewhere in the house,
so he'd checked to make sure she hadn't fallen asleep and
just hadn't heard him calling. Then he'd searched the outside property, thinking she might have fallen and hurt herself. At that point he'd decided to contact her friends and
see if she was out visiting. He'd just finished talking with
their closest neighbors, but none of them had seen her, either.

He stood in his front hall, a mass of gnawing fear grip-
ping his insides. If anything happened to Amelia, he
wouldn't know what to do. He'd built his life around her
needs, making her life the best he possibly could. Everything he'd done or dreamed had been for her. He hadn't
felt this type of fear since the day Felicia disappeared. The
scariest part was that Amelia's disappearance was so sim-

ilar to her mother's. He'd looked for his wife in the same way he was looking for Amelia, but he hadn't been able to find Felicia, not until it was too late and she'd come home to die. He couldn't survive if that happened a second time with Amelia. Where could she have gone?

Though he didn't know where to start, he knew he couldn't just sit at home and do nothing. He was just grabbing his hat when the front door opened and Amelia appeared on the threshold, smiling over her shoulder at someone standing behind her.

"Oh, Papa. I'm so glad you're here. Look who I've brought with me for a visit."

"Amelia," he said, his voice filled with relief. He wanted to rush over and take her in his arms and never let her go.

Relief quickly replaced his fear but was just as quickly supplanted by anger, anger at her for scaring him so, for not telling him where she was going, for acting just as her mother had. Maybe the last offense was the most damning of all.

"Where have you been for the better part of the day?" he demanded, his voice harsh and tight. And then he saw Lily.

"Papa!" Amelia said in a scandalized voice, shocked by his lack of manners in front of a guest.

"I want to know where you've been," he persisted. This was too important an issue to be brushed aside. If anything, Lily's presence fueled his worst fears, for there was only one place Amelia could have met her. His tone of voice must have signaled his daughter to answer, for she quickly replied, "At the circus," though without her earlier enthusiasm.

"The circus! You mean to tell me that you left this house without telling anyone to go to the circus?" Gray repeated, making no attempt to mask his feelings. He'd thought Amelia had put the circus in perspective: as a passing entertainment she could indulge in on occasion, not as something central in her life. That was why he'd taken her to the parade. But her actions today proved him wrong. The circus was more to her then an idle pastime and that scared him.

"But, Papa, you don't understand. You were out at the ranch, and Mrs. Bellows wanted to spend time with one of her friends. You know how boring that can be; you said so yourself that one time we both went with her. All I wanted was to have a little fun—and I did." Her voice rang with enthusiasm once again. "I can't tell you what a wonderful time I had. It was so exciting. I saw—"

"I'm not interested in what you saw, Amelia. You broke all the family rules." So he was right. She had gone there all on her own, unable to resist its allure. He would never have believed her capable of disobeying his wishes like this, at least not before she'd met Lily.

"But I was perfectly safe, Papa. I was with Lily."

She said it as if being with Lily would make all his fear and pain disappear, but she was wrong. Knowing Lily had only increased the appeal of the circus, attracting his daughter like a moth to a flame. Before Lily entered their lives, he'd never even considered that Amelia was anything like her mother—now he saw signs of Felicia at every turn. But this time he knew what to do; he wouldn't lose his daughter the way he'd lost his wife.

"I think you'd better go to your room," he said.

"But, Papa, Lily's—"

"Now." Gray knew his voice betrayed him. He could see the surprise in Lily's eyes. But she didn't know, she could never fully understand what was driving him.

Amelia gave him a stricken look, then rushed out of the room, not even taking a moment to say good-bye to Lily.

He could see her wiping the tears from her cheeks as she fled.

"Gray, I—"

"Don't," Gray interrupted.

"I just wanted to say I was sorry."

"You have nothing to be sorry about."

"If I could have gotten her back home before the performance, none of this would have happened."

"Do you think I'm upset just because she's late?"

"Well, you did say—"

"It's more than her being late, it's . . . You wouldn't understand."

She bit her lip, then said, "But I want to. Please, try to explain."

Gray sighed and ran his hand through his hair. How had life gotten so complicated? He thought he'd left the past behind when he came out West, but now it seemed to have caught up with him in the worst possible way. How could he explain it all to Lily without hurting her? If only he'd had more time with her on Saturday, they'd have a stronger bond, one that could withstand the strains of his ambivalent feelings about her life. But they hadn't had that time. Hank had cornered him after the performance and urged him to go out to his ranch to check on his security. Hank's men had overheard some strangers discussing the rustling in a saloon, and Hank didn't want Gray to be the victim of another foray on his property.

Now he had no choice but to explain what he was feeling—and why. Motioning Lily into the front parlor, he followed her in, wondering how to tell her the world she came from was the world he most wanted Amelia to avoid.

"Please sit. This may take some time," he said and gestured to the sofa. Their gazes met and he could see the confusion and vulnerability in the depths of her brown eyes. He smiled wanly as he sat across from her and knew in his heart that nothing less than the truth would do, no matter that he had to bare his innermost secrets. "There are things that happened before Amelia was old enough to understand," he said, looking down at the floor. "Things that make me want to keep her away from anything theatrical."

"Theatrical?"

"Like the circus."

"I don't understand. What's wrong with the circus?"

"I don't want to lose her to a sudden infatuation."

Lily heard the anguish in his tone and the same fear she'd noticed the very first time they'd spoken of Amelia and the circus. She still didn't understand, but the urge to comfort him was strong inside her.

"Oh, but, Gray, Amelia's infatuation with the circus is only a passing fancy. I've seen it in lots of other children. They all think they want to be a part of the fantasy they envision for the circus, but when they find out what hard work it is, they always back off. Otto's very good about showing them the less romantic side. Do you want me to ask him to talk with her?"

"I don't think it would do any good."

"It can't—"

"Amelia isn't a child, and no matter what your Otto told those other children, they didn't have Felicia for a mother."

Lily felt a coldness invade her body. The mention of Gray's wife brought to the fore images she'd tried to keep from her mind. Was he still in love with his dead wife, so in love that her memory prevented him from ever loving someone else? Though she dreaded hearing the wrong answer, she knew she had to know the truth.

Gray must have sensed her need, for he continued speaking. "When Felicia and I first married, everything was wonderful. We were happy together, at least for a while. Then she began to change."

He told her of Felicia's dissatisfaction with married life and maternity, with their social position and its limitations. And then he told her of Felicia's entrancement with the traveling actors' troupe, how she followed them, leaving behind her frantic husband and very young daughter. As Lily listened to his story unfold, she began to realize what he had been through and to appreciate his protectiveness of Amelia from what he perceived to be a threat to her well-being. Would she have been any less protective herself? Hadn't her own sister done the same thing in a sense, going to extreme lengths to protect her younger sister from the hurts she herself had encountered?

What surprised Lily the most was the difference in the stories she'd heard from Gray and Amelia. Though Lily could hear the bitterness and betrayal underlying Gray's words, he'd kept all of that from his daughter. She couldn't help but be impressed by his generosity of spirit, fostering his daughter's love for her mother by painting a much prettier picture than what had really happened.

"Is there anything I can do?" Lily asked after a few moments of silence. Although she could understand Gray's pain, she wasn't sure how to help.

"I'm not even sure there's anything *I* can do," he said with a sense of defeat in his voice.

"Amelia's a wonderful girl. You've done a marvelous job raising her. She's sweet and kind, understanding and sympathetic. I think you can trust her to do what's right."

"I wish I had your faith, but I have to wonder if I can counteract whatever urges were bred in her."

"There are wonderful qualities bred in her, too, you know. And while I can see why you don't want Amelia to join the circus, it really is a wonderful place to grow up."

"I didn't mean—"

"It doesn't matter," Lily said, but she knew it did. "I must get back. I promised Elena I'd help her with a new costume."

As she stood, Gray also rose to his feet. "Do you have to go?"

"I think I'd better." She knew there wasn't anything else to say. Now that she understood his fears, she knew there was nothing she could do to relieve them, for she was a part of them.

Gray walked along the public promenade of the circus grounds and watched the people milling from one end to the other even though it was after ten o'clock. They must have figured they'd paid their fifty cents and were going to get their money's worth. He, on the other hand, had paid the money so that he could get a glimpse of Lily. He'd hoped to catch her act but had arrived too late. He'd taken Amelia and Mrs. Bellows to the ranch right after Lily had left this afternoon and had only gotten back into town a scant half hour ago.

His decision to have Amelia return to the ranch had been a hard one. While he hoped that having her away from the circus would dull its glittering allure, he didn't like having her apart from him. But he needed to be in town for a while to see what he could learn about the rustlers. Hank's men had heard strangers talking openly in town, which meant the rustlers were getting careless in the face of their success. Now was the time to be most vigilant when the chances of catching them in a mistake were the greatest.

At least Sam would be at the ranch to watch over Amelia. The young man was responsible beyond his years, and Gray knew he could trust him to keep an eye on his daughter, especially with Mrs. Bellows around. So far the rustlers had stayed well away from the homesteads, preferring to do their dastardly work out on the range in the more remote locations, so Gray wasn't worried that the ranch house would be in any danger. Still, he was gratified that Sam promised to stay close by and insisted on driving Amelia into town for school.

Amelia had been hurt by his decision, but he stood firm in the face of her objections. He had no choice. Now he had to talk with Lily. Just as he'd anticipated, his words had hurt her. She'd tried to cover it up when she left, but he'd seen the pain in her eyes. His heart was torn in two directions, wanting to be with Lily and wanting to save his daughter from her mother's fate. Those two desires were at odds, and he didn't know how to put everything right. All he knew was that now he needed to be with Lily, to make her know he didn't blame her or think less of her because of her circus upbringing. Somehow, when she'd left earlier today, he'd had the distinct impression she was walking away from him forever, and he wasn't ready to face that.

He walked from one end of the public promenade to the other, past the ornithological thoroughfare at one end and the zoological avenue at the other. At any other time the exhibits might have interested him, but in his present state of mind he wanted only Lily. He couldn't find her in any of the public areas, so he decided to look in the back lot where the private wagons sat.

Unfortunately, he hadn't paid much attention to their path when Dun had escorted him to her wagon the other day, and now he had no idea which way to turn. Since most of the circus folk were still out in the public areas, he didn't spot anyone to ask, so he wandered around aimlessly, looking for anything familiar that might spark his memory. Then he saw Bryce Mason exiting a small wagon.

"Mason," Gray called out. He had no desire to meet the

man with whom he'd had the altercation on his last visit, but he was desperate to find Lily.

Bryce turned at the sound of his name, and Gray walked over to him. When Bryce recognized him, the other man's expression changed from pleasant to hostile. "Yeah, what do you want?"

Gray refused to let the man's nasty tone dissuade him. He'd simply get his information and leave this man's company. "Could you point me in the direction of Lily's wagon?"

"Ain't it kind of late to be visitin'?" the shorter man asked with a sneer in his voice.

"I don't want a scene, Mason, just directions."

"I bet you don't."

"If you're not going to help . . ."

"Far be it from me to keep you two lovers apart," he said, his lip curling over the words. "Go to the main tent and then take a left by the museum tent. It'll be straight back from there. You can't miss it since it's red, but then, you probably know that. Seems like a pretty appropriate color for her, don't it?"

Gray reached out and grabbed Mason by his lapels, pulling him up until their eyes were level. It was all Gray could do to keep from punching the man. Instead, he pulled him close so he wouldn't miss a word. "If I ever hear you say something like that again, I promise you it will be the last thing you'll say because I'll break your jaw. Is that clear?" Gray's voice was hard and menacing.

When Mason didn't say anything, Gray gave him a slight shake. "Do you understand?"

Bryce nodded and Gray put him back on the ground. "Good," he growled, and then in a more pleasant tone, he added, "Nice talking with you, Mason. Thanks for the directions."

Mason gave him a dirty look but didn't say another

word. He turned and stalked off in the opposite direction without a backward glance. Gray headed toward Lily's wagon, wanting nothing more than to be in her arms and smell her sweet scent, to explain why he hadn't seen her since his first altercation with Mason and make sure she understood their conversation this afternoon. He didn't want to end things between them though he hadn't yet figured out how else to shield his daughter from her mother's fate. But there had to be an answer, and if they talked it over, maybe they could find one together. All he knew was that he had to see her—and soon.

NINE

LILY SAT IN her wagon, alone and lonely, but preferring her loneliness to the company of others. Ever since her conversation with Gray, she'd felt a deep sense of loss. All this time she'd thought he mourned the loss of his beautiful, talented wife, a woman who sounded so loving and giving in Amelia's telling that Lily could never hope to compete. The truth was just as devastating.

Felicia had left her husband and daughter to carve a career for herself as an actress, to be the center of attention. Lily couldn't understand her. To be the center of Gray's life would be all Lily would ever need, and having a daughter like Amelia would only make life more special.

Until recently the applause from the audience had always been fulfilling to Lily, satisfying the dream she'd first envisioned the day she saw Hilda on her beautiful white steed. But in the last few days she'd acquired a new dream, a new sense of what a fulfilling life would entail—and applause from an anonymous crowd was the least of her needs. But how did Gray see her? Did he think she lived for the limelight like his dead wife, and that she, too, would desert him for the siren song of fame?

She flopped down onto one of the armchairs and leaned her head back, heedless of the wrinkles she was undoubtedly pressing into her one remaining costume. How could he think otherwise? It was the only side of her he'd really seen, the only side of her she'd had the opportunity to show him. Circus life was more than just performing, but only the members of the troupe ever got exposed to the other aspects. The circus was like a small town with all of the complicated interrelationships that a large family experienced: the loving and hating, the giving and back stabbing, the nurturing and competing, every side of life that existed anywhere else.

Gray had had no opportunity to see her long-standing friendships with Elena and Roberto as well as other circus folk, to know she still kept in contact with performers around the world, people who had toured a season or two with Bruner's show and then moved on. She had rarely spoken of them, for in mentioning her friends she would also be mentioning the circus, and from the very first she'd known of his distrust of it even if she hadn't known the reason.

The whole thing was hopeless. Circumstances had worked against them from the very beginning, bringing them together only to drive them apart. She closed her eyes and tried to imagine the rest of her life going on in the same pattern as before. Instead of a world shiny with promise, she saw a world of sadness and dark, of herself going through the motions of living because she had no other choice. Who would have thought that the stop in Cheyenne could have changed her life like this?

A knock sounded at her door, but Lily ignored it. The last thing she needed was to cope with the worried looks from Dun or Elena, or worse, to have to pretend a cheerfulness she did not feel for the benefit of some other member of the troupe. The knock came again, persistent and brisk, not taking her lack of response as a sign to depart.

"Lily? Are you in there?" the familiar voice called out.

Gray! In an instant she was out of her seat ready to fling open the door. Then she stopped, smoothed down the skirt of her costume and remembered her thoughts of a moment ago. Regaining her composure, Lily opened the door.

"Gray, I wasn't expecting you." He stood on a step below her, his eyes just level with hers. She could only stare at him, her heart beating wildly in her chest. After their talk this afternoon she thought she'd never see him again. Despite the internal reminder that whatever she and Gray had was over, her knees were turning weak with relief.

"May I come in?" he asked, his gaze studying her face as if he was searching for something important.

"Yes, of course." She stepped back, giving him room to enter.

He followed her in, tall and dark like the night, smelling of the evening dew and a scent uniquely his. He was wearing a coat to ward off the coolness of the evening, and he reached up to undo the buttons.

"May I?" he asked, and she nodded, afraid he would hear the trembling in her voice if she spoke. He took off the coat and placed it on the hook behind the door, then hung his Stetson on top of it. "It's cozy and warm in here."

"I lit the stove," she murmured and gestured toward the corner where the little potbellied stove sent out waves of heat. Her nerves were strung taut. Why had he come? It was hard enough getting used to the idea that she was never going to be with him again. Seeing him, having him so close she could touch him, made it all too much to bear. "Why are you here?" she blurted out, then was appalled by her rudeness. "I'm sorry." She ran a hand over her hair, nervously checking that it was still in place. "Please, have a seat. Would you like something to drink?"

He sat on one of the chairs, and she relaxed a little. Seated, he wasn't quite as imposing. His shoulders were still broad and his body as lithe and hard as ever, but looking down on his face gave her the illusion of being in control, an illusion he shattered with his words.

"Come here," he said in a voice almost soft enough to turn the phrase into a request rather than a demand. She looked around wildly, seeking an avenue of escape, then he closed the trap with a single word. "Please."

Like a sleepwalker in a trance, she obeyed him, approaching his outstretched arm, letting his embrace enfold her until she sat stiffly on his lap. His thighs were firm and hard beneath her legs, though she sat as primly as a schoolgirl with her back straight and her shoulders squared, her hands knotted tightly in her lap.

He tugged her closer to his chest until she could feel his heart pounding as furiously as her own. She looked away from him, unable to handle the myriad sensations flooding her body and mind—his scent and feel, his closeness; her excitement and the heated swirl of emotions rocketing through her—sudden desire and enervating fear.

"What do you want?" she whispered.

"To talk, for a moment. To explain," he answered to her surprise. She had thought he wanted something far more elemental.

"Like this?" she asked, letting her doubt bleed into her tone.

He chuckled. "Not exactly. I thought you'd be a bit more pliant."

She tried to pull away from him then, indignant. And again he stopped her with a word, a single, soft-spoken plea: "Don't."

"Why? Why like this?"

"Because I want to know what you're thinking, what you're feeling, and I don't want the words to come between us."

She looked at him, deep into his eyes, and saw honesty and vulnerability and something else, hidden in the dark blue depths. The small oil lamp on the chest next to them threw sharp shadows on his face. This close, there was little he could hide, and she understood the elemental needs were there, too, waiting.

"What do you want to talk about?" she asked, still tense.

"You. Me. What happened today. I want you to understand."

She stiffened, but he wouldn't let her move away. "I do understand."

"Do you? I think not. I think you heard only part of what I said and imagined the rest."

She didn't want to hear more, not if it meant he would put into words her worst fears. But from the way he held her, firmly though without causing her the slightest pain, she knew he would not let her go until he'd had his say.

"All right, then. Talk."

He talked but without words. Instead he leaned forward and nibbled gently on the back of her neck, sending frissons of awareness prickling down her spine and raising tiny bumps on her skin. His breath was warm and carried his fresh scent to her nostrils as he worked his way from her nape to one ear.

"Can you feel what I'm saying?" he whispered before catching her lobe in his mouth. "Do you understand?" he added a moment later.

She shook her head, afraid to let her body rule her mind, to let it fool her into believing what she wanted to without hearing the words spoken aloud.

"Are you willing to listen, then? Really listen?"

His tongue swirled over the folds of her ear, and his breath came in quickening gasps, blowing tiny puffs of air against her skin. She closed her eyes and leaned into him. "That's better," he crooned, and placed his arm around her, cuddling her close before she realized she had relaxed. His mouth traced a path along her jaw as he turned her so his lips could meet hers.

"Listen," he murmured at her mouth, "and let my heart speak to yours. Look into my eyes and hear me."

She sensed as much as heard his words, and a languid feeling came over her, loosening her shoulders and spine, flowing down her arms and legs until she had no more resilience than a rag doll. Her insides also heated and flowed, responding to Gray's every touch, to the sound of his voice more than the meaning of his words, to his scent that mixed with her own and permeated her skin so that she didn't know whose scent filled the air she breathed.

She brought both arms around his neck, entwining them behind his back as she twisted to face him. Her breasts brushed against the wall of his chest, and in her light performance costume she felt him as though she were bare, as if nothing at all came between them. The fabric chafed against her engorged nipples, making her shiver and moan as a wave of pleasure crested inside her.

He captured her moan with his mouth and slipped his tongue past her lips and her teeth to explore the cavern behind. His hands tangled in her hair, sending hairpins flying. Her hair cascaded down past her shoulders and his fingers combed through it, separating the coiled strands, before he once again cupped her face and tipped her head to a better angle.

Lily couldn't get enough of him, of his heat and his passion, of his touch and his taste. She ran her tongue over his lips and felt him shudder, his breath coming as raggedly as her own. Soon she wanted more—more contact, more closeness. Her hands crept around to the front of his shirt, the texture of the cotton fabric feeling rough against her sensitized fingertips. When she reached the front, she undid his collar and the top buttons of the shirt.

His skin felt hot when she slipped her hands inside the

opening, hot and silken. She could feel the pulse in his throat, vital and racing just beneath her fingers. Her own heart tripped, scattering extra heartbeats. And still their mouths clung, until they simply had to catch their breath. She laid her head on his shoulder, her chest rising and falling in rhythm with his.

"Now do you understand?" he asked again. "I never meant to hurt you. I just wanted to protect my daughter, but that doesn't mean I think less of you." He put a hand on each of her shoulders and raised her so she could look at his face. "I thought that meant I couldn't have you, but I was wrong. Do you see?"

She nodded, knowing deep inside that he spoke the truth. His daughter had been his life since the day she was born. He could not let anything happen to her, but that did not mean he blamed Lily.

"I understand," she said and stroked his cheek with one hand, savoring the velvet feel of his cleanly shaved face. "But there is more than just that."

"Nothing we can't solve. Believe me."

The rational part of her mind knew it wasn't that simple—nothing in life had ever been—but her heart listened with a different ear. And it believed.

His hand moved to cup her chin and draw her toward him. She closed her eyes and let him guide her again into the sweeping vortex of need and desire that spun around them every time they touched. He held her in place while he licked and sucked at her lower lip, tantalizing her with unspoken promises of more, keeping her on edge with his gentle teasing until she thought she would do anything if only he would kiss her again as he had before.

The tiny sounds that came from her throat seemed to inflame him, for suddenly his mouth was on hers, plunging and plundering while his hand stroked down her throat and beyond, slipping around to her back. She felt him fumble

with the button. Then the straps of her bodice slipped
down her arms, baring her flesh to the tops of her breasts.
His mouth kissed a path down her throat to that softer,
more sensitive skin and instinctively she threw her head
back, giving him greater access.

Her bodice gave way, and Gray lifted his head as the
fabric slid to her waist. She was beautiful, even more
beautiful than in his dreams. In the shadowy light from the
lamp, her skin looked white, like a fine-veined alabaster,
and her hair gleamed like the darkest copper. Her lips were
swollen and pouty, red from his kisses. She tasted sweeter
than the sweetest strawberries, headier than the finest
wine.

Her breasts were firm and full, the nipples puckered
from desire, beckoning him, crying for his touch. With her
head thrown back she was the quintessential female, a vital feminine force that made him think of the mythical
Sirens—a womanly beauty no mere man could resist, nor
did he want to. With a muffle groan, he buried his face between her breasts, kissing first one, then the other.

She was soft and sweet and oh, so responsive, arching
her back and pressing her flesh into his hand, against his
mouth. Her hands threaded through his hair, holding him
to her, then pulling him away when it became too much.

"Oh, God, Lily, if we don't stop now, I don't know if
I'll be able to later." He wanted nothing more than to
make love to her, to plunge into her heated warmth and
become one with her, but he wanted her to be sure, too.

She tensed at his words, and he lifted his head to look
into her face. He saw desire and need . . . and a whisper
of fear. He couldn't believe it. He hadn't really meant his
words; he could stop at any time. It was just his way of
letting her know how she made him feel: so full and so
much a man, so ready to explode, to take her with him on
the most intimate journey a man and a woman could share.

Surely she understood that it was just the passion talking, not the man? If she wanted to, she could stop him at any time with just a single word.

"Tell me," he whispered hoarsely. "Why are you afraid? Should I stop? Is that what you want?"

She shook her head and bit her lower lip. The confusion in her eyes increased, a mixture of want and passion . . . and reticence. He didn't understand. She'd been as ready as he, a burning fire in his arms, flaming hotter than the sun.

"Are you afraid?" he asked at last.

"A little," she whispered back, her voice so soft he could only hear it because he was so close. She didn't even look at him. She was shy, she was scared . . . she'd never done this before. The thought jumped full blown into his reeling mind. Of course! What a fool he was.

"This will be your first time?"

"I . . ."

He didn't need her to tell him she had kissed someone before. He'd sensed it the first time their lips had met. She hadn't been this hesitant, this unsure of herself, but in his passionate desire he'd failed to notice when that had changed, when she started following him into uncharted territory.

"It's all right. We really can stop at any time, you know," he said to reassure her and gently stroked her back. "Do you want to stop now?"

"No." Her voice trembled over the softly spoken word, and he had to admire her honesty and trust. He curbed his urgency as he coaxed her lips to part again. Her mouth opened to him, and when he stroked her breast with his fingers, she did not pull away. The breath eased out of him. He didn't know what he would have done if she'd really wanted to stop. Deep in his soul he felt they belonged together.

Emboldened by her response, he held her away from him for a second while he shucked both his shirt and undershirt in a single movement. The heat from the small stove was nothing compared to the heat his body was generating. And when her breasts nestled against his chest, the heat began to burn from the inside out. He shifted on the armchair so that the side of her leg brushed against his engorged flesh. He closed his eyes and held his breath, afraid that even the slightest movement would make him come apart.

The softness of her skin was incredible; the sweet smell of her hair filled him. He lifted her breasts with his palms gently bringing them together so he could nuzzle the fragrant skin between. He felt her fingers thread through his hair, holding him close. Then her hands moved down his neck to his shoulders, and he knew she was learning his textures as he was learning hers.

He dipped his head and mouthed one turgid nipple, feeling the shudder that traveled through her. He suckled her delicate flesh, slowly shaping her to fit him, then switched his attention to her other breast. She tugged more frantically at his back, begging for more. He raised his head and swiftly conquered her mouth again, spurred on by her heated response.

He stroked her from shoulder to waist, but when he wanted to go beyond, her dress got in his way. He fumbled with the clasp at her waist, and the filmy blue fabric parted, dropping to her lap.

"Come with me," he said, lifting her off him and standing in one smooth motion. Her short-skirted costume pooled at her feet, leaving her naked from the waist up. He led her across the small wagon to the bed, then he pulled back the covers and laid her down. After quickly removing his trousers, he lay beside her. The bed was too short for him, so he shifted to lie diagonally across it, snuggling her close by his side.

When he kissed her, Lily lost all her inhibitions. In the tight cocoon of her bed, they were in a new world, a world belonging to just the two of them. She ran her hands over his chest, marveling at the tantalizing feel of his skin, resilient over steely muscles. The textures fascinated her: the silky smoothness of his shoulders, the wiry roughness of his chest where the golden brown hair grew, the tiny diamond points of his masculine nipples. He groaned when her hand gently brushed one, and she felt the first surge of feminine power.

Her mouth followed her hands, as his had earlier, and his whispered encouragements let her know how much he enjoyed her ministrations. He was busy, too, stroking her back and her sides, then easing under her arms to once again cup her breasts. Ribbons of need arced from her breasts to her very center, making her ache in ways she had never known. The ache grew until it throbbed and her legs moved restlessly on the bed.

Gray pulled her over on top of him, her legs falling to either side. She could feel the muscled hardness of his frame, the strength of his arms, and then she pressed urgently against the ridge of his manhood. He moved his hands beneath her pantalets to her buttocks. Gently he rocked her back and forth. She gasped as one wild sensation after the other raced through her. She hungered for him without knowing exactly what she hungered for, knowing only that he was the source of both the pleasure and the need, the satisfaction of one ache and the birth of another, greater one.

He groaned, and she felt the vibrations deep in his chest. "Don't move," he pleaded, suddenly stilling her, "or this will be over before it starts."

She raised her head and looked down on him, arching

her back. He groaned again as the movement pressed her hips closer to his. His face was flushed and lightly beaded with sweat. His eyes looked nearly black, the pupils expanded to fill the whole iris. His hair was tousled, softening the harsh angularity of his features, an angularity brought on by desire. He looked into her eyes, and she wondered what he saw—was her face as flushed, her skin as luminous, her eyes as slumberous with desire? And then the time for wondering was past as he brought her head down and captured her lips.

He shifted her to one side and deftly stripped her of the rest of her garments, sliding them down her legs with a firm hand, then trailing his fingers back up in a gentle caress.

"Hold on," he whispered. "We're almost there." He removed the last of his clothes, then rolled his body half over hers. His lips touched hers in the same instant that he slid his hand down her stomach and tangled it in the nest of curls below. She lifted her hips involuntarily off the bed as his hand stroked her inner thigh, and he gently parted her legs.

Wave after wave of excitement poured through her when he touched her most secret spot. His name escaped her lips in a voice she barely recognized, husky and dark and mysteriously feminine. He responded in kind, telling her all he felt, all he wanted her to feel.

"Come to me," she cried at last, unable to wait another moment for the fulfillment her body craved. She tugged at his neck and shoulders, and he yielded to her need, making a place for himself between her legs, urging her knees up so that she lay beneath him, pliant and willing, aching and needing to be filled. He moved slowly, deliberately, until she felt him nudge her in the most intimate way possible.

He was larger than she'd thought and burning hot. The anticipation rose in her again, a feeling not unlike the thrill she experienced before doing a dangerous trick—knowing that her whole life was at risk and the reward would be worth it. The rush of energy built and built. She could feel his arms tremble as he held himself back, his eyes darker than she'd ever seen them.

Suddenly she didn't want him to hold back. She felt the moment grow and expand just the way it did when her horse approached the ring of fire. The blazing circle lay ahead, and she urged him on, but felt him pause when her body resisted. Then he plunged through, making her body irrevocably his.

"I didn't want to hurt you," he whispered anxiously between gasping breaths, brushing her tangled hair off her face.

"You didn't," she murmured in response. Deep inside her there was a craving for something more, for that burning ring and its promised delights, but she didn't know what else there could be beyond this fullness, this sense of peace with its underlying need for more.

And then he moved, slowly at first as if testing her readiness, then gathering momentum. And as he thrust, driving more and more deeply, the ring burned brighter, the flames glowing, twisting, beckoning her, drawing her ever higher. With every passing second the pleasure grew and swirled inside her, lifting her, lifting him, until suddenly they burst through the ring in a shower of blinding light and heat.

Afterward she floated down, held safe in his arms, her breathing as wild and desperate as his, her sides heaving as she came back to herself to find he was still with her.

"Are you all right?" he asked, his eyes glowing with the heat of their lovemaking.

She nodded, overwhelmed by the reverberating waves of pleasure that still crested and broke inside her. He smiled with that masculine arrogance she found so endearing. She traced his smile with one finger, first his upper lip, then the lower one, fuller and more sensuous than its mate. When her fingertip reached the tiny flat area right in the center, he opened his mouth and captured her finger, sucking on it and rubbing it with his tongue. Shivers of delight ran across the surface of her skin, tightening her nipples again and replacing the feeling of satiation with a renewed hunger.

She ran her hands over his back and down past his waist, exploring new territory, places she hadn't had a chance to explore before. His skin was velvety smooth, his muscles sleek. He worked hard, and his body had been honed to perfection by his labors. She pushed gently on his shoulder, and he rolled off her, keeping her in his embrace. The musky scents of their lovemaking aroused her again, making her bold, bold enough to look at him, to see for herself the source of all the pleasure he'd shown her.

"You're beautiful," she said, in awe of his masculine perfection.

He laughed. "You're the one who's beautiful," he countered and combed his fingers through her hair. It felt like silk and smelled of wildflowers—lilies, like her name, wild and free and blazing with the color of fire. Having her near him like this was like holding a wildfire in his hands.

She was an exquisite lover, like none he'd ever known, and in his heart he understood the difference. His union with her had not been to assuage a primitive and passing male need. If anything, it had been even more fundamental, a claiming and a joining, a uniting of two people in the most intimate way possible. Inside her, he felt safe and sheltered, accepted and desired. She healed him from wounds he wasn't even aware of having suffered; she made him whole and wholly male. Even now, sated though he'd been, he could feel the stirrings of renewed desire.

Her hands touched him with shy hesitation, and he reveled in each caress, each gentle stroke setting him on fire once again. Her hands moved lower, closer to his center. And then she touched him, softly, like the whisper of the wind. A muffled sound of pleasure ripped through him, and she withdrew.

"I'm sorry. Did I hurt you?" Now she sounded as anxious as he had before. It brought a smile to his lips.

"It hurts more when you don't touch me," he said and sighed when her hand returned to run along his length. Her touch nearly undid him, and when he couldn't take the pleasure any more, he rolled her onto her back and once again claimed her, more quickly this time as she arched into him, showing him the way where before she'd been content to follow. This time the ride was quick and wild as first he let her set the pace, and then, when he realized nothing he could do would frighten her, let his passion rule, driving them both beyond control until they cried out together in climax.

In the aftermath she lay snuggled by his side like a trusting cat, all silken and warm. They drifted off to sleep, waking once to add wood to her little stove before making love again, and yet again. Each time was different, each uniquely sublime. And by morning no problem seemed too difficult to surmount, no chasm so deep they could not cross it. All they needed was time. . . .

The next two days passed like a dream, a dream Lily wished could last forever. In the early mornings she and Gray would walk to the outskirts of the city and beyond to watch the sunrise. Arm in arm they greeted the day, sharing kisses as the dawn gave way to morning. Then they would return to the circus tents so Lily could feed and groom her horses and Merlin. Lancelot seemed a little better, and Gray could find nothing wrong with him, either, but since the horse seemed improved, Lily didn't worry.

During the afternoons Gray went about his business, planning for the coming roundup, hiring hands and exchanging information with the other cattle growers. In the evenings, as soon as Lily finished her last performance, he joined her again, and it was as if the time between had never existed. She had never felt so free-spirited, so attuned to her world and happy with her life. Gray made her feel cherished and feminine and—dare she think it?—alluring, not only when they made love, but at other times as well, sometimes just by the way he looked at her, the sudden darkening of his eyes, the blaze of color along his cheekbones.

Her heartbeat would quicken, and a liquid heaviness would claim her insides, starting low in her belly and working its way to the tips of her fingers and toes, until her whole body was ready for him. The more he fed her hunger for him, the more it grew. He was always in her thoughts, always on her mind, whether she was in the room with him or alone, in the middle of her performance or mucking out a stall. It didn't matter: She had just to close her eyes and she saw him, his dark hair tousled from her hands running through it, his blue eyes darker than midnight with desire.

He touched her and she quivered in anticipation, reaching for him with joyful abandon, holding nothing of herself back. She ignored Elena's warnings and Dun's misgivings, knowing in her soul that they were wrong. They'd never been in love the way she was, they'd never known the ecstasy she found with Gray, the delight she found in pleasing him, the joy in having him please her.

The only shadow of her happiness was the series of disturbances between the circus and the townspeople. For the first time the circus was plagued by a barrage of complaints from visitors, protesting everything from pickpockets to rigged games. Bryce denied there were any unusual problems. Still, Lily worried, and her worries increased when she walked past the sideshow pavilion and found Bryce once again engaged in a shouting match with some paying customers. Except this time the customers were a family, and judging by the threadbare quality of their clothes, they had scraped together the admission fee by dint of hard work.

"What's going on?" she asked, even though she had promised herself she would not intervene in Bryce's business again. She'd kept that promise the past few days, but today with Gray gone to see Hank, she was more aware of Bryce's inappropriate behavior.

"Nothing you need to get involved in," Bryce said, his voice tight with warning.

"My boy here's been cheated out of his money, and I'd like to see him get it back," the father replied. There was an innate dignity to the man that had Lily wanting to believe him.

"What happened?" she prompted, ignoring Bryce's glare.

"One of the clowns told him he'd show him something special if he gave him all his change. Tyler didn't know no better and gave him the money. Then, when he took him behind the curtain, there wasn't nothing there 'cept a bearded man."

"He said there'd be a lady," the boy put in. "With hair like a dog all over her face."

"Now, I want the boy's money back. He's worked more'n two weeks over at Rafferty's ranch cleaning out the barn and grooming the horses, on top of his chores for me, to get his money. I don't take kindly to seeing him swindled."

"Them's strong words, mister," Bryce snarled. "You got any facts to back them up? If not, you'd better leave before I call the sheriff."

"Wait, Bryce, that's unfair," Lily said, appalled at his outburst. Otto would never have allowed a paying customer to be threatened like this, especially a twelve-year-old boy.

"I'm warning you, Lily, this is none of your concern," Bryce snapped back.

"At least listen to their story. Please, can you describe the clown?" she asked the boy.

The boy described a tall, thin man in full white face makeup, but the design on his face resembled that of no one in their troupe.

"There's no one here like that," Lily said. "At least, no one who officially belongs to our troupe. And we haven't hired on a bearded lady, either. Where'd you say he took you?"

The boy led her to a curtained-off area that was usually used to store supplies. She pulled back the curtain, but the small enclosure was empty.

"What'd I tell you?" Bryce demanded. "You can see as well as I can that they're lying. They just want to make money off of us."

"That's not true!" the boy yelled. "There was, too, someone here. He sat right there."

The lad pointed to the center of the room. Lily could see four round indentations set in a square in the dusty ground.

"He's right, Bryce. Someone was here." She pointed to the marks. "You can see where the chair was. Now, what I want to know is how someone managed to set up an exhibition in here without authorization." Lily felt the fury rise in her chest. This, more than anything else, was

Bryce's job during the run of a show: to keep the grafters and cheaters out, to check and check again to make sure no one was taken advantage of on their visit.

"You don't know for sure," Bryce countered. "I still say the boy is lying."

"Whether he is or not, there's enough evidence here to give him the benefit of the doubt. Are you going to refund his money or shall I?"

"Damn bitch," Bryce muttered under his breath. "You'll be sorry you crossed me. Just you wait and see." He left the enclosure with furious strides.

As soon as he was gone, Lily escorted the family to the ticket wagon and got back their money, pitiful though the amount was. She apologized for their inconvenience and sent them on their way.

When they'd left, she went in search of Otto. Maybe this time she could talk some sense into him before it was too late, before something happened that brought real trouble down on the circus. But no matter where she looked, she could not find him.

Sighing, she decided to check on Lancelot once again. At least being with her animals helped pass the time until Gray's return.

Gray rode out to Hank's spread. The place looked better than when he'd last seen it. Clearly Hank was beginning to show some profit and was doing the right thing: turning it back into improving the ranch. The outbuildings were no longer in the same state of disrepair, and the few animals out in the corral looked sleek and healthy. Gray only recognized one or two of the horses. Things must be going very well for Hank to have purchased new stock.

He tied his horse near the watering trough in the shade of a cottonwood tree and crossed the yard to the house.

Hank's house was a large wooden cabin with two rooms upstairs and a large living area divided into three rooms on the first floor. He'd bought it off a family of homesteaders who'd decided the area had gotten too crowded for their taste and had headed farther out where a man could still walk for a day without seeing another living soul. Hank had gotten a good deal, but it had still used up most of his capital. He'd been working since then to build up his herd and turn the ranch into a profitable business.

Gray called out to announce his presence, then opened the door and let himself inside. The room was fairly neat, maintained by a widow woman Hank had hired to cook and clean for him three times a week. Today there was no sign of her. Instead, Hank was sprawled on the large chair in the corner, his arm in a sling.

"My God, Hank! What happened to you?"

Hank looked up, and Gray could see a bruise high on his cheek and another near his mouth. His lip was scabbed over where it had been split, probably in the last day or so.

"H'llo, Gray." He grimaced in what Gray decided was a lopsided attempt at a smile. " 'Fraid I messed up. Thought I'd be clever and lie in wait for those rustlers. Instead, they jumped me."

"You what?" Gray couldn't believe his ears. "That wasn't part of our plan at all. You should have told me!"

Hank shrugged. "I didn't think it would have made a difference. Besides, it seems to me you've had more important things to do lately."

Gray felt a stab of guilt. Since meeting Lily, he hadn't devoted as much time or concentration to his ranch or the problem with the rustlers. If he'd thought about it, he, too, might have tried to do more than merely bait the trap.

"I'm still sorry I wasn't here. You look pretty beat up."

"It ain't nothin' much. I'll be as good as new in a few

days." He sat up a bit in the chair. This time his grimace was from pain.

"Can I get you anything?"

"No, I'm fine. Edith should be back before dinner. She's been lookin' in on me the past couple of days." Edith was the woman who cleaned for him. She lived in a small ramshackle hut on the outskirts of Cheyenne, the only place she could afford after the death of her husband.

"So what happened?"

"I went out to the hollow where we took your two bulls to keep an eye out. I guess I musta dozed off or somethin'. Next thing I knew, my horse was whickerin' and pawin' at the ground all nervous like. I got up to look around, and someone hit me from behind, not enough to knock me out, but I saw a few stars, I can tell you. So I twisted around and punched him. Trouble is, I missed . . . and he didn't." He fingered the bruise on his cheek, then tried to smile again. "I'm afraid I lost that one." His expression became serious. "That's not all I lost. By the time I got my senses back, they were gone—and your bulls, too."

"They?" Gray asked sharply. "How many were there? Did you get a good look at them?"

Hank started to shake his head, then winced. "The one hittin' me had the lower part of his face hidden by his bandanna, and I never got a glimpse of the others."

"Damn." Gray paced across the room. If only he'd been here! "Well, at least we know one thing."

"What's that?"

"Someone at the Cattlemen's Club must be involved."

"I still don't believe that, Gray. Those men are our friends. Why'd any one of them want to do somethin' like this?" His eyes narrowed as he watched Gray, but Gray had no reason to offer beyond his earlier suspicions.

"I don't know. Greed? Desperation? Someone wants to

get rich even quicker than most, without putting in any hard work. It's not impossible."

"Maybe not. But it sure seems unlikely to me. If I were you, I'd look in some other direction. It's probably outlaws from another part of the territory. They just want to make money fast and get out of here."

"Well, I hope we get them first. If I find out who's caused all this trouble, there'll be hell to pay."

Hank paled suddenly, and Gray wondered just how serious his injuries really were. "Have you seen a doctor?" he asked.

"No need," Hank replied. "Edith's checked me over. She knows a fair amount of doctorin'. I'm just a little worn out, is all. Be up and about in a day or two, none the worse for wear."

"Well, I'm going to ride out to the hollow and look around. You never know what I might turn up."

"I think you'll be wastin' your time. There won't be anything there. Nothin's been found before, has it?"

"Not that I know of, but that doesn't mean there won't be a first time. I'll check on you again on my way back."

Gray rode out to the hollow. All he found were some hoofprints interspersed with the footprints of his bulls. The prints disappeared over a rocky expanse as the animals and riders climbed out of the hollow onto drier, harder ground. Gray couldn't pick up their trail. Frustrated, he rode back down into the hollow, intending to cross it one last time.

As he rode, something shiny glinted in his eye. He stopped his horse, then backed it up a couple of paces. There it was again. He dismounted and walked toward the shiny object. It was smaller than he'd thought, and as he picked it up, he realized why it had glinted so brightly. In his hand he held a highly polished and intricately engraved gold sleeve link. It seemed familiar, but he couldn't immediately place it. Undoubtedly he'd seen it at the Cattlemen's Club or perhaps at some social gathering in Cheyenne. But who had worn it?

He placed it in his vest pocket and searched the immediate area to see if he could find anything else, but there was nothing more to be found. After mounting his horse, he slowly walked the animal across the hollow, his eyes constantly searching, but to no avail. It had been pure luck that he'd found the link, and his luck had run out.

On his way back he stopped at the ranch as he'd promised. Edith was there, preparing a stew for Hank's supper.

"You find anything?" Hank asked.

Gray shook his head. For some reason, he was unwilling to share his discovery quite yet, not until he knew who owned the gold sleeve link and how it had gotten out to the hollow.

"Let me know if you need anything," he said to Hank. "I'm staying in town if you need to send for me."

"I doubt they'll be back," Hank said. "After all, I didn't get a good look at anyone, so I should be safe. I'm sorry about the bulls. I sure never meant for them to disappear when I thought this up."

Gray shrugged. "I knew I was taking a risk when I agreed to the plan. I only wish we'd learned a little more."

"I doubt the rustlin' will continue too much longer," Hank said with a confidence Gray sorely lacked. "Once the cattle are branded, it'll be a lot harder to take them."

"Depends on whether the rustlers know how to doctor a brand or not. But you're right. Once the roundup's held, it's harder to claim someone's cows. I'm thinking of starting things up a bit earlier than usual myself. If you like, I can send my men over to your section as well."

"I'd be grateful," Hank said.

Gray nodded. "Let me know when you're ready."

He left soon after, his thoughts troubled. Could he have

done something more to stop the rustlers? He just didn
know. They always seemed a step ahead, as if they kne
what he was planning to do almost before he knew him
self. He dreaded investigating any of the possible reason
but the gold sleeve link in his pocket gave him very littl
choice.

TEN

WHEN GRAY RETURNED that evening, he was preoccupied and tense. Lily suggested they take a walk even though the air had turned brisk. Was he feeling the way she was—that time was running out? Soon the circus would depart for Denver, and they still hadn't talked about what would happen then.

"Is everything all right?" she asked once they had left the circus grounds behind them.

He sighed and took her hand in his, intertwining their fingers. "No. I visited Hank today."

"Oh?" Though Hank was one of Gray's close friends, Lily herself hadn't succumbed to his charm. Perhaps it was because he used it so freely, as if all a woman needed was the glow of his attention to fall at his feet.

"The rustlers stole his new cattle. Worse, he tried to stop them and nearly got himself killed."

"He what? How badly was he hurt?" She couldn't believe it. Though she'd realized the rustlers could be dangerous, she'd put those thoughts aside. Now she had to face the fact that Gray was in danger, too, particularly if he continued to pursue them. And she had no doubt that he would.

"He's a bit banged up, and his left arm may be broken. It could have been worse. If they thought he'd gotten a good look at them, God only knows what they would have done."

"What did the sheriff say?"

"The same as always: He's working on it, and we should leave the investigation to him other than keeping our eyes open and watching our livestock."

Watching livestock on the open range was no easy task, Lily knew. The cattle roamed at will, following their instincts to the best grass and water. Though they traveled in small groups, those groups were scattered and intermingled with those of other ranchers until the spring roundup sorted everything out again.

"What are you going to do?" she asked, afraid to hear the answer but knowing she had to ask.

"Keep looking," he answered and clenched his jaw.

"You've found something, haven't you?"

His hand tightened on hers, so she knew her guess had surprised him. "It's better that you not know, Lily. Those men are dangerous. I don't want them to think they have any reason to come after you."

"And what about you? Isn't it dangerous for you, too?"

He stopped walking and turned to face her, pulling her close. "Are you worried about me?"

She slid her arms around his waist, holding him tight, as if she could keep him safe within her embrace. "You know I am. I don't know what I'd do if anything happened to you."

He smiled, his teeth gleaming white in the moonlit night. "I like hearing that you care."

"Of course I care! I love you." The words burst out of her and hung in the air between them.

"Oh, Lily, I love you, too. That's why I want to protect you from all this."

Lily couldn't breathe. His voice was full of passion. Joy welled up inside her as his mouth came down on hers.

By mutual consent they headed toward her wagon. By the time they reached it, she was out of breath and giddy with excitement, eager to touch him once again, to feel his flesh against hers and know the ecstasy of their ride through the flames. They undressed, and then, without a word being spoken, they yielded to hungers as old as time, to the rhythms of male and female, until once again the ring of fire claimed them.

Lily walked Lancelot around in a circle, noting his lack-luster gait. His head hung listlessly, and his eyes had lost all interest in the outside world. Even Merlin was unable to shake the horse from his painful lethargy. The animal had seemed so much better just a day ago. What could have happened in the interim? She'd been spending so much time with Gray, she hadn't been keeping as close an eye on the livestock as she should have. Had she been too distracted to notice the subtle changes that might have warned her Lancelot was in trouble sooner?

She was glad that Gray promised to get one of his friends to look at the horse. The sooner, the better, she thought until she looked up at the sound of approaching footsteps and saw Hank Farrell coming toward her.

"Well, well, pretty lady, I heard you have a mighty sick horse. Anything I can do to help?"

"Did Gray send you?"

"He mentioned you might have a problem. I took it upon myself to come down."

His face was still bruised, Lily noted, and his arm was in a sling of black silk. She shuddered. If Gray had been with him, he, too, might have been hurt.

"Are you feeling better?" she asked.

"Why don't you come over here and check?" he offered with a rakish smile as he leaned against a water barrel in the corner.

She gave him a quick look. His expression was open and friendly. She wasn't sure what he was after.

"Maybe you should sit. I can get you a chair."

"No need. I'll just check out the horse, and then we can both go someplace and sit. How does that sound?"

"All right," she agreed more because she hoped he would know what was wrong with Lancelot—and how to fix it—than because she wanted to spend more time with him.

He came to her side, crowding her a bit as he looked at the horse's eyes and mouth, then felt along his legs and belly. "What's he been eatin' lately? Anythin' new?"

"Not that I know of," Lily replied. "We're very careful with the show stock. They're too hard to replace, especially horses like Lancelot. It took a long time to train him."

"I can imagine. I saw you perform the other day when that yellow dog burst out of the stands and came runnin' through the ring. It was a miracle your horse didn't shy. You could have been killed."

"That's exactly what I mean. We don't just train them to run steadily around the ring when everything goes as planned. They also have to be trained not to shy at unexpected sounds and events. It takes a special personality in the animal, too. I was lucky that day. Galahad is pretty placid most of the time. If Lancelot had been with me, he might not have taken it so well, especially with the way he's been feeling lately."

Merlin came running up at that moment and tried to butt Hank. "Hey, what's this?" he exclaimed, jumping out of the animal's way.

"Oh, I'm sorry," Lily said with a gasp as she ran after the goat. "He's very protective of Lancelot. Let me put them both away."

She led Lancelot back to his makeshift stall and shooed Merlin in with him. She'd isolated the horse from the rest of the stock in case he had anything contagious. When she came back outside, Hank was waiting for her.

"I'm sorry I can't tell you more about the horse, but I'd watch what he's eatin', especially if none of the other animals are gettin' sick."

"Thank you for coming." She knew she should be more gracious, maybe offer him a cup of coffee or something to eat for his trouble, but he made her feel uneasy, so she didn't want to prolong his stay.

"No thanks necessary. It's not every day I get to spend a few minutes with a woman as vibrantly beautiful as yourself." He took a step closer to her and fingered a lock of her hair that had escaped its bonds. "So beautiful, like a blazin' fire. Tell me, Lily, are you as hot-blooded as your hair makes you look?"

Before she could guess his intent, he had backed her into a small opening between two of the large props. Then his mouth was on hers. For an instant she stood stock still, unable to believe this was happening. Then, overcome by fury and revulsion, she put her hands up to his arms and shoved hard. He resisted for a moment, trying to deepen the kiss as if he couldn't believe she would reject him, but when she pushed harder, he fell back a couple of steps.

At that instant Dun came round a corner. "Is everything all right?" he asked, looking assessingly from Lily to Hank.

Lily felt disheveled and unclean, as if Hank's touch had sullied her in some way. She edged past Hank, then said, "Mr. Farrell was just leaving. Could you show him the way out, please?"

Without questioning her, Dun turned to Hank. "If you'll follow me?"

But Hank wasn't ready to leave. "Wait, Lily!" he cried. "You don't understand." He took a couple of steps in her direction, but Dun stepped in front of him.

"I think it would be better if you came this way," the shorter man said and gestured in the opposite direction with one hand while holding his coat open just enough for Hank to catch a glimpse of the gun at his waist. Hank looked down and nodded once. Much to Lily's relief, he followed Dun with no further argument.

The episode had shaken her. She ran to her wagon and scrubbed her face and arms everywhere Hank had touched. A knock on her door startled her, making her drop the facecloth she was using.

"Are you all right?" she heard Dun call from the other side of the door.

"Yes," she replied as she unlocked it, and he came inside. "Thank you for getting rid of him for me."

"What'd he want?"

"Gray sent him to look at Lancelot, but he has no more idea than we do what might be wrong. I guess I should have brought Lancelot out to the front instead of letting Hank corner me that way."

"It wasn't your fault, Lily. A true gentleman wouldn't have taken advantage, regardless of the circumstances. I'm just glad I came by when I did."

"Were you looking for me?"

"I thought you'd want to know that Iola Parsons is down at the changing tent with Elena."

"Yes. I wanted to talk to her about that new costume she's been helping me with."

"You still want to see her now, or would you rather have some time alone?"

"I think I'd prefer the company." If she stayed by herself, she would just brood about what had happened. With Mrs. Parsons and Elena she could get something positive accomplished, and with the circus scheduled to leave town in just a couple of days, every minute they could get of Iola's time and skills was precious.

When Lily reached the changing tent, she found Elena and Mrs. Parsons stitching away on new costumes.

"I can do that for you, Elena," Mrs. Parsons was telling the younger woman when Lily walked in. "I don't rightly think you should be doing all that running around in your condition."

"What condition?" Lily asked as she dragged a straight-backed chair across the floor and placed it by the others.

Elena looked at Mrs. Parsons and then over at Lily. "I am *enceinte*—with child, I think you say."

Before the words had left Elena's mouth, Lily was off her chair and flinging her arms around her friend. "A baby! How wonderful. When did you find out? What does Roberto have to say? Do you want a girl or a boy?"

"Give the gal a chance to catch her breath," Mrs. Parsons said with a laugh as she watched the two younger women hug and kiss.

"Oh, I'm sorry," Lily said, jumping back. "Are you all right?"

"I'm fine. Madame Parsons was talking about all ze questions. Ze 'ugs, zey are no problem." She smiled up at Lily, who couldn't resist giving her friend another hug before holding her at arm's length.

"So?" Lily prompted.

"So what?" Elena asked with a puzzled expression.

"When did you find out? What does Roberto have to say? Do you want a girl or a boy?"

"Oh, I see," Elena said with a laugh. "Your questions. I 'ave suspected about ze baby for two months. I was not sure, but Madame Parsons, she says it is true. So now I will tell Roberto." She looked a little worried.

"He'll be so happy," Lily said, guessing at the most likely cause of her friend's concerns.

"I 'ope you are right."

"I know I am. A new baby is a blessing. Everyone will

be thrilled." But would she be here to see it? Lily wondered. When Gray had talked about their being together, she hadn't realized how it might affect all her friendships and ties. This baby would not be born before the fall. Where would she be then?

"Madame Parsons and I were talking about 'ow to let out my costumes."

"Let them out—but you can't be thinking of doing your act much longer," Lily said, all thoughts of her and Gray's future overshadowed by Elena's statement.

"I must. What will Roberto do without me? The act needs two people. As long as I am well, I do it."

Lily didn't know what to say. No wonder Elena had delayed talking to Roberto. She knew her husband would have stopped the act immediately. "The decision is yours, yours and Roberto's, I know. Just let me know if I can help. Otto will see that Roberto still has an act, maybe with another partner."

"*Alors*, you think that Monsieur Bryce will allow that?"

"I don't care what Bryce thinks. It still isn't his circus, and I won't let him interfere in this."

"You are a good friend, Lily," Elena said. "I will not forget what you 'ave said."

Lily picked out a costume to work on and had just started sewing when the flap on the tent was pulled aside and Otto walked in.

"Excuse me, ladies. I hope I'm not interrupting anything."

Lily smiled. It was so good to see Otto more like his old self. Now that she thought about it, he'd been out mingling with the troupe and the customers much more frequently lately. There was a spring to his walk she hadn't seen in a long time.

"Otto, come in. We've been wondering if you would drop by," Iola said. She smiled up at him, and Lily marveled. Apparently she'd been so wrapped up in Gray these past few days, she'd missed the changes that had taken place.

"How could I not, when I knew you would be here, working your fingers to the bone for me."

"Oh, Otto, you're such a tease," Iola replied, a faint blush coloring her cheeks.

"I was not teasing, *Liebchen*," Otto said, taking one of her hands in his. "You work very hard. We would have serious trouble without you."

"What you think of the costumes, Otto? *Très chic*, no?" Elena asked, holding up one of the newly finished garments in front of her.

"*Ja*, they are wonderful. I am sorry this happened. I should have been working harder. Bryce is a good boy, but this work he not do good. I have been a *Dummkopf*."

When Lily heard his accent thicken, she knew he was upset. Normally he worked diligently on perfecting his "American accent," as he called it. It was only in moments of stress that his origins showed in his speech.

"It's not too late to fix things," Lily said. "What matters now is that you're ready to see us on to the next stop. And with Mrs. Parsons's help, our new costumes are going to be even better than the ones we had before. Don't you agree?"

Otto nodded, and Iola looked away, her blush deepening, but with a pleased smile lighting her face. "*Ja*, she is right. These are the best costumes we ever have. I will stay and help."

Otto pulled up a chair beside Iola's, and the four settled down to work. As she watched the older couple exchange glances when they thought no one was looking, Lily realized what had brought Otto back to life. She was happy for him until she remembered he now faced the same agonizing decisions she did—how to reconcile two disparate lives without having to give up on each other.

They'd been working for about an hour when Roberto came running in. "Otto, you come quick! Big trouble!"

"What trouble?" Otto asked, pushing his chair back and coming to his feet.

Roberto answered in a spate of heated Italian.

"No, *mon cher.* English, English," his wife prompted him.

"The law people have come, Otto," Roberto repeated slowly in English, but there was more than a hint of panic in each word. "You must stop him."

"What?" Otto said in astonishment.

"Yes. Out there. Come, come!" Roberto urged.

Otto ran out of the tent, followed closely by Roberto. The women chased after them, equally anxious to find out what was going on.

Lily was frightened. This didn't sound like a friendly visit from the local sheriff. While Roberto could be excitable, he was levelheaded and didn't cry wolf unless the animal was on the doorstep.

By the time the group reached the main gate, a large crowd was gathered, with townspeople on one side of an invisible line and circus people on the other. In the absence of any other circus leadership, Dun was trying to talk with the sheriff, but he was having trouble being heard over the shouts and epithets flung by each side against the other.

"But, Sheriff, I'm sure you're mistaken," Lily heard Dun telling the large man who towered over him.

"I have the broken chairs and glassware to prove it!" a man yelled out from the crowd.

"And I know some people who had their pockets picked when they were walking the grounds," a new voice added.

"And that's not all," a woman called out. "My husband said you took him for five dollars."

"Are you sure it was done by our people? We don't like to see our customers abused," Dun said, trying to ward off the verbal attacks and deflect some of the crowd's animosity, though Lily was sure he'd rather be someplace else.

The sheriff turned and looked back at the crowd. "Any of you have proof of what you're saying?" he asked, ready to concede that Dun had a point. He obviously didn't want trouble any more than the circus.

"Yeah, Gertie, your husband probably told you he was five dollars short because he lost his money in a poker game."

"Gertie may not know her husband's business, but I know mine. Think I don't know who comes into my place?" said the first man who'd spoken in reply to the sheriff's question, then he turned to Dun. "Your people came in last night, and it ended with my place being turned upside down."

Before anyone else could add their voices to the argument, Otto joined Dun and the sheriff, hoping to stop the trouble before it started. "If there's been any damage, of course we'll pay for it," Otto said loudly enough for the crowd to hear.

Lily knew that the one thing the circus couldn't afford was to have the town angry at them. Goodwill was a necessity when you needed the patronage of the town to keep the money flowing in. If a circus got on the wrong side of the law, a town could put a lien on its property, forcing it to stay in town until all bills were paid or enough circus property and livestock had been sold to cover them.

"Well, if they're willing to pay . . ." the sheriff said, backing down on hearing Otto's offer.

"But Fred here wants his money now," a voice called out.

Lily could hear the crowd murmuring its approval and knew the only choice Otto had was to pay the man off and hope nothing like this happened again. As for the pickpockets, they would have to put more people out on the promenade to watch for them.

"Let me get the money box out of the ticket wagon, and I'll take care of it right now," Otto said.

"Fred, you come with us. The rest of you stand back and give us some room," the sheriff told the group.

Fred and the sheriff followed Otto to the red ticket wagon. Otto knocked on the door and called out Bryce's name.

"Bryce! Are you in there?" Otto said as he knocked again. With his second, harder knock the door flew open.

"What the . . . ?"

The ticket wagon was never left unlocked. It housed the company office as well as all the records and ledgers. The door was always padlocked unless someone was inside, and then it was bolted from within. Bryce and Otto were the only ones with keys, and Bryce had strict orders never to let anyone in without Otto's approval. Lily knew something was wrong, as much from the expression on Otto's face as that the door was not locked. She ran to Otto's side and looked in the wagon, then gasped. The cash box was lying on the floor wide open—and empty. There would be no money for Fred and the damages to his business. There'd be no money for anything else, including salaries.

"What happened here?" the sheriff asked.

"This is where we keep the money," Otto replied, sounding dazed.

"So what's the problem?"

"See for yourself." Otto gestured toward the empty box.

"All your money was in there?" he asked. "Every last penny?"

"Yes. Where else would we put it? This wagon is built

extra strong. No one has the key except for me and my manager."

"Well, let's get him and see what he has to say."

Otto and Lily turned to search the crowd for Bryce, but neither saw him.

"What's going on?" some of the men in the crowd started asking.

"Does this mean I don't get my money?" Fred demanded to know as he stared at the empty cash box in Otto's hands.

"You'll get your money, I promise you," Otto said. "It'll just take a little longer than I thought."

The sheriff looked around the inside of the wagon. "I don't see anything in here that'll be much help in finding out who did this. Where's your manager?"

"It looks like he's gone," Otto said in a weary voice.

The sheriff scratched his head. "Well, you know what that most likely means?"

"Yes," Otto said, defeat showing in his voice and his posture. "He probably did this, but I don't know why."

"Greed, I'd guess," the sheriff opined.

Otto shrugged. "It makes no difference now."

Lily hated seeing him like this. Only a few minutes before he'd almost been the old Otto, and she didn't want anything to push him back to where he'd been.

"I saw Bryce inside there early this morning," Dun said, "right after breakfast."

"Who's this Bryce fellow?" the sheriff asked.

"He's our general manager. Bryce Mason by name," Otto said, his voice unsteady.

"Has anyone seen him since this morning?" the sheriff asked.

A murmur went through the circus part of the crowd, but no one else had spotted Bryce all day.

"It looks like he's your culprit, all right," the sheriff

said. "Any idea of where he might be headed? Not that I think you'll get the money back."

Lily looked around at the others. No one had an answer. It seemed Mason had kept to himself and revealed few personal details. Lily looked over at Otto and wished she'd told him her misgivings earlier.

"It's water under the bridge," Otto said, his voice stronger and more forceful than before. "Mr. ... uh, Fred, I want you to rest assured you'll get your money. We'll extend our engagement, *ja*? With the city's permission, of course, and make sure you're paid in full."

Fred looked over at the sheriff.

"Best do as the man says," the sheriff told him. "You can't get blood from a stone."

"All right," Fred agreed grudgingly.

"What about us?" a few others groused.

"Come back to my office and we'll make a list. If you can prove your claim, I'll take it up with Mr. Bruner here. Can't be fairer than that."

When the townspeople split up into small groups and started wandering back to their carriages, Otto asked all the members of the circus to meet him in the main tent in fifteen minutes. "I know you all have questions. Be sure to let anyone else know who isn't here."

Lily watched as Iola walked over and talked quietly with Otto. He nodded at whatever she said and then walked back to the ticket wagon. Iola must have noticed Lily's interest for she came over.

"I can tell you're worried about him," she said, coming to stand beside Lily and nodding in Otto's direction. "From all Otto has told me, you two are very close."

"He was like a father to me until—" She broke off, unable to betray Otto by putting everything into words.

"I understand," Iola said with a sympathetic smile.

Lily gave her a questioning look.

"We've had a lot in common, Otto and I. You see, I lost my husband five years ago and felt much like Otto. I didn't turn to drink, but I did things that were just as bad. Nothing could take the place of Jim, and he was all I wanted. We were married thirty years. It might have been different if we'd had children, but we only had each other."

"You told Otto all this?"

Iola nodded. "After Elena mentioned what he'd been going through. Don't seem right, somehow, that the Lord takes such good people, but who am I to say? I just told Otto what I've learned, and it seemed to help."

"It did more than help. I can't tell you how happy I am. My heart was breaking for him, but I couldn't seem to help."

"He told me how much you mean to him. He thinks of you as his daughter. Sometimes it takes an outsider to do some plain talking."

Lily put her arms around Iola and gave her a hug. "Thank you. You've given us back a wonderful man. I just hope this situation with Bryce Mason doesn't set him off again."

"He was just telling me he's going into town to send off some telegrams. He's not just going to sit back and let that young scalawag get away with this. Said there weren't that many places that Mason feller could head where he didn't know someone."

"It would be nice to see Bryce get his comeuppance," Lily said, but she wasn't sure that would ever happen. For Otto's sake, though, she hoped it would.

The troupe settled down and planned what they would be doing for the next few days. All of them were willing to give up their salaries, but Otto wouldn't allow that. He simply asked for a delay in paying them, until the circus could bring in more money. He had already begun rearranging their schedule, posting a rider to go to Denver, their next stop, to explain the delay and sending telegrams to later stops in their itinerary announcing the changes. Everyone got ready for at least four more days with an additional show each day to help make up the lost money more quickly.

By the time Gray arrived at her wagon that night, Lily was in a state.

"I heard what happened," Gray said after their first kiss. "The talk is all over town. Come sit here and tell me about it."

He sat on one of the chairs and motioned her to the other. She sat and told him everything, starting with Roberto's panicked visit to the changing tent and ending with the troupe's decision to put off getting their wages until Otto paid off his debts in Cheyenne. By the time she was finished, she was no longer in the chair.

"And that's not the worst of it," she added, pacing in the narrow space in front of him. "You're not going to believe what else I discovered. You know all the trouble I've been having with Lancelot?"

"Yes. In fact, I mentioned it to Hank. Did he have a chance to drop by and have a look?"

Lily knew if there was one thing she didn't want to talk about, it was Hank Farrell's visit. "The reason none of us could find anything wrong with Lancelot," she said, completely ignoring Gray's question about his friend, "was because of this." She pointed to a small plain box lying on the chest.

Gray looked at it carefully, then gave her a puzzled look.

"It's arsenic," she explained. "And it looks like Bryce was giving doses of it to Lancelot."

"You're sure?"

She nodded. "Young Bobby said he saw Bryce around Lancelot's quarters on a number of occasions. And they found three more packets just like this one in Bryce's wagon."

Gray swore. "I can't believe it. Didn't he know how dangerous that stuff is? He could have killed half the troupe with that amount of poison. No wonder we couldn't figure out what was wrong with Lancelot. None of us ever suspected someone could be deliberately harming him."

"I know. It's so awful. I'm so angry that if Bryce were here, I'd ... I'd ..."

"I'd do it for you," Gray said grimly. "The man was totally unscrupulous."

"There's more. Iola Parsons told us she's heard in town that he purposely started a lot of the trouble himself. She says there're rumors that he hired the pickpockets and cardsharps from Cheyenne's mean streets. What I don't understand is why he did it. I mean, if all he wanted was to take the money, why did he cause all the trouble first?"

"I don't know. Obviously he wanted to discredit Otto, or keep him and the circus so preoccupied that no one would go after him."

"He must have been planning this for a long time. I never liked the man, but Bryce was good at making Otto think everything was going along nicely. It wouldn't surprise me if Bryce didn't encourage Otto's drinking. The rest of us were always so careful, yet he never improved, at least not until recently."

"You may be right. But at least one good thing's come of all this."

"Oh?"

He held out his arm when she passed in front of him, and she put her hand in his. "While I would never wish these ills on your friends, at least we'll have more time together, time to make our own plans."

Slowly he pulled her closer to him, then eased her onto his lap. Lily smiled up at him as she cuddled in the crook of his arm, her heart pounding with excitement, not only at his nearness, but at the images his words evoked. Plans. A future. Things she'd secretly dreamed about her whole life were starting to come true.

"I like the thought of more time together," she said, reaching up to give him a quick kiss. But a quick kiss was not enough for either of them, and one kiss blended into another. Lily's breath quickened and her heart skipped a beat the way it always did when her lips touched his. Desire swamped her, and she could think of nothing but Gray.

He'd loosened the belt of the wrap she was wearing, and his hand had started to slip inside, his fingers just grazing her skin, when he suddenly stopped and drew his lips from hers.

"Lily, no."

The unexpectedness of his words shocked Lily from her state of euphoria. She didn't understand. She knew he wanted her as much as she wanted him. She could feel the evidence of his desire pressing against her. Why had he stopped?

"I mean . . . yes, I want you, but we have to talk first," he explained. "Every night I tell myself, 'Tonight's the night.' But then we end up like this." He nodded at the way they were sitting, entwined in each other's arms. "We have to make plans, but once we're like this, I can think of nothing but making love to you."

Lily knew he was right. They did have to talk, but she was afraid, afraid there wouldn't be a way for them to have a life together, afraid Gray would find her lacking, just as her father had. She didn't want to face that, in fact had been avoiding the issue since the day they'd met, first using the circus and then Cybil as excuses. It had been easier to find outside reasons for why she and Gray might never have a permanent future rather than deal with her fears.

"Lily, are you all right?" Gray asked.

She nodded her head as much to signify her answer as to clear her mind. She'd promised herself she wouldn't let her father's treatment hurt her anymore. After all, it had all happened so long ago, and her sister had always told her to forget what their life had been like before they'd escaped to the circus, but it was easier said than done. She'd never realized the importance of her sister's advice until this moment. She would have to forget, to put the distant past behind her, if she really wanted a new life.

"I'm fine and you're right. We do have to talk." Her voice sounded strained even to her own ears. She tried to get off his lap, but he held her in place. Since her struggles were futile, she turned her head away and looked anywhere but at Gray.

"Dammit, Lily, what's wrong?" he asked with a touch of bewilderment. "You can't believe I don't want you. My God, I know you can feel my desire even now. Tell me what's wrong."

How could she? She wasn't sure what it was herself. "I don't know."

"All you have to know is that I want us to be together. I know it isn't going to be easy. Do you think I'll expect you to give up the circus?"

In some far part of her mind, she had thought he would, and the idea appealed to her. She would miss all the people, but as she'd thought so often, it would be nice to have a real home.

When she didn't answer, he took her silence for agreement. "Please, Lily, I'd never make you give up your life with the circus for me. I know how much it means to you.

We can work this out, as long as you come back to me. That's all I really want. Please believe me."

Lily heard his words but was having trouble taking them in. This was what she'd waited for all her life. "I do believe you. I'm just not sure I can believe my luck," she said, tears pooling in her eyes. She knew if she blinked they'd spill over and down her cheeks.

"I'm the lucky one, you know. I found you."

His words were all it took to make the tears tumble down.

"Oh, my sweet Lily. Why tears? I thought this was what you wanted."

"It is. I'm just so happy."

Gray lowered his head and kissed the tracks the tears had left on her cheeks and then moved to her lips, caressing them ever so tenderly until their mutual passion demanded more. They could talk about their plans later. Right now they needed to confirm their love, not with words, but in the most elemental way, with their bodies and their souls.

The next day when Lily's performance had just finished, she came out of the main tent with Galahad on his lead to find Sam. From the look on his face, she knew there was trouble.

"Amelia's been hurt," he said without preamble.

"What did you say?" she asked.

"Amelia's had an accident out at the ranch," he said, confirming her fears.

"How did it happen?"

"I'm not quite sure. Something to do with Cleo. All I know is I found her on the ground inside the corral. When I saw her, I thought . . ." His voice broke, but he quickly regained control. "If anything happens to her, I don't know what I'll do."

Lily looked at the pain emanating from Sam's eyes and saw something she'd never seen before or else had overlooked: a look of love so sweet and true, it seemed almost a crime to witness it.

She placed a hand on his arm. "Sam, is she badly hurt?"

"She came to by the time I got her into the house, but I don't know. Gray left for the ranch immediately. He asked me to let you know."

Lily looked around frantically, hoping to catch sight of Otto. "I promised Otto I'd help him with the papers for the sheriff. We're supposed to meet him this afternoon. Can you wait while I see if I can find him? Maybe we can postpone all this till tomorrow, and I can come with you."

Sam nodded. "Okay, Lily, but hurry."

Lily ran from one tent to the other until she located Otto in the food tent.

"Oh, Lily, it's good to have you here," he said as soon as he spotted her. "I was getting worried about our visit to the sheriff."

"Why?" she asked.

He lowered his voice. "I have counted my money, the money Bryce did not find. You know how I always hide some here and there?"

She nodded.

"Well, some of it is gone. That devil Bryce must have followed me when I hid it." He sounded so unhappy that Lily knew he was once again blaming himself.

"You couldn't have known," she told him reassuringly. "He had most of us fooled."

"But not you, eh, Lily? I remember all the times you came to tell me what was happening, and I did not listen. You are like Hilda, Lily, you read people. That is why I need you so much today. The sheriff will believe you. He won't try to cheat us. And now that I have discovered how little money I have, I can't afford to let him make us pay for everything. We'll go broke, Lily, and then what will happen to everyone?"

Lily swallowed her gasp. She hadn't fully realized how precarious the circus's situation had become. Instead of telling Otto that she couldn't go with him, she made plans to meet him in half an hour so they could see the sheriff together. Then, excusing herself, she ran back to Sam.

"I can't come today," she said near tears. "I tried to talk to Otto, but, Sam, he's so distraught. And the circus is in much worse shape than I thought. What should I do?"

"You do what you have to here. I'll ride back to the ranch. If there's a serious emergency, I'll be sure you get word. Otherwise, tomorrow's soon enough."

"Thank you, Sam. You don't know how much I appreciate all you've done."

"I'd better get out there, just in case I can do something more to help."

Lily nodded her agreement. "Tell Gray I'll be out as soon as I can."

As Sam walked away, Lily had the uncanny sensation that her life had suddenly changed again and nothing would be the same. She shivered and looked up at the sky to see if a cloud had covered the sun, but all was clear. There was no reason for her to have this uneasy feeling, yet it lingered, making her feel helpless and inexplicably sad.

She worried about Amelia the whole time she was with Otto in town and even during her evening performance. Her only solace was that Sam had not had to send anyone to see her. That meant Amelia's injuries, however serious, were not life-threatening. But it was a small solace, indeed.

That night she felt lonely and bereft. Her dreams were plagued with violent images, and she awoke feeling more tired than she had the night before. At least she no longer had to wait. There was nothing to prevent her from going out to the ranch right away. She borrowed a buggy from one of the other performers and headed out of the city, pushing her horses as hard as she dared.

ELEVEN

THE TRIP TO the Whispering Winds seemed longer than Lily remembered, probably because she was so anxious to get there, not only to see Amelia but also to make sure Gray was all right. His daughter was such a central part of his life, Lily wasn't sure how he would handle her being hurt.

When she pulled up in front of the ranch house, Mrs. Bellows came out to greet her. "Lily! How good to see you. Did you come all this way by yourself?" she asked.

"Yes, it's an easy ride."

"But I don't like your being alone, what with all these tales of rustlers. You can never be too careful out here."

"I know, but I was just so worried about Amelia. Is she all right? Is Gray inside with her?"

"No, he went out to the far pasture. Since Amelia was doing so well, he figured he could get some of the things done out here that he's been neglecting since he's been in town."

"Then Amelia's all right?"

"Right as rain. As a matter of fact, she's in the parlor working on some embroidery. Come on in. One of the men will take care of the buggy."

Lily followed the older woman into the house. Everything was just the way it had been the day she left. It seemed so long ago now. She was relieved to hear that

Amelia was up and around. Her nightmare visions had been filled with images of Amelia's pale, broken body lying on the bed, a grieving Gray by her side. That Amelia was well enough to be out of bed and Gray was gone from the house was a surprise.

"Amelia, honey, look who's come to visit," Mrs. Bellows called from the front hall.

"Who?" Amelia asked in an excited voice.

Lily smiled. At least the younger girl sounded like herself. Thank goodness the accident hadn't been serious. It seemed her worries had been for naught. A heaviness lifted and Lily smiled in anticipation, eager to see the girl's welcoming expression.

"Is it Cybil?" Amelia continued. "When she left last evening, she said she'd come back first thing this morning. There are so many things we have to talk about."

"No, it's not Mrs. Heath. It's Lily. Come all the way from town to see how you're doing."

So Cybil had been out yesterday, Lily thought. She certainly hadn't wasted any time in getting to the ranch and Gray. Lily wasn't surprised, but now was not the time to worry about Cybil; it was Amelia she'd come to see. She was stepping into the room as Amelia began to speak.

"Oh, tell her—" the younger girl started to say and then, seeing Lily, stopped in midsentence. "Why, hello, Lily," she continued, her tone cool and formally polite.

Lily wasn't sure what to make of it. Where was the eagerness she'd always associated with the younger girl? Maybe she was more injured than was apparent.

"I'm glad to see you up and about," she said, standing awkwardly just inside the door of the room.

"I'm feeling quite well."

"From what Sam said, I was afraid you were badly hurt."

233

"Oh, Sam just worries too much. As you can see, I'm fine."

"Why don't I get you both some coffee and cake?" Mrs. Bellows asked. It was obvious the older woman was as uncomfortable with the conversation as Lily.

When Amelia didn't say anything, Lily took over. "I could use a cake or two. As usual, I missed breakfast again this morning." She smiled over at Amelia, hoping to share the memory of their time at the circus food tent, but the young woman was busily stitching away, her gaze trained downward.

Mrs. Bellows hurried out to the kitchen to prepare the refreshments, and silence reigned in the large room, Amelia at one end, Lily at the other.

Something wasn't right. Amelia's tone and whole bearing were different from what they had been just days earlier. Slowly Lily walked across the room to the short sofa where the other girl was sitting. "So, what have you been doing out here all week?"

"Oh, this and that," Amelia said in a dismissing voice.

"Amelia, is something wrong?"

"Why would you think that?" she replied, her tone snippy.

"I thought we were friends. Now you're acting different."

"Different? I don't know what you mean."

"Why won't you look at me?" Lily implored. Suddenly a cold lump formed in her stomach. Did Amelia resent her relationship with Gray? Was that what this was all about?

The girl raised her eyes from her handiwork and looked directly at Lily. "There. Are you happy now?"

"Amelia!" Lily couldn't believe the younger woman's insolence.

"Well, what do you want me to say?"

"I guess I want you to tell me what you're really feeling." Though she said the words, she wasn't sure they were true, not if Amelia's detached expression was anything to go by.

"I've found that the circus isn't quite the right appearance I want to present to the world."

"Appearance?"

"Yes, you know—it's not how I want my friends to see me. Cybil says that women of breeding never associate with such . . ."

"Such what?" Lily was quite sure she knew what Cybil thought of people like herself, but she wondered if Amelia would have the nerve to tell her to her face.

"It doesn't matter. Suffice it to say, I've decided that in my own best interest I need to find more suitable activities for someone of my station in life."

"I see." Lily couldn't believe what she was hearing. "And what might these more suitable activities be?"

"Anything that will improve my mind and position me properly in society. I can't afford to have my reputation sullied, you know. A mistake at this point will have dire consequences for the rest of my life."

The more Amelia said, the worse Lily felt, but she couldn't keep from asking the next question. "How will you know what is a mistake and what isn't?"

"Cybil has graciously offered to guide me. She knows about these things. That's why she's so sought after as a hostess and a guest by all the quality people in Cheyenne. With her help I'll be sure to do all the right things."

"I'm sure she knows all the proper activities for a young woman entering the highest social circles." Much better than I ever would, Lily thought. She'd known that there would be obstacles when it came to loving Gray, but she had never thought Amelia's attitude would be one of them.

The silence that followed was broken only by the entrance of Mrs. Bellows with the coffee tray. "So, have you girls had a nice chat?"

"I'm feeling rather tired. I think I'll go up to my room and rest," Amelia said, pushing herself up off the sofa. She was walking toward the door, when Mrs. Bellows blurted out, "But I've just brought the coffee and cakes. And Lily has only gotten here."

The girl's steps faltered for an instant, but she didn't stop, and then she was gone.

"Well, I never!" Mrs. Bellows said in bewilderment. "She was feeling fine. I just don't understand it."

"You know how it is. Sometimes a headache comes on very suddenly."

Mrs. Bellows merely shook her head.

"Amelia and I didn't get much of a chance to talk about what happened. How did she hurt herself?"

"Seems she was trying to do some tricks on the back of that horse of hers."

Lily was aghast. "You mean on Cleo?" She'd warned Amelia not to try anything on the horse yet, and *never* when no one was around to watch and make sure everything went well.

"Yes, that's the one. Had us all worried nearly out of our minds. Mr. Benedict nearly took a piece out of her hide, and Miss Cybil backed him, too. Mind you, that was after he found out she wasn't badly hurt."

"I just don't understand why she would try such a thing," Lily said, a deep-seated anguish forming inside her. What if Amelia had been seriously hurt? Riding an un-trained horse was extremely dangerous, even for a profes-sional. There was no telling how it might react the first time it felt its rider leap off its back and then land with a thump.

"That's exactly what Miss Cybil said. She told Gray the girl needed more guidance in the womanly arts. I must say

I have to agree. I never took with a young lady like Miss Amelia fooling with such big, ill-tempered animals myself."

Lily found no comfort in Mrs. Bellows's words. After all, she "fooled" with horses all the time, although that fact seemed to have escaped Mrs. Bellows's attention at that moment. Nor did she find much to reassure her in hearing that Cybil Heath had managed to get out to the ranch yesterday while she herself was stuck in town.

"Mrs. Heath must have arrived right after Amelia's injury, then."

"Oh, no. Miss Cybil was here when it happened. She's been spending quite a few afternoons with Amelia. It's nice for the child to have company. She took it hard when her father sent her back to the ranch while he stayed in town. Here, let me pour you a cup of coffee. You must be thirsty after that long dusty drive out here."

Lily thanked her and sipped the coffee, but her mind was on what she had just learned. Cybil's interest in Amelia didn't surprise her, not if she thought it would be a way of getting close to Gray. The woman had made her intentions clear the night of her party. It was equally obvious that she was doing her best to undermine Amelia's friendship with Lily—with great success.

What worried Lily most, though, was Amelia's rebellion, first in doing the circus tricks in such a dangerous way and now in snubbing her the way she had. Maybe it had been a mistake to banish her to the ranch, especially since Gray stayed in town. Showing an interest in the circus was certainly one of the quickest ways to get Gray's attention from Amelia's perspective. Lily still remembered his anger on her first morning at the ranch, when Amelia had shown such interest in her life.

What must Gray be thinking, after learning his daughter risked serious injury by trying to do circus tricks? He must have thought his worst nightmare had come true. While losing Amelia to a wandering life would be painful, having her seriously injured or even killed by that life would cut him to his very soul. How she wished she could have been here to comfort him last night!

She lingered at the ranch, hoping either Amelia or Gray would return. Mrs. Bellows was eager to hear the gossip from town and the circus, and Lily was glad to oblige her. But as the time grew close for the start of the afternoon performance, Lily knew she had to leave.

"Tell Gray I'm sorry I missed him," she said as a ranch hand brought her buggy to the front of the house. She was deeply disappointed, but there was nothing she could do now.

"I'm sure he'll be sorry he missed you, too. But with all this thieving going on, he doesn't give himself a minute to do anything but hunt for who's behind it all. Why, we've hardly seen him at all this whole week, he's been so busy."

Lily nodded and climbed up onto the seat of her buggy. Mrs. Bellows's words only added to her confusion, for it seemed the other woman didn't realize how close Lily and Gray had become. She was not at all suspicious that he wasn't there to greet Lily and hadn't left her any message.

The uneasy feeling that had been plaguing her since the night before returned full force. Where was Gray? she wondered. And when would she see him again?

"This way," Gray said as he rode beside Sam. He turned his horse up a steep grade, and Sam followed suit, both horses slowing to a walk. "I hope this isn't just a wild-goose chase."

"No matter," Sam replied. "It's worth checking. How'd you hear about this place?"

"There was talk in town. A couple of men mentioned

seeing activity out here, and I was kind of surprised. Besides, we know those rustlers have to be hiding the stock somewhere. They sure haven't been turning up at anyone's ranch, or we'd have heard of it by now."

"So you figure they must be collecting the cattle out here?" Sam asked.

"It's a good place for it. There's water and enough grass for a short stay, especially at this time of year. And it's isolated. Almost no one comes out here. Once they have a small herd put together, they can take it out west with no one the wiser."

"That's true enough. I don't think I've ever been this far out."

The area was rocky and drier than most. The ground was hard and barren except in a few isolated areas where the lay of the land collected run-off water from the surrounding countryside. In those hollows scrub grasses grew in abundance around natural sinks that now served as water holes but would dry up before the end of the summer, leaving the entire landscape inhospitable.

"I wouldn't have dragged you along except that I'm not sure how many men might be out here. After what happened out at Glader Canyon with Jud, I didn't want to take any chances by coming alone," Gray said.

"Yeah, that was a nasty knock on the head, all right. They couldn't have known how badly injured he was or if he survived. I don't think they much cared."

"They beat up Hank, too. I just hope they haven't moved on already. It's past time they were caught."

Gray spurred his horse into a gallop on the downward side of the ridge they had just climbed. Sam followed him, but at this pace conversation was no longer possible. Still, Gray had more than enough worries to occupy his thoughts. Amelia's accident had shaken him deeply. He'd rushed to the ranch, pausing only to ask Sam to contact the doctor and let Lily know what had happened.

The time he'd spent riding out from town had been the worst in his life, until he stood beside Amelia's bed and saw for himself that she was all right. When she'd opened her eyes at the sound of her name and smiled up at him, he'd breathed his first unconstricted breath since Sam first told him of her plight.

Then Amelia had told him how she'd hurt herself and something within him died. She'd been practicing tricks Lily had shown her—*circus tricks*. If there was one thing he'd trusted Lily with more than anything else, it was to look out for his daughter. She knew what Amelia meant to him, knew how he felt about his daughter having anything to do with the circus. Yet she had gone behind his back and taught Amelia exactly those things he'd feared most when she'd first come to the ranch. He couldn't believe that she'd done it, not after all they'd been to each other. He thought she understood his pain and fear, both for himself and his daughter, but obviously she didn't, and now he had nothing.

Feelings of betrayal raged through him, betrayal by the one woman he'd thought he could trust with his very soul. How could he have been so wrong? How could his judgment have been so faulty? It seemed his marriage to Felicia had taught him nothing about the fickleness of women.

Two nights ago he'd been ready to give Lily everything. Their lovemaking had been so rare, so intoxicating, he'd thought nothing could ever come between them. Now the pain of her betrayal stabbed at him like a knife.

He glanced over at Sam, seeking some distraction to take his mind off Lily, when suddenly he heard a horse whinny. Sam looked at him, and they both took off in the direction of the sound. This might be just the break they'd been seeking—a chance to get close enough to the rustlers to catch them.

Within seconds they crested a rise and looked down on a small herd of cattle and the figures of two men. As they watched, a shot rang out and one of the men fell to the ground, then the other bent over him.

"Ain't that Hank Farrell?" Sam asked in surprise.

"Sure looks like it." They kicked the sides of their horses and raced toward the two men at a gallop. What the hell was Hank doing out here? Gray wondered. He'd thought his friend had been laid up at his ranch.

"Gray! Am I happy to see you!" Hank called out as the two riders drew close.

"What the hell happened?" Gray asked as he and Sam dismounted and came to stand over the body lying at Hank's feet. Sam leaned down and turned the man over. He looked up at Gray and shook his head. The man was dead, a bullet hole in the middle of his chest. His gun lay on the ground near him.

"I'm not sure . . . what happened," Hank answered, rubbing his left arm cradled by his side, the one injured by the rustlers.

"I guess you heard some of the same rumors I did," Gray said, looking around, but he couldn't see anyone else in the area. This wasn't a place you'd expect to find someone taking in the scenery.

"What rum— Oh, yeah, the rumors," Hank answered in a somewhat dazed voice.

Gray looked at him more closely. Hank was acting strangely, but then he'd just shot a man. "How'd you hear about this place?"

"Why . . . at the club. That's where you heard about it, right?"

"Right," Gray confirmed, then looked down at the dead man. "Do either of you know him?"

Both Sam and Hank shook their heads.

"But he knew what he was doin'," Hank said. "He was keeping watch over these cows, and I know some of their brands."

Gray looked over at the herd and recognized one or two of the brands on the rumps of the animals himself. "Do you remember who was talking about this at the club?"

"Don't rightly recall. But I thought it couldn't hurt to check it out. I just came by to see if there was more to the story than just rumor. I've a stake in gettin' these guys, you know." He rubbed his sore arm more vigorously.

"You were damn lucky not to get yourself killed. Didn't you think about bringing someone with you?"

"I didn't expect to find anything. Hell, I thought I was makin' the trip for nothin' and didn't want to look like a complete fool in case I was wrong. This was all just a long shot."

"Dammit, Hank. You're in no condition to try this by yourself."

Hank stopped rubbing his shoulder and said, "After I lost your cattle, I couldn't let any lead slip by. I had to try to do somethin'. After all, it was my idea to graze your bulls on my land."

Gray nodded, understanding that Hank felt responsible for losing his animals. In Hank's shoes he might have done the same thing, but with the man's injuries this excursion didn't make sense. Nor did this shooting. Gray looked around but could see nothing except a small herd of cows and a secluded valley. "What happened exactly?"

"I came up real quiet like, just in case, so this guy didn't hear me until I was almost on top of him. Unfortunately, at the last minute he turned, and when he drew on me, I couldn't do anything but shoot to save myself."

"I take it he didn't say anything?"

"Wasn't any chance. Hell, he turned on me before I knew what was happenin'."

Gray took off his Stetson and ran a hand through his hair. "Let's get him up on his horse and take him into town," he said to Sam. "Someone might recognize him. Until then there's nothing more we can do. We'll send a couple of hands out to keep an eye on the cattle and watch for the rustlers in case they return."

"Do you want me to stay, boss?" Sam asked.

"Not on your own. They seem to be a pretty violent bunch. The cattle will be fine, and I doubt they'll go anywhere on their own. This land's too inhospitable."

"I think I'll head back into town with you and drop in on the club," Hank said. "Maybe I can learn somethin' else."

"Just don't go off on your own again. If you learn anything, take someone with you."

"I've learned my lesson," Hank returned with a nervous laugh.

They mounted up and headed for town, leading the horse that carried the body of the slain rustler.

When they reached Cheyenne, they dropped the body off at the sheriff's office, and then Hank and Gray headed over to the Cattlemen's Club to grab a bite of lunch. Sam had gone back to the ranch to organize a group of men to stand guard over the cattle.

Gray and Hank were both quiet as they decided what they'd have to eat, each lost in his own thoughts.

"How're things with your pretty lady?" Hank asked after they'd ordered their lunches. The club was pretty empty for a Saturday so they sat alone.

"We're not seeing each other anymore," Gray said, and realized it was true. He had no plans to see Lily again, other than to tell her his decision. His fear for his daughter outweighed his own need for happiness. He couldn't risk losing Amelia, and if the only way he could stop it was never to see Lily again, then that's the way it would have to be. Besides, the sting of her betrayal still resonated within him.

"What happened?" Hank asked.

Even though Hank was one of his closest friends, Gray didn't want to talk about it. Everything was still too fresh in his mind. "I decided it was for the best, that's all. Besides, this rustling is taking its toll. I don't have time for other things now."

"Maybe the sheriff will turn up somethin' on the fellow we brought in."

"I wouldn't count on it. His pockets were empty, and there was nothing about him of note. Besides, he's just one of the hired guns. He might not even have had contact with the leader of the bunch."

Gray was just about to ask Hank if he could remember anything else about the shooting when Dixon and Prescott walked in.

"I say, old man, you're looking a bit under the weather," Prescott began, clapping Hank on the shoulder.

"Didn't you hear?" Dixon asked as he looked from Hank to Prescott.

"Hear what?"

"Why, Hank's had a run-in with the rustlers."

"Not just one," Gray added, looking closely at the two new arrivals. Every man was a suspect, he now felt, and he didn't want to miss any of their reactions.

"What are you saying?" Dixon asked and then turned to Hank. "Have you had another run-in with them?"

"'Fraid so. Only this time they got the worst of it." Hank's tone was almost boastful as he described what had transpired at the rustlers' hideaway.

"That's a stroke of luck—luck that you weren't hurt,

that is," Prescott said as he listened to the story with wide-eyed amazement.

"Damn right, he was lucky. He could have been the one who came home slung over the back of a horse, instead."

"How'd you hear about this place?" Prescott asked.

"Why, here at the club. Ain't that right, Gray?"

"At the club!" Dixon exploded. "Again? Dammit! I don't like it at all that this information seems to be coming out of this club. You hear it here, too, Gray?"

"This is where I traced it back to. One of my men heard about it and brought me the information."

"Did he say who it came from?" Hank asked.

"Didn't remember who told him, only that some men had been out that way and there was speculation that maybe the cows were being stashed there until they could be moved out."

"I think we'd better have another meeting. Someone else might have heard something, too." Dixon turned to Hank. "Who'd you say you heard it from?"

"It was you, wasn't it, Prescott?"

"What?" the Englishman asked in surprise.

"Weren't you the one who told me about the hiding place?"

"Certainly not." His voice was full of indignation that Hank would even think of such a thing. He drew himself up to his full six feet. "I haven't even seen you since you met up with the rustlers the first time."

"I could've sworn it was you, but if you say it wasn't . . ."

Prescott was about to protest further when Dixon suggested they set a date for another meeting and not too far into the future.

Gray looked from Hank to Prescott. His hand came up and felt the gold sleeve link still in his pocket. He felt sure it was connected to all this in some way. He was close to getting to the bottom of this mystery; he could feel it in the tension in this room. Someone here knew more than he was telling.

Each time Lily rode around the ring, she searched the section where Gray usually sat, hoping to catch a glimpse of him, but she was having no luck. If she didn't pay more attention to her act, she was going to end up on her bottom on the hard ground of the ring.

She'd taken special care tonight when she'd dressed for her performance. Her costume was one of the new ones Iola had made, a pale green that Elena said suited her perfectly. The filmy, flowing material hugged her body like a second skin, and the soft color complemented the fiery wildness of her hair.

The crowd also seemed to approve, giving her rousing applause as she finished each of her tricks. So far she had done the easier parts of her repertoire: standing on Galahad's back as the horse cantered around the circus ring; dropping to her knees and then jumping up again, balancing on one foot and then the other; and juggling balls as the horse set his pace in a controlled canter. Now she knew she would have to sharpen her concentration, as the somersaults required her complete attention.

The backward somersault looked very complicated, but it was actually one of the easier movements because she started facing forward and landed facing forward, able to see exactly where to place her feet. The forward somersault was much harder to perform, because she landed blind, having to trust Galahad to be where she expected at the right moment. For both somersaults, her starting position on the horse was extremely important. If she started too far back, she could miss the animal entirely on her landing; too far forward and she might land on the horse's neck and topple off. In both instances the ground would be her final resting place, with the risk of injury to herself if not her mount.

Lily positioned herself carefully, and Galahad evened out his steps as he cantered around the ring. Her somersaults went without a hitch. Then two clowns came out carrying a four-foot-wide banner and placed themselves on either side of the ring, each holding one end of the banner so that it lay flat between their two stations.

On her first pass Lily ducked down and allowed the blue banner to pass over her head. The second time around she jumped over it, landing flawlessly on the horse's back. The crowd roared its approval. On the third pass she performed a backward somersault, clearing the cloth banner in perfect form as the crowd roared again, clamoring for more.

If Lancelot had been back to health, she would have had him jump through a blazing ring. That trick that always brought the house down. But Galahad was skittish around the flames, so instead the clowns came out with four paper-covered rings holding them aloft around the ring.

She jumped, bursting through the first ring, and landed on Galahad's back while the crowd shouted its approval. After each succeeding leap, the applause grew louder until she exploded through the last hoop and everyone surged to their feet, stomping and yelling their approval. She took her bow, riding the circle on the back of her horse, but the whole time her eyes were searching the faces in the dimly lit seats. None was Gray's.

The band played her closing music, and with one last seeking glance, she rode the horse through the opening in the ring and out of the tent. After sliding down from Galahad's back, she led him over to the tent that housed the animals. When she'd seen to all his needs, she walked over to Lancelot and checked to make sure he was still doing well.

She had just started patting Lancelot's nose when Merlin came over and butted her, not hard enough to hurt, only firmly enough to remind her he was there. Smiling, she started to push him away as she'd done so often in the past, but the sight of him brought Gray to mind.

Suddenly she was remembering the two of them together as they groomed her horses and laughed over Merlin's antics. Those mornings were the best she'd ever spent, preceded by the most wonderful nights; nights filled with passion and tenderness, ardor and gentleness. When she closed her eyes, she could imagine Gray beside her again, the touch of his hand on hers, his scent surrounding her, familiar and unique. Memories flooded her.

She had found something with Gray that no one else had ever given her: a love that went beyond anything she'd ever imagined. They could almost read each other's thoughts, instinctively knowing exactly what the other needed and wanted. More than anything they understood each others inner needs, needs that weren't met with a touch or a smile but that came from somewhere deeper as if they were two halves of a perfect whole.

Lily opened her eyes, half expecting Gray to be there simply because she needed him so much. But she was alone. A chill passed through her. Where could he be? And why had he made no attempt to contact her? Surely by now he knew she'd been out to see Amelia, didn't he? And then it came to her.

Gray must blame her for what happened to Amelia. After all, she'd been the one who had taught Amelia circus tricks, and behind his back, too, even though she'd never allowed Amelia to do anything on the horse. But Gray couldn't know that. She'd knowingly joined Amelia in the conspiracy of silence when she should have anticipated something like this happening.

Her eyes filled with tears, and one escaped to spill down

her cheek. She laid her head against Lancelot's neck, taking comfort from his large, warm presence, even though he was a poor substitute for what she really wanted. Even Merlin seemed to sense her heartbreak, for instead of butting her away, as was his habit, he nuzzled his forehead against her leg.

"Lily? Are you 'ere?" she heard Elena call out over the whinnying horses and the various growls and snorts of the other animals.

Wiping her eyes, Lily took a deep breath and stepped out into the aisle. Thinking the worst would not help her. She would have to meet Gray face to face and see where she stood. In the meantime she couldn't stay in hiding. "I'm over here," she called back.

"Oh, I am so 'appy to find you. What I tell you, you won't believe." Elena's voice was high-pitched with nervous excitement.

"What's happened?" Lily asked warily. So much had gone wrong lately, Lily already expected the worst.

"You will not like to 'ear it. This day I 'ave received three telegrams."

"Three telegrams?"

"Oh, my English. She is as poor as Roberto's. We, Roberto and I, 'ave three telegrams. You know, for The Santellis."

Elena's point was finally sinking in. The telegrams had to do with their act. "And what did the telegrams say?"

"Zey knew we would look for ze new job and zey 'ave place for us."

She should have guessed. Word was out already about Bryce and what he had done, and like vultures, the other circuses were wasting no time in trying to strip Bruner's circus of its top acts. She'd hoped they'd have more time. In another week or two Otto would be in a better position to handle a siege on his most prominent performers.

Though everyone had agreed to go without their salaries this week, she wasn't sure how strong their commitment to Otto would be in the face of these enticing offers.

"And?" Lily was almost afraid of Elena's answer. With a baby on the way, she and Roberto couldn't afford to be without money or risk keeping a job with a circus in trouble.

"Of course we say no," Elena said, shaking her head. "We love you and Otto very much. You are my excellent friend, no?"

"Best friend," Lily automatically corrected.

"*Oui*, best friend and you must be with us when our *enfant* comes to zis world," Elena said, putting her arm through Lily's. "Come, we go to our wagon and 'ave something warm to drink. It is much cold out 'ere. Ze 'orses, zey are all right?"

"Yes, they're fine," she replied as she followed Elena to her wagon, hurrying to escape the cool night air. The Santellis' wagon was bigger than most, roughly twice as long as Lily's. Half of it had been converted into a parlor that rivaled the rooms in some of the best homes in Cheyenne and befitted the Santellis' status as one of the star attractions of Bruner's.

Elena had worked hard to get the wagon decorated perfectly. Since both she and Roberto were what she considered "foreigners," it was important that their home be truly American. When they were doing the eastern circuit, Elena had bought the finest furnishings from the best manufacturers at each stop on the tour, including two overstuffed chairs, a sofa, various shelves filled with knickknacks, and a Persian carpet. Lily always felt a little overwhelmed by the sheer magnitude of the furnishings, not to mention the vibrant colors. Even the windows were elaborate, each covered with delicately woven lace curtains overlaid with the finest crushed velvet. The overall effect was in keeping with the opulent homes Elena was trying to copy.

When Elena and Lily entered, the two chairs were occupied, one by Roberto and the other by someone neither of the women had ever seen before. The men rose from their seats when the ladies entered.

"Roberto, we 'ave guests?"

"*Sì*, this is Bernard Sawyer. This is my wife, Elena Santelli."

"*Monsieur,*" Elena said, nodding her head. "May I introduce my *best* friend, Lily Avenel."

"Mrs. Santelli. Ma'am," Mr. Sawyer said, then added, "You wouldn't be the same Lily that has the equestrian act?"

Lily nodded her head.

"Then I'm mighty pleased to meet you," he said with a new enthusiasm.

"Signore Sawyer is with Cooper's Circus. You know?" Roberto looked over at Elena and Lily.

"*Mais oui*, ze Circus of Cooper is world famous." Elena looked over at Lily and raised her eyebrow.

"What brings you out here, Mr. Sawyer?" Lily asked, though she knew what he wanted. He'd come to raid, to take the best Bruner's had to offer and leave before anyone could stop him.

"Mr. Santelli and I were just talking business." The sentence implied it was none of hers.

Lily could see Elena's face and knew Bernard Sawyer had said the one thing that would set her friend off. Elena and Roberto shared everything equally, the work and the business, particularly the business, and she was very proud of that fact.

"Per'aps you don't understand, Monsieur Sawyer, but Roberto and I share all the decisions of business."

"I figured it won't hurt to start the discussion and let your husband know some of the basics."

"And what are ze 'basics,' as you call zem, Monsieur Sawyer?"

"I have an offer from Mr. Cooper himself. For all of you." His gaze took in Lily as well as the two Santellis. He then went on to describe the terms Cooper was ready to meet.

"Your offer is very, 'ow you say, interesting, and we will certainly talk between us. And you, Lily?"

"I agree. I have one question, though. Why did Mr. Cooper pick this particular time to make these offers?"

Sawyer shifted from one foot to the other, looking uncomfortable. "Well, to tell the truth, Mason said I should come out here and talk with you. He put word out at the beginning of the week you might be looking for new jobs."

So Bryce was behind this. It didn't surprise her. "Why did he think we'd leave Bruner's?"

"Said Bruner was having trouble. That's all."

"The only trouble Otto had was Bryce Mason," Lily stormed, suddenly not caring whether she got any more information from the man or not.

"Hey, I'm sorry. I didn't know. Cooper's didn't have anything to do with this. I only got my information third-hand. Graham's put in an offer to buy Bruner's a while ago. Mason's been working with them since. He's the one who said there were problems here, not me."

"Well, tell your friend at Graham's Circus that we're doing fine and most of the acts are staying. Those that aren't, we'll tell them who they can go and see."

"Don't bother sending them to us. We're only interested in very special acts. We have enough talent and don't need any more. Sorry to have wasted your time—and mine," Sawyer said as he put on his hat and stomped out the door.

Lily didn't even wait for the door to shut behind him. "Did you hear that? I can't believe it." She closed her eyes in frustration. "Why didn't Otto ever mention that Graham's had wanted to buy him out? If we'd known that, we might have been suspicious of Bryce from the start."

"You can't blame yourself, Lily," Elena said. "You tried your best."

"Yes, but if I had known what was going on, I would have been able to convince Otto not to trust Bryce so much."

"Ah, Lily, you forget. Otto, he know about Graham's. He could 'ave stop Mason."

"I guess you're right." She sighed. "At least now I understand why Bryce went to such lengths to cause the circus trouble, arguing with our paying customers and hiring all those pickpockets and cheaters."

"And don't forget our costumes," Elena put in.

"He must have been disappointed when we hired Iola and put this circus back on its feet. It sounds like he had the competition all lined up in Cheyenne to take over when Otto gave up. It's ironic that, if anything, his actions helped pull Otto out of his slump and got him back on his feet."

"*Oui*, and Madame Parsons, too." Elena had a twinkle in her eye as she put her arm around her husband. He responded immediately, hugging her close.

"Yes, I've noticed," Lily admitted. Cheyenne had certainly yielded its share of romance. She wondered if Otto was faring better in his than she was. Dun was right to warn her back on the ranch: Circus folk did best if they stuck to their own. Look at Elena and Roberto. They traveled together, worked together, and now were about to embark on the greatest adventure of all—having a baby. Seeing the loving look that passed between them was almost too much for Lily. She said her good-byes and hurried out.

"Do not worry much, Lily," Roberto called out after her. "Time fixes everything. You will see."

She wished she could believe him. And maybe she would have if Gray had been waiting for her at her wagon. But as she drew close, she saw it looked dark and deserted, no light burning in the small window to tell her he had come.

Slowly she stepped up into the wagon and pulled the door shut behind her. With practiced movements she lit the candle sitting beside the door and carried it to her bedstead. She was so tired she wasn't sure she had the energy to undress.

Gray's continuing absence spoke volumes, especially as he'd sent no message. He must, indeed, blame her for Amelia's accident, and while the girl hadn't been seriously injured this time, luck had played a major role. Even now Lily felt a chill run down her spine at the thought of what might have happened. How much worse Gray must feel every time he thought about it!

Shivering, she wrapped herself in her bedclothes. Without Gray her heart felt empty, her soul lost, but she knew she would have to go on. She'd done it before, when she and Rosemary had first come to the circus. Then, as now, she'd thought nothing would remove the memories. But memories dim, and she could only hope her memories of Gray would fade. She closed her eyes and remembered him as he'd been two nights ago. She'd come back from her performance and waited up for him, but to no avail.

When midnight came, Lily undressed and crawled into her narrow bed. Her worry about Gray kept her awake at first. But then she fell asleep, and the dreams came. The scenes were so vivid, she thought they were real, but she had no control over what was happening. All she could do was watch and wait. She saw the door opening and a figure fill the doorway.

"Who are you?" she called out, but there was no answer.

The figure moved across the narrow width of the cabin and stopped beside her bed. She felt the covers lift from her body and found she could not pull them back. A hand came out of the darkness and began opening her nightdress, starting at its neck and working down, one button at a time. The cool night air invaded the warmth of her skin, sending tingles of excitement through her. She tried to force her gaze from the hand and look into the face beyond it, but could not. It was as if she were frozen but knew and felt everything.

The hand stopped before the buttons were completely undone. With just the slightest motion, the fingers slid beneath the material of her nightdress and touched her skin. Her breath quickened. The fingers rotated ever so slowly in small circles across the slight rise of her breast, but went no further. Desire built steadily within her. The mere absence of movement made her crave more. Her body gyrated in urgent question, seeking something she could not find.

She knew the touch, yet couldn't identify it. She knew what would come next, but was surprised when it happened. Then the fingers covered the tip of her breast, and she heard his quick intake of breath. He took her nipple between his finger and thumb and rolled it to hardness before passing over to the other breast and doing the same.

The dream was becoming more real. Was she asleep or awake? It no longer mattered, for in one quick movement her nightdress was gone and she lay bare before him, wanting only to feel his body covering hers. His hands caressed her from shoulder to calf and back. Her limbs trembled with need, shifting to allow him entrance to the center of her desire.

And then the spell had broken and she'd opened her eyes. It had been Gray, her lover, her love, and they'd spent the rest of the night entwined in each other's arms, reality and dream merging in a kaleidoscope of color and magic.

Lily came awake with a start. Last time she'd awakened and found Gray; this time she had awakened to emptiness and loss. Tonight had been only dream, a dream of things past. With a wrenching cry, she turned over in her bed and buried her face in her pillow.

TWELVE

GRAY STOOD ON the corner, pulled his watch from his pocket, and checked the time. It was just past eleven, but Cybil was always late. He should have realized that and not worried so much about being on time. If he had, he might have gotten to see Lily after all. Instead, he'd only been able to leave a message for her with Dun.

The last three days had been some of the longest in his life. He had felt trapped between his past and the future. When Amelia had first injured herself performing circus tricks, his first reaction had been to blame Lily's world, but having had time to reflect, he realized how unfair he'd been. More than that, the hours had dragged, empty and dark even on the sunniest day. The rest of his life would be like that if Lily left.

He shuddered at the thought. In a short time Lily had changed his life, breaking through barriers he'd forgotten were there, filling his days with light and hope, daring him to dream again. Now that he had banished her from his world, he found he couldn't resurrect his barriers. Nothing seemed worthwhile without Lily in his life, sharing his dreams and challenging him to make new ones. The only question was what could he offer her to make her want to stay—and was it even fair of him to ask?

Nothing could be resolved until he and Lily talked. After his experience with Felicia, he knew the disastrous consequences of two people trying to blend lives when they had different dreams. Somehow he had to find a way to satisfy both their needs. If he pressured Lily into a role she neither wanted nor desired, their love would be doomed.

He looked at his watch again and cursed silently. He wanted to be with Lily, to apologize for disappearing from her life and convince her they could work things out. He didn't have much time; in a couple of days the circus would be leaving town. He had just decided to leave when he saw Cybil rushing up the opposite sidewalk. He crossed the street and hurried up the block to meet her.

"I'm sorry I'm late," Cybil offered in a frazzled voice, "but I couldn't find anyone to take care of the children."

"I don't understand why we couldn't just meet at your house."

"I thought it would seem less conspicuous if we met like this."

"What do you mean, less conspicuous?"

"You know, more like we just happened to run into each other by chance."

Gray looked closely at Cybil and noticed she was pale beneath the rouge she'd used on her cheeks. "What's wrong?"

Cybil looked to her right and left, then moved in closer to Gray and whispered in a confidential manner, "There's a problem."

Something in Cybil's voice told him this wasn't one of her frivolous and nonsensical emergencies.

"With Prescott?" Gray knew as soon as he asked the question that he was right. He'd had a niggling suspicion about the man ever since he and Hank had gone to the club on Saturday and he'd realized the sleeve link he'd found out on the range belonged to the Englishman.

"How did you know?"

"I thought there might be a problem last time I spoke with him."

For a moment Cybil looked puzzled. "Oh, no, I'm sure this is about something that came up very recently. Only yesterday Prescott was fine. It wasn't until this morning that he insisted I come talk with you."

"Did Prescott tell you what the problem was?" Gray felt sure Prescott would have kept this kind of business from Cybil and wasn't surprised when she was puzzled by his claim to be privy to Prescott's problem.

"No, he said it would be best if I knew nothing about any of this. I pleaded with him to let me help, but nothing I said would sway him. I'm really worried, Gray." Cybil placed her hand on his arm to emphasize her distress.

Gray patted her hand and then looked around. He had the feeling someone was watching him. Cybil had thought it a good place to "run into each other." He peered into the window of the shop behind them, but could see nothing because of the sun's glare reflecting off the glass.

"Everything will be all right," he said to reassure Cybil. "I'll do everything I can to help."

"Thank you. I know Prescott will appreciate it. He said if you agreed, he wanted to make plans to meet with you."

"I can go over to the house right now," Gray offered.

"No," she said in some alarm. "He says it has to be in secret. That's why I had to meet you here on the street. He doesn't want anyone to know that we're talking with you."

Gray thought for a moment. Everything Cybil was saying helped strengthen his notion that Prescott was involved in the rustling. "Where does he want to meet, then?"

"Out at the ranch. He thought that would be the last place people would look for him."

Gray would have laughed at the other man's reasoning if this didn't appear to be so serious. Everyone knew Prescott didn't go out to his ranch unless he absolutely had to.

The Englishman was not a rancher by choice. "Is he out there now?"

Cybil shook her head. "He wants you to meet him tomorrow. He says there's something he has to do today, and if you could meet him at the ranch about noontime . . ."

Cybil's voice trailed off and she looked at him with such hope in her eyes, he couldn't very well tell her this was the most ridiculous idea he'd ever heard. If Prescott had a problem, why was he dithering so? Why all the secrecy? But Gray had no choice but to agree to Prescott's plan, since the man himself wasn't around to discuss it.

"I'll be there."

"Thank you. Pres has been in some scrapes before, but I think this one may be really dangerous. I've never seen him quite this frightened. He's insisted that the children and I come out to the ranch with him. He says he doesn't want us staying in town by ourselves. We're leaving as soon as I get home."

It would seem that Prescott was certainly up to his neck in trouble. If Gray was right in what he suspected about the rustling, Prescott had a lot of explaining to do. Gray just wondered what Prescott thought he could do.

"Please don't tell anyone about this. Prescott was adamant about that. He said *no one* else should know you're going to see him."

"Don't worry. I'll make sure the wrong people don't find out. Now, let me walk you home," Gray said, putting his hand under her elbow and starting to walk down the plank sidewalk.

Cybil complied, but with a restriction. "Only as far as Converse and Warren's, though. Prescott said it was important for us not to be seen together."

Gray couldn't understand Prescott's need for such secrecy unless he was involved with someone else and that other person didn't know what he was planning to do.

Gray left Cybil by the dry goods store and headed back to his house to get his horse. He'd hoped to get back over and see Lily before heading out to the ranch, but now it didn't look as if that would happen. Since the circus wasn't leaving for another two days, he had time. As soon as he had this mess with Prescott cleared up, he'd be by her side. Filled with impatience, he headed for the Cattlemen's Club to see Hank, eager to get this business behind him so he could find Lily and convince her to stay.

When Lily had arrived at Iola's dress shop, the street was deserted. She had only come at the older woman's insistence, sure that Elena had told her about Gray's absence and that she was trying to cheer her up with thoughts of something new. Lily only wished it were that simple.

Sunday and Monday had come and gone, and she'd waited for Gray in vain. Today she had finally decided her conclusions had been correct and he blamed her for Amelia's accident. Now it seemed he didn't want to see her at all, not even to say good-bye.

Thinking back, she wondered if there hadn't been signs all along that their relationship wasn't as strong as she'd thought. Except for the one evening at Cybil's party, he'd never again introduced her to any of his friends. They'd shared a life on the circus grounds, but not beyond. He'd never taken her to his club for dinner, though she knew that it was a popular place to dine and meet with friends. Had it been at his insistence or hers that they work with the horses, that they hurry off to her wagon whenever they had some time alone together? Until this moment she'd never questioned his actions or his motives. Now the veil of secrecy over their relationship seemed ominous.

He hadn't even told his best friend about their relationship. For if Hank Farrell had known his best friend was interested in a certain woman, he would've treated her with respect, not tried to claim her the first chance he got. The only thread of hope that still ran through her was that Gray would have enough honor and respect to tell her he didn't want to see her again. Iola interrupted her thoughts as she opened the door of the shop.

"Lily, my dear! I'm so glad you could make it," Iola greeted her as she entered the shop.

"It's really nice of you to let me have the material for my dress at your cost," Lily said, smiling at the older woman, unable to tell her she'd wanted the dress when she'd thought she and Gray would be having a life together.

"I have some very nice satins over here near the window. Come and see what you think."

Lily walked over to a table filled with bolts of cloth. It would be hard to choose from the bright array, and she wasn't sure these were the colors that suited her at the moment. A dark brown or black might be more consistent with her mood.

"Do you have any color or fabric in mind?" Iola asked.

"I really hadn't thought . . ." Lily's voice trailed off as she caught sight of two people talking in front of the shop. Her heart stopped and then started again with a jerk. She felt a pain so acute it nearly doubled her over. Just outside the window of Iola's shop stood Gray and Cybil immersed in conversation. She stepped back away from the window, not wanting to be seen while she fought to retain her composure.

"Don't you see anything you like?" Iola asked, not realizing what had pulled Lily away from the table.

"I'm not sure."

"Well, I have lots more in the back. Wait and I'll bring some out. The light is better out here than in the storeroom. I'll only be a moment."

She left the main room, but Lily was oblivious; all her attention was centered on the couple outside. While she couldn't hear what they were saying, she could guess their conversation was of a personal nature by the way they stood, heads close together as they shared intimacies. She wanted to look away because seeing them together caused her so much pain, but she found she couldn't.

She hadn't seen Gray in four days and just the sight of him filled her with both gladness and despair. The wind tousled his dark hair, and he lifted a hand to brush it back. It was a gesture she'd seen so many times, found so endearing. An ache started at her center, and she placed her hand over her heart as if she could keep it from shattering into a thousand pieces. Seeing Gray with Cybil hurt her as she had never been hurt before. She wanted to be in Cybil's place, with her hand on Gray's arm. She wanted Gray to look at her the way he was looking at Cybil, with caring and gentle concern in his eyes.

Gray patted Cybil's hand and leaned closer toward her as if he were trying to catch her slightest word. Hadn't Cybil warned her this would happen? Foolishly Lily had chosen not to believe her. Lily remembered well the scene at Cybil's party when the other woman had cornered her and hinted very strongly that while Gray might dally with someone new, he always came back to Cybil. Lily wouldn't be the first, nor would she be the last, Cybil had warned in that haughty way she had. At the time Lily had felt almost sorry for the older woman. To Lily she had seemed desperate, clinging to a relationship that had ended.

Now, looking at the couple outside the window, Lily felt like the desperate one. Gray and Cybil seemed made for each other. Cybil was golden as the sun, tall and willowy, a perfect foil for Gray's rugged, dark looks. No one seeing them together could ever imagine a better match.

Lily's dreams faded away like daylight fading into night, and that was how she felt—as if all the light had been taken from her life and there was nothing left but a terrible, never-ending darkness. Tears filled her eyes, and through a shimmery haze she watched Gray and Cybil move off across the street. She wouldn't cry, she told herself. She'd gone through harder things and never cried before. Besides, she couldn't allow Iola to see her in such a state. She had some pride.

"Look here, Lily. Don't you think these are lovely?" Iola asked, plopping several bolts on the table.

Lily forced herself to turn her attention to the collection before her and forget what she'd seen outside the window.

"What do you think about this green satin?" Iola continued. Lily nodded, not really seeing the fabric. "With your red hair, this should be perfect. Do you see a matching velvet?" Iola asked as she pulled a length of material off the bolt and draped it over Lily's shoulder. "Mmmm, that is nice. Let's see, what kinds of trim do I have?"

Iola was clearly in her element, and Lily surrendered to her skills, letting her make most of the decisions. After much consideration, the materials were picked. Lily was thankful that Iola already had her measurements so she wouldn't have to spend more time at the dress shop.

After hurriedly giving her thanks, she made her way back to the circus. When she reached the circus grounds, she breathed a sigh of relief, happy not to have met anyone on her way home. If she had run into Cybil and Gray, she wouldn't have known what to say.

She'd barely had time to remove her hat when a knock sounded on her door. The temptation was great to let her visitor think she wasn't home, but she knew that in all likelihood whoever was at her door also knew she was inside.

"I hope I'm not disturbing you," Dun said when she reluctantly opened the door.

"Of course not," she said, but there wasn't much conviction in her voice.

"Are you all right?" Dun asked, eyeing her closely.

"I'm fine. Like everyone else, I'm just tired. Doing three shows a day instead of two takes its toll."

Dun nodded his head in agreement. "Even with my ribs feeling better, the third show is a strain, but it's been worth it."

"Oh?"

"I've just spoken with Otto, and we've made enough money with the extra shows to head out to Denver sooner than we thought. First thing tomorrow we'll be pulling down the canvas and packing up. No need to stay until Thursday."

The news should have cheered Lily. Once she was out of Cheyenne, she could begin to forget about Gray and the precious time they had shared. But inside her heart was a small voice that cried out at the pain of never seeing Gray again, of knowing there was no longer any hope that he'd suddenly show up and say that his absence the past few days had all been a mistake.

"Oh," Dun added, "I almost forgot the reason I came by. Gray was here earlier."

"Gray? Here?" Lily couldn't believe it. She felt as if one of her secret wishes had come true.

"About two hours ago, I'd say. I tried to get you, but you were nowhere to be found."

"I'd gone to town and stopped in at Iola's shop to pick out some material for a dress she said she'd make me. Did he say what he wanted?" Her heart leapt, anxious and excited.

"Only that he needed to see you. He seemed pretty anxious to find you."

She couldn't allow herself to hope. Not after all she had seen today. But one tiny place in both her head and her heart refused to give up hope and pounced on Dun's words as if they were the gospel offering salvation to the barbarians.

"Did he say when he'd be back?"

"No. Only that he'd see you later this afternoon."

Lily knew she should consider that he might be coming just to say good-bye, that after what had happened with Amelia, he didn't see them having a future together, but the last bit of her dream refused to fade away.

"Do you need any help getting your things packed?"

Dun's question brought her out of her thoughts. "No, thank you. The main thing I want to make sure of is that Lancelot is loaded with both Galahad and Merlin. I don't want them separated. Even though Lancelot seems much better, there's no sense taking any chances."

"I'll tell Gustav to make sure they're all put together. If you're sure I can't help you, I'll see if Otto needs me for anything."

"Watch out for your ribs."

"I will. It'll be hard enough traveling a hundred miles on the seat of a bouncing wagon without any additional problems."

Dun took off to find Otto, and Lily went into her wagon to begin packing things away so they wouldn't fall in a jumble if the roads got rough. Her thoughts churned as she went through a routine so familiar it no longer required her attention. Why had Gray come? When would he return? Why had he been with Cybil? Round and round her thoughts spun, but no answers came to her. All she could do was wait.

Despite the fatigue of the performers, the afternoon performance went smoothly, maybe because they knew they were reaching the end of this grueling schedule.

Only one more show remained, the one scheduled for this evening, and then they would move on. At this time of day Lily missed Gray the most, for this was when he had come out to meet her whenever he had the time. Would he come out today? she wondered, afraid to hope too much.

She settled Galahad and gave him an extra portion of oats. He'd done a good job today and deserved a rest before the evening show. She had just finished wiping him down when she heard her name called from the front of the tent.

For a brief moment she thought it might be Gray, but immediately realized her error when Hank walked up the center aisle.

"Thought I might find you here," Hank said.

His tone was friendly, Lily thought, far too friendly for what had happened between them the last time they'd met. She looked around, hoping to see someone else caring for their animals, but they were alone.

"I don't think we have anything to say to each other," Lily said in what she hoped was a dispassionate tone.

"I can think of quite a few things to say." He gave his off-center smile and moved in closer.

Lily wanted to take a small step back, but didn't want him to see how uncomfortable she felt in his presence after the last time. "Why don't you just tell me why you've come."

"Maybe I just wanted to see you again."

"Well I don't want to see you."

"That's not a very friendly thing to say after I've come all the way out here."

"I don't feel very friendly toward you."

"Maybe you'll be a little friendlier after I tell you the message I've come to deliver."

"What message?"

"From a friend of yours. I was sure you'd want to hear it."

"Is the message from Gray?"

"Ah, so now you're interested, aren't you?"

Lily wanted to scream at him to tell her what he knew, but he was enjoying his little game too much to be goaded into answering quickly.

"If you have a message, I'd appreciate your giving it to me. Otherwise, please leave." She turned her back on him and took a step closer to Galahad's side.

"Don't you sound hoity-toity. What a laugh. I gave you a chance, and you turned me down flat. Shouldn't have been so particular, should ya?"

"What are you talking about?"

"Gray's message for you," he said, watching her closely.

Lily couldn't quite believe Gray would have sent a message with Hank, but then Gray didn't know about her first encounter with him, either. Though she was sure that Hank's claim was all a trick of some sort, she couldn't resist asking, "What message?"

"The message he gave me for you after he didn't find you here. He had to get back out to the ranch and didn't have time to come back himself after all."

Hank's final words told her that he was speaking the truth despite the way his eyes had narrowed, giving him a sly and calculating look. How could he have known Gray had already been to see her if Gray hadn't told him?

Lily stood silently, waiting for him to speak. She wasn't about to give him the satisfaction of asking again.

Hank looked down at her, a slight smile on his face, and shrugged his shoulders. "I'd think you'd be a little more obligin', what with you havin' passed me up and now not havin' a man of your own."

"What does that mean?" she demanded, tired of his manipulative games.

"It means Gray's decided you aren't good enough for him and his daughter. He'd a told you so himself, but he had other things to do."

The color drained from Lily's face and a terrible sinking feeling filled her stomach. It was like the first time she'd walked the wire and fallen. She'd been lucky then, someone had caught her. Not so today.

When Lily didn't reply, he continued, "I may not be as rich as Gray, but I have more goin' than you think. If you jump on my wagon, it'll be goin' to better places than you might imagine." He took a step closer to Lily.

"I want you to leave now," she said quietly. She was surprised at how normal her voice sounded, for on the inside she was shaking like a leaf.

"Don't be stupid. Why not take what you can?" he countered and reached out to run his fingers up and down the bare skin of her arm.

She jerked her arm away from his hand and tried to rub off his dirty touch. "Don't ever touch me again."

"You don't have to play hard to get, honey," he said, stepping forward until he cornered her by the side of Galahad's stall.

"Get out, dammit, and don't come back." This was his last chance. If he didn't leave quickly, she was going to start screaming and let whoever got here first take care of him.

"Do what the signorina says." Roberto's voice came from directly behind Hank.

Relief surged through Lily. Roberto must have come in unnoticed while she was arguing with Hank. Edging past Hank, she ran over to the other man.

"You fine?" Roberto asked as he motioned her to stand behind him.

She nodded. Roberto was neither tall nor big, but he was very strong; the act he performed with Elena required phenomenal muscles. Once she was behind him, she felt safe and secure. She only hoped Hank would leave without causing more trouble.

"The signorina has asked you to go," Roberto reiterated

"This business is between her and me," Hank replied not moving an inch.

"She no want to talk business anymore. You go."

Hank looked as if he were about to argue, and then he looked at Roberto more closely. The acrobat was still in his costume and the powerfulness of his body was plainly visible.

"You'll be sorry for this, Miss High and Mighty," Hank threatened. "Your precious beau will be in big trouble."

With those words he stormed off, leaving Lily bewildered and confused. What had he meant—*her beau* would be in trouble? Surely he didn't think that Roberto was her beau, did he? But something about his last statement made her very uneasy.

Gray lingered at the Cattlemen's Club, hoping Hank would show up. Dixon was there, though, and kept him talking over the plans for the meeting he was trying to set up. Although Gray suspected there was no need for the meeting, he couldn't very well tell the other man until he had more information. So he swallowed his impatience and let the man talk.

By the time he left the club, it was late afternoon. Hank had not appeared, and Gray debated what to do, then decided to ride out to Hank's ranch and talk to him there. This business with Prescott was a surprise, even if Gray had nearly convinced himself someone at the club was at fault. Having suspicions was one thing, but seeing those suspicions confirmed, especially with a friend as close as

Prescott had been, was something else. He wanted to check with Hank on how to handle this latest development.

Why did everything have to come to a head at the same time? he wondered. With a longing glance in the direction of the circus, Gray headed for Hank's ranch. By the time Gray rode into Hank's front yard, it was early evening. He called out a greeting, wanting to let the other man know he had a visitor.

Hank came out onto the porch. "Well, friend, what are you doing out in this neck of the woods?" He came down the steps and met Gray as he dismounted.

"I had the strangest meeting today and thought you might like to hear about it."

"Somethin' to do with the rustlin'?"

"Maybe. Thought I might get your opinion on it."

"Come on inside and I'll get Edith to fix us some coffee," Hank offered.

"Sounds good. I could use some." Gray followed him into the house.

"I'll just go talk with Edith. Make yourself at home," Hank said on his way to the kitchen.

Gray walked around the room, unable to settle down. He looked at Hank's collection of guns and realized he'd added quite a few new ones since the last time Gray'd been here, expensive ones at that.

Hank walked into the room carrying two cups of coffee and motioned for Gray to take a seat.

"You're able to use your arm, I see. Is it feeling better?" Gray asked, taking the cup of coffee Hank held out.

"Oh, right," Hank said, flexing the arm he'd injured. "Must have been only a sprain."

"You were luckier than we thought."

Gray took a swallow of his coffee and then nodded to

271

the guns. "You've added some new ones to your collection, I see."

"Yeah, I've run into some real good deals," Hank said, but quickly changed the subject. "Now, what was it you were sayin' about the rustlin'?"

"Seems Prescott wants to have a private meeting with me."

"You don't say. What do you think he wants?"

"I didn't mention this to you before, but I found a gold sleeve link out at that spot where the rustlers ambushed you and stole my bulls," Gray said, reaching into his pocket and pulling out a handkerchief.

"A sleeve link, you say?" Hank asked, eyeing the white cloth in Gray's hand.

"Here, take a look." Gray unwrapped the object and held it out for Hank's inspection. "I'm sure I've seen Prescott wearing a pair just like this. What do you think?"

"Yeah, sure looks like one of his."

Gray sighed. "I thought as much. When I go out to see him, I'll show this to him and see what he has to say."

"I'm not so sure that's a good idea."

"Why not?"

"He'll just deny it's his, and then he'll know you have evidence against him. It'll just give him time to make up some story to explain it all away. No telling who he'll blame."

"You may be right, but this is the only proof we have, and I want to see how he reacts."

Hank looked as if he was about to disagree again, then shrugged and said, "It's up to you."

"Might as well get this done. Think I'll just head out to his place tonight instead of waiting until tomorrow," Gray said. The sooner he saw Prescott, the sooner he could get back to town and see Lily. Since he'd made his decision, he wanted to talk with her and ask her to forgive him for being so stupid and not seeing everything more clearly from the beginning.

"You're going to Prescott's tonight?"

"Yeah. The sooner this gets done, the better for all concerned."

"You're right about that. Where'd you say you heard about all this?"

"From Cybil. She was worried about him and came to talk with me. As a matter of fact, she and the children will be out at the ranch with Prescott. He's certainly scared about something. What difference does it make?"

"It's just that I heard something, too, and thought I'd check it out tonight."

"What did you hear?" Gray asked.

"About another spot where the rustlers might be keepin' some cattle."

"Are you sure?"

"I was right about the last one," Hank returned. "Besides, I don't think we can let any stone go unturned."

"I know," Gray said. "If there's a chance to get those bulls back, I can't afford to miss it. They were the keystone of my new breeding program."

"Can't you replace them?" Hank looked upset, and Gray felt bad. He shouldn't have said anything, knowing how responsible Hank felt for the loss.

"I hope so," he said. "It just takes time . . . and money, of course."

"Listen, Gray, that only makes it more important that we check this out. What if your bulls are still around here somewhere? It'd be terrible to have just missed findin' them. Besides, didn't you say Prescott doesn't expect you there until tomorrow? He might not even be there himself yet. What time is your meetin'?"

"Around noon."

"There, you see? For all you know he's only gonna go

there in the mornin'. You know as well as I do how much Prescott hates bein' at that ranch of his."

Gray had to agree. Besides, if his assumption about Prescott was all wrong, then they'd be back where they started. All he had was the sleeve link and the fact that Prescott was acting suspiciously. Not a whole lot to go on. He looked at Hank. He couldn't let him go by himself. Look what had happened the last time. He'd damn near got himself killed.

"I could use your help if you think you could spare the time," Hank added, rubbing his arm.

"All right. I'll leave Prescott for tomorrow," Gray decided, "and head out with you tonight. I don't want anything happening like the last time."

"I appreciate that, Gray. Why don't we get movin' while we still have the light."

By the time they made it back to Hank's spread later that night, the sun had been down for a couple of hours. The ride had been long, tiring, and futile. If Gray had known exactly where Hank had planned on taking him, he might have tried to talk Hank out of going. He'd sent some of his own men up into that area less than a week ago, and they'd found nothing. Not that the rustlers couldn't have set up something over the last few days.

"Sorry about that," Hank said yet again.

"You don't need to keep apologizing. This could have turned up something; you just never know when you're dealing with rumors. Every piece of information helps us. Now we can eliminate that area as a place the rustlers are using."

"I know, but I feel real bad about your not goin' out to Prescott's like you wanted."

"It doesn't matter. But at least you can understand why I wanted to check the gold sleeve link with Prescott. It's the only real clue we've found."

274

"Yeah, I can understand. When are you goin' over? Not too early, I hope, after that ride we had tonight. I don't think I'm going to be out of bed much before noon, myself, and your week's been at least as bad as mine, what with that scare over Amelia and all."

"Most probably I'll go tomorrow around noon like Cybil wanted."

"That's probably best," Hank said and then muffled a yawn. "I don't know about you, but I'm beat. Even though my arm's better, I'm still not feelin' up to snuff. I'm about ready to turn in."

"Sounds like a good idea. I'll let you know what happens with Prescott tomorrow."

"Make sure you do that. I'm real interested in what he has to say."

Gray turned his horse and headed back to his ranch. Though he couldn't quite put his finger on it, some instinct was making him uneasy. He thought back to his conversation with Cybil. She had seemed scared. Had she known her brother was involved in the rustling or was it something else? It was so hard to know what to think. Ordinarily he wouldn't have suspected Prescott. The Englishman seemed too wrapped up in himself and his socializing to think up the rustling schemes. Still, that could be a facade to hide what he was really doing.

Hank had been of little help, having no more idea than he what might have motivated Prescott. If anything, Hank had seemed reluctant to have him confront Prescott. Did he, too, share Gray's doubts that the other man was capable of conceiving of such activities, let alone planning them?

Gray wished now that he hadn't let Hank drag him along all night to no purpose. Then he would already have the answers to his questions. Well, there was nothing he could do now, but he'd be damned if he'd wait until noon tomorrow. Nope, first thing in the morning, he'd get over to Prescott's and see what was going on.

By midnight Lily had finished the last of her packing and knew that Gray would not be coming. Somehow, she'd kept her hopes up throughout the interminable hours since Hank Farrell's departure, unable to believe Gray could have disappeared so completely from her life without a word. But now there was no denying the facts—tomorrow Bruner's Munificent Menagerie and Family Circus would depart Cheyenne, and she would never see Gray again. With any luck, Otto would secure their old bookings in the East for next season, and she would never even return to the Magic City of the Plains.

And for her, their stay in this city had truly been magic—until the past few days. Here she had learned the meaning of love and passion and desire fulfilled. Here she had learned to dream, to look beyond the narrow confines of her life and see a larger, fuller world. Here, too, she was coming to learn the pain of heartbreak and shattered dreams—and she very much feared no magic in the world could put her heart back together, to say nothing of her dreams.

Already she could hear the sounds of the circus readying itself for departure, the shouts of men, the bellows of Old Bess, the clanking of equipment. By morning only the largest of the tents would still be standing, waiting to be taken down at first light. Usually she felt excitement when the circus was about to move on. She enjoyed the exhilaration of going to a new town, of seeing the grown-ups' eager faces and hearing the children's excited shouts.

But tonight the circus sounds only fed her pain. With each second that passed, she was moving farther from Gray, farther from her dreams, even though the circus had yet to take a step. By morning the distance would become real as the circus turned its back on Cheyenne and moved to its new location, a barrier that time and space could not bridge. But a part of Lily would be here forever, even if she never returned. For she knew now that her heart was Gray's, and she would never forget him.

The knock on her door was faint, but she recognized its cadence.

"Come in, Elena," she called. "The door is unlocked and I'm still awake."

Elena came in. "You are all packed?" she asked, looking around the small wagon.

"Yes. And you?"

"Oh, you know Roberto. From the moment 'e learn 'e is to be a papa, 'e don't let me 'elp with anything."

"He looked so happy after you told him," Lily said, ignoring the shaft of longing that speared through her.

"Yes, 'e was. 'E will get a new partner for a while. Otto say 'e can do other things. The Santellis will still be 'ere for a long time."

"I'm glad for you." She smiled at her friend, relieved that Cheyenne had brought only blessings to her and her husband.

"But I am not so glad for you. Roberto, 'e tell me about what 'appen today."

Lily looked away, her eyes filling with tears. She'd hoped Hank Farrell was lying when he said Gray no longer wanted her, but time had shown her the truth of his words. "I guess it wasn't meant to be," she murmured, her words catching in her throat.

"Your Gray, 'e is a fool if 'e let you go like this."

"He has his reasons," Lily defended.

"Do you love 'im so very much?" Elena asked, her voice soft and sympathetic.

Lily could not reply as tears ran down her face. Yes, she loved him, but that had never been the question. Sometimes, though, love was not enough, not enough to overcome the fears of the past, not enough to overcome the fears for the future.

THIRTEEN

THE LOW MORNING sun was shining in Gray's eyes as he and Sam rode in a southeasterly direction toward Prescott's ranch. True to his decision the night before, Gray had refused to wait until noon to visit the Englishman. With any luck this business would be over soon, and he could get back to town and see Lily. Missing her as he had yesterday gnawed at him. It was as if the fates that had conspired to bring them together were now working equally hard to keep them apart. But Gray had learned his lesson where fate was concerned. He was going to make his own destiny, not let a few misunderstandings and mistakes stand in the way of his happiness and Lily's.

Squinting into the distance, he saw the first signs of the Warford-Smythe homestead and slowed his horse. Turning to Sam, he said, "I don't know what to expect, so let's approach carefully."

"This is some outfit," Sam muttered as his gaze scanned across the horizon, taking in the generously built outbuildings, the acres of fenced paddocks close to the house, the imposing ranch house itself. "You think he's built all this up by rustling?"

"Not all of it. I'm sure he came out here with enough cash to get started, but he and Cybil like to live in high style. They travel all the time and stay in town whenever they can, entertaining and going to all the latest shows and parties. It takes a lot of money to live like that; maybe he couldn't get enough just out of his ranch and his holdings in England."

"What should we do?"

"Let's leave the horses here. I'd rather no one sees us until we figure out how many people are here and what their connection is to this rustling business."

They dismounted, tying the horses by a row of young trees planted as a windbreak. Hugging the edge of the line of trees, they worked their way close to the front yard.

"Doesn't look like there's anybody around," Sam said as they both looked over the barns and paddocks.

"No, it doesn't," Gray agreed, wondering what Prescott was up to. "It looks like he sent all his hands out. I'm beginning to like this situation less and less. Come on, let's see if we can find anyone up at the house. You go around the front, and I'll head this way. If you find anything interesting, meet me round the other side. If you can't get through that way, let's meet back here in, say, twenty minutes. Okay?"

Sam nodded and they took off in opposite directions to begin skirting the house. The place seemed deserted, though from what Cybil had said yesterday, Gray was sure she and the children were coming out to join Prescott. Could they have had a last-minute change of plans?

He crept around the corner of the house and along the back wall. As he reached the area near the open kitchen windows, he heard a murmur of voices, but couldn't make out whose they were. A covered porch separated him from the rear wall of the house and the windows. Checking to the left and right, Gray decided to take the risk and quietly vaulted over the wooden railing onto the porch floor. The wood creaked softly beneath his feet, and he froze, but the voice inside kept talking, oblivious to the sound.

Gray flattened himself against the near wall and slowly

inched closer to the window. The voice became clear, but Gray's mind refused to accept what he was hearing, the shock was so great.

"You won't get away with it," Prescott responded, sounding desperate.

"Sure I will," said the other, his voice brimming with assurance.

"Gray will come after you," Prescott said.

The other man laughed. "I doubt it. Why, I killed a man with Gray standing almost closer than you are now, and he never suspected a thing."

"I don't believe you."

"Believe what you want. It makes no difference to me. Now, are you gonna sign this?"

"No."

"You fool."

Gray heard the sound of fist hitting flesh followed by an unmistakable grunt of pain. His stomach clenched. Though he had often thought the rustling was coordinated at the Cattlemen's Club, never in his wildest imaginings had he considered Hank Farrell as a possible suspect. But there was no mistaking it now. No wonder Hank had tried to keep him from coming out here yesterday. He'd wanted to be sure he got here first. A sick feeling washed over Gray.

"Hey, Hank, you 'bout done?" a new voice asked.

Gray sneaked a peek through the window and recognized one of Rafferty's men, the same man who had attacked Lily on her first day in Cheyenne. If Blackie was here, chances were his buddy Travis would be around somewhere, too. What a mess! Gray pulled his head back before the others could see him.

"Give me a minute more," Hank replied. "What's with the sister?"

"I've finally got her subdued. Real wildcat, that one.

Travis is out in the shed with her. What you want us to do?"

"That's up to old Prescott here. You listenin', Pres, old friend? We've got your sister all trussed up in the shed. Will you sign, or would you rather I let the boys use her for their own enjoyment?"

"All right. I'll sign." Prescott's voice sounded weaker than before, his words slightly slurred. Gray guessed that Hank must have punched him in the mouth. There wasn't much time left. Once Prescott signed, Hank would have no further use for the man, or for Cybil.

A sound to Gray's right made him look up suddenly and whip out his gun. Sam was standing by the edge of the porch. Gray motioned to him to stay put and reholstered his gun. Then he made his way across the porch, jumping lithely over the railing and pulling Sam back away from the windows.

"Did you find anything?" Gray asked in a whisper.

Sam shook his head. "I thought I saw some movement over by the large shed, but I wasn't sure. When I didn't see you at the other side of the house, I thought I'd better swing around back here and see what happened."

"Hank is behind the rustling," Gray said dispassionately, still numb from the realization of his friend's betrayal.

"Hank Farrell!" Sam looked as shocked as Gray felt. At least he wasn't the only one fooled. "But that's impossible. Why, they stole from him, too—and they beat him up."

"So he had us think. We can talk about this later. Right now we better do something to stop them."

"How many do you reckon are here?"

"Three that I know of—Blackie's inside with Hank. They've got Prescott. From what I overheard, Travis is out in the shed with Cybil. Blackie just came over from there."

282

"You want me to come in the house with you or handle things out at the shed?"

"You'd better take the shed. I don't want old Travis getting nervous if things start coming apart at the house. I'll take care of Blackie and Hank."

"Blackie's a big man, boss, and not above fighting dirty. Watch out."

"I will. I figure surprise will be on my side. I'll give you a head start, then go in myself."

They checked their weapons, then Sam crept back the way he had come, and Gray followed him, heading for the front of the house when Sam veered off to go to the shed. The front door was unlocked, as Gray'd expected, and he let himself in. He could hear the voices from the back of the house and knew all three men were still in the kitchen.

"That's fine," Hank was saying. "Now sign this confession, and we'll be on our way."

Stall, Prescott, Gray prayed silently as he eased his way through the house. *Just keep them talking and preoccupied so they don't notice me.*

As if the other man heard his plea, he said, "I will not. I may have been willing to give you my ranch, but never my honor."

"It's a little late to worry about your honor now, you foolish English prig. It's your life you better hope to save, yours and your sister's."

"And after I sign it?"

"Why, I told you. You and your sister will leave town. Go back to England or find some other place to live. Just don't come back to Cheyenne."

"How do I know you'll let us go?"

"You don't. You just have to take my word for it."

"Your word!" Prescott drawled contemptuously, then spat in Hank's face.

Hank drew back, furiously wiping his face. He raised

his arm to strike Prescott just as Gray entered the large kitchen.

"I wouldn't do that if I were you," Gray said, his gun in his hand, ready to fire.

Hank stopped and slowly looked around as if nothing out of the ordinary was happening. "Why, Gray, what are you doin' here?" he asked, his voice warm and friendly.

"Came to see who's been doing all the rustling. Seems I came to the right place."

"You sure did." Hank gave him the same friendly smile he always did. "Prescott, here, was just goin' to tell us all about it."

"Was he now? And what's Blackie doing here?"

"After all your warnin's about not goin' out alone, I figured I better bring along some protection, so I asked him to come with me."

The explanation sounded as plausible as any Hank had ever given. To look at the man, you would swear he was telling the truth despite the fact that Prescott was bound to a chair, a trickle of blood running from one nostril, and his left eye swelling shut.

"And why didn't you ask me to come along?"

Hank gave him a sheepish look. "Well, to tell the truth, I was kind of embarrassed after last night, takin' you on that ride to the back of beyond. I didn't want to drag you out for nothin' again."

"Even though you knew I was planning on coming here anyway?"

"Not till later. I figured I'd have everythin' finished up by the time you got here, one way or the other. Sorta redeemin' myself, you might say."

"I see. Well, I guess you won't mind my asking Prescott a question or two, will you?" Gray lowered the barrel of his gun so that it pointed to the floor, figuring the gesture would make Hank feel he was winning him over.

"There's really no need," Hank said. "He's already told me and Blackie everythin'. Most of the cattle he stole are long gone. Those few we saw the other day are the last remainin' head. Isn't that right, Blackie?"

Blackie grunted, a scowl on his face, his body poised for action. Gray noticed the man had his hand on his gun, though he hadn't drawn it from the holster. He still wasn't sure which way this conversation was going, but so far, he was following Hank's lead. That gave Gray more time to position himself and keep Hank off guard. "You mean the cows up where you shot that man?" he asked.

"Yeah, where that rustler tried to jump me," Hank said easily. "I sure was glad when you and Sam rode up. I was half afraid one of the man's cronies would show up with revenge on his mind."

Gray could have almost been lulled into believing this was his old friend Hank he was talking to, but he caught the slightest twitch of the man's eyebrow smugly signaling to Prescott that he was in control, reminding him of how well he'd drawn the wool over Gray's eyes, enough to get away with cold-blooded murder. But there was no wool there now, only a horrified appreciation of Hank's manipulative skills and sheer amorality.

"So, Prescott, have you anything to add to what Hank said?"

Prescott sat wearily in his chair, his shoulders slumped, defeat written in his eyes. Gray wished there was some way to let the man know he didn't believe a word Hank was saying without revealing anything to Hank, but it was too risky to try a secret signal.

"Would it make a difference?" Prescott asked, his tone indicating he thought it wouldn't.

"I don't know. If you don't mind answering one question; I have been curious about something."

Prescott looked at him listlessly.

"I have a better idea," Hank said. "Why don't you go get the sheriff while Blackie and I guard Prescott. Once he's in jail, you can ask him anythin' you want. I'm kind of worried about stayin' out here too long. What if the rest of his gang comes along? They're a pretty ruthless bunch."

"This won't take long," Gray said, and reached into his vest pocket to retrieve the gold sleeve link he'd tucked there before leaving home. "This yours?" he asked Prescott, moving to stand next to the seated man.

Prescott looked at Gray's face, and for the first time this morning Gray saw a spark of hope in his eyes. "At one time. Lost it in a poker game. About a month ago or so."

"Play poker a lot, do you?"

"For goodness' sake, Gray, what's this all about?" Hank demanded. "Time's a-wastin'."

"I don't think so, Hank. I remember you telling me how well you'd done at poker just about a month ago. As I recall, you were bragging about how much you took 'old Pres' here for."

"What are you sayin'?"

"I'm saying that you won this sleeve link off of Prescott." He raised his gun, pointing it straight at Hank. "And that you're the one who lost when my bulls were supposedly stolen."

"You can't believe that. Why, you know damn well they beat me up."

Gray stepped to the side so Blackie fell into his line of sight. "Drop your gun, Blackie," Gray ordered before the other man could draw. "Mine's already out, and I won't hesitate to use it. I haven't forgotten what you tried to do to Miss Avenel."

Blackie ignored the warning, drawing his Colt and firing in Gray's general direction and then vaulting out the door. At the same instant Hank lowered his head and charged at Gray, taking him down in a tackle. They

286

fought, fists swinging, two longtime friends turned enemies.

Gray's gun went off, the bullet hit Hank in the shoulder, and the other man collapsed. Gray quickly sprang up ready to defend himself.

"You shot me!" Hank exclaimed in surprise. "I'm bleeding."

Gray could see Hank had only been nicked. He spotted an extra length of rope on the floor by Prescott's chair and quickly tied Hank's arms behind him and left him on the floor.

"I'll bleed to death," Hank whined.

"With any luck," Gray muttered under his breath, then in a louder voice added, "Why, Hank? Why did you do it?"

"You don't understand. Everythin's always come easy to you. I've had to stand by and watch while you got richer and richer and I just stayed the same."

Gray didn't know what to say. Hank knew as well as he did how hard Gray worked. Gray wasn't the one who spent so much time at the Cattlemen's Club or felt compelled to impress all the single ladies in town with expensive gifts. "I was willing to help you. So were the others."

"I got tired of your help. I wanted to do it on my own."

"By rustling?"

"It worked, didn't it? And it would have kept on working if you'd done like you were supposed to and waited until noon to come."

Gray turned away in disgust. "I'd better go after Blackie," he said, then added to Prescott, "I'll be back in a minute to untie you."

As Gray ran out into the yard, he saw Blackie coming out of the barn at the gallop, the horse's saddle tied on with a rope. Gray realized Sam must have gotten to the

287

barn and cut the cinch with his knife, delaying the man's escape.

Blackie took one look at Gray and raised his gun to shoot. Gray somersaulted out of the way of the bullet, then raised himself to one knee and sighted. When Blackie turned in the saddle to shoot again over his shoulder, Gray fired. The big man fell onto his horse's neck, and after a couple more steps, the big bay slowed to a walk, unsure what to do with the dead weight on its back.

Gray ran over to the horse, slowing his pace as he neared the animal. He spoke softly, and the horse stopped walking and looked at him quizzically. Blackie groaned, and the horse's ears twitched backward, but he did not bolt. Gray grabbed the reins and started leading the animal back toward the house. As he neared it, Sam came running out of the shed across the yard.

"I got Travis tied up!" he shouted. "You okay? I heard shots."

"Yeah, I winged this guy as he tried to take off, and Hank got shot in the shoulder after he jumped me. He's tied up in the house. You find Cybil?"

"I heard her moaning, but I wanted to make sure you were okay. You want me to take care of him while you check on her? She might prefer someone she knows."

"Okay. Check on Prescott, too. He's in the kitchen. They roughed him up quite a bit. And be careful of Blackie. He might come to any minute."

Sam nodded and took the horse's reins, freeing Gray to go to the shed. Before he reached it, though, a piercing, haunting wail rent the air. Both Gray and Sam stopped in their tracks and looked at each other. The sound had been almost inhuman, though neither truly believed in ghosts. The cry came again, from inside the shed.

Gray ran for the building. He threw open the door, and Cybil came out, but a very different Cybil from what Gray was used to. Her hair was in complete disarray, her clothing torn and dirty. Worst of all was the expression in her eyes. It was as fierce and feral as her piercing wail.

With the rope used to restrain her still loosely attached to her ankles, she stared frantically around the front yard, tears streaming from her eyes. Gray caught up with her and placed his hands firmly on her shoulders. "Cybil, you're safe now. Let me help you," Gray beseeched, but she didn't seem to hear him.

She shook her head violently and tried to escape. He tightened his grip just enough to keep her from getting away. She was so hysterical he was afraid she would hurt herself.

"I'm going to take her inside," he called to Sam, who was returning from the shed where he'd taken Blackie and secured him. "See if you can get some cool water from the well."

Cybil fought him every inch of the way until he finally lifted her over his shoulder and carried her inside, laying her on the morning bed in the second parlor.

"Hush, now, Cybil. It's over," he told her again and again, but she continued to fight him.

"I have to go," she kept repeating over and over, pushing at his hands.

Where the hell was Sam? he wondered, just as the younger man burst into the room. "Gray, you have to come! I heard voices from inside the old well!"

"What?" He turned to look at his foreman.

"I went to get the water like you asked," Sam said breathlessly, "and I heard these funny noises coming from nearby. I didn't see anyone, so I ran around looking. And then I found it—the old well, I mean. It's just a hole in the ground. The cover was lying nearby. God, Gray, what do you think is down there?"

In a horrific instant shocked comprehension rushed

through them both. Cybil's children! Gray hadn't given them a thought, assuming they were still in Cheyenne, but all of a sudden he understood her desperation. "Stay with her," he ordered. "Let me go see."

He raced outside and tore across the yard to the old well. As Sam had described, it was just a hole in the ground. As he neared, he could hear muffled cries. At least they were still alive, he thought as he fought the feelings of panic that threatened to overwhelm him. He had to keep a clear head and figure out what to do. He approached the opening cautiously, not wanting to kick any dirt down the hole.

Only one voice could be heard, and Gray wasn't sure whether it was Peter's or Lorna's. Dropping to his knees beside the well, he tried to look in and gauge its depth, but it was dark enough that he couldn't make out the bottom. Scrambling back to his feet, he looked around the yard but saw nothing that would help him. Sam appeared by the front porch of the house.

"I untied Prescott. He's taking care of Cybil. How can I help?"

"Bring our horses up. I'm going to have to go down the well. I don't see any other way of getting them out."

"Are they all right?"

"I don't know. I could hear one of them crying, but I'm not even sure which one. How did this happen? Did Cybil or Prescott say?"

"Apparently Hank and his thugs wanted to convince Prescott to turn the ranch over to him, so they threatened the children. I don't think Prescott believed them. He nearly collapsed when I told him what I found."

"Well, as long as he can handle Cybil, we'd better get to work. I don't know how much time we have. The children may be hurt and I don't know if there's water down there or not."

"I'll hurry," Sam said and took off on the run.

Gray ran back to the well to listen for the children's voices and plan his strategy. He called down, hoping to soothe the children, and told them he would come for them as soon as he could. His only reply was a faint whimper, no more identifiable than the earlier sounds.

Sam galloped up at that moment, leading Gray's mount. He yanked the two horses to a skidding stop and ground-tied them. "How should we work things? You want to go down, or you want me to?"

The younger man was slimmer and slightly shorter than Gray, probably the better choice of the two, but Gray needed to go down himself. "I'd better go. The children already know and trust me. They're scared enough already. If I'm there, maybe they'll feel safer."

"Okay. I saw some extra rope in the shed. Let me get it and we can start."

"See if there are any candles or a lantern. It's darker than pitch at the bottom of the well."

Gray positioned his horse while Sam got the rope. They made a double loop at one end of the rope so Gray could put his foot in it while being lowered, then tied the other end firmly to the saddle horn. Sam took the horse's head, and Gray filled his pockets with the candles Sam had found, then went over to the hole. Sam pulled the rope tight as Gray stepped onto it and suspended himself over the opening, only his head and shoulders above ground level.

"All right. Start lowering me. Go slow."

The horse took a couple of steps forward, and Gray lurched down, the ground collapsing around him in a shower of dirt and stones. He yelled out, barely catching himself on the rope as he fell the extra feet. The rope swung madly, bumping him against the walls of the shaft as the dirt continued to rain on him.

"You all right?" Sam called from the surface.

"Stay back. I don't want this thing to collapse even more!" he shouted back. His muscles ached from the strain of catching himself in mid-fall and the effects of his struggle with Hank. His breath came in gasps. He tried to control it so he could listen for the children, but heard nothing aside from the sound of the wind whistling past the top of the well.

"Should I keep lowering you or do you want to come back up?" Sam yelled from a greater distance.

As the rope stopped swinging, Gray looked up. The opening of the well looked larger and the dirt had more or less stopped falling. Unfortunately, it looked as if his rope was draped over the weakest part.

"You might as well lower me. Whatever damage is going to occur will happen whether I go up or down, and I want to check on the children. The dirt probably fell right on them."

"Okay," Sam called back. "Hang on."

The rope lowered again, at a steadier pace this time. A few more rocks were dislodged, but for the most part the well wall seemed to hold. Gray breathed a sigh of relief when he finally hit the bottom.

"Is everything all right down there?" Sam called down.

"I don't know yet," Gray answered, and pulled a couple of candles from his back pocket. "Give me a second or two."

"I'm going to see if I can get more help. I don't see how we're going to get you and the children out of there without the whole well collapsing."

"All right!" Gray shouted up.

He lit one of the candles and looked around. The well was dry except for a small trickle of water in one corner. The two children were huddled together. Gray knelt next to them. The boy was whimpering quietly and sucking his

humb as he clung to his sister. Gray ran his hands over
he boy, checking for broken bones and other injuries. The
boy flinched when Gray touched his arm, and Gray could
feel the ragged edges of the bone beneath the skin.

"Hey, Peter. Come here, son," Gray said, being careful
o support the boy's arm. "I need to check your sister."

The boy refused to budge, crying more loudly and ask-
ng for his mother. Gray made soothing noises and decided
o leave the boy where he was. Though the well shaft widened a bit under ground, it was still pretty cramped. Gray
checked the parts of Lorna he could easily reach without
dislodging the boy. She didn't appear to have any broken
bones, but she was unconscious and had a good-sized
lump on her head. He called her name and tried to rouse
her.

Gray started making a mental list of supplies Sam
would need to lower to him if he was to do anything about
he broken bones. Impatient, he checked his watch. Sam
had only been gone fifteen minutes. How long would it
take him to get to the nearest neighbor's and back? Gray
ried to ignore that thought. However long it took, he
new Sam would be doing his best to make the time as
short as possible.

He wet his handkerchief in the trickle of water and
wiped the children's faces clean. Lorna felt cool to his
touch, so he took off his vest and covered her with it. He
wished now that he had thought to have Sam lower some
blankets and food down the shaft before he left, but knew
Sam was worried about the collapsing well walls. Gray
pulled Peter to his side now that he had calmed down and
snuggled Lorna in his arms, thinking he could at least give
hem some body heat while they waited for Sam's return.

The circus caravan slowly made its way down the dusty
road. A crowd of Cheyenne citizens, mostly young men

and older boys, followed it out of town, cheering on the elephant and other animals, using the warm day as an excuse to cavort in the sun and spend a few more minutes with the circus before it disappeared. Lily watched their antics and wished she could feel as innocent and carefree.

The bright, sunny day and clear blue sky seemed to mock her, for inside she felt anything but bright and cheerful. She was going from Cheyenne, but she was leaving the best part of herself here. Elena and Roberto had tried to comfort her. Elena even offered to send Roberto out to the ranch to be sure Gray knew they were leaving, but Lily refused their generous offer. This was between her and Gray, and no one else could help, at least not while her feelings were so raw, so near the surface.

A commotion at the front of the slow-moving caravan caught her attention. A cloud of dust indicated that a rider had just come down the road from the opposite direction. A couple of minutes later the rider careened past her, then pulled up his mount and came charging back.

"Lily, is that you?" he called out.

"Sam! What are you doing here?" That something was wrong was clear from his strained expression and the lather that had built up on his mount's shoulders and flanks. The horse was winded as if he'd been ridden hard over a distance.

"I need help, Lily. Gray's at the bottom of a well at Cybil's place. I can't get them out alone."

"What?" The story made no sense, except that Gray and Cybil were together. For a moment she wondered how long it had taken Gray to go back to Cybil, then she quelled the thought when what Sam had said finally registered.

"What's going on here?" one of the roustabouts asked, coming up to her wagon. "He bothering you?" he asked Lily.

"No. He needs help."

"What 'appen?" Elena asked, walking back from her wagon, which had pulled up just a few feet ahead of Lily's. When she recognized Sam as Gray's friend, her expression hardened and she turned to Lily. "What 'e want?"

"I need help," Sam cried. "You've got to come. There's a man and two children stuck in a well near here. I can't get them out. The walls are crumbling."

"Who?" Lily cried, her heart filling with dread. "Who's in the well?" But she knew.

"I told you. Gray. I lowered him to get to the children, but the whole thing is collapsing. Can you help?"

"Oh, my God," Lily whispered.

Elena patted her hand. "I tell Otto. You find out what we need. 'Urry." She ran back to her wagon calling for Roberto.

Lily looked at the roustabout and said, "We'll need Old Bess. Tell Gustav. Also get some of the men together and see what equipment we can quickly unpack. How far do we have to go?" she asked Sam.

"About three miles up the road."

"Okay," the roustabout answered. "We'd best split a group off the main caravan so we can move quickly. The rest can catch up with us later. Come on," he said to Sam and led the way up the line to the equipment wagon.

Elena came running back to Lily's wagon, medicines and bandages in hand. " 'Ere, take zese. You don't know what you will need. We will follow you."

Dun came up at that point. "You planning on taking our wagon?" he asked Lily.

"Yes, I guess. We may need it."

"All right. I had them saddle a horse so you can go on ahead with the others. I'll bring your wagon. Sam told me where to go. Now, you better get going. The men are ready to leave."

"Don't worry, Lily. It will be fine. *Le bon Dieu*, 'e will not let anything 'appen to your Gray. Now go."

Tears filled Lily's eyes as she ran to get her horse. What would she do without such loyal friends? The circus folk were good people—they always helped anybody in trouble. But she knew today they were doing it especially for her.

When she reached the horse, she found a half dozen roustabouts waiting with Sam. A light wagon had been emptied and loaded with blocks and tackle and poles of various lengths. One of the roustabouts sat on the seat, ready to drive, while the rest were mounted on various horses from the working stock—large, muscular beasts trained to haul the heavy freight of the circus without complaint.

"Let's go!" one of them shouted, and they rode off ahead of the wagon.

The big horses moved with surprising speed, and the ride took only minutes, but they seemed like hours to Lily. As they reached the ranch yard, Sam showed them the location of the crumbling well. "Stay away from the well shaft. I don't know how much weight the ground can support."

The men nodded and approached the area cautiously. Lily dismounted, intending to join them when a sudden noise to the side distracted her. Cybil came running out of the house, making a beeline for the old well.

"Stop her!" Prescott shouted from the door.

Lily saw she was the closest and ran to head Cybil off. The woman plowed right into her and would have continued on except that Lily grabbed hold of her arm.

"Let me go!" Cybil cried, striking at her with her free hand. Her fingers became entangled in Lily's hair and she pulled hard, yanking Lily's head back.

"Damn you!" she shrieked. "Let me go. If you hadn'

come, everything would be different. Damn you! I hate you!"

Prescott reached them and threw his weight into subduing Cybil. When he finally had her pinned to the ground, he said, "Hush, now, Cyb. You're only making things worse. Let's go inside and leave the men to rescue Peter and Lorna. That's what you really want, right? Come on, now, love. Promise me you won't run away again, and I'll get up."

Cybil started to cry in low, keening sobs, and Lily stepped away, giving the brother and sister the privacy their sorrow merited. Her hair spilled down past her shoulders, her hairpins scattered all over. She shook out the bright locks, then quickly plaited them, leaving the braid to hang down her back. Her heart still pounded furiously, but she was beginning to catch her breath. As soon as she was sure Prescott had Cybil under control, she ran toward the well site.

"The ground's in bad shape, Lily," one of the roustabouts said as she approached. "We're setting up a scaffolding to brace the block and tackle, but we don't want to get too near the shaft."

"Who was that?" another asked, looking back at Cybil and Prescott.

"The children's mother," Lily explained.

"Ah," the man replied, as if that explained everything. And it did. Lily knew how she felt about Gray trapped down in that dangerous situation, and he was an adult. How much worse it must be for a mother to know her children were trapped and maybe hurt.

"Any word from down the well?" she asked.

"Not much. Ground's too chancy to get close."

She nodded, then left them to their work and walked around the well in a large circle, careful to stay far from the edge. The roustabouts were hard at work, sweat beading their brows and turning their shirts dark as they fought the equipment, trying to save every minute. Sam was on the far side of the well, talking to the crew chief about how to proceed once the scaffolding was up.

"How can I help?" Lily asked, needing to feel useful so her fears wouldn't overwhelm her.

"See what you can find in the house," Sam said. "Blankets, candles, ropes. I don't know. Whatever you think we might need."

She nodded and raced to the front door. Prescott and Cybil were nowhere in sight, so she ran up the stairs to the bedroom wing of the house. She heard muffled voices behind one of the doors and knew Prescott had taken his sister there. She went into another bedroom and flung open the chest at its foot. It was filled with blankets and clean linens. Lily grabbed a couple of each and ran back down the stairs.

As she came back out of the house, she saw Old Bess lumbering up the drive to the house. Dun followed with her wagon. He turned off the road by the side of the house.

"Is this a good place to set up?" he called out.

Lily nodded, then ran to catch up with Gustav and the elephant. "The well is in bad shape," she told him and explained how the men were setting up a scaffold that would be anchored on the ground far from the crumbling walls.

The crowd of townspeople who'd been following the circus had gathered around the well, and a couple of the roustabouts were trying to move them back. There was an air of utter confusion about the scene, with people moving at cross-purposes. As Gustav guided Old Bess to one side, out of the way of the workers, the group of boys and men from Cheyenne gathered around, eager to get close to the elephant.

"Lily, what have you got?" Sam called. She worked her

way through the crowd and showed him what she'd scavenged. "Good. Gray's worried about Lorna. She's unconscious and her skin is wet and cold. He wants us to send down some blankets. Also some lengths of wood to use as splints."

Sam approached the chief of the roustabouts' work gang. "How should we do this?" he asked.

"We'll lower the blankets first, then we'll send someone down to help out," the crew chief answered. Then he looked at Lily. "You're pretty lightweight. You want to try walking across the pole and then going down?"

Sam began to protest, but the crew chief cut him off. "I'm afraid to put anything too heavy out there," he explained. "It'll be hard enough pulling Mr. Benedict out. This whole thing is not that strong, but we don't have time to build anything stronger. You said yourself that the dirt is still crumbling. And it sounds like those children need help fast."

"Are you sure you can do this?" Sam asked Lily. She saw concern and fear in his face and a glimmer of hope that somehow this would all work out. She took a deep breath before she answered. Could she do it? she asked herself. But if she didn't go down, who would? Only Dun was lighter than she, and he had yet to regain his full strength from the beating he received. There really was no choice; she'd have to handle the task.

"Yes, I'm sure," she said, and gave him what she hoped was a confident smile.

"What do I have to do?" she asked the crew chief.

"The easiest way is to walk across on that pole to the center, right above the well"—he pointed with his hand along the top of the scaffolding—"then we'll get Old Bess to lower you slowly."

Lily nodded. She'd walked a wire many a time, even sharing in one of the high-wire acts before Hilda let her perform with the horses. Though she'd never mastered the most difficult tricks, she'd been quite competent as a funambulist. Walking on the pole would only be easier. She hurried to her wagon to change into a pair of pants and switch her shoes while the emergency supplies were lowered to Gray. Then she prepared to make her own descent.

FOURTEEN

GRAY LOOKED UP to the distant circle of light so many feet above his head, waiting for some sign that Sam had returned. The cool temperature even had him feeling cold and damp, so he couldn't begin to imagine its effect on the children. Lorna worried him the most, lying so still with her face pale and white even in the golden light from the candle. Where was Sam? he thought for the hundredth time, and then he heard Sam's voice.

"I got help," Sam called from somewhere beyond the circle of light. "How are things down there? You need anything?"

"Blankets," he called up.

"Okay. It'll be a while up here. We're hurrying as fast as we can."

"We," he'd said, and Gray wondered how Sam had found help so quickly. The steady rain of pebbles and dirt clods had him worried. He'd moved the children to shield them from being hit, but there was no way to shelter himself from the constant barrage. He was simply too big for the small well.

The blankets came down first, then the splints with some clean linen strips from what must have been a bed sheet. Gray wrapped the blanket around Lorna, then gritted his teeth as he began to set Peter's arm. The boy screamed

301

in pain as the grating sounds of bone slipping into place echoed in the dimness.

"Okay, we're ready up here," Sam called down. "Look out for falling debris. Help is on the way."

Gray looked up in time to see a head of fiery-red hair blocking the opening. Lily! What the hell was she doing here? He wanted to protest, to tell her to go back and not put herself in such danger, but it was too late. The rope was already lowering her down into the shaft. His heart caught in his throat as he watched her descend, praying the well would not collapse. He would never forgive himself if something happened to her.

Regret filled his heart as he thought of all the time they'd lost this past week. He'd let his fears overtake his life and nearly lost the best thing that had ever happened to him. Amelia would be gone in a year or two, facing the challenges life threw her, as he had taught her to. Could he do less himself? He loved Lily and wanted to be with her. He only wished he'd told her, especially after Amelia's accident. Lily probably blamed herself more than he did. And now, despite the way he'd treated her, withdrawing without an explanation and leaving her to draw her own conclusions, she was risking her life for him.

He watched as the rope slowly lowered her, and suddenly he sensed that all was not well.

"Lily?" he called out.

She did not answer.

He stood slowly, careful not to jostle the children who were lying on one of the folded blankets.

"Lily? Are you all right?"

"Yes. It's just so narrow," came her voice as if from a distance. She sounded frightened, not like the vibrant Lily he knew.

"It's not too bad," he said soothingly, understanding

how overwhelming the dark, crumbling channel could be. "There's a candle down here."

"I can't see anything down there."

"I'll light another candle." He suited his actions to his words, quickly lighting three more candles. "There, is that better?"

"A little."

He recognized now that she was on the edge of panic, but doing her best to overcome it.

"Good," he said, keeping his voice even. "You should be down in a couple of minutes. Just hang on tight."

"Okay," she murmured, and for a few seconds the only sound was the creaking of the pulleys at the top of the shaft. "You still there?" she asked.

"Yup. Ain't nowhere to go except straight up. How're you doing?"

"Okay now."

"Just a few more feet," he said. And then she was just above him. He reached for her, placing his hands on her waist to steady her for the end of the descent. "There. You're down."

"Thank you." Her hands still held the rope in a death grip. He could feel her breath coming in shaky gasps.

"Are you all right?" he asked softly.

She took a deep breath, and nodded. He could feel some of the tension inside her ease.

He wanted to hold her—to ease the pain he felt radiating within her, but now was not the time. As if to prove his point one of the children moaned. Lily let go of the rope, and Gray tugged on it sharply twice to let the people aboveground know she was down safely.

"We'd better see to the children," she said.

But they stood together for another moment, the air filled with unspoken promises, until Peter moaned again. Gray let her go, and bent over the boy while Lily went to check on Lorna. "She's unconscious. Has she been like this long?"

"Since I've been down here," he replied.

"And the boy?"

"A broken arm. I've set it, but he needs a doctor, too."

"How will we get them up?"

"I've put together a harness from the extra rope they sent down. I'll secure Peter, and then you can take him up."

"And the girl?"

"I'll do the same with her once you're safe."

"Okay. Tell me how to help."

Just like that, with no fuss, she set about helping him. Together they lifted Peter into the rope harness, tying it around his shoulders and between his legs before fastening it to the rope hanging from above. Lily positioned herself on the main rope, her arms around the boy.

"You ready?" Gray asked her. She nodded. "Okay, I'll signal them, just—" He couldn't resist. Her lips were so close to his, and who knew if he'd make it out of this alive. Despite their care, the well was slowly disintegrating, a constant trickle of dirt falling in one them.

He bent his head, and his lips touched hers. A sweet rush of memories raced through him. She smelled fresh and clean even in this musty well, a ray of sunshine here in this dank abyss. She moaned deep in her throat, and he opened his mouth to swallow the sound. He put his hand behind her head to hold her while he plundered her secrets. He kissed her as if there would be no tomorrow, telling her everything he felt but could not put into words. It would have to do. There was no time for more.

"You about ready down there?" came the cry from above.

"Yes. Pull her up—and be careful. She has the boy." He held on to her arm as the rope started its ascent, then let

304

his hand slowly trace a path down her leg until she was too high to touch. And still he stood there, watching her slowly move away from him.

As she reached the top, Peter suddenly flailed out with his legs, setting the rope swinging.

"No, Peter, stop!" he heard her call out, but it was too late. The boy's foot hit the wall and dislodged a flurry of rocks and dirt. Gray threw himself over Lorna as the side of the well continued to collapse on him, sending down a torrent of dirt and rocks. By the time the avalanche stopped, Gray was coughing from the dust and lying underneath a good six inches of rubble.

Lily hung on to the boy, trying to keep him from dislodging any more dirt. He fought her, crying for his mother and angrily trying to escape her grasp. Old Bess pulled them out of the hole, and Sam grabbed them with a large animal hook, swinging them away from the opening. As soon as Lily's feet touched the ground, a crowd of people swarmed around her.

"Are you all right?"

"How's the boy?"

"What's going on down there?"

"What about Lorna? Is she okay?"

This last came from a familiar voice, only instead of sounding snippy and cold, today it sounded scared. Lily looked into Amelia's face and saw all her own fears reflected there. Sam took Peter from her arms and began loosening the knots that held him in the harness.

"Here, let me help," Prescott said, kneeling by the foreman's side. "Shush, Peter. As soon as we get you untied, I'll take you to your mummy."

The boy calmed down at the sound of his uncle's voice and soon was freed. Prescott picked him up, hugging him as close as the awkward splint on his arm would allow. His eyes glistened, and he blinked rapidly. "I'll just take

him inside," he said and started toward the house. Several
people followed, including the doctor.

"Is Lorna okay? And my father?" Amelia asked again.
The girl kept her distance, though Lily could see she
wanted nothing more than to have someone hold her and
take away her fears.

"I don't know about Lorna. She's unconscious and has
a bump on her head. Your father's fine—at least, he was
when I left."

"But?" Amelia's face paled, and her blue eyes looked
huge in her face.

"More dirt fell. Let me just check with Sam. Come with
me."

She held out her arms, and Amelia ran into them. "Oh,
Lily," she said, tears flowing. "I—I'm so scared. Will he
be all right?"

"He has to be. Come on. Let's find out what's going
on."

The crowd had grown since Lily first went down the
well. People had come in from Cheyenne and the neigh-
boring ranches. They gathered in groups all around the old
well site.

Lily found Sam with a couple of the roustabouts fitting
out the rope with a narrow board.

Sam looked up as they arrived. "Amelia, how did you
get here?" He looked startled to see her, and a red blush
highlighted his cheekbones. "Are you all right?"

Amelia nodded and wiped away her tears. "Jackie
Glover rode over to tell me what happened. Said he'd been
following the circus out of town when he heard what was
going on. Thought I should get over here. How's my father?"

"So far he's fine. We're trying to figure out a way to get
Lorna up without setting off another avalanche. Gray sug-

gested we send down a board so he can secure Lorna better than you could Peter," he added to Lily.

"Is she still unconscious?"

"Yeah, from what I could tell."

"Stand back, everyone," the chief roustabout said. "We're ready to send this down."

Amelia looked fearfully from Lily to Sam. "Now what?"

"Now, you come with me, and we'll wait where we won't get in the way," Lily said.

"I don't want to leave." Her eyes started to tear again, and she chewed on her lower lip.

"We won't. We'll just go over here a couple of steps."

Amelia let Lily lead her away, and Sam went back to join the work crew by the well.

They watched with bated breath as the board was lowered, then waited anxiously until Old Bess started pulling the rope back up. The wait seemed endless, and then the top edge of the board appeared above the ground.

"Where's Papa?" Amelia said, her voice rising. "He's not there!"

The men at the well site had taken the board carrying Lorna off the rope.

"What happened? Where's Gray?" Lily asked.

"He's still down there. He thought it would be safer for Lorna if he helped guide the board up."

"What do you mean? How could he guide it when he didn't come up himself?"

Sam looked up then. "We tied a second rope to the bottom of the board, and Gray held on to it as Old Bess pulled Lorna up, making sure the board didn't hit the edges of the well."

"But what about getting Gray himself up?" Lily was beginning to share some of Amelia's desperation. Even from this distance she could make out the sounds of falling dirt and knew the well was slowly collapsing. It was just a matter of time before the entire shaft caved in.

"He's next. Hang on. It'll only be a couple more minutes."

Even as he spoke, the rope was going down the shaft yet again as Old Bess lumbered closer to the well, Gustav guiding her steps.

Lily stood with Amelia, their arms around each other's waists, as if they couldn't stand alone without support.

"Oh, Lily, what if something happens to Papa? I'll never forgive myself. None of this would have happened if I didn't try those tricks on Cleo." She started to cry again.

Lily turned the girl to face her. "Stop this, Amelia. You're right, you shouldn't have done those tricks, not because they caused this, but because they weren't safe for you."

"I remember you warned me not to, but I was so angry at him for making me stay at the ranch. I wanted to hurt him, don't you see?" She cried even harder.

"If wishes worked that well, we'd all have exactly what we want."

"Maybe you're right," Amelia conceded. "But I did lie to him." Her voice had dropped to a hoarse, tear-filled whisper.

"What are you talking about?" Lily asked, her heart almost breaking for Amelia.

"I told him you taught me those tricks, Lily. I was afraid he would be even madder at me if he thought I'd ignored your warnings. And then, when you came to see me, I was afraid. You were trying to be so nice, and I was feeling so bad. I didn't want you to stay and talk to Papa, so I was mean. You must really hate me now."

"Oh, Amelia." Lily drew the girl into her embrace and stroked her back. "You poor dear. Now, listen to me. You didn't do anything so terrible an apology or two won't fix. What's most important is that you weren't hurt. I don't think your father could have stood that. Everything else can be taken care of easily enough."

"Does that mean you forgive me?"

"Me?"

"For lying about you and making you feel so bad that day. I really am sorry."

"Yes, I forgive you. These things just happen sometimes, even between friends. And we are friends, aren't we?"

"Oh, yes," Amelia said and gave Lily a fervent hug.

"Then that's all that matters. What happened in the past can't be changed, so there's no point in dwelling on it. It's the future that counts and what you do with it."

At that moment Old Bess started her slow walk back, pulling the rope up inch by inch. The scaffolding creaked as it took on Gray's weight, and both Lily and Amelia stood like statues, watching the slow progression of the rope, their hearts stopping every time there was another sound.

And then, when Lily felt she just couldn't take the tension another minute longer, his head appeared just above the surface, and then his shoulders. As he had with her, Sam used the animal hook to pull Gray to safety. At that moment Amelia bolted from her embrace and ran to his side, flinging herself into his arms.

Gray looked down into Amelia's concerned face and gently wiped the tears from her cheeks.

"Oh, Papa, I was so scared. What would I ever do without you?" she asked, holding him tight.

He'd always feared how he would go on if something happened to her, but now he saw that she had the same feelings for him. And yet, she'd never tried to limit him the way he'd done with her, never told him not to do what he felt was right even if, like today, it put him in jeopardy. She trusted him to do what was right, and maybe it was time he trusted her.

"You don't have to worry about that now. I'm here and safe."

"When you were down in that well, it seemed like an eternity."

Gray felt her tremble with the memory. "It did for me, too," he said lightly, wanting to alleviate her fear, then on a more serious note added, "I'm just glad we're all up and safe. How are the children?"

"I don't know for sure. The doctor went inside with them and the last I heard, they were doing fine. I've never seen Cybil act like this before."

"Most times people aren't always what we expect. And you have to remember that it was Cybil's children in that well. She's already lost a husband—imagine how she must feel about a threat to her children's lives. I know how I'd feel if it were you."

"I know that, but they needed her when they came out, and she couldn't get herself composed enough to take care of them. You wouldn't have done that." She looked up at him with an admiring gaze that warmed his heart. No matter what misunderstandings they'd had these past few weeks, she still seemed to love and respect him.

"I'm glad you have such faith in me," he said and gave her a hug. "Just give Cybil some time. I'm sure she'll be back to normal before you know it."

The men who helped with the rescue gathered around, congratulating him and each other. Word had come from the house that Lorna was finally awake, and though she was a bit dizzy, the doctor thought a couple days of bed rest would be all she needed.

Gray looked at the crowd, searching for that one special face. He knew Lily had been at the mouth of the well when he'd been brought up. Where could she have gotten to? "Did you see where Lily ended up?" he asked Amelia.

"No. After I saw you come out from the well, I don't remember anything but wanting to be near you and making sure you were all right." Amelia looked up at her father, staring intently at his face. "You love her, don't you?" she said in a quiet voice.

The complete change of subject knocked him slightly off balance, and then he realized telling Amelia would be the first step in starting a new life with Lily. "Yes, I love her."

"And she loves you." It was more of a statement than a question.

"I hope so, for I love her more than I ever thought possible," Gray said, knowing it was true and wanting Amelia to know exactly how he felt. He also wanted her to feel the same way, but since Mrs. Bellows had told him about Lily's visit to see Amelia, he wasn't as sure how his daughter would react. "How do you feel about that?"

"I have to tell you something—something about Lily."

Gray felt his heart begin to pound. What could it be that had Amelia so concerned? "You can tell me anything. You know that."

"Did you know that I was very angry with you and Lily? That I blamed you both for my having to stay at the ranch?"

Gray shook his head.

"Well, because of my anger I let other things and other people influence me. The short of it is I lied to you. When I fell, I told you Lily taught me those tricks, but she didn't. I did them on my own. Lily told me never to try the tricks on a horse, but I did it anyway." Amelia ducked her head. "I'm sorry."

"Was that why you were so mean to Lily the day she came to visit after your accident?"

"Mrs. Bellows told you?" There was no accusation in her voice, only an acceptance and understanding of her own shortcomings.

"She mentioned it, but only because it was so out of character for you." And now he knew why. Amelia's guilt had driven her to act the way she had.

"I'm so ashamed. I apologized to Lily when we were waiting for you to come out of the well, and she said we were friends and sometimes things like that happened. She said what had happened in the past wasn't really important, it was how you met the future that mattered."

"She's right." How very right Gray was only starting to learn. He'd let the past play too large a part in his life, but today's events had taught him the folly of that approach. He'd nearly lost the most important chance in his life for lasting happiness, and he wasn't going to make that mistake again. "I'm glad you made your peace with her."

"What about you? Are you going to make your peace with her, too?" Amelia's eyes sparkled, and Gray was glad to see some of her old impudence back.

"I certainly plan to," he conceded with a smile. "Provided I can find her."

"Why don't you ask Dun if he's seen her?" Amelia suggested.

"I'll do that. But first I need to make sure you get home in one piece."

"Oh, Papa. There are any number of people who will see that I get home safely."

"But not many I deem qualified." Gray looked about and spotted Sam standing and talking with one of the roustabouts. "Sam?" he called out. "Can you do me a favor?"

"Sure, boss," Sam answered as he joined them. "What is it?"

"Will you make sure Amelia gets back to the ranch?"

"Papa, I don't need anyone to take care of me," she whispered in protest. "I'm not a baby." Despite her words, Amelia snuck a shy look in Sam's direction.

"I'd be honored to escort you, Miss Amelia," Sam offered gallantly.

Gray watched as Amelia smiled up at Sam, and with a jolt Gray noticed the speculative gleam in her eyes as she assessed Sam, not so much as a possible friend, but as something more. And Sam was looking back at her in much the same way. Then Sam looked up at Gray. "Don't worry, sir. She'll be safe with me." There was a promise in the young man's eyes, a man-to-man message Gray could not miss. He could trust Sam beyond a doubt, but when Amelia was ready, really ready to look for a man, Sam would be there, waiting.

Gray nodded once, accepting this state of affairs. He knew Sam well enough by now to know his daughter could do worse, and he trusted him not to hurt her. More than that, he was starting to trust Amelia's judgment. If she chose Sam, it would be because he deserved to be chosen.

"I'll see you both at the ranch," he said to the young couple.

"When?" they asked in unison.

"As soon as I can convince Lily to marry me."

Lily made her way through the raucous crowds to her wagon. She felt apart from all the noise and excitement, relieved that the emergency was over and no one was hurt, but drained by the events of the past few days. Seeing Gray emerge safely from the well had been the answer to her most heartfelt prayers. She'd watched Amelia run to her father and wished she could be a part of their love. When his arms closed around his daughter, comforting her after her ordeal, Lily looked on with a touch of envy.

More than anything she wanted to be wrapped in his arms, to be comforted and loved.

Gray had said things at the bottom of that well that had given her hope, but now she felt they were said out of fear. In moments of extreme danger you did things you normally wouldn't, and that's what had happened with her and Gray. Now that the emergency was over, he would recall the problems between them, the threat he felt she posed to his daughter's well-being, and he would once again put his happiness aside for his daughter's sake.

Lily knew she couldn't face hearing that. It was bad enough knowing she had to leave Gray's life forever, to hear him tell her the reasons she wasn't good enough would destroy what little control she had left. She had to get away. After climbing up onto the driver's seat, she pulled her wagon onto the road and drove back to where Sam had found them and where the rest of the circus camped.

Once there she didn't have the heart to talk to anyone, but went inside, locking the door behind her. She sat on her bed, her head buried in her hands, overwhelmed by her emotions.

As if her thoughts had conjured him up, Lily heard Gray call out her name from outside her wagon. She sat quietly, convinced he would go away if she pretended she wasn't here. Instead, he began pounding on her door.

"Dammit Lily, I know you're in there!" he called out. "Please open the door. I need to talk to you."

She sat stiffly on the bed, trying to block out his voice. Her heartbeat quickened, but she forced herself not to call out. She couldn't bear the pain of another parting. It would be easier if she didn't see him again.

"Lily, I don't want to tell the whole world our private business. Please open the door!" Gray shouted and resumed his banging.

Then, abruptly, the knocking stopped. The sudden quiet had more impact than the pounding. Lily stood up and started toward the door. Suppose he had gone? She stopped. But wasn't that what she wanted? She was so confused, she couldn't decide what to do. And then the choice was taken from her. She barely had time to identify the metallic-sounding scratching at her door, when suddenly it was flung open and there stood Gray and Dun.

Her gaze moved from one to the other and then down to the thin piece of metal in Dun's hand. He had picked her lock! She couldn't believe he would do such a thing. Her accusing eyes must have said as much, for he quickly defended himself.

"I did what I thought was right." He pulled himself up to his full height.

"Breaking into someone else's property is the 'right' thing to do?"

"In this case."

"Lily, this is between you and me," Gray interrupted. "Don't take your anger out on Dun. I'm the one you're upset with."

Lily had refrained from looking in Gray's direction after her first quick glance. She knew if she did, she'd be lost. He had that effect on her.

"I'm not upset," she said in a soft voice, still not looking at him.

"Hurt, then?"

Yes, she did hurt, and she was sure having to face him again was only going to make the pain worse, the final parting harder to bear.

"Please, can we talk?"

She looked around, knowing it was inevitable. She couldn't run any farther. She'd have to face up to what Gray was going to say. Taking a breath, she nodded and then motioned for him to have a seat. She was barely aware of Dun slowly backing away, and closing the door behind him.

"I don't want to sit, Lily," Gray said, taking her by the shoulders. "We need to talk. There are things I need to tell you and things I need to know."

"You and Dun haven't given me much choice in the matter," Lily answered, using her belligerence to keep from breaking down in front of him and telling him how much she still loved and needed him.

"I love you, Lily."

"What?" she asked, sure she had heard him wrong. She had expected him to say many things but never this.

"I love you and I want us to be together." His hands moved up and down her arms, warming her.

"Oh, Gray." She wanted to believe him with every fiber of her being, but she was afraid he was still feeling the influence of what they'd just been through. "This could just be a reaction to your brush with death," she said, voicing her fears. "When things like this happen, people often have strong reactions, then a short while later they go back to their old feelings."

"What old feelings?" Gray repeated with a puzzled expression.

"The feelings Hank told me about."

"Hank? What the hell does Hank have to do with us?"

"He came to see me yesterday and said you'd come to tell me you didn't want me, that I was a bad influence on Amelia and you didn't want to see me again."

"And you believed him?" he asked, his hands tightening on her upper arms.

"He was very convincing. He knew you'd been to see me."

"Hank has always been convincing. He fooled me as much as anyone. But I hope you don't believe a word he said. Anyone could have seen me at the circus, but he had no idea why I was there."

"I didn't want to believe him, but when you didn't show up . . ."

"Hank led me on a chase to a nonexistent rendezvous with phantom rustlers. I must confess I never suspected him. And that was my mistake, but don't let that mistake ruin the rest of our lives. Hank isn't worth it—he's tainted everything he's ever touched. Don't let him ruin us."

Lily could see the pain Gray was suffering because of his friend's betrayal. "Don't blame yourself for what Hank did, Gray. You had no way of knowing. He was always so charming when other people were around."

"But?" he asked, apparently sensing she'd left much unspoken.

"But inside he wasn't a good man. Not like you."

His eyes lit up with hope at her words, and she felt her barriers weaken. How she wanted to believe him! The only question was, could she? Could she put the past behind and look forward to the future. As if he read her mind, Gray said, "I can't change what happened the past few days, Lily. I can only go on from here. Isn't that what you told Amelia after you got out of the well? That it was the future that mattered, not the past?"

"Yes." So Amelia had told her father what she'd said.

"I do love you, Lily. And I'm not going to let you go. That's what I came to tell you yesterday before Amelia even confessed about the tricks. I've learned a lot about myself these last few days, and I've had a good chance to think about what scared me about having you in my life and in Amelia's."

"And?" Lily was almost afraid to ask.

"And I realized that you weren't anything like Felicia. Felicia was a spoiled child, irresponsible and flighty. She thought about no one but herself." Gray stopped talking

317

and looked down at her. "And . . . though I told you most of what happened, I left out the most important part."

Lily stood silently, waiting for Gray to continue. She could tell this was hard for him, but she didn't know how to help.

"Felicia didn't just join a theatrical troupe; she ran off with another man, their star actor. Until lately I don't think I ever truly faced that. I always blamed the theater for luring Felicia away, when in all truth it was a man. I must have failed her somehow, and I guess I tried to hide from that fact."

"Oh, Gray," Lily said, seeing his pain. "We can't hide from the past. You can't, and neither can I. And as you said before, we can only go on from here."

"Is that what happened this morning at the well? Did you face up to your past?"

For a moment Lily didn't speak, then in a quiet voice, she replied, "Yes, I think I did."

The darkness of the well shaft had reminded her of all she'd run away from as a child—and survived.

"Can you tell me about it?" Gray asked, his arms moving up and down her arms, warming her.

"My sister Rosemary and I ran away from home, you know. I was young, but I remember some things—like hiding with Rosemary in the closet to get away from my father."

Lily stopped, trying to decide how best to say what had to be said. "After our mother died, my father started treating Rosemary just like he'd treated our mother, beating her when he was drunk and . . . other things, things she wouldn't tell me."

Gray closed his eyes, unwilling to imagine what those other things might have been, how a father could so abuse his daughters that they would run away from him—and to a precarious life with the circus. "And then?"

"One day he looked at me funny, and Rosemary yelled at him. I'd never seen her like that, like she was going crazy. He turned on her, told her she couldn't stop him. That night she came to me, and we ran away. She was all beat up, but she never told me about what had worried her."

"Thank God you met Hilda and Otto." When he thought about what could have happened to them, two young girls with nowhere to turn, it made his stomach turn. No wonder Lily never spoke of those days. A rage against her father rose in him and he wished he could get his hands on the man for just a few minutes. He remembered all the times she'd sidestepped Amelia's questions about fathers and understood now why she thought he was such a good one.

And maybe he was, he now conceded. Maybe he had worth as a human being even though his wife had chosen another over him, even though her parents had blamed him, thinking him below their station.

"If there's one thing I've learned from this, it's that you can't let other people's mistakes control your life," Lily said. "I don't think there are any excuses for my father, but Felicia was young and she made mistakes. That can happen to any of us—we all have to make choices. If it had been me, I'd have given everything in my life to have won your love and Amelia's, but each of us is different and wants different things." The words tumbled out unguardedly in her eagerness to ease his hurt and possibly her own. She didn't give a thought to all she was revealing.

"You have our love, Lily," Gray replied. "The question is, do we have yours?"

For the first time since the circus left Cheyenne, Lily dared to believe her dreams just might come true. As hope fluttered wildly in her heart, Gray touched his lips to hers, softly, tenderly.

"What I feel for you is unlike anything I've ever felt before," he told her. "I'll do whatever it takes to keep you in my life. If you can't stay with me on the ranch, I'll join you with the circus. I want you to marry me—say yes, and you'll make me the happiest man alive."

Lily thought her heart would burst with joy. Gray's gallant offer to join the circus wouldn't be needed, for she wanted nothing more than to live her life with him on his ranch. Her dreams had changed since meeting him; the winds of fate had blown her from one place to another for long enough. She was more than ready to settle down, to let the winds blow past, whispering their secrets, while she stayed in one place and built a new life.

She smiled up at him and touched his cheek with her fingers. "Unless joining the circus is one of your lifelong dreams, I want to spend my life with you on your ranch. I can't wait to plant a flower garden and be there to watch it bloom, or to see the tree outside my window change from green to red with the seasons."

"And watch me grow old, too."

"That's going to be the best part," she said and threaded her fingers through the few strands of silver at his temples.

Gray wrapped his arms around her and covered her lips with his, sealing her words with a kiss of promise for their future together. Then the kiss became more than a promise; it grew and heated, lighting a fire within them—a wildfire that blazed out of control in a burst of heat and passion.

"I want you. Right now," Gray said, his voice rough and dark with intent.

"And I you," she returned, pressing her mouth to his with equal fervor.

At her words, Gray knew he'd found true happiness.

Everything he'd ever wanted had finally come together in his life. He looked down into Lily's face, unable to believe his luck.

"God, you're beautiful." His hand came up to her hair and unbraided the long plait hanging down the middle of her back. The brilliant red strands slipped like tongues of fire through his fingers. He looked down the length of her body, admiring the fullness of her figure, the curves that fit his hands so well. He'd never seen a woman in pants before today and was surprised at how appealing he found them—at least when Lily filled them.

Slowly his hands moved to the front of her shirtwaist and began unfastening the buttons. When he had the last of them undone, he pulled the two sides back to reveal her thin chemise. The material was so transparent he could make out the soft shape of her breasts and the darker shadows of her nipples.

"Will the circus be moving on to Denver today?" he asked, his voice rough with need.

"No, they'll wait and start tomorrow morning."

"Good." He swept Lily up into his arms and carried her to the quilt-covered bed, gently placing her in its center.

With fingers that fumbled he tried to undo the buttons that ran down the center of the chemise. His desire for her was so great that for a moment he feared he might lose control too quickly and not bring Lily fulfillment. Abandoning the buttons, he simply pulled the lacy garment off over her head. Seeing her bare body lying in wait made him feel he would burst from his own longings.

At the waistband of Lily's pants he found more buttons and groaned in frustration. "After these buttons, there aren't any more, are there?"

Lily glanced up at him with a tantalizing smile and began on the buttons of his shirt. When she reached for his own pants, he knew he couldn't let her be the one to unfasten them. Quickly he finished the job she had started and pulled them off, dropping them onto the floor. Her pants quickly followed, landing on top of his.

He wanted to take her slowly, to give her time to savor their newfound intimacy, but his need for her threatened to overcome his control. And then she reached for him, pulling him to her with the same intensity he felt, urging him forward so that all thought of control was gone, and he took her quickly and fully. Her movements matched his, inciting him to ever greater heights. She was hot and tight and her sweet scents surrounded him. Suddenly everything came together, only to fly apart in an explosion of heat and light. He collapsed on top of Lily, his breath coming in gasps.

He closed his eyes, wishing he'd lasted longer, wishing he'd been able to take her on the journey with him. "I'm sorry. I just wanted you so much."

She covered his mouth. "I didn't want to wait, either. Besides, we have all the time we want, at least until morning."

She smiled up at him, her face filled with anticipation. Gray smiled back, then leaned down and kissed her, suddenly hungry for her all over again.

FIFTEEN

LILY STOOD OUTSIDE her wagon for a moment before going in. She'd awoken at dawn just as the sky was starting to lighten, and now her early morning mission had been completed. While her decision to stay with Gray brought her only joy, she hadn't been sure how her circus friends would take it. She'd spent the past hour finding out.

Her worries had been groundless. Otto had kissed her and given her his blessing, saying he wanted her to follow her heart as he was following his with Iola Parsons by his side. Elena and Roberto had also wished her well though they were disappointed she wouldn't be there for their baby's birth, but they'd promised to visit the first chance they got.

Filled with a quiet elation, Lily tiptoed into the wagon not wanting to wake Gray. She moved on silent feet, pulling the door softly shut behind her. When she turned toward the bed, it was empty. Before she could even wonder where Gray might have gone, his arms snaked around her waist, enclosing her in their embrace.

"Do you know how disappointed I was that you weren't here when I woke up?"

"How disappointed?" she asked, joy welling inside her as he rubbed his beard-roughened cheek against hers.

"Very," he said as his hands moved upward, cupping her

323

breasts. The sensuous movement made her breath catch. "All my plans were spoiled, you know."

"Were they? I wasn't sure you'd be up to any *plans* this morning."

Gray pulled her body tighter against his own and she realized just how successful his plans would have been. "I see I was wrong," she admitted huskily. "I'm sorry I wasn't here. Do you think your plans could still be put into action?"

"Mmmm," he murmured as he kissed the side of her neck. Shivers of anticipation shimmered down her spine. "Where were you?" he whispered against her skin.

"I had to talk with Otto and let him know I wouldn't be going on with the circus."

"And what did he say?"

"That he knew someday I'd leave and settle down. Don't you find that strange? I mean, I dreamed of that happening, but I didn't realize anyone else knew."

"Otto's been like a father to you, and like any good father he knows what's best for you." Gray began unplaiting the braid she'd hastily put together this morning. "But now he's given you over to my care."

She turned to face him and draped her arms over his shoulders. "Does that mean you know what's best for me now?" she asked saucily.

He rubbed against her and grinned. "Care to find out?"

"Mmmm," she managed in the second before his mouth closed on hers. For the next half hour he showed her that he did, indeed, know what was best for her, in every possible way.

When Lily was finally able to catch her breath, she leaned her cheek against Gray's chest, enjoying the freedom that loving Gray had given her.

"You'd better stop that if you want to move outside this

wagon anytime today," Gray warned as her hand ventured lower and lower.

She merely smiled.

"You'll want to take your horses and Merlin back to the ranch, won't you?" Gray asked when she didn't answer.

"If that's all right with you," she said, unsure of how he felt about the horses since Amelia's attempt at trick riding.

"You love those horses and that old goat. Even Amelia's got a soft spot for Merlin. There's no way I'd let you leave them behind." Gray smiled down at her and then the smile turned to a sensuous grin. "I hope you're not planning on leaving this wagon behind, either."

"I hadn't really thought about it," she confessed. All she'd thought about was being with him. She was pleased to find that he didn't consider her a threat to Amelia any longer. He really had put the past behind him. But one thing puzzled her. "Why do you want this wagon?"

"I've become very attached to it. Besides, it will give us someplace to go whenever I have new plans."

"New plans, huh? Like now?" Her hand had found her goal, and to her surprise, he was hot and hard, ready for her, as insatiable in their loving as she.

"Like now and forever." He rolled her onto her back.

Lily smiled and silently agreed, knowing that no matter where they were or where they lived, they would be happy as long as they were together.

Diamond Wildflower Romance

A breathtaking new line of spectacular novels set in the untamed frontier of the American West. Every month, Diamond Wildflower brings you new adventures where passionate men and women dare to embrace their boldest dreams. Finally, romances that capture the very spirit and passion of the wild frontier.

__**COLORADO TEMPEST** by Mary Lou Rich
1-55773-799-1/$4.99

__**GOLDEN FURY** by Deborah James
1-55773-811-4/$4.99

__**DESERT FLAME** by Anne Harmon
1-55773-824-6/$4.99

__**BANDIT'S KISS** by Mary Lou Rich
1-55773-842-4/$4.99

__**AUTUMN BLAZE** by Samantha Harte
1-55773-853-X/$4.99

__**RIVER TEMPTRESS** by Elaine Crawford
1-55773-867-X/$4.99

__**WYOMING WILDFIRE** by Anne Harmon
1-55773-883-1/$4.99

__**GUNMAN'S LADY** by Catherine Palmer
1-55773-893-9/$4.99 (May 1993)

FROM THE AWARD-WINNING AUTHOR OF
RIVERS WEST: THE COLORADO, HERE IS THE SPRAWLING
EPIC STORY OF ONE FAMILY'S BRAVE STRUGGLE
FOR THE AMERICAN DREAM.

THE HORSEMEN

Gary McCarthy

The Ballous were the finest horsemen in the South, a
Tennessee family famous for the training and breeding
of thoroughbreds. When the Civil War devastated their
home and their lives, they headed West—into the heart
of Indian territory. As horsemen, they triumphed. As a
family, they endured. But as pioneers in a new land,
they faced unimaginable hardship, danger, and ruthless enemies...

If you enjoyed this book, take advantage of this special offer. Subscribe now and get a

FREE
Historical Romance

No Obligation (a $4.50 value)

Each month the editors of True Value select the four *very best* novels from America's leading publishers of romantic fiction. Preview them in your home *Free* for 10 days. With the first four books you receive, we'll send you a FREE book as our introductory gift. No Obligation!

If for any reason you decide not to keep them, just return them and owe nothing. If you like them as much as we think you will, you'll pay just $4.00 each and save at *least* $.50 each off the cover price. (Your savings are *guaranteed* to be at least $2.00 each month.) There is NO postage and handling – or other hidden charges. There are no minimum number of books to buy and you may cancel at any time.

Send in the Coupon Below

To get your FREE historical romance fill out the coupon below and mail it today. As soon as we receive it we'll send you your FREE Book along with your first month's selections.

Mail To: **True Value Home Subscription Services, Inc., P.O. Box 5235 120 Brighton Road, Clifton, New Jersey 07015-5235**

YES! I want to start previewing the very best historical romances being published today. Send me my FREE book along with the first month's selections. I understand that I may look them over FREE for 10 days. If I'm not absolutely delighted I may return them and owe nothing. Otherwise I will pay the low price of just $4.00 each: a total $16.00 (at least an $18.00 value) and save at least $2.00. Then each month I will receive four brand new novels to preview as soon as they are published for the same low price. I can always return a shipment and I may cancel this subscription at any time with no obligation to buy even a single book. In any event the FREE book is mine to keep regardless.

Name	
Street Address	Apt. No.
City	State _____ Zip
Telephone	
Signature	

(if under 18 parent or guardian must sign)

Terms and prices subject to change. Orders subject to acceptance by True Value Home Subscription Services, Inc.

883